The Blackbird

The Blackbird

TIM WEAVER

MICHAEL  JOSEPH

MICHAEL JOSEPH

UK | USA | Canada | Ireland | Australia
India | New Zealand | South Africa

Michael Joseph is part of the Penguin Random House group of companies
whose addresses can be found at global.penguinrandomhouse.com.

First published 2022
001

Copyright © Tim Weaver, 2022

The moral right of the author has been asserted

Set in 13.5/16pt Garamond MT Std
Typeset by Jouve (UK), Milton Keynes
Printed and bound in Great Britain by Clays Ltd, Elcograf S.p.A.

The authorized representative in the EEA is Penguin Random House Ireland,
Morrison Chambers, 32 Nassau Street, Dublin D02 YH68

A CIP catalogue record for this book is available from the British Library

HARDBACK ISBN: 978–0–241–41871–0
OM PAPERBACK ISBN: 978–0–241–41872–7

For Jo and John

They should have been dead.

That was what people kept telling me in the days before I went out to see the scene for myself. I spoke to family and friends, to the medics and fire crews who were actually there on the night it happened, and they all said the same thing – there was no way Cate and Aiden Gascoigne should have been able to survive a crash like that.

On the morning I was due to drive down to what was left of the scene, I got up early and, over breakfast, used my laptop to repeatedly inch back and forth along the road where it had happened. It was on the eastern edges of the Surrey Hills and the route I saw online was a sloped two-lane stretch of tarmac, hemmed in by trees on both sides, with a ravine to the west – the Gascoignes' right as they travelled down the hill – although the ravine wouldn't have been visible from their vehicle. Top to bottom, the road was less than a mile long, with a junction for the M25 at one end and a village called Gatton at the other. There were two minor bends en route, the road itself was in good condition, and the night the Gascoignes had plunged ninety feet into the ravine, it had been a dry evening in early January. No frost, no ice, not a hint of rain.

So it wasn't the weather that had caused the accident.

And it wasn't the layout or the quality of the road either.

Their car had been a black Land Rover Discovery, two years old. The history on it showed no issues and it had only just been through its service, so everything – including the tyres – had been checked literally days beforehand. Yet three minutes after exiting the M25, and only ten seconds after a CCTV camera halfway down Gatton Hill captured the two of them on film – apparently untroubled inside the car – Aiden Gascoigne lost control of the vehicle and the Land Rover nose-dived off the road.

The photographs of the scene in the casework, taken by forensic techs in the aftermath, were certainly better than nothing, but the portrait they painted wasn't as lucid as it could have been. The crash had happened at dusk, so a lot of the shots were too dark, even when I adjusted the levels on them, or they were the opposite: bleached by a flash, or over-saturated because of the big mobile lights that had been craned in and erected in the gully. Other pictures in the file were physical prints that had been pinned to a board some-where in an office at Thames Valley Police. Overall, they were better quality but, by the time the case wrapped up – still unresolved – and the pictures were scanned in and then taken down from those boards, they'd accumulated a mesh of hairs, creases and pale coffee-coloured water damage.

There was, however, one clear shot.

It had been taken from the flank of the ravine, about twenty-five feet up from the crash, by an accident investiga-tor. They had climbed part of the way up a sloping carpet of scree to try and get a better angle on the wreckage. There were a couple of trees in the way – both stripped to the bone by winter – and a very light spotting of frost at the foot of the chasm, although none around the Land Rover itself. Instead, there was only a pitch-black ring, the grass, ferns and overhanging branches all scorched by the fire that had started in the engine and ripped through the car.

The Land Rover – on its roof – barely looked like a car at all. It had been transformed into a ragged tangle of metal, the front concertinaed all the way into the dashboard, every single window smashed. Investigators had drawn an illustration of how they believed the descent had gone, the impact points on the slope of the ravine, but in the end, maybe it didn't matter all that much. The damage was obvious from just a single photograph, its severity stark and brutal, and however many times the Land Rover had turned, whichever part of its chassis had crunched against the scree – however hard its roof had hit the floor of the gully at the end – there should only have been one outcome for the husband who'd been driving, and the wife beside him.

They should have been dead.

But that was the thing. That was why the photographs of the crushed, charred Land Rover had spent so long pinned to a board at Thames Valley Police. It was why the media began labelling it 'The Mystery of Gatton Hill' and why the CCTV footage of the Gascoignes had got over three million views on YouTube. Everyone knew they should have been dead, that the accident should have crushed them or broken them in half; it should have severed limbs, and arteries. It should have started turning their bodies to ash.

But it didn't.

Because when members of the emergency services got to the bottom of the ravine ten minutes after the crash, there was something wrong with the Land Rover.

It was empty.

The Gascoignes had vanished.

PART ONE
The Crash

I

The family lived near Runnymede, in a house on the banks of the Thames.

It was half a mile from the motorway, less than three from Heathrow Airport, but it was easy to imagine that you were in the countryside somewhere, and London was a distant memory. The weather helped: it was the first Monday in July, searingly hot even this early, and as boats glided lazily past me, there was almost no traffic noise at all. All I could hear was birdsong and the sound of kids on their way to school as they played in the long grass that lined the fringes of the river.

I got out of my car and took in the house itself, a mock-Tudor mansion with a double garage and a black wrought-iron gate at the front. The gate had been left ajar and, in the middle of the gravel driveway, an old retriever was lying down, panting in the sun. The second I arrived at the gate, its gaze pinged to me.

'Hey,' I said, and got down on to my haunches.

It was a girl. She eyed me for a second, clearly wondering if I was worth getting up for, and then she must have decided that I was because she hauled herself to her feet, one of her legs stiff, and trotted across to me. I ran a hand through her hair, along her flank, and she rested her muzzle against my thigh.

'She's never been much of a guard dog.' I looked up. A man in his late sixties was coming down the driveway towards me, a half-smile on his face. 'But we still love her, don't we,

Jess?' He was smartly dressed in a powder-blue button-down shirt and cream chinos. 'I'm sure you've guessed this already,' he said, 'but I'm Martin Clark.'

He held out his hand to me.

'David Raker,' I said, standing. 'But I'm sure you knew that too.'

We shook hands.

'Thanks for coming, Mr Raker.'

'David.'

He nodded. 'Martin.'

I gave Jess another stroke and glanced at the river again. All that lay between the Clarks and the water on this side of the house was a band of long grass, a knot of oak trees and an old, rickety jetty at which a rowing boat bobbed gently. 'This is a beautiful spot,' I said.

He smiled. 'We've always loved it.'

'How long have you been here?'

'We moved here from Islington when the girls were still young. It was a happy home for a long, long time . . .' Something flickered in his expression. *But not any more.* He cleared his throat, forced a smile. 'We used to take the girls out on the river a lot.' He pointed to the rowing boat.

'They must have loved it,' I said.

'They did. We all did. It takes on a bit of water now, so you can't go very far, but back then, the four of us used to row miles.' The four of them. Him, his wife Sue, and his two daughters: Georgia, who was the eldest by two years, and Catherine.

Cate, for short.

'Why don't you come in, David?'

I followed Martin into the house, Jess plodding along behind us. Immediately inside was a foyer with a staircase in the centre. It was lovely, made from glass and timber, and

8

gently spiralled up to the first-floor landing. Circling the staircase like the spokes of a wheel were five doors. I could see a living room, a kitchen and an office from where I was. There was light pouring in from all directions thanks to a series of windows high up on the walls of the foyer.

He led me into the living room, which then opened out on to a deck elevated over a sloping garden. The garden was immaculate and hemmed in by perfectly sculpted laurel bushes. It only added to the sense of being somewhere remote. Even the soft drone of a plane, taking off from Heathrow, couldn't tarnish the effect.

A woman was waiting for us out on the deck, standing to the side of some grey patio furniture, hands in front of her. She looked worried, or scared, or both.

'Mrs Clark?'

She smiled. 'Sue, please.'

'David.'

We shook hands. Her skin was clammy.

'Can I get you something to drink, David?'

'Something cold would be lovely, thank you.'

Sue disappeared into the house and Martin gestured to one of the patio chairs. Above me, I saw that the deck had a cover, which appeared to be able to slide back and forth along its runners, depending on where the Clarks wanted their shade. It was another smart, expensive feature. But that, and the pristine house, and the flawless garden, were all just illusions. Everything here was near perfect on the surface but turbulent as a storm below. The house, the garden, it was all distraction.

'I hope you don't mind,' Martin said, 'but I did a little reading up about you. I saw some of the cases you've had. It seems like it can get pretty hairy at times.'

'At times. But not always.'

9

'I suppose there are all sorts of reasons why people go missing.'

'No two cases are exactly the same.'

'Do you ever get a gut feeling one way or another?'

'About where a case is going to go?'

He nodded. 'Do you ever sit down like this and hear the story from the family and then think to yourself, "This is going to be a difficult one to crack"?'

As Jess wandered out from the living room and slumped on to the decking, I turned Martin's question over. In a disappearance, especially when it came to runaways, sometimes the object wasn't to vanish, it was simply to break free. In those cases, I was usually employed by children's homes, or councils, or foster families. Occasionally, you might get work from the biological family, but generally – by the time a teenager reached the stage when they were trying to escape – the biological family had long been erased from the picture. Those searches tended to stick to a rigid pattern, tended to involve doing the same things on repeat, so I suppose it was true that in those cases I'd get an idea right out of the gate of where things would go.

But it wasn't always like that.

Sometimes you caught a case where there was no pattern and no recognizable shape to it, where the answers appeared unreliable or non-existent. And in almost all the investigations that I'd never had a gut feeling about – and which had hurt me the most – there was always a liar at the centre.

Liars were why cases were unpredictable.

Liars got you killed.

Looking at Martin, I said, 'Sometimes you might get a feel for where a case is going to go, yes – but every case is different. I try not to prejudge them. And even if they *are* tricky to crack, it doesn't mean I won't.'

It was an attempt to reassure him because the catalyst for the question was obvious: he'd spent the last two and a half years facing down nothing but failure, of being tortured with dead ends and unanswered questions, and now he wasn't sure if he'd made the right choice. *What if my search just brought them more suffering?*

What if I never found Cate and Aiden Gascoigne?

'I guess you know a little about them already?' he asked.

'Only through what you told me on the phone and what's been reported.'

He put a hand flat to the table that separated us and looked out at the garden. 'The reports were pretty accurate. I probably read every single one of them – I suppose I was trying to find some sort of answer, some explanation of where Cate and Aiden might have gone. But what the media put out there matched what the police told us.'

He looked at me, a shimmer in his face.

The car was empty.

'So, as I understand it,' I said, 'Cate and Aiden were heading to some friends in Reigate. A CCTV camera confirmed they exited the M25 at the Gatton Hill turn-off. From there, they crossed the roundabout and connected to Gatton Hill itself, and halfway down *that*, another surveillance camera filmed them again.'

'That's right.'

'Ten seconds later, something happened.'

We looked at each other. *Something happened.* That made it sound minor: a mishap, not a sudden catastrophic event where a car plunged ninety feet into a gully.

'No one saw them leave the road?'

'No. The first witnesses arrived after.'

One, travelling south from the motorway, was a student called Zoe Simmons. She told police she saw tyre marks on the road and a piece of the Land Rover's bumper; when she started to slow her Suzuki, she saw the spot where the car had exited the road. The other driver – heading north – was a 61-year-old retiree called Audrey Calvert. Even before Simmons had seen the tyre marks and the bumper, Calvert was already slowing her Fiat 500 because – for a few seconds, as she travelled up the hill – the layout of the road allowed her a brief, uninterrupted view down the slope of the ravine, into the foot of the gully.

There she could see a vehicle.

It was on its roof.

Both she and Simmons parked up, dialled 999 and, about two minutes after the crash, walked up to where the tyre marks bled off: some of the foliage had been torn, allowing them both to see down the slant of the ravine.

Soon after that, the Land Rover caught fire.

I'd requested a copy of the police investigation from a contact of mine in the Met, so I'd confirm all this for certain in the next twenty-four hours. But the details reported by the media *did* seem to be pretty accurate; as I continued to go back over the events of that day with Martin, he basically repeated what I already knew.

'The witnesses never saw Cate and Aiden get out of the car?'

'No,' Martin said.

According to the media, in nine minutes, the witnesses never took their eyes off the car and at no time did they see the Gascoignes leave the vehicle. Both women had been upset because they believed Cate and Aiden were still inside and there was nothing either of them could do. It was too dangerous to go down the slope, so they just stood there the entire time, watching the car cremate.

But that was the thing.

The Gascoignes *weren't* inside.

'We just need to know what happened,' Martin said quietly.

'I know.'

'If she's . . . if she's . . .' He stopped.

Dead.

As Sue came back out on to the deck, she saw her husband and the tray she was holding wobbled in her grip. She set it down and went to him, as if drawn to him, his torment, because they were both trapped in it, moths fluttering in endless darkness.

'I'll find out what happened to her,' I said.

You shouldn't be making promises.

But it was too late.

Their pain had already become mine.

'I'll find out what happened to Cate and Aiden.'

2

'The last time we saw her was a week before she disappeared.'

I had my notebook out on the table and my phone recording beside that. Martin and Sue had gathered themselves again, their tears gone for now, the two of them slipping on the same disguises they'd worn every day since Cate vanished – a show of strength that dissolved the moment they were alone again.

'So let's go back to the 3rd of January,' I said.

Martin nodded. 'Two years, six months and one day.'

He glanced at Sue, taking her hand, and she looked back at him: for them, this was a sentence, every day a mark on a cell wall.

'You saw Cate and Aiden over Christmas?'

'Right,' Martin said. 'They came to stay with us on Christmas Eve and were here all the way through until the Saturday, the 28th. Georgia was here too for Christmas Day with her boyfriend, Will, and our little granddaughter, Talia. It was so nice.' He blinked a couple of times. 'I mean, we just loved having them all.'

'Where did Cate and Aiden go after they left here?'

'They went to some friends near Bristol for New Year.'

I asked for the name of the friends, just in case. Cate and Aiden had returned safely to London on New Year's Day, and Aiden had returned to work on the 2nd at the design agency in Soho where he was the creative director, so I didn't expect that line of enquiry to be relevant. But these were all boxes that needed to be ticked.

'Cate and Aiden lived in Twickenham, is that right?'

'Yes.'

'How long had they been there?'

'Ooooh, what would you say, Sue?'

'Seven years,' she replied without hesitation, and then smiled, although it was a little sad, the pain flickering in and out. 'Mart isn't the only one who can remember dates,' she added, trying to make light of the fact that this was yet more time, more events in her daughter's life, she'd marked out on that same wall.

'How long had they been together?'

'Almost nine years,' Sue replied again, 'five married.'

'Where did they meet?'

'It was through some work Cate did at Aiden's company,' Martin said, picking things up again. 'They were creating this campaign which needed some photography. Aiden found Cate online, they worked on that project together – and then Aiden asked her out.'

'Cate was a full-time photographer, correct?'

'Yes. She made a really good career out of it.'

'What sort of stuff did she photograph?'

'We have some pictures inside if you'd like to see them.'

'That would be great.'

Martin hauled himself out of his seat and headed back inside the house, and then Sue also got up, going to a sideboard in the living room, bringing back more photographs. Except none of these were professional shots, and none of them were taken by Cate. They were all taken by Martin and Sue.

They were all of their daughter.

I'd seen pictures of Cate already, of Aiden as well. They were a good-looking couple, both thirty-eight at the time they went missing: Cate was tall and fair-skinned with a beauty spot above the left arc of her lips; Aiden was athletic, shaven-headed, bearded, his eyes brown, his skin olive. I knew already that both his parents were dead, that he was an only child, and that his father had been Irish and his mother was from Turkey.

I kept going through the pictures. They seemed to cover most of the nine years Cate and Aiden had been together, but there were also shots of Cate with her sister Georgia – she looked much more like Martin, whereas Cate was the spitting image of Sue.

As Martin returned to the deck weighed down with albums and opened the first of them, he and Sue physically leaned in, drawing themselves closer to the portraits mounted inside. I studied the two of them: both appeared to be fit and healthy, their skin lightly tanned from the long spell of hot weather, their clothes smart, brand names. Sue was in a dark blue cotton dress and had a thin gold chain at her neck with one half of a heart as a pendant. Unlike her husband, who had lost most of his hair – and what remained had coloured silver – hers was thick, honey blonde, cut into a modern style that allowed her fringe to hang longer on one side of her face. I wondered if the fact that she and Cate were so alike physically made it harder for them.

For Martin, because every day he could see the echoes of Cate in his wife.

For Sue, because those echoes were written into her.

'This is some of the stuff she used to do,' Martin said, and pushed the albums across the table towards me. There was a grimace on his face now, and as soon as I saw the first page of the first album I realized why.

It was a photograph of a helicopter crash.

The site had mostly been cleared but some of the wreckage remained, perhaps because it was in a narrow chasm between two sheer rock faces. In the background was a jagged wall of peaks, some snow-capped, and a handwritten note was underneath: *'Fragments Pt 1' – Beinn Sionnach, Scotland, October 2015*. I turned the page and across the next spread were two more shots, each a variation on the first. *'Fragments Pt 2'* had been taken a month later, this time under bright clear skies; the full horror of the accident – the scorched angle of the rotors, the crushed, blackened cockpit, the snapped tail – impossible to look away from. The scale of the destruction, the perfection of its framing in the chasm, was hard to articulate. I didn't want to think of it as beautiful, because people would have died – and yet it was. There was something about the shot, about the third one as well, that was almost hypnotic: *'Fragments Pt 3'* had been photographed the following month and the crash seemed to have mutated again, a thick blanket of snow hiding the worst of it now, with only the occasional twist of metal reaching out.

Sue pursed her lips, her eyes on the pictures, as Martin poured himself some more iced water. 'It wasn't all like that,' Sue said. 'She photographed lots of other things – but she always said she was drawn to the tragic. In fact, one of her exhibitions was actually *called* that. Well, "Tragic, Drawn".'

'Where did she exhibit?' I asked.

'A gallery in London,' Martin replied. 'We can get the name for you if you like. She did a lot of work for photo agencies too, covering big news events, but the stuff she did for herself, that was her real passion.'

'We don't want to give you the wrong impression of who Cate was,' Sue added quickly. 'She wasn't some emotional vampire who went around feeding off other people's misery. She was the complete *opposite* of that. She was so kind, and gracious, and funny. But she always used to say that she found a certain beauty in things that other people might not. You'll see it repeated throughout that album.'

I started turning pages. More mundane images followed that I assumed had been shot for magazine covers or for websites. But then the mood started to change again. An abandoned railway station, the roof collapsing in on itself, every blade of grass at its front crested by gold light. An old house on the edge of the sea: empty and dark, windows gone, the swell of a wave captured at its rise, almost as if it were about to swallow the house whole. And then a roller-coaster track – almost entirely rusted through – disappearing into the dark of a dilapidated building.

'I know they're not to everyone's tastes,' Martin said.

'I think they're amazing.'

Both of them seemed surprised – and perhaps it was true, not everyone would find them appealing. But in the time I'd been working missing persons, even before that when I was a journalist, I'd been to many places like this, to forsaken houses, to lost villages, into the darkness of old hospitals and boarded stations. I'd searched for people in them and I'd hunted killers in their shadows, and in all of them I'd found a kind of symmetry. Because, in a way, after the death of my wife, Derryn, these places had echoed my own life: the emptiness I felt, the parts of me I didn't want to go into.

'You must have been so proud of her,' I said, my gaze still on the last shot of the roller coaster and the building, my thoughts on my own daughter now. Annabel was a teacher down in Devon, and every time we talked on video-call, or I went to visit her, I'd listen to her and think to myself, *I'm so lucky to have this.*

I'm so lucky to be in this moment with her.

I looked up at the Clarks, their eyes glimmering even in the shade; they were so proud of their daughter, they could barely even put it into words.

But Cate was gone.

There was no moment to be in any more.

I turned another page and found a portrait of her and Aiden. Cate had set it up in a hall of mirrors somewhere, and they were both sitting down, cross-legged, their backs to one another, looking into reflections that repeated endlessly.

'What was Aiden like?' I asked.

'He was a lovely kid,' Sue said without any hesitation. 'Very kind, good-natured. He absolutely worshipped the ground Cate walked on, which made us very happy. She'd have to boss him around sometimes because he was so laid-back' – both of them were smiling – 'but I don't think he minded too much. He was close to his parents, so when they died shortly after one another, he took it really hard. He got very down. But I never had any worries about them: him and Cate, they were always rock solid. They were both creative, both shared the same sort of passion for art, and books, and travel. Most of the time, they were glued at the hip.'

'So they seemed okay in the days before they disappeared?'

'Yes,' Sue said. 'I talked to Cate the day before she went missing and we had a text conversation on the morning of the crash.'

Sue took out her phone, found the messages and slid it across the table towards me. Their last text exchange was short, perfunctory, a question from Sue about what Cate was up to, a reply about how they were meeting friends in Reigate for dinner. As I scrolled down, I noticed that next to every single reply Cate had ever sent her mum was a red heart: Sue had saved them all.

Every message. Every word.

'I understand their mobiles were in the car?'

'What was left of them after the fire, yes,' Sue said.

'Wallets, purses?'

'Fragments of them were in the car too,' Sue confirmed.

It seemed highly unlikely any of the bank cards would have been taken out and used over the past two and a half years. The police would have put an alert on both Cate and Aiden's accounts and any activity on them would immediately have been flagged.

I asked if they'd be all right with me downloading the conversations between them and Cate. I didn't expect to find much, but it needed to be checked off. Mobile phone statements for Cate and Aiden were where my interests really lay, because it would give me an idea of who they were talking to and how often in the days preceding the crash. But there was just as much chance that the phone statements I'd requested would go absolutely nowhere, the same as everything else had in the hunt for answers about the Gascoignes so far.

At the moment, a lot rested on two major unanswered questions.

One was the cause of the crash. Was it a lapse in concentration by Aiden? Did he take his eyes off the road? Could they have been arguing, or laughing, or distracted? I knew already from media reports that there had been no phone calls to them in the seconds before the accident, but it could have been something that happened outside the car. Maybe the slight bend in the road surprised Aiden, or perhaps an animal ran out in front of them. Police said that, although it was cold, they found no evidence of ice, and – as had been underlined already – there had been no evidence of a mechanical failure in the vehicle either.

Yet something had happened.

One thing I was absolutely certain about was that they didn't exit the Land Rover in the time between them being captured on CCTV and the point at which the Land Rover came off the road. The timings were set in stone because crash data captured from the car showed the impact happened 11.9 seconds after they passed the camera. That just wasn't enough time to slow to a halt, get out, push the car to the edge of the ravine – for whatever reason – and then roll it off. And even if they *had* somehow done that, there was no way that could have resulted in the kind of damage the Land Rover sustained. It was damage that could only have come from leaving the road at thirty-plus miles per hour.

In the same way, I was pretty dismissive of the idea that they might have leapt from the car as it was moving. Even if the car had only been doing thirty miles per hour, if they leapt from it, they'd probably be travelling about forty feet per second in the air: that meant they'd land like a dead weight at the same speed the car was going – at best, they'd painfully tear skin, twist ankles, maybe suffer a minor fracture or break; at worst, they'd injure themselves so badly it would be impossible for them to even get up off the tarmac. And that didn't factor in the car itself; in order to get it into the ravine, Aiden would have to direct it that way, and he would have had to have done that at the last minute given the bends in the road. That, in turn, would have given him and Cate almost no time to exit the car.

So if they were still inside the car when it landed, whatever happened in the ravine happened inside those first two minutes. Because after two minutes, once they'd dialled 999, the witnesses got to the lookout point and were peering down at the burning vehicle. They didn't take their eyes off the scene until the fire crews and police arrived – and that was when the car was found to be empty. So the Gascoignes *had* to have crawled, dragged or climbed their way out of the vehicle in the first two minutes, before the witnesses got to the edge of the gully. There was simply no other window of time in which to get out of the car without being seen.

And that was the second major unanswered question.

Where did they go?

Did they hide in the gully? That would seem hard to do, especially with cops and fire crews at the scene, but until I took a drive out and had a look at the ravine myself, I couldn't discount it. Did they exit at the other side? That, from some of the photographs I'd seen in newspapers, seemed possible because the opposite bank was much less steep. But with both theories the question was why? Why hide? Why go anywhere at all after the crash? And, even then, how were they in any state to do so?

'You said you wanted to talk to Georgia?' Sue asked.

'Yes,' I said. 'She lives in Hounslow, doesn't she?'

'Yes.' She pushed a set of keys across the table towards me. 'These are for Cate's place. The silver one with the blue dot on it is for the front door, and the alarm code is 0188. I'm sure Georgia would be happy to meet you there if you want.'

'Thank you,' I said, and made a note of the code.

I looked at Sue, at Martin, their expressions anguished now, the searing light of summer making no impact on the sudden pallor of their skin.

'Georgia's the one who looks after it for us,' Sue said softly.

And then she stopped and the rest of the sentence played out on her face.

Because we can't go back to where Cate lived.

To us, that house is haunted.

3

I got straight on to the motorway and headed south to Gatton Hill. On the way, I called Georgia to set up a time to meet at Cate and Aiden's house. I hadn't spoken to her before, but it was clear that her parents had already prepped her because, as soon as I gave her my name, she knew who I was. We didn't talk for long – she was on a shift at the Marylebone gastropub she worked in – so we quickly agreed on 5 p.m.

After that, I dialled an old friend of mine and the source at the Met who was getting me the casework on Cate and Aiden's disappearance: Ewan Tasker. He'd spent a large proportion of his career working in the NCIS and SOCA – precursors to the National Crime Agency – and much of his supposed retirement shuttling back and forth to the Met, where he had an advisory role, and for twice-weekly meetings at Scotland Yard. We were going to meet at the scene.

I drove the rest of the way in silence, with not even the radio for company, going over everything Martin and Sue had said. They were hurting and they were lost, and I'd seen both those things, on repeat, in every case I'd ever worked. But they also carried a perpetual sense of dislocation that was unique to missing persons searches. They would have received comfort from others, from people who had also had to suddenly and painfully say goodbye to the ones they'd loved – but the warm words, even if well intended, could never recognize the singular nature of a disappearance, where there was no body to bury and no answers. When the person you loved was missing, you didn't move forward and you didn't move on. You were on a Ferris wheel that you could never get off.

I left the motorway and turned on to the two-lane road that was Gatton Hill. It was quiet, so I slowed a little, wanting to get a sense for the place. I'd seen photos of it online, had been back and forth using Street View, and had pored over newspaper reports and photographs released to the media – but being in a place was different.

It was where the small details were.

Straight away there was a gentle gradient to the slope, which then became marginally steeper as it fed into the first of the two bends on the hill. The first bend wasn't sharp and was signposted in advance, so I doubted it would have presented much of a problem to Aiden, even if he hadn't been paying full attention. Just before it, I spotted the CCTV camera the Gascoignes had passed ten seconds before the crash. It marked a subtle change in topography: once I was past the camera, the trees started to clot together on one side – the side that the unseen ravine was on – and on the other a high red-mud bank rose up from the tarmac.

In my head I counted down the ten seconds, assuming that the foliage damaged where the Land Rover had come off the road would have mostly grown back.

I was wrong.

The impact point was still obvious, a torn, pronounced hole in a series of vines and branches, and while the tyre marks had mostly washed out of the asphalt, I could still see a very faint echo of them, a pale almost ghostly arc suddenly veering right.

I knew, from my research, that the layby the witnesses had stopped at was five hundred feet further down the hill, so I parked there and returned on foot, following a narrow trail up the edges of the road.

It was so hot I was already sweating by the time I got back, and as I looked down the sloping carpet of scree, I realized that, although there was little growth here at the edge of the road, there was tons further down. It was tricky to even see the gully clearly; once you cleared the shelf of scree, it was just brush – tangled, dense.

My phone buzzed in my pocket.

Going to be late. Accident on the A23. E

I texted Ewan Tasker back and asked him how long he thought he might be and, as I waited for a response, weighed up getting down into the ravine.

Tasker replied. He wasn't sure.

Could be ten minutes. Could be an hour.

I let him know I was parked up and going to take a closer look at the scene and then pocketed my phone. Stepping off the road, the ground immediately started to cant and I moved on to the bed of scree. The sun was beating down hard and – even after only a few steps – I could feel sweat streaming down my face and back. Just as bad as the heat was the unreliability of the scree itself; the rocks moved constantly, shifting, my ankles turning and jarring, my whole body lurching as I tried to balance. If I'd ever been willing to believe that Cate and Aiden had, for whatever reason, leapt from their car as it was moving and made a break into the ravine itself to hide, I dispelled it once and for all. The scree was a nightmare. There was no way they'd be able to get down, even uninjured, in the time before the witnesses arrived.

When I reached the bottom, I heaved a sigh of relief and looked back up in the direction I'd come from. I knew that fire crews and police had used ladders to move up and down the scree, and that the brush had been cut down here in order to make access easier. I also knew that a lot of what had existed here had been burned away by the fire, which had helped investigators too. It made me wonder if it was worth coming back with a pair of shears, or a blade, because – as it was right now – it was going to be difficult to get a proper sense for the area where the Land Rover had come to rest; everything that had burned had regrown, the fire just a memory now. Even as I palmed away some of it, pushing at the heavily laden branches hanging down like arms, it made no difference to my sightlines. It was just too dense on the ravine floor.

There were plenty of pictures online – and, I was assuming, in the casework Ewan Tasker was bringing to me – that chronicled the way the gully had looked that night. And while I would have liked to have had an unobstructed view of the ravine – just to satisfy my curiosity – it was going to be impossible to do so without a major clearing operation.

But the opposite bank was different.

I'd hardly seen any pictures of it at all in news reports, but if the car had landed here with the Gascoignes still inside – which I believed to be the case – the opposite bank seemed an obvious place for them to have gone. It was easy to reach, simple to climb, and provided the quickest route out.

I headed up the bank.

There were trees all the way up, weaved through with more growth, but – compared to edging my way down the scree – it was a simple ascent. The undergrowth was thick but it wasn't as unyielding as in the ravine and I could walk it, unhindered.

At the apex of the bank, I stopped and checked my watch. It had taken me fifty seconds to get to the top.

Was it realistic to think that Cate and Aiden could both have crawled out of the vehicle in the first sixty to seventy seconds after it hit the ravine? Because, factoring in the fifty seconds it took to climb the bank, that was what would have had to have happened. There was maybe *some* wriggle room in terms of exactly when the eyewitnesses got to the ravine edge – the two-minute time frame was an estimate by investigators, based on data, 999 calls, CCTV footage and statements – but I doubted it was far off. All of which meant that, even if the Gascoignes really had managed to escape the crushed vehicle inside that time frame, they'd then *immediately* have had to traverse the gradient of the bank in fifty seconds or less, in order to disappear from view before the witnesses arrived. I just didn't see it. They'd have been dazed, at worst badly injured, perhaps completely trapped by the malformed vehicle. Plunging ninety feet into a ravine was going to be incredibly traumatic, physically and emotionally. It wasn't the sort of thing you'd simply shrug off.

And yet . . .

From the top of the bank I studied where it went from here.

Dropping away in front of me was another much sharper slope dominated by hundreds of pine trees. It looked like a sustainable forest: the trees were in straight tightly packed rows and, off to the right, I could see piles of timber. In the distance, at the bottom of the slope, it looked like there might be some kind of access road, although it was hard to be sure. The pine trees were so close together they were keeping out the sun, so all I could see was a faint grey trail.

I followed one row of trees all the way down. It *was* an access road, a mixture of gravel and mud, coming from my right and snaking off into more trees to my left. There were no signposts anywhere, and when I looked back up the slope – to the top of the bank – I could barely make it out. I must have travelled half a mile, maybe more.

I looked at my watch.

It had taken me six minutes to get down to the access road.

I carried on walking – following the road to the left as it dipped down – further into the woods. Fifteen minutes later, after a couple of switchbacks, I arrived in a car park. It belonged to the Forestry Commission and was off a tree-fringed B-road, with signs for Reigate and Crawley next to the exit gate. I looked for CCTV cameras but there weren't any, and took in the car park properly. It was empty except for a single green Toyota, an old couple in the front, sharing coffee from a flask.

I grabbed my notebook and wrote down *21 minutes from the top of the bank to the car park*. It was a mile and a half, maybe a little more, but that would feel a long way with the sort of injuries you might sustain in a major car wreck. Plus, if the Gascoignes came here, why hadn't there been a sighting of them?

Perhaps no one was parked here that day.

'Perhaps,' I echoed quietly, but – like the timings back at the ravine – it didn't feel right. They could have left a second car here to pick up, but if they did, if that was the plan, why do something as insanely dangerous as driving the first one off a road into a ravine? Why would anyone choose to make that the starting point for a disappearance?

It risked failure from the first second.

I returned the way I'd come and, at the point I joined the access road, walked the other way to see where it went. It ended in an impasse, at a swathe of forest whose trees had been felled. It looked barren and there were no surprises or hiding places.

It was simply a dead end.

I hoped it wasn't a sign of things to come.

4

When I got back to the ravine, I could see Ewan Tasker waiting for me at the lookout. He waved but didn't attempt to come down: he was six-three and sixteen stone, but he was also seventy-three and, although he was in good health, he wasn't about to put it all on the line by negotiating his way down a carpet of scree.

I took some photographs of the ravine floor, trying to push back some of the brush in an attempt at clearer shots, and then started the climb back up to the road. It wasn't quite as arduous as coming down, but by the time I got to the top, the sweat was pouring off me and I had cuts on my shin, forearm and hand where one of the loose rocks had tilted and taken me with it.

Tasker said hello to me. I pointed to his blue tailored shorts and boat shoes and said, 'What time do you set sail?'

He laughed. 'Cheeky bastard.'

We embraced. Not only had it been a while since we'd seen each other in the flesh, but Tasker was also my best friend. He'd started out as a source back when I'd been a journalist, and now he was so much more than that I sometimes forgot that was the way things had begun for us. After Derryn died, Tasker had been immense, the person who'd been there for me when it was darkest.

In his hands was a brown A4 envelope. He passed it to me and then looked down through the trees to the bottom of the gully. 'Looks like you should have brought your machete.'

'It's like the Amazon down there now,' I said, peeling the

flap on the envelope and sliding out the file. It was eighty pages, all black-and-white printouts except for a colour section at the back featuring photographs. 'I really appreciate this, Task.'

'As always –'

'I didn't get it from you.'

His eyes were still on the ravine. 'So they really just disappeared?'

I looked down into the gully myself. 'Their car comes off the road, hits the bottom of the ravine on its roof. Two minutes later, there are two eyewitnesses standing in exactly this spot here. Pretty soon after that, it all goes up in flames.' I leafed through the file again, trying to find a timeline of events. 'It says here the response time was nine minutes, forty-three seconds and, by the time the fire crew arrived, the Land Rover was an inferno. The eyewitnesses told investigators the vehicle had "been on fire for approximately eight minutes".'

'Was that backed up by the FSI?'

The FSI was the fire scene investigator, who worked in conjunction with the SIO from Thames Valley Police, the forensic teams and the fire crews to establish exactly what had happened and why. I flipped back a couple of pages, trying to find the answer. 'Here we go. The FSI found the witnesses statements to be "accurate".'

Tasker waved a hand at the ravine. 'You can discount any idea of your couple somehow climbing out of the car *after* the fire crew arrived. They didn't hide out down there and evade every fireman, copper and forensic technician at the scene. I mean, those things sound ridiculous even *before* you consider the fact that – in order to do any of that – they'd have had to have crawled out of a burning wreck.'

'It *had* to have happened in that first two minutes,' I said.

'Thing I can't figure out, though – or *one* of the things – is how. It would have required them to basically have sustained no serious injuries at all, *and* to be lucid enough to have instigated an immediate escape. And even if that was the plan – to vanish, I mean – there are about a million easier ways of setting it up than veering off the edge of a sheer drop.'

'Any blood found around the car?'

'I don't know,' I said, holding up the file. 'I'll need to check. But if there was, if there was some convenient trail leading away from the scene, I seriously doubt we'd be standing here two and a half years later still trying to work out where they went.'

Tasker nodded.

I briefly went through all the reasons why I didn't think it was possible that the Gascoignes could have exited the car before it left the road, and then, reluctantly, said, 'Of course there might be something else that I need to face up to.'

Tasker looked at me. 'What's that?'

'The eyewitnesses.' I glanced at the file in my hands. 'The only account of what went on in that ravine during those first eleven minutes is provided by them.'

We both stood there for a moment, silent.

'What if they were lying?'

5

I went to a local pub for a proper catch-up with Tasker and then drove back up the motorway towards Twickenham, where Cate and Aiden had lived.

It was still a couple of hours before I was due to meet Georgia at the house, so I found a parking space and headed to a coffee shop on King Street. The temperature hadn't eased even a fraction, so I decided against sitting outside and found a space inside in a corner booth at the back, got out my laptop and connected to the Wi-Fi.

I laid the file for the crash investigation out on the table.

Much of what I read – although covered in greater detail, down to things like paint flakes from the car and precise angles of impact – matched what I already knew, which at least proved that Martin and Sue's recall of events was reliable, and that the media had reported the facts as they were. But that also meant that I was adding little new to the overall picture.

I found mobile phone records included for both Cate and Aiden, as well as for their landline, but they only went back a month, to 1 December, and I always liked to go back further. I'd requested two additional months – the October and November before the accident – through another source of mine, but was still waiting on those, so for now I concentrated on what I had and looked for anomalies.

I searched for frequently dialled numbers, recurrent incoming calls, calls at odd times of the day and night, but nothing stood out. I double-checked for calls made in the thirty minutes before the crash too, and – just as had been stated in the media – there hadn't been any. I hadn't expected the crash to have been caused by Aiden trying to take an incoming call, but now I had my proof.

I paused on a photo of Cate and Aiden at her parents, the Christmas before they disappeared. Alongside the picture was a note from one of the investigators, listing some of the possible motivations for why one or both of the Gascoignes might have organized their own disappearance. It was a pretty standard list: money issues, although bank statements contradicted that theory; and domestic problems, of which there was no evidence either. Martin and Sue certainly didn't paint a picture of Cate and Aiden having had a turbulent, unpredictable marriage, and even if they had, it was more likely that only one of them would vanish in those circumstances – after all, it wasn't much of an escape from a spouse if the spouse came with you.

As well as theories about why they might have disappeared, the investigators also worked through ideas of how, and then where, Cate and Aiden might have gone.

All of it went nowhere.

The police, like me, dismissed the concept of them finding a hiding spot in the ravine somewhere and watching the whole thing play out: the way the fire had burned, its radius and ferocity, and the number of emergency services personnel in the gully at the time made it impossible for two people to find cover and not be noticed. They had also, like me, walked the pines beyond the ravine, even going as far as drawing a map of the area, with all the trails, including the one that eventually led to the car park. Again, they couldn't definitively dismiss the idea of Cate and Aiden making it to the car park, but – considering everything – it seemed unlikely.

The police spoke to three separate experts – a fire scene investigator with over twenty years in the service; a two-decade veteran of crash scene investigations; and then a trauma specialist from the Royal London Hospital – and their basic overview was pretty similar: Cate and Aiden would probably have been severely injured. More likely, the trauma specialist commented, 'we're talking spinal injuries and neurological damage, both of which impair rapid, lucid decision-making.'

I flicked through to the witness statements.

As my eyes lingered on the names of Zoe Simmons and Audrey Calvert, I thought back to what I'd asked Tasker earlier: what if they were lying?

I read Simmons's statement first: she'd approached from the north, seen a piece of the Land Rover's bumper, and, when she slowed some more, saw the tear in the greenery where the car had gone off the road. She told police she didn't really know the area, she lived in Horsham and was coming back from visiting friends in Croydon. Given that she had no record and no red flags, and that what she'd said in her interview tallied with indisputable evidence like surveillance footage, it was easy enough to see why the cops had trusted her account of that day. Of course, they trusted it because they saw no reason for her to lie.

Audrey Calvert's statement mirrored Simmons's closely.

Sixty-one, she had a grown-up son, was retired and lived in Streatham. She told police that she'd been to see an old friend for lunch, who lived close to Gatwick Airport – so her route home, via Gatton Hill, made sense. I couldn't find anything at all online for Audrey Calvert, but Zoe Simmons I found quickly and easily: like most kids her age, her life was played out on social media. It looked like she had Instagram and TikTok accounts, and there may well have been other apps she was using, but for now I scrolled through her wall of photographs.

Almost immediately, I noticed something.

Before the accident, her Instagram was absolutely full of pictures of her, her mates, parties, pub gardens, memes, the life of a young woman in her late teens and early twenties playing out on repeat. She was posting something at least twice every week. But after the date Cate and Aiden disappeared, it all stopped.

I checked her posts again just to be sure.

But I was right.

Before the accident two and a half years ago, she'd posted three hundred and forty-six photographs over a period of thirty-four months. That was ten every month.

Since the accident, she'd posted nothing.

Not one single picture.

6

I got to the Gascoignes' house a couple of minutes early. Georgia hadn't arrived yet, so I walked along the street, getting a sense for the road and its surroundings.

The area was nice, mostly terraced houses. Cate and Aiden's, and the ones either side of it, were easy to spot because thick sweeps of emerald-green ivy were growing between the ground and first floors. It was now two and a half years since they'd lived here, but none of the ivy had overgrown, which seemed to back up what Martin and Sue had said to me: Georgia looked after things here.

She was the only one who could enter this ghost house.

'David?'

I turned, recognizing Georgia straight away from the pictures that Martin and Sue had shown me. Physically she didn't share much with her sister, her brown hair threaded through with silver, the angles of her face a little less striking, but she had a beautiful smile and the most perfectly blue eyes.

'Georgia,' I said, shaking her hand. 'I really appreciate you meeting me here.'

'I'm sorry I'm late,' she replied, her cheeks flushed. The heat of the day had eased off a little, but it was still warm. 'I was only meant to be covering a few hours.'

'Honestly, don't worry.'

She started going through her bag.

'Your parents gave me keys if it's easier,' I said.

'Ah, brilliant. I've got the other set in here somewhere – but alongside my first boyfriend, this bag has to be one of the worst decisions I've ever made.' She smiled, took the keys from me and then unlocked the house, punching in the alarm code on a pad just inside the door. Handing me back Martin and Sue's set, she said, 'Come in.'

The house had the appearance of a country cottage, with red-tiled floors in the hallway, an ornate wooden staircase and – through a living-room door on my left – a large stone fireplace with a wood burner. The furniture was rustic, a theme that continued through to the kitchen, where there was an Aga, a big dresser, shelves decorated with plates and jars, and a white ceiling with dark beams.

'They always wanted to live in the sticks,' Georgia said.

That much was clear. What was also clear was that, in the time her sister and brother-in-law had been missing, Georgia had shown the house a lot of love. It smelled nice, despite how long it had gone without being lived in, the floors and carpets were all clean, the worktops spotless. It wasn't all that unusual in missing persons cases to find family members treating an empty home with the same care as their own, as if it were soon going to be lived in again.

'I'm afraid the water is off, so I can't offer you a cup of tea.'

I told her not to worry and we went to the end of the hall-way where the living room wrapped around from the left into a sunroom with a set of huge bifold doors. The garden, like the house, was well kept, although it was simple, perhaps deliberately so: the flower beds were empty, the patio clean. I didn't know Cate, but I imagined it would have meant a lot to her to see how much effort had been put in by her sister.

The angle of the sun had created a shaded corner in the living room, so we sat at the table and enjoyed what little breeze wafted through the doors from outside.

'How did it go with Mum and Dad?' Georgia asked.

'It was good,' I said, and then started to ask her the same

sorts of questions I'd asked her parents: when she last saw Cate, how she seemed, any changes in her sister or moments that stuck.

'You two were close?'

'Very. I mean, don't get me wrong, we were sisters, and as teenaged girls in the same house we had our fair share of meltdowns.' But a flicker of a smile edged across her lips: even the meltdowns were good memories for her now. 'Cate went to university here in London, to do her photography, and I . . .' She stopped. 'I wasn't as academic, put it that way. I suppose I gave Mum and Dad a few more sleepless nights than Cate did.'

'In what way?'

'Oh, typical teenage stuff, the type of thing that'll give me a coronary when my own daughter gets to that age.' She laughed a little. 'I liked the bad boys, let's just say that. Probably went to too many parties and didn't work hard enough at school. But Cate . . . she only had two boyfriends before Aiden, both long-term. And she worked her arse off at school. She got As across the board at GCSE and A level.'

'What were those two relationships like before Aiden?'

'In what sense?'

'I mean, were they good? Turbulent? Did they end badly? I'm just looking for angles.'

'Oh, I see. Well, she was with Aiden for nine years – so I suppose any fallout from her exes would have happened way before the accident.' It was true, but I asked again if the relationships were good. 'Yeah, I don't remember them *not* being.'

'Why did they end?'

'The first was at school, but they split about two or three months after they both went to different universities on opposite sides of the country. The other one she went out with for about five years in her mid-twenties. They split because he got drunk and shagged some woman on a stag do – and Cate found out.'

On the surface, it was true that neither relationship seemed relevant, but I got the men's names from Georgia anyway, and made a note to follow up on it.

'So you said Cate always knew that she wanted to be a photographer?'

'Oh, she always knew *exactly* what she wanted to be, from as far back as I can remember. She always loved taking pictures, even when we were kids. Mum and Dad bought her this second-hand Polaroid camera back when she was maybe nine or ten, and she just took it everywhere with her. I mean, *everywhere*. It used to piss me off actually' – Georgia was smiling again – 'because you'd hear the whir of that bloody thing, and then turn around, and you'd realize she'd been watching you for ages, just trying to line up the perfect shot.' She'd been pretty stoic up until now, but as the memory formed and played out in her head, there was the first glimmer in her eyes.

She looked at me and then away again, as if embarrassed, so I gave her a few moments. 'She loved stories,' she said finally. 'She used to say all the time that her pictures were stories, not photographs. She'd never press the button until she saw it.'

I thought of the shots Cate had taken of the downed helicopter, and what Sue had said: *She was drawn to the tragic.*

'She loved writing too,' Georgia added.

'What did she write?'

'It was all tied into the things she photographed. Often, when she took a picture, she then went and really dug down into the details behind it. So, for example, one of my favourite series was the one she took at that theme park. Did you ever see them?'

'I saw the picture of the roller coaster.'

'There were quite a few others, but yeah. I thought they were really eerie; like, you just don't expect a theme park to look like that, do you? Anyway, she did an exhibition where all of them were on display, and next to the photos – on the wall – there would be a plaque or a board, or whatever, with something she'd written on it.'

'Something like what?'

'Like, where it was shot, what she was trying to capture, that sort of thing.'

'So, kind of like background?'

'Exactly. It would aim to support the picture. The story.' She frowned, as if she'd confused herself. 'That sounds so airy-fairy, but she was really clever with it. You'd look at the photograph, and then look at the words on the wall next to it – maybe only a paragraph – and it was like you then had a full grasp of it. I suppose what I'm saying is, she was a really bloody good photographer, but I reckon she could just as easily have been a writer. She was so good at both. It made me sick.'

It was another joke, another broad smile, but while it was clear she'd adored her sister, it felt like a comment that was tinged with some element of truth. I made a mental note of it. 'So did she ever try to get into photojournalism?'

'I think, ultimately, that was where she saw herself, yeah. She never had anything major published in terms of her writing, but she contributed a few pieces to some photography magazines. You know, how-to guides. And she had her website.'

I'd come across it already in the background I'd done on Cate.

'It was more like a blog, though, right?'

'Right,' Georgia replied. 'Just a place where Cate liked to put down her thoughts. Mostly it was photography stuff.'

There wasn't any obvious connection between what had happened two and a half years ago on Gatton Hill and Cate's job, but these were important steps in getting to know her, how she thought and where her interests lay. I switched tack to Aiden, trying to do the same with him, and asked Georgia to describe what he was like.

'He was easy-going,' she responded, echoing what Martin and Sue had already told me. 'Maybe *too* easy-going some-times. He was pretty focused at work, but I know Cate could get frustrated with him around the house. He was . . .' She stopped and looked at me. 'No offence, but he was a typical man. Basically thought, outside of his own responsibilities, life magically ran itself. But one of the things we all loved about Aiden was that you could bring him up on anything and he'd never take offence. He was just really good fun. I mean, I was *always* taking the piss out of him.'

'About what?'

'Oh, all sorts of stuff. Like, he got this haircut about a year before he and Cate disappeared and the hairdresser left a huge step at the back of his head. It was *awful.* So obviously none of us let that go for a while.' She chuckled to herself. 'And he used to be into open-water swimming – was really good at it too; he competed in all sorts of competitions – so he'd wax his whole body before a race, and inevitably that was a source of enjoyment for us as well. We used to call him the "Karate Kid".'

' "Wax on, wax off." '

Georgia chuckled again. 'Right.'

'Did Cate joke with him too?'

'Oh yeah. She was the ringleader most of the time.' She paused for a moment, remembering it all, and then her smile faded a little. 'I miss all of that. I miss them.'

'Did you all spend a lot of time together?'

'Tons. Me and Will – that's my other half – and Cate and Aiden, we all got on great. And Cate and Aiden were amazing with Talia, our little girl.'

'Did they ever talk about wanting kids?'

'Not really, no. They were way too career-focused, I think. Cate had her thing; Aiden was high up at the design agency he worked for. His company did all sorts of stuff for these huge brands, and he was always zipping about here, there and everywhere, making presentations and meeting people. So their jobs often meant time apart in different places – but when they were together, they were tight. Hardly ever argued, never seemed to get sick of each other. My sister was lucky. Aiden worshipped the ground she walked on most of the time.'

Her choice of words stopped me. '"Most of the time"?'

She shrugged. 'They had a bit of a rough patch once.'

'When was that?'

'Maybe six months before they went missing.'

'Did your mum and dad know?'

She shook her head. 'No.'

They hadn't mentioned it, so I'd guessed not.

'Why do you think Cate didn't tell them?'

'I guess because she didn't want to stress them out unnecessarily. I think she only ever saw it as a temporary thing. She and Aiden, they *were* really solid the rest of the time. But there was a month or two there where it just got a bit rocky.'

'What was the catalyst for it?'

Georgia opened out her hands. 'I don't know. She never wanted to talk about it – which was unusual for Cate, as we normally shared everything. But, whatever it was, she said they'd worked through it.'

I tapped my pen against the pad.

'I remember a couple of things, though,' Georgia went

on. 'One time, Cate said Aiden was pushing her to do something she wasn't ready to do. I asked her what, but she didn't want to say. I just assumed it was starting a family or something like that.'

'And the other thing?'

'We met for a coffee in Kew, right in the middle of their rough patch, and I could tell she'd been crying. Then she got this call on her mobile.'

'From who?'

'I don't know. But when she looked down at the phone and saw who was calling, she didn't want me to see the screen.'

'She tried to stop you from looking at the phone?'

'She turned it over. But it was more than that.'

'What do you mean?'

'I mean, there was this look on her face as well, this expression. Maybe someone who didn't know her like I did wouldn't have even noticed. But I did.'

'What did the expression say to you?'

'That she was worried about something but trying to disguise it.' She paused. 'Maybe it really *was* nothing. But it didn't *feel* like nothing.'

'So she didn't pick up?'

'Not then, but whoever it was phoned back a few minutes later.'

'And she took the call then?'

'Yes. She apologized and left the table.'

'Did you hear any of her conversation?'

'No,' Georgia said, but then paused. 'Well, maybe one word.'

'And what was that?'

'I could be wrong, but I'm pretty sure she said "dunes".'

7

'"Dunes"?' I asked. 'As in, "sand dunes"?'

'Yes,' Georgia said, 'I think so.'

I took a second to think. *Dunes* sounded pretty similar to a lot of other words, and when I tried to remember if I'd seen any shots of sand dunes in Cate's albums, I couldn't recall a single one. Even if there were, though, and Georgia was right, why would that have anything to do with Cate and Aiden's disappearance?

'You said this was right in the middle of their rough patch?'

'Yes.'

'And she didn't share *anything* with you about her marriage?'

She shook her head. 'No, not really. She just said they were going through a difficult time – "working things out". I kept trying to press her about it – but she just kept telling me not to worry. I've got to admit it did hurt me a little. It was the first time that she'd ever *not* been open with me. It made me feel . . .' Georgia paused, searching for the word. 'I don't know. Confused, I guess.'

'You said their rough patch only lasted for a month or two?'

'About that, yes.'

'How did it resolve itself?'

'One day she told me that things were better. I kept asking her what had happened, but she said it was just something that she and Aiden needed to work out for themselves.' Georgia shrugged. 'I mean, what else was I supposed to say? It was clear she didn't want to get into it and, afterwards, things just went back to normal.'

'And that was six months before the crash?'

'Approximately, yes.'

'Did you tell the police all this?'

'About the dunes thing, yes – but I forgot about the other thing. You know, Aiden trying to push her into something she didn't want to do. I think because, in my head, I thought it was about having kids, I kind of dismissed it.'

'What did the cops say about the dunes thing?'

'They didn't seem to think it was important.'

I wrote down *dunes* and underlined it a couple of times, and then moved on again. 'I know Aiden was an only child, but does he have any family he's close to?'

'He's got a couple of cousins – but they both live up north. One of them came down after the crash, but I don't know . . .' She paused, pushing her lips together. 'I know cousins can be close, but it's not the same as brothers or sisters – or parents.'

'And I understand both his parents are dead.'

'His dad died before he met Cate, and his mum passed on four years later. Cancer, both of them.'

We talked more about Aiden's extended family and Georgia said she'd dig out the contact details of his cousins for me.

'Have you ever watched the YouTube video?' she asked.

I looked at her. 'You mean the CCTV footage from just before the crash?'

She nodded. I *had* watched the video of Cate and Aiden that had been posted, many times over, but as an investigative tool it was basically worthless. Ten seconds before the crash everything was fine. It wasn't that part that was going to get me the answers I sought, it was what happened after the car hit the ravine. But that didn't stop Internet commenters making the video seem like a vital piece of evidence. Online, in the hands of anonymous posters, that short few seconds of a Land Rover appearing and passing the camera was the key to unlocking everything.

'"The Mystery of Gatton Hill",' Georgia said, the disdain heavy in her voice. 'I hated that the media called it that. It made it sound like an episode from a TV show, like this fun puzzle everyone should get involved in. I mean, that video barely lasts any time at all and it's got three million views or something.' Her head dropped a little. 'I hate myself for doing it, but sometimes, when things get a bit desperate, I find myself going on there and reading the comments.' She looked at me, shook her head. 'I don't know why I do it.'

'You're looking for answers. It's understandable.'

'But there are no answers on there. It's just people saying shit that hurts me. All this crap about how Cate and Aiden faked it, got out of the car and pushed it into the ravine themselves. Or how they owed money to people, which was why they had to go on the run. Or how Aiden deliberately crashed the car because he was trying to kill Cate for the insurance. It just goes on like that. None of it makes any sense, none of it holds up to examination – but that doesn't stop it from hurting. I'm just glad I've kept Mum and Dad away from it – especially Dad.'

'Why especially him?'

'He had a massive heart attack ten years ago. We thought we were going to lose him. Honestly? All this stuff online, all the lies and conspiracy theories – I genuinely think it would be the death of him.'

I remembered seeing some of the user comments myself. I agreed with everything Georgia had said – comments on the Internet, more often than not, didn't lead anywhere good – but I'd scrolled down all the same, wading through the swamp in the remote possibility that there might be something worthwhile, a line to help spark off an idea or theory.

46

What interested me most now, which I didn't think about at the time, was how few question marks had been raised online about the witnesses. If there was ever a place for baseless accusations and unprovable conspiracies it was within the relative anonymity of a website's comments section. And yet, even among those people who seemed to have studied the case quite closely, there was very little mention of Zoe Simmons and Audrey Calvert. Everyone, from cops to commenters, seemed to have believed the story the witnesses had given. And maybe that was because it *wasn't* a story, but an actual, genuine account of what had gone on in the ravine.

Again, I tapped out a rhythm with my pen, trying to see between the lines. 'Do you think one of them might have had an affair?'

'Cate? No way.'

'She hid that phone call from you.'

'I know but . . . I really don't see it.'

'What about Aiden?'

'Cate wouldn't have taken him back.'

'She might not have known.'

'I think she would have found out. She always told me there were never any secrets between them and, away from their work, they lived in each other's pockets. I think it would have been hard to hide an affair.'

Hard but not impossible, I thought.

'And if Aiden *was* cheating on her, she was decisive and single-minded about stuff like that. After her second boyfriend did the dirty, she just cut him off. They were together five years and she ended it right there and then, not even a flicker of hesitation. He used to turn up at the flat they had, begging her to take him back, and she wouldn't even let him in. I mean, she was *upset*, don't get me wrong, but she never wavered. Not even once.'

We were quiet for a moment, the house silent around us. And then, finally, she looked out at the living room, at the photos on the wall, and said, 'What do you think happened to them?'

This was the heart of it.

The *what*.

The *how*.

'I don't know,' I replied softly. 'But I promise you, I'm going to find out.'

8

I left Georgia in the living room and did a search of the house.

Away from the breeze coming in through the back doors it was hot, stuffy, the air still as a tomb. As I came up the stairs on to the landing, a thick shaft of light poured in, motes of dust in the air, not a single one moving. There were three bedrooms up here, two opposite one another and a third at the other end of the landing, which I could see had been turned into an office.

I concentrated on the first two bedrooms, looking inside wardrobes, drawers, kneeling at side tables. I spent time going through clothes and shoeboxes full of detritus at the bottom of a built-in cupboard, and then worked my way around to a bookcase in the second bedroom. I paused for a moment, wanting to see the types of books on display, trying to get a sense for Cate and Aiden as people, and not just as faces and names in a file. Thrillers, sci-fi, history, art – which could have been the choice of either of them given that Aiden worked for a design agency – and then a copy of *No One Can See the Crows at Night* by Eva Gainridge. My eyes lingered on that one; it always reminded me of Derryn, always brought home how little time we'd had together in our marriage and how long she'd been gone.

I headed through to the office. It was well lit by a huge bay window, but because the sun was on the other side of the house, the office didn't quite have the stifling heat of the bedrooms or the landing. Under the window was a built-in seat filled with cushions, each cushion cover a black-and-white print of one of Cate's photographs. A couple I recognized from her albums, but most were new: a shipyard, a lonely hill, a Spanish taxi.

There were two desks next to one another, chairs pushed under them. On one was a pencil pot and a cutting board and a few photographs in a pile; on the other an iMac, some more design books and some sort of pitch document for an advertising campaign. Above them was a corkboard but it was empty. I booted up the Mac and moved to the cupboards. On the front of one of the doors was a calendar, the date still set to January 2020, the last month anyone had seen Cate and Aiden alive.

Inside were a series of shelves, laden with camera equipment. Folded tripods. Lenses. Memory cards. Reflective panels. Batteries. There was so much of it, it filled every shelf front to back. When I opened another door, I found more of the same.

Behind a third door, though, were stacks of old boxes. A lot just contained more equipment – I recognized a lens pen and an air blower from my days as a journalist – but some contained random items like Christmas baubles. Others had books in, computer leads and USB sticks, pens, rulers and scalpels. In a smaller shoebox I found tons of old receipts, and as I began to go through them I saw that they were separated according to month, each month stapled together, and that the receipts covered the period between April 2019 and January 2020. The last receipt was for two coffees at a Starbucks on the M4 and was from New Year's Day.

Forty-eight hours later, Cate and Aiden were gone.

I tilted the box to see if there was any kind of label and there was: *Tax & VAT*.

Maybe there's something in here.

I set them aside and bagged up all the memory cards and USB sticks. It would be an arduous task to go through them all, but if there was a small chance it might lead somewhere, it was a job worth doing. I then returned to the Mac. There was no login screen so, once it had loaded, I was able to start exploring the desktop.

It looked like it had belonged to Aiden. He had all the projects he'd been working on in folders on the right-hand side – but most of it was stuff like mood boards and prototypes for corporate web pages. Next, I opened Photos. There were a lot of pictures of him and Cate, on holidays, with friends, with family. There were some of him doing the open-water swimming that Georgia had mentioned, some of him at the football with mates, a lot of him and Cate with Georgia and her partner Will. I closed it and went to his browser, to the History. The last site he visited, the day before he and Cate disappeared, was about football transfer rumours. As I went back through December, and then November, and then October, I found more of the same, basically on repeat. Aiden loved his football, his sport, mountain biking, and things like architecture and art too. Beyond what he was doing on the computer for work, he seemed to spend a lot of time looking at holidays and travel, something I'd already seen echoed in the photographs of him and Cate.

But then, just as I was about to close the computer down, I spotted something. I'd deliberately gone back six months from the date of their disappearance, in order to look at Internet activity around the time of the 'rough patch' Georgia had described – and that was where I found it. It was a Google search and a subsequent URL, both hidden among a ton of other more mundane links.

The Google search was for *local police station.*

The URL was for a page on the Met website.

I clicked on it but then realized there was no longer an Internet connection at the house, so used my phone as a hotspot to bring the page up on the Mac. It was an address and map for Twickenham Police Station.

Why would Aiden search for that?

'How are you getting on?'

Georgia had appeared in the doorway. I could see she'd been crying. Her eyes were puffy and she was clasping a screwed-up ball of tissue.

'Is it all right if I take these things?' I asked gently, and held up the shoebox, its lid off, showing her the receipts and the bag of SD cards and USB sticks.

She nodded and then handed me a scrap of paper. 'Here,' she said. It was the numbers for Aiden's cousins up north. 'Like I say, I don't really know them all that well – we only talked for the first time after Cate and Aiden went missing – but, you know, maybe they might come up with something that I can't.'

I pointed to the screen. 'Any idea why Aiden might have wanted to know where his local police station is?' I asked. Georgia shook her head, confused, and said she had no idea at all. 'You said Cate told you that Aiden was pushing her into doing something she didn't want to do?'

Georgia nodded, and I returned my gaze to the monitor. Could that thing have been going to the police? Why would he want her to do that?

It was obvious that Georgia had no idea either way, so I shut the Mac down, and when I turned to her, she looked like she might be about to cry again.

'Are you okay?' I asked.

The answer was clear – it wasn't just in her eyes, or in the tissue she held, it was like it was written into her skin – but she smiled all the same, even seemed oddly appreciative of me asking. It made me wonder if it had been a long time since anyone had asked her that. 'I'm fine,' she said softly, 'it's just, sometimes, it's all a bit much.'

'I know. I get it.'

She eyed me for a moment.

'I read that . . .' She stopped, swallowed. 'I read that your wife died.'

'She did,' I said simply.

'I'm really sorry to hear that.'

'Thank you.'

'How long has she been gone?'

'Ten years.'

We both looked at each other.

'What happened to Cate and what happened to my wife isn't the same,' I said, smiling at her. 'For starters, I'm hoping for good news about Cate . . .' I paused, looking around the office. Cate was everywhere here: in the equipment left behind; in the photos on the walls and on the cushions; in the furniture she chose, in the colour she painted the walls. My home still felt like this, even now. I'd struggled with it for years, being in the same place that my wife and I had lived in, laughed in, cried in; sleeping in the same bed I'd nursed her in during her last months. Maybe Georgia's memories were different in this home, but they came from a similar place. I looked at her. 'I guess what I'm saying is, whatever happens from here – and especially if the news is difficult – what you're feeling won't go away for a while. But, over time, like it did with me, it starts to become less oppressive.'

She nodded again.

And as we lingered there, both of us lost to different people, in different places at different moments in time, my eyes returned to the box of receipts, and I noticed that a couple from the November batch had shaken loose from the pile.

I took one of them out. It was dated 6 November. A chicken mayonnaise sandwich. A side portion of chips. A fruit tea.

But that wasn't what had got my attention.

It wasn't the business – the Castle View Café – either.

It was, instead, the address of the café, listed under its name, that had snagged me. As I stared at it, my thoughts racing, I remembered what Georgia had said about hearing Cate say *dunes*.

And I started to wonder if I'd just found a lead.

9

I looked at the receipt, at the black printed logo for the Castle View Café – a spidery ornate design with the *t* of *Castle* a turret – and then at the address printed below it.

Bamburgh, Northumberland.

I didn't know that part of the country well but I knew enough. Bamburgh was a picturesque tourist spot on the North Sea coast, renowned for its iconic castle, which was perched on a dramatic crag overlooking the town. From memory I knew that that part of the country was home to something else too. The thing Cate had mentioned.

Sand dunes.

Along that frill of the Northumberland coast there were acres of them.

Georgia had told me she'd meet me downstairs when I was done, so I took another quick look around the office and then gathered up everything I was going to take with me and returned to the living room. Georgia had moved out to the garden and was now turning over the earth in the empty beds. I watched her for a while from behind the glass of the patio doors, wondering how much I should tell her about what I'd found.

These moments were always the hardest.

A lot of the time the families had gone so long without answers, without any hope at all, that I found the lure to give them something, even something minor, very powerful. But I almost always resisted. Worse than giving someone no hope was giving them false hope, and I'd probably already gone too far in my assurances to the family – to Martin and Sue, to Georgia as well – that I would bring them the truth. I believed I would with every bone in my body, but believing it and delivering on it were two different things. I'd let my emotional connection to the work that I did get the better of me, so when Georgia finally noticed me, put down a trowel and came over, I said to her, 'I've just been going through some of these receipts that Cate was saving for her year-end tax. She seemed to travel quite a lot in the time before she vanished.'

'My sister was always on the move.'

'So her being in a place like Northumberland was pretty normal?'

'Absolutely. She travelled all the time.'

The mention of Northumberland didn't seem to register with her. Instead, she looked around the living room, at some of the framed pictures on the wall. One was of the two sisters, a portrait in black and white that Cate must have set up. As Georgia's gaze lingered on it, there was a faint tremor in her lips.

'She was always on the hunt,' she said quietly.

'The hunt for what?'

Georgia looked at me. 'For the perfect story.'

I opened up the car, slid behind the wheel and then watched Georgia head back in the direction of the Tube station, thinking for a moment about some of the things we'd talked about, particularly Cate's mention of *dunes*. There was every chance that Georgia might have misheard and that Cate hadn't said it at all. And even if she *had* said it, it didn't necessarily have anything to do with her and Aiden going missing. The same was true of Aiden's search for his local police station. All of it could have meant nothing so, for now, I didn't want to become too fixated on any of it.

Instead, I switched my attention back to the file on the Gascoignes' crash, and specifically the two witnesses, checking over their personal details and the addresses besides their names. Horsham was an hour away, a straight drive down the M25 and M23. I could be there for seven fifteen if the traffic was kind. And, after, if I took the route back home to Ealing that avoided the motorway, Streatham would be on my way too. But it was still a detour – and neither of them might even be home.

I thought about whether the journey was worth it now.

But not for long.

A minute later, I was heading south to see Zoe Simmons.

Amelia

30 Years Ago

Amelia checked her watch again.

Three minutes had passed.

It felt like three hours.

She looked around the room, at the other women waiting for their scans. She counted seven seated, and then an eighth standing, who was moaning slightly, rubbing her belly, unable to sit because it appeared to be too painful to do so. Just watching her, the way her face would crease up, was making Amelia nervous. Amelia didn't have any pain, but that didn't mean everything was rosy: when she'd woken up that morning, she'd found a spattering of crimson spots on her bed sheet.

She was only nine weeks.

Bleeding early in pregnancy couldn't be good, could it?

She didn't know, that was the truth. She was nineteen and didn't know anything of the world, really. She readily acknowledged that herself. This whole pregnancy had been a mistake, a stupid drunken consequence of a stupid drunken night out. The worst thing was, she barely remembered the name of the guy she'd slept with. He'd been a friend of a friend, just another face at a party, and when she'd asked around about him in the days that followed – and especially, a few weeks later, as she missed her period and, hands shaking, took a test – no one could remember him. One of her friends seemed to think he was called Phil, but given that everybody at the party was pissed, Amelia wasn't sure how reliable that information was. But 'Phil' was a starting point at least, even if a couple of months on from the party, she could barely even recall how Phil looked.

That was when it hit her again: she was having the baby of a man she couldn't pick out in a crowd.

No wonder she hadn't told her parents yet.

Amelia had been thinking about it all day every day since she'd taken the test and she reckoned that, after the initial shock had died down, her mum would probably be okay. Disappointed in her possibly; angry maybe – but okay. It was a female thing. 'We women adapt and survive,' Amelia's mum said to her once when she found out Amelia's dad was having an affair. The way Mum had adapted and survived was to refuse to chuck Dad out – and, instead, she made him suffer. He asked for her forgiveness, but she wouldn't give it to him. He offered to do anything to make it up to her, and she let him without ever saying thank you.

So her mum would probably be okay eventually – but her dad would hit the roof. He'd probably try and apply for a gun licence just so he could buy a rifle and then hunt Phil Whoever-He-Was down. The thought, the image of her dad in that way, made Amelia smile – but the smile only briefly flickered. The woman in the corridor was starting to moan again – actually it was more like a wail now – and her partner was at the reception desk, angry, on edge.

Amelia tried to tune it all out again.

But it was impossible to look around the waiting room and not feel scared. It wasn't just the thought of having a baby at nineteen, of having no job and an education that was about to go no further than the two Cs she'd scraped at A level. It wasn't the thought of missing out on parties or clubs, or on holidays with her mates. It wasn't even the thought of telling her parents. It was the thought that if everything was still all right, if she wasn't bleeding because something had gone wrong, she was doing this on her own. Sure, her parents would be there – even Dad, in the end, would come round – but there would be no partner. Telling herself that, repeating those words, sent a shiver of panic through her, and she started thinking that maybe it really would be better if something was wrong inside her. Maybe it would be for the best if this was the start

59

of her losing the baby. Because how the hell was she going to cope with being a mum –

'Amelia Robbins, please.'

She looked up.

The nurse was searching the waiting room for her, so – heart beating hard in her chest – Amelia gingerly raised her hand and stood. 'Yes,' she said. 'That's me.'

'Great,' the nurse said, smiling.

It felt like everyone in the waiting room was staring at her, like every face was silently judging her – for being so young, for being so alone, and stupid, and naive.

She followed the nurse to the ultrasound suite.

10

An hour and fifteen minutes later, I pulled into Zoe Simmons's street.

At the time of the crash, Simmons had been a twenty-year-old student, studying Sport and Leisure at a college in Crawley. I'd imagined the address would be for her parents' place and when I pulled up outside the house – a red-bricked semi-detached near the train station – I discovered I was right. I knocked on the door and a woman in her fifties answered. She had bushy blonde hair and looked just like her daughter.

'Mrs Simmons?'

'Yes.'

I got out a business card. 'My name's David Raker. I'm an investigator.'

She took the card from me, studying it.

'I'm looking into the disappearance of Cate and Aiden Gascoigne.' I could see straight away that she recognized the names. 'I was hoping to speak to Zoe.'

'Oh, Zo just moved out,' she said. 'A couple of weeks back.'

I got out my notebook. It had always been a risk turning up unannounced, but I still felt frustrated at having made the journey all the way down here for nothing. I tried not to show it, and said, 'Whereabouts does Zoe live now?'

'In London, at her girlfriend's flat.'

'Which part of London?'

'Dulwich.'

It could have been a lot worse. Audrey Calvert lived in Streatham, which was only three miles west of Dulwich. In fact, depending on the time, if I went to Dulwich first to find Simmons, then to Streatham, I hardly had to deviate from my route home at all. When I glanced at Mrs Simmons, she was still staring at my card.

'Is everything okay?' I asked her.

She almost jerked out of whatever thought or memory had pulled her in, as if I'd physically grabbed her – and then she looked over her shoulder, into the hallway behind her, and inched towards me, on to the front step, pulling the door behind her.

She eyed me but didn't say anything.

'Mrs Simmons?'

'I, uh . . .' She paused. 'I just don't want my husband to hear this.'

'Okay.' I waited.

'Do you know much about that car crash?'

'I'm still filling in details. Why, do you?'

'No, not much. Just what was reported.' She looked at my business card again, then at me, as if weighing up whether to say any more. 'Zo, she was such a good kid, you know?' She stopped. 'I mean, she'd only just turned twenty when this thing you're investigating happened – so, obviously, she could be a bit sullen some days. But most of the time she was good as gold.' She checked behind her again, making certain the door was shut. 'My husband . . . he doesn't think any-thing changed afterwards. That's not surprising because when the kids – Zo and her brother – were growing up he'd often miss the little things in their behaviour that told *me* something was up.' She looked at me. 'What I mean to say is Zo . . . after that crash, she changed.'

I thought of Zoe's Instagram page, the lack of posts after

62

the day Cate and Aiden disappeared. 'In what way did she change?'

Mrs Simmons took a moment, as if gathering herself.

'She became much quieter. Zo was always pretty boisterous growing up. She played football and hockey, went on nights out with her mates, did all the things teenagers her age *should* have been doing – and a few things she probably shouldn't have.' A hint of a smile. 'But after the accident, something just . . .'

'Altered?'

'Yeah.'

'Was it *just* that she became quiet – or were there other things?'

'She just wasn't as open with us as she was before. I mean, I'm sure there were lots of things in her life that she didn't share with us – I didn't expect her to tell Greg and me every little thing she got up to. But she and I, we had a close relationship.'

'But it didn't feel like that after the crash?'

'No.' She shook her head. 'She *never* talked about that day. Ever. If you tried to bring it up, she'd shut you down or just leave the room. I don't know how to explain it, but I just . . . I knew . . .' She faded out.

'You knew her better than anyone.'

She nodded. 'She was my daughter.'

And then she looked at me, as if she realized she'd unwittingly said *was*, not *is*. Something had happened to Zoe two and a half years ago – and, after the crash, it wasn't the same daughter that came back.

It was someone else.

Someone who might have been keeping a secret.

The flat that Zoe Simmons lived in was the top floor of a semi-detached house near Dulwich Park. I found the only space at the end of the road and then walked back. There were two cars in the driveway, one of them a blue Suzuki Swift. It was the same vehicle Simmons had been driving that day on Gatton Hill.

I buzzed the flat and waited for a response.

'Can I help you?'

Above me a window was open and a woman in her early twenties was perched on the sill. She was an attractive brunette with dark eyes, her cheeks slightly flushed. It could have been the lingering heat of late evening, but more likely it was because she was in the middle of exercising: she was wearing a sports bra and a pair of leggings.

This must have been Simmons's girlfriend.

'Hi, my name's David Raker. I'm an investigator.' I didn't bother showing her any ID. She was too far away to see it, anyway. 'I was looking for Zoe.'

'An investigator?'

'That's right.'

She frowned. 'What are you investigating?'

'The disappearance of Cate and Aiden Gascoigne.' I waited for a reaction, but there wasn't one. It was possible she and Simmons hadn't been together at the time of the crash. It was also possible that Zoe had chosen not to tell her girlfriend anything about it.

'I don't know who they are,' she confirmed.

'Sorry, I didn't catch your name.'

'Becky,' she said.

'Hi, Becky.' I smiled, trying to put her at ease. 'So Cate and Aiden were involved in a car accident a couple of years ago.'

Still nothing. This wasn't going to go anywhere.

'Is Zoe in?'

'No, she's at work.'

Her mother had mentioned that after leaving college she'd landed a job at a sports centre in Croydon.

'What time is Zoe due home?'

I looked at my watch. It was 8.45 p.m.

'Not until at least ten,' Becky said.

Again, just as with Zoe's mum, I tried not to let my frustration show, even though this whole trip had been a waste of a couple of hours. The sun had set already and, by the time I got to Streatham, and Audrey Calvert's address, it was going to be even later. It didn't feel like the sensible option turning up there at night: people tended to be more guarded after dark and knocking on her door at 10 p.m. was only going to put Calvert on edge.

'What's any of this got to do with Zoe?'

Becky was leaning a little further out of the window now, her one hand on the edge of the frame. Even from where I was I could see her brain going.

Maybe this is something I can use.

'I'm going to post my card through the letterbox here,' I said. 'It's got my name and details on it. Maybe you could pass it on to Zoe when she gets home?'

'I still don't get it. What's this got to do with her?'

I didn't want to damage their relationship, especially if they *had* been together at the time of the crash; after all, there may have been good reasons for Simmons not to have told Becky about what happened two and a half years ago. So it felt like my best option was to leave a business card with the girlfriend there was a good chance Zoe had kept all this from. That way, in front of Becky, Simmons could pretend she didn't know what I wanted and protect the sanctity of their relationship. But she also couldn't ignore me. The card was a message: call me, or next time I'm honest with your girlfriend.

'I'd really appreciate you giving her my card,' I said. 'It's nothing to worry about. Just let Zoe know I called by.'

12

By the time I arrived back in Ealing, it was completely dark and the air had cooled. I pulled into my driveway and turned off the engine, then sat there, looking at my house. At the edge of the lawn was the FOR SALE sign that had been there, on and off, for over eighteen months. I'd had offers, I'd even accepted two of them, but both times the buyers had pulled out and I'd genuinely started to believe that, perhaps, I wasn't destined to leave these walls, that maybe the ties binding me to it – the fact that it was the house that I'd bought with my wife, that was supposed to have been the place we had kids in – made it impossible to pass on.

Then, five months ago, I got another offer, and so far this one had stuck. I'd asked the estate agent not to change the FOR SALE sign for SOLD, because I didn't want to jinx it, but as determined as I was to move on, to begin again somewhere new where I could remember my wife but not feel her in every part of the house, there were still doubts. Mostly they came in these moments, when I pulled on to the driveway. I'd sit and look at my home and it would feel as if I were betraying her somehow – leaving her, forgetting her. I knew that I never would, not for a single second – but it didn't make the feeling any less real. Sometimes the thought of change seemed so big, so frightening, I'd found myself putting the estate agent's number into my phone, ready to pull out of the sale.

But, in the end, I always stepped back from the edge.

I unlocked the front door, the air inside thick with the heat of the day. I opened windows and doors and let the night cool the place off, and once I'd showered, made myself something light to eat. I sat on the back deck listening to the music playing next door and to the gentle hum of traffic out on Uxbridge Road.

As I ate, I thought about Zoe Simmons, about Audrey Calvert too. I'd drive out to see Calvert in the morning, but for now I'd sown a seed with Simmons by leaving my business card with her, so things were moving with at least one of the witnesses.

After dinner, I phoned Aiden's cousins, Ted and Barbara, apologizing for the late hour. The first call was to Ted who told me he was a night owl, anyway. He filled me in on some of the family background: Aiden's parents had both died of cancer, four years apart, when Aiden was in his twenties; both Ted's parents – his dad and Aiden's mum had been brother and sister – were gone too. Which just left him, Aiden and Barbara, Ted's sister.

'We're a pretty small family now,' he said.

'Did you used to see Aiden a lot?'

'Not tons, but, you know, on and off. The last time I saw him was a few months before he and Cate disappeared. I had a couple of work meetings in London, so we met for a pint and a pub lunch. It was just nice to catch up with him.'

'What was he like?'

'Fun, pretty much up for anything. When we were younger, Aid and I used to run marathons together. We did London, the Great North Run, we even went over to Berlin and ran that one year. He was great company. He was someone I'd have liked even if he wasn't my cousin. He had solid values too. He could drink you under the table and he liked a laugh with the lads, but he was all about family. When his dad died, that hit him really hard. At least when his mum

68

passed on a few years later, he had Cate to help him get through it.'

'Cate's family described them as a tight unit.'

'Yeah. I met Cate loads of times and you could see it. He doted on her, her on him. It was nice to see, you know? Too often couples are at each other's throats.'

I lingered on that last sentence. Cate and Aiden were never at each other's throats based on what I'd heard – other than six months before they vanished, when something had been briefly off in their marriage. I thought about Aiden's Internet search for a local police station, then said, 'So no skeletons in the closet as far as Aiden's concerned?'

'In what sense?'

'In any sense that might help me find him.'

'No. Not that I ever knew of, anyway.'

We talked a little more and then I thanked him, hung up, and called Barbara. The conversation echoed pretty much everything I'd already been told about Aiden, by Martin and Sue, by Georgia, and by Ted. He was a clever guy, he loved his work at the design agency, he was easy-going, funny, serious about his exercise. There were still friends and work colleagues of his that I'd need to chase down – but somehow, in my gut, I felt that if Aiden was carrying a secret, it was something he'd even hidden from the people he knew best, perhaps including Cate.

Shortly after I was done with Barbara, my phone went.

On the display, it said SPIKE. He was another old contact from my paper days, a software developer who didn't do much in the way of software development and whose real name wasn't Spike. In fact, despite knowing him – at least via a telephone line – for almost fifteen years, I didn't know what his real name was. That was the way he liked it, given that he made his money these days as a hacker.

'How you doing, Spike?'

'Hey, David. I thought I'd take a chance on you still being up.'

'I'm still here. You got some good news for me?'

'I've got phone records for October and November for Cate and Aiden, and I've gone through the numbers – both the ones they called, and the ones that called them – and have done a search on who *those* numbers belong to. That information is all in what I'm about to send you, including home addresses. I've also included December as well, running through to the day they disappeared. I know you have those already, but it's just easier to pull it all.'

'You're a rock star, Spike. Thank you.'

'You got it. The new combination is 4077.'

I wrote it down. He meant the combination for the locker he was using as a drop-off for the money I now owed him. The locker changed location all the time, but for the last six weeks it had been in the changing rooms at a country club down in Richmond. Spike and I never met, I just drove the cash to the locker he gave me within forty-eight hours of the work being sent to me.

While I waited for his email to arrive, I spent some time looking again at the website Cate had created. It was really just a place where Cate could talk about her photography: the type of images that inspired her and how she captured her own; equipment she used; technical breakdowns; and news about her exhibitions. She'd written a blog – back in June 2019 – about the series Martin and Sue had mentioned, 'Tragic, Drawn'. That collection had exhibited at a gallery off Covent Garden called The Memorial and Cate had described it on the blog as 'a selection of portraits from the justice system that are truly some of the most personal I've ever shot.' There were a couple of photos posted to the blog – one of some courthouse steps, another taken on the bottom floor of a prison, cells running down either side of her. It made me wonder if it might be worth speaking to the gallery and seeing if there was some kind of record of – or, even better, visual guide to – the pictures she'd put on display, because they weren't in her albums, as far as I could tell. Maybe it wouldn't lead anywhere, but at the very least, it would help fill in a little more of Cate for me.

Fifteen minutes later, the email from Spike pinged through.

While the attachment was downloading, I grabbed a beer from the fridge and, heading back outside, realized how low the temperature had dropped. I didn't mind the cool, though. In fact, often, it gave me exactly the clarity I needed.

But then my mobile started buzzing across the table again. It was late now – well after 11 p.m. – and, as I scooped up the phone, I tried to imagine who it could be.

The number said WITHHELD.

The second I saw that, my heart sank.

Healy

It was just gone 8 p.m. when he noticed the security light flick into life at the front of the cottage. He was in the kitchen making himself some tea, and he paused there, teaspoon hovering above the mug, looking out through the window at the driveway. Sometimes people would walk past on the lane beyond the gate and set the light off, but he hadn't heard any voices and it was so quiet up here that anyone approaching normally announced themselves – like an alarm call – from halfway down the hill. That probably meant it was an animal, a rabbit or a fox, or it could even have been a cat – maybe the plump tabby that lived with the woman in the next house down from his. When it could be bothered, it sometimes ambled up this way looking for birds or voles.

Healy waited a moment, saw nothing, and then took his tea through to the living room. The last time Raker had come to visit him, he'd brought a huge stack of DVDs and a box of books. Healy had slowly been working through them all. He remembered that one of the books, *No One Can See the Crows at Night*, had been one of Raker's wife's favourite novels, so he'd read that first and had liked it. Now he was reading a pulpy sci-fi novel about two men who were exactly alike.

The DVDs, however, he'd been trying to eke out, because it would be another ten weeks before Raker returned with more. Books weren't as much of a problem, as there was always the library in the next village if Healy got desperate. They had DVDs there too but, over the course of the two years he'd been hiding out here, living under the alias Marcus Savage, he'd already been through the entire collection. Really, Raker was it.

Raker was how Healy maintained his sanity.

It was why he so looked forward to their weekly phone calls, even if all they talked about was Raker's work, or the boring shite Healy did with his own life: his job on the trawler, his memories of his old life as a cop. He just wished Raker was able to come up more often, but he'd insisted that they stick to four times a year because he felt it was too risky to do it more frequently. Much as he didn't enjoy the solitude, Healy understood.

He was, after all, supposed to be dead.

Shrugging out of his thoughts, he reached to the DVD pile and looked at the cover of the one on the top. *Anzio* with Robert Mitchum, about an Allied assault on the titular Italian port. He had the vague notion he might have watched it before, but he put it on anyway and collapsed into the sofa. As the disc loaded, he thought about how much he'd give for a phone right now or a laptop, some way to connect himself to the outside world that didn't involve trudging into the next town and using the computer at the library there. But he didn't spend too long on the idea because, once that sort of thing lodged, it made him frustrated, and when he got frustrated, he got angry.

A noise.

Healy swivelled on the sofa, looking out into the kitchen. Had it come from in there? He paused the film – which had automatically started playing – and listened.

The noise came again, this time more clearly.

Someone was knocking at the door.

He got up. The layout of the cottage didn't conform to modern design, and Healy liked it that way: access through the kitchen and the fact that it had two windows, one looking out at the drive, the other down the hill to the village, meant he didn't bring the stink of fish from his bib and braces any further into the house, and he also got an unimpeded view of the only two approaches to the cottage.

Who the hell would be knocking on his door?

He stepped right up to the window facing the driveway. To his surprise there was a woman in her fifties there – tall, lean, her eyes on the front door. Was it the woman who lived in the next house down with the cat? He'd never even said a proper hello to her the few times they'd passed in the lanes, and would barely have been able to pick her out in a crowd. Involving himself in the lives of others, making friends, all endangered his situation here. So he just passed through the village every day, spent no time in it – never went to the pub or the small general store – rarely even put on interior lights at night, just so it would look like no one was home. He and Raker agreed to monitor the set-up here day by day, and they'd organized it so they could react quickly if he had to move out and move on. As a result, he'd never exchanged a single word with anyone from the village. No one seemed to care, or even realize, that he was living here now.

No one, it seemed, except for this woman.

He thought about not answering, but she glimpsed him at the window when she turned to look, a hint of a smile in her face. Nodding to her, he realized he didn't have a choice now; if he didn't open up, this exchange would stay with her – it wouldn't be a brief forgettable conversation with a neighbour, it would be him seeing her out there and refusing to answer the door. She might tell her partner if she had one. She might speak to other people in the village.

'Shit,' he muttered.

Swallowing his frustration, Healy stepped away from the

window, flicked on the kitchen lights and then, taking a couple of deep breaths, pulled open the door.

Just remember who you are now.

Warm air escaped from the night into the house, followed by the scent of her perfume. She was holding a basket of apples down by her side and looked a little older up close – early sixties maybe, six or seven years beyond Healy's age, rather than the three or four he'd first thought. A flowing floral dress hid much of her body, but he could see she was slim, and she was definitely attractive.

'Oh, hi,' she said, her voice soft, and her accent – like his – not local. 'I keep seeing you walk past, but we never get a chance to speak to each other. So I thought I'd put that right.' She had blue-grey eyes tagged with fine age lines, and shoulder-length blonde hair. Holding out a hand, she said, 'Nice to meet you. I'm Paula.'

He took her hand. 'Marcus. Nice to meet you too.'

'I love your accent. What part of Ireland are you from?'

Dublin. 'Cork.'

'That's a beautiful part of the world.' She paused, and then seemed to remember she was holding the basket of apples. 'Oh, these are for you. I've got a huge Bramley tree at the bottom of the garden, and I can't keep up with it. They're cookers, obviously, so you'll need to whack them in a pie, or just stew them.'

He took the basket from her. 'Thank you,' he said.

They stood there for a moment.

'Uh, anyway, I don't want to take up too much of your time,' she said. The security light had flicked off, but now it erupted into life again.

Would you like to come in?

That's what he *wanted* to ask her. Something fizzed in his guts, the weight of the words on his tongue, the desire to say

75

them like a rope around his waist, tugging him closer to them. He wanted to talk to her. It wasn't just because she was attractive. He just wanted to have a conversation with someone. He wanted to be normal, *feel* normal. But he stopped himself as he watched her eyes go past him, into the kitchen, to where his bibs and braces hung.

'Oh, are you a fisherman?' she asked.

'Yes.'

'On Anglesey?'

He wondered what the best response was. He'd done such a good job of keeping his head down that she didn't even realize the trawler he worked on tended to get moored overnight at the village's only jetty. But if he lied to her, and she saw him down there one day, what then? Would she think anything of it? Or would his lie register with her and then make her look more closely at him?

'I work all over, really,' he said finally.

She nodded and seemed fine with the response.

'What about you?'

'I work from home,' she said. 'Marketing. It's very boring.'

Another smile, and he was struck again by how lovely she was, her face half lit by the light coming from the kitchen. He tried to gather himself, to bring down the shutters, knowing he was being led somewhere he wasn't meant to go. But this was the first close physical contact – beyond the father and son he shared a boat with, and the occasional visits by Raker – that he'd had with anyone for a long, long time.

'Anyway,' she said, 'I didn't just come up here to give you some apples.'

He eyed her. 'No?'

'No.' She shook her head. 'I mean, those apples are great in a pie, don't get me wrong, but the real reason . . .' She paused, frowned. 'I guess it could be nothing at all.'

Healy's stomach knotted.

'Yesterday, a man came to your house,' Paula said.

'A man?'

'In the morning. It's probably nothing, but it just struck me as . . . odd. I can see some of your driveway here from my back step, and I was in the garden hanging out some washing and happened to look up. And I could see this man, about where I am.'

'Knocking on my door?'

'No,' she said. 'Looking through your windows.'

Another twist in Healy's stomach.

'I guess you were out on the boat at the time, and I just figured that maybe he was a friend of yours, or one of those annoying door-to-door salesmen who can't handle it when someone isn't actually home.' She smiled again, joking.

But Healy hardly noticed it this time, his mind racing.

'Thing is, though, that wasn't the end of it.'

He looked at Paula again. 'No?'

'No,' she said. 'Because he came back again later on.'

13

'Some guy was snooping around the house?'

I knew that an unscheduled call from Healy, after 11 p.m., and on a day that we didn't normally speak, was never likely to be good news. But I hadn't expected it to be this.

'That's what she reckons,' Healy replied.

'What did he look like?'

'I didn't ask. I didn't want to seem too desperate for an answer.'

I realized he was right. Too many questions, too much hint of panic, and it just drew more attention to him. The whole reason he was living in a tiny village in north Wales was to vanish. And, as I thought of that, I thought about how we'd ended up here.

It had begun with Healy being fired from the Met, after spending a decade and a half as a detective. But that had only been the start of his spiral. He buried a daughter he loved even more than his job, he became a drunk, his family disowned him, and then he suffered a near-fatal heart attack. For a time he was homeless, which I didn't know about until after, and then the only way he felt he could ever begin again was by becoming someone else entirely. He believed closing the chapter on Colm Healy and beginning with a new name in a new place would wash him clean of everything that had come before. So he'd faked his death, and – because I'd recognized something in him: his grief, his suffering – I'd helped him do it, perjuring myself in front of the police as I did. And now here we were: having to move him every time something looked even slightly off, constantly on edge about our secret escaping into the open.

'Who is she?' I asked. 'This neighbour, I mean?'

'I don't know. Tonight's the first time we've ever spoken.'

'You haven't spoken to her in two years?'

'Two years and three months,' he said. 'I thought you'd be pleased. Isn't this what you wanted?'

The comment annoyed me but I let it go. In part, it was true: it was exactly what I wanted, because it was the best way to keep us both safe. But there were days where I regretted deeply what we'd started. It wasn't just the lies I'd had to tell after helping him fake his death. It wasn't the way Healy had emotionally blackmailed a forensic tech who'd owed him a favour into swapping around DNA samples – although those were certainly a part of it. It was that – even though everything I felt for him at the time had been real, all the grief, mirrored in him, that I felt myself – sometimes I wondered if it was a burden I shouldn't have helped him carry. If I'd just let him destroy himself, I wouldn't have had to lug the weight of this around. There would be no persistent low-level alarm buzzing at the back of my head. I wouldn't be paying rent on a place in north Wales I'd never live in myself and I wouldn't have to drive up every three months to collect the cash I was owed. I wouldn't have to go out and get fake IDs, and I wouldn't have to deal with the fire that still burned in Healy, the caustic nature of him that he'd never quite quelled.

But then he'd be dead.

Is that what you want?

'Raker?'

I tuned back in.

'Have you been talking to anyone else in the village?' I asked.

'No,' he said.

'What about the people you work with?'

'The father and son?' He made it sound like a joke. 'The father's monosyllabic and the son's an arsehole. I don't talk to them unless I have to.' He paused, and then I heard him take a tired breath. It was a common refrain. He hated working on the trawler, even though he knew it was the perfect way for him to exist below the radar. He was out at sea the whole day and it was cash in hand, so no one except the father and son spent any time with him, and no bank had an account of what money he did or didn't have. But those things were hard to square when the only job he wanted, and had truly loved, was one he could never go back to.

He couldn't be a cop again – not now, not ever.

'Can you think of any reason at all you might have compromised yourself?'

'No.'

But had there been a minor hesitation this time?

'Healy?'

'No,' he repeated, his hackles up again.

'I'm only asking because I need to be one hundred per cent sure.'

'And I'm telling you, I've been careful.'

I paused again, thinking. The most obvious decision would be to move him on again – send him to another part of the country and get him a new name – but that was also the hardest option. It was hard for me, because it took time to enact big changes like that and erase the evidence of his two years in north Wales, and it was even harder on him – small as Healy's life there was, it was a life of sorts.

I tried to think of any reason why someone would be snooping around the house if it wasn't because of us. Maybe it had been the owner, wanting something, although I couldn't think what. Maybe the owner had put the house on the market, and just hadn't informed us yet, and it had been someone from the estate agency. Or maybe the neighbour had been right: the man had been selling something, just going door to door. Did door-to-door salesmen keep coming back, like this guy had? It was possible. Did they peer into people's windows? That felt more unlikely.

And then I stopped.

'Shit,' I said quietly. 'What if it's McCaskell?'

Silence. I could almost feel Healy's blood chill.

Connor McCaskell was a journalist at the *Daily Tribune* who had been on my trail for over four years. I could barely remember how his interest in me had begun. But he worked for the country's bestselling and most salacious tabloid, and whatever the genesis was, he believed that my public persona, such as it was, was a lie. The few times I'd appeared in the press – reluctantly, after a big case – seemed to have riled him somehow. He believed there was no way that I could do what I did just because I wanted to help people. He believed I was hiding some dark secret.

He just didn't know that my secret was Healy.

He didn't know about the blackmail and the perjury.

Perhaps until now.

'He's been quiet for months,' Healy said.

'I know. That's what worries me.'

'How would he even know about me?'

'He *shouldn't*,' I replied, my mind still turning, 'but he's been looking into me, so he's probably been looking into things I'm connected to.'

'You think he's got hold of your financial records?'

'He works for the *Tribune*. I wouldn't put it past him.'

'But we've insulated ourselves, right?'

'He shouldn't be able to connect me to the house you're

in, no. All the contact I've had with the landlord is done over the phone, via a call box, and the financial stuff – the rent, anything else – isn't on my statements because it's paid through a holding company. It should be impenetrable. Spike set it all up for me and there's no way McCaskell has the skill-set to break through a wall like that.'

'So what do you want to do?'

I looked out into the blackness of the garden. I felt cold now, although I wasn't sure what was making me shiver: the coolness of the night or the thought of a tabloid journalist unearthing my secrets. I didn't want to move Healy if it really was just some door-to-door salesman.

But what if it *was* McCaskell?

I could get Healy to install a doorbell camera, but that required the Internet, and it also required him to have a mobile phone, and both those things would make him eas-ier to locate, trace and to follow. One of the ways we'd kept Healy hidden so successfully was by leaving no digital trail.

'Raker, you keep going silent on me.'

'I'm still here,' I said. 'I'm just thinking.'

'I vote we sit tight for now.' He didn't want to move again either, which I didn't blame him for. 'This neighbour,' he continued quietly. 'She told me that she works from home.'

I was already shaking my head. 'No.'

'What's the alternative?'

'We don't know her.'

'She could keep an eye on the house for us when I'm out.'

'We don't even *know* her, Healy.'

'What's the alternative, then, Raker? Because I'm all ears.'

'We could move you again.'

His silence said everything.

And that was just the problem: I couldn't think of another alternative.

He continued: '*She* was the one who told *me* about this guy being at the house. If I spoke to her about it, it doesn't have to be some big thing. I'll make it casual. Give me some credit here: I'm not a total idiot. I can make it work with her if we need to.'

It was this. Or it was uprooting him.

And why do that until we knew who this guy *really* was?

'Okay,' I said eventually. 'Speak to her.'

'Okay, good.'

'But be careful.'

'I will.'

'I mean it, Healy.'

'I know,' he said. 'Trust me, I'll find out who our snooper is.'

14

Tired, but wanting to get back to the phone records that Spike had sent me, I grabbed a second beer from the fridge, returned to the deck and opened up the PDF.

It was divided into about thirty pages for each month. October had a little more than November and December but not by much. Spike had given me a foot-up by organizing each page according to the number that either Cate or Aiden had called or been called by, the name of the person or company associated with the number, and then their address.

Before I started going through it all, I again went to my Inbox and found the list of names and contact details, where possible, for friends and work colleagues of Cate and Aiden that Martin, Sue and Georgia had put together for me. I wasn't about to discount the idea that one of their friends might know what had happened to the couple, but – if I could cross-check everything against a list of close contacts – it would be easier for me to spot one-off calls or calls to or from new numbers.

I went through the data meticulously, noting names and numbers that weren't on the family's list. The list obviously gave me more of an advantage with Cate than with Aiden, though Georgia had done her best to add some friends of Aiden's, some work colleagues she'd met or heard Cate talk about. The truth was, though, without parents or siblings to help me, I was probably going to have to do some more leg-work in that area.

Even so, I kept going, and the next time I looked up, it was half past midnight, and I'd gone so deep into the numbers that I didn't see that I'd emptied the second bottle of beer. I was cold now too, so I went inside and grabbed a hoodie, then made a cup of tea and returned to the work.

It was one thirty by the time I was done.

There were things I could run down, like names – especially related to Aiden – of potential friends and colleagues who might be worth speaking to. But, based on the phone calls he made and received in those last three months, I didn't see a lot to worry me. Most of his calls had been to the same small group of friends, or to a series of mobiles that started with similar numbers to his, which suggested they were work associates on company handsets.

By contrast, because she was self-employed, Cate didn't have colleagues in the traditional sense, but there were some galleries and studios I could chase up. More interesting to me were phone calls she'd made to places outside London. When I ran the numbers down, they tended to be hotels, car hire places and airlines, which suggested they were locations that she was travelling to for her work.

One grouping of calls particularly caught my eye.

They'd all been made in early November, two months before the crash – and as I looked at them, I immediately thought of the receipt Cate had for the café in Bamburgh, dated 6 November, and of Georgia hearing her sister say *dunes*.

That date fitted with what I was looking at now.

The calls were all to the north-east. One was even to a hotel on the A1, the road that ran from Newcastle all the way up the North Sea coast to Edinburgh, passing Bamburgh on the way.

I went back into the house and grabbed the pile of receipts for November. I'd been through them all once already – but only very briefly – and, after some digging, found an invoice for a hotel called the Coast Inn on the A1. The invoice didn't have a header or a logo; the name was just printed small at the bottom of the receipt, which is why it hadn't particularly lodged with me on a first run-through. But now I looked closer. The invoice was for a three-night stay from Tuesday 5 to Friday 8 November 2019. That would have coincided with two other calls she'd made to north-east numbers on 4 November, the day before she'd driven up.

One of the calls was to someone called Tom Swainswick.

When I googled him and the address that Spike had provided me with, I quickly found out who he was: a senior crime reporter for the *Northumberland Star*.

But that didn't interest me as much as the second call she'd made.

That one had been to Northumbria Police.

Why would Cate have been phoning the cops before she made the journey north? And was it connected to the Internet search Aiden had done for police stations?

Contacting the reporter at the *Northumberland Star* could be explained, at least on paper, by the fact that Cate was a photographer. Maybe she'd done some freelance work. Maybe she was pitching for opportunities. Although, in truth, both those arguments failed to sit comfortably with me. If she was just pitching for work, why did she call a reporter covering the crime beat? And why would she then call the police headquarters in Tyne and Wear straight after?

I went to my laptop and cross-checked the number Cate had used against the number listed on the force's website. I expected the numbers to be the same, for it to have been a switchboard.

But it wasn't.

I grabbed my mobile, punched in the number that Cate had used, even though it was late. After five rings, a voicemail message kicked in. *'Hi, this is Detective Superintendent Leon Coetzer. Please leave a message after the tone.'*

I hung up.

Pulling my laptop towards me, I put in a Google search for Coetzer. I found plenty of photographs of him behind microphones at press conferences, as well as official shots of him in uniform, used by the force in media packs. I clicked on a couple to see where they took me and I ended up embedded in news stories that featured him.

What interest would Cate have in a cop like Coetzer?

Her exhibition on justice – 'Tragic, Drawn' – had taken place five months before the call, and if she wanted to see day-to-day police work in action – the aftermath of crimes, cases being worked – a superintendent wasn't going to be the most visual of focal points. At his rank most of Coetzer's professional life was going to be spent chained to a desk.

So *had* she called him because she needed access?

An official sign-off from a senior cop?

And if so, a sign-off for what?

I backed up, switching tabs in Google from Images to All, then scrolled down the wall of results. They were all links to local news stories, the headlines as dull as the images I'd already found and followed: Coetzer talking about budgets, about the strain on the force during Covid lockdowns, about training and recruitment. He seemed to get wheeled out a lot, even for things that might have been the remit of the chief constable or his assistants, which suggested that management liked Coetzer and trusted him. His history would no doubt have also played into their thinking. The idea of a veteran detective was a lot sexier to the public than a cop who hit the heights because they'd been the best at administration.

Then, at the bottom of the page, something stopped me.

The very last hit was for a story that had run in the *North-umberland Star* almost three months ago, towards the end of April. I clicked on it. It was a retrospective of sorts, written to coincide with the thirty-year anniversary of a local crime that had never been solved. The byline was for Tom Swainswick, the same journalist Cate had called.

But it was the headline that caught my attention.

THIRTY YEARS ON, WHEN WILL THERE BE
JUSTICE FOR THE GIRLS IN THE DUNES?

Dunes

30 Years Ago

Makayla gunned her car along the coastal road.

Off to her right, still at a distance, she could see activity in the beach grass, the white specks of a forensic team moving around, constables further out, their dark uniforms like swishes of paint at the edges of the crime scene. They were trying to push the media back, off the sand and on to the tarmac. In the end, it wasn't going to make much difference. The media already had a perfect view: against the grey of the sky she could see two helicopters circling the dunes, like crows hunting for carrion.

Two minutes later she arrived, stopping her Volvo at the edge of the circus, where three marked cars and a mobile forensic lab were in a line. There was a news truck off to the left of those, a cameraman watching back footage he'd taken already. She recognized the presenter in the front of the truck, talking to someone on a car phone, but she couldn't recall his name, and soon her focus shifted elsewhere. Grabbing her coat from the back seat, she checked her pockets for her warrant card, then made a beeline for a bleached uneven boardwalk. On a normal day there would have been few, if any, vehicles parked here, and – at this time of year – the boardwalks and dunes would have been deserted, the thick braid of protected coastland empty.

But this wasn't a normal day.

As the sand dunes rose and then flattened off, she could see the scene more clearly. A tent had been erected about a hundred and fifty feet ahead of her; beyond that was the North Sea, tormented and sullen, breaking hard on to the sweep of beach that bled into the dunes. The closer she got, the more she could hear of conversations along the boardwalk and its edges. A TV crew had already started broadcasting. An official from the council, concerned about ecological damage, was complaining about the metal plates that the scene of crime officer had laid across the sand in order to get officials from the boardwalk out to the body. And in front of the crime scene tape, as it whipped and twisted in the wind, was another journalist. Her name was Abi Salaya – but back at the office, they'd taken to calling her Abi's A Liar, because most of what she wrote in her tabloid was fiction.

'Detective Jennings! Detective Jennings!'

Makayla held up a hand. 'No comment.'

'Can you confirm whether this is –'

'No comment,' Makayla said again, pushing aside a Dictaphone that was being shoved into her face. She showed her warrant card to a waiting uniform and ducked under the tape. A camera flash went off behind her somewhere, and she heard heavy footsteps on the boards, which she assumed was a TV crew trying to catch up with her before she got too far away. But she didn't look back. She hated seeing herself in print but hated being on TV even more, despite it always giving her kids a thrill. The last time it happened, her husband Tyler recorded her appearance on the BBC and made her watch it back with them after dinner one night. Her boys – seven-year-old twins – had danced around the room singing 'Mummy is a film star, Mummy is a film star' so perfectly in unison that she knew it had to have been Tyler's idea, because he'd clearly made them practise before she got home. But then, later, when she and Tyler had cuddled up on the sofa, he'd said to her, 'Not that I don't like you being a film star – but please promise me you'll stay safe out there.'

It was hard to know what was safe any more.

She certainly wasn't in any danger here – but it would be hard to describe any crime scene as safe. Safe was certainty, security. It was where no one came to harm.

Makayla looked at the tent ahead of her.

That place wasn't here, she thought.

She finally deviated from the boardwalk and made her way across the metal plates, feeling them sink under her weight into the sand. The day was unseasonably cold, a frigid morning at the end of April, and while the wind was light, it was bitter. As it rolled in off the sea, carried all the way down from Scandinavia, her eyes began to water and then, as she wiped them clean, something else hit her: the first wave of decay. Makayla held her breath for a second – in all the years she'd been doing this, she'd never got used to it – and then forced herself forward to the tent, to the smell.

Leon Coetzer was waiting for her at the entrance.

The two of them had worked together for twelve months but couldn't have been more different: Makayla was a trim and diminutive 42-year-old woman from London, attractive and well dressed, a mum first, a wife second, a cop third; Coetzer was a heavy 26-year-old single guy from Sunderland, who had one good suit and a second for when the good one was in the wash. He had no kids and had already been divorced once. Makayla could see today was a second-suit day – it was getting small for him, the stitching of the jacket starting to strain.

'Sorry I'm late,' Makayla said, even though she was Coetzer's DI.

'The school run?'

'How did you guess?'

Coetzer did a quick round of introductions, although Makayla already knew the pathologist, then they both moved past the group gathered outside and into the tent.

The body was in the middle.

Makayla, conscious of not contaminating the scene until forensics had officially cleared it, stayed at the edges of the tent with the back of her hand to her nose. Techs danced around the body – buzzing like the insects that had already long done their work here – dusting, digging, picking up, photographing. But, even with them partly obscuring her view, she could see enough: the woman had been concealed in landscape fabric, brown hessian wrapped around her like bandages. Over time, the hessian had started to unravel, perhaps picked at by the red foxes living

91

along this stretch of the coast, or the crows, maybe the gulls. Or it could have been the weather that had loosened the covering; the previous week, the coast had been battered by gales.

Makayla could make out a hand – the fingers facing up towards the sky – and part of a face: an eye socket, the eyes starting to liquefy, and the hint of polished bone in the forehead where a wound must have been picked at. The rest of the woman was either still hidden under the hessian, or by the thickness of the beach grass that she'd been shoved into and covered with. Not only that, but two months without discovery had been enough time for her to start to become part of the grass itself, the blades flourishing around her. As she'd continued to hollow out, they'd even fused with her body. She'd been so well hidden, and so far away from the boardwalk, that no one had seen her. With the spring growth, if she'd been here much longer, it was possible she might never have been found at all.

'Is it definitely her?' Makayla asked the pathologist.

He nodded. 'Looks like it. There was a handbag with the body – it's got her driving licence in, her bank cards and other stuff belonging to her.' He faded out.

'So it's her, is what you're saying.'

'Yes,' the pathologist said. 'It looks like it's Lilly.'

Lilly Andrews was eighteen when she disappeared. On the morning of Thursday 27 February, she'd left her home in North Shields and taken the Metro into Newcastle where she worked at a record store at the bottom of Dean Street. She'd never gone to college, much less university, because her family couldn't afford it, and she still lived at home – but she absolutely loved music. She played the keyboard and guitar, both self-taught, was never seen anywhere without a Walkman and headphones, and had an encyclopaedic knowledge of bands and artists. Her parents told Makayla and Coetzer that Lilly had still harboured ambitions of studying music, despite the fact she played everything by ear and from memory, and could barely read a note.

Somewhere between leaving T-Bridge Records after it closed and the time she should have been home – 7 p.m. – Lilly disappeared. Makayla and Coetzer tried to follow Lilly's route back on surveillance film, but coverage wasn't anywhere close to good enough in Newcastle city centre, and certainly not once Lilly had exited the Metro in North Shields.

If she'd even got the Metro at all.

They spoke to eyewitnesses and that led nowhere: no one remembered seeing her on the train she always returned on; no one saw her at Central Station before she left Newcastle. Sometimes, her parents said, she would bump into old school friends in North Shields, but none of the friends had seen her on that particular day. And in the days beforehand they hadn't seen her with anyone new and hadn't noticed any unusual behaviour. As a result, Makayla and her task force ran down thousands of leads – but, eventually, all of them proved to be dead ends.

And so, despite Lilly being on the local news for weeks after, on the front pages of regional newspapers – even the nationals for a day or two – the investigation stalled. It was never far from the thoughts of Makayla Jennings, never far from the desk where she and Coetzer had mounted a MISSING poster on the wall, Lilly's face looking out, the edges adorned with yellow Post-its full of facts and hypotheses.

Never far, but far enough that they had never found Lilly.

Not until this morning when – forty-five miles away from where Lilly was last seen leaving the record store, and two months after she first disappeared – the owner of a Labrador followed his dog into the protected scrub of some sand dunes on the Northumberland coast. He wanted to see why the animal was barking, because the dog was normally so quiet; 'as placid as a millpond' he would tell police afterwards.

There he saw something in the grass.

A pale hand.

After she got home that night, after seeing the kids and eating dinner with Tyler, Makayla got a call from Coetzer, who'd gone back to the office.

'I just heard from Rebin,' Coetzer told her.

Rebin was the scene of crime officer.

'What did he say?'

'He decided to expand the search, just to make sure they didn't miss any evidence. He'd already got uniforms to walk those sand dunes within a quarter-mile radius of the dump site, but he expanded it out to a half-mile.'

'Okay,' Makayla said. 'Did they find something?'

'Yeah, they found something.'

'More of Lilly's things?'

'No,' Coetzer said. 'They found two other bodies.'

16

THIRTY YEARS ON, WHEN WILL THERE BE JUSTICE FOR THE GIRLS IN THE DUNES?

By Tom Swainswick | Senior Reporter
Families no closer to answers after three decades

On 28 April 1992, the body of 18-year-old Lilly Andrews was uncovered by a dog walker in a two-mile stretch of sand dunes north of Bamburgh. She'd been missing for two months.

The confirmation that Lilly had been murdered was terrible enough – but later on the same day, as the search area was expanded to include a larger section of dunes known as 'The Hook', police made a further grisly discovery. Two more bodies had been dumped there – Felicity Sykes, 19, from Jedburgh, and Maggie Wilkins, 21, from Carlisle. Felicity had been missing since 15 January, and Maggie two weeks before that, since New Year's Day.

All three had been strangled.

The search for answers, and the person responsible, turned into one of the most expensive investigations in the history of the force: over 7,500 leads were pursued, 91 persons of interest were brought in for questioning, and – at its height – over 150 people were working on the case across various departments.

Ultimately, all the effort was to no avail.

Despite interviewing what at the time were referred to as 'several promising suspects', Northumbria Police never ended up making an arrest. In fact, according to one insider, the task force didn't even get close to identifying the killer. 'The so-called "promising suspects" – that was just hot air. We brought a couple of guys in who had records we thought might be relevant. But

I don't think, even for a minute, that we genuinely believed any of them killed those girls – plus they all had alibis. We had another one who ran a local business, who *could* have been our guy, but we had nothing to tie him to any of the women – just some weird behaviour, and being weird isn't a crime.' Another former detective who worked on Operation Red, as the murders were then codenamed, agrees: 'I think most of the time we were just wheeling in these men so we could make ourselves feel better.'

Yet another former cop goes further: 'That case was cursed.'

This isn't just superstitious talk. A number of detectives and personnel who were assigned to the case said it was afflicted with continual bad luck. 'Someone, somewhere must have broken about fifty mirrors the day we found those girls because it was just one thing after another,' says a former detective sergeant in Northumbria Police. 'Forensically, it was a washout. We had nothing of any worth. Those girls had been dumped in those dunes, wrapped up in hessian sacks, but the sacks had unravelled and become loose over time, so animals had been at them, sea spray, sand. The weather was bloody awful for weeks running up to their discovery. If there was evidence left on them, it had been contaminated or destroyed. And remember this was before the days of DNA testing in every case as well. So we started with nothing on that beach. Meantime, the media were all over us like a rash, and had been ever since Lilly first vanished, which generated this insane pressure for us to do something, anything. That forced us into mistakes, into rushing things through, into opting for desperate moves, like bringing in men for questioning that we *knew* didn't do it. We wasted weeks trying to pin it on one guy because of some local fire he might have been involved in. It was a mess, and *then* you had a jurisdictional problem. The other two girls weren't even from the north-east – Felicity was from Scotland, and Maggie was from Cumbria. Cooperation between forces was at best laboured, at worst non-existent. So that was all playing out, and was bad enough – but then the guts got ripped out of the team as well.'

That last part plays into talk of a 'curse', and refers to a series of tragic events that befell the core team: one, Detective Constable Leon Coetzer, who was only 26 at the time, suffered a heart attack in the July following the discovery of the bodies; a civilian member of the major crimes team, Anne Glass, who was responsible for inputting key details from the investigation into HOLMES, the police database, was killed in a fatal car accident seven months later; and then, perhaps most prominently, there was the senior investigating officer – and the face of the 'Dune Murders' in print and on TV – Detective Inspector Makayla Jennings. Even when the hunt for the person responsible was scaled back, Jennings still spent her days trying to keep the search for answers alive – for herself as much as for the families of the three murdered women, according to the people who knew her.

But all that came crashing down close to the two-year anniversary of the bodies being discovered when Jennings was delivered a cruel hammer blow in her personal life.

Questions

28 Years Ago

Makayla found a space on the street outside the school and switched off the engine. She could hear a man singing 'Baby Got Back', very badly, out of a window in the block of flats opposite St David's Primary.

She checked her watch, knew she was early for the twins, so retrieved some paperwork from the back seat on a hit-and-run she'd been working in Gateshead. She leafed through the pages for a while, trying to look for new leads, but – after a while – she started to lose focus. That was happening more and more. She didn't know if she was falling out of love with the job – or still hung up on what happened two years ago in the dunes outside Bamburgh.

Or maybe it was neither of those things.

Maybe I'm in denial, she thought.

Snapping the file shut, she dropped it into the passenger footwell and got out of the car. As she headed across to the school gates, where some of the other parents were waiting, she tried to stop thinking about what might really be going on with her. Not her falling out of love with her job. Not what happened at the dunes two years ago. Something worse than both of those. But then she took a long breath and switched faces: cop to mum. Her boys didn't need to see her disappointment, anger and guilt. They didn't need to see her scared.

'Mad hour's about to start,' a voice said from behind her.

Makayla turned to find a woman at her shoulder, one of the other mums. She was in her early thirties, slight, dark-haired.

Makayla smiled at her. 'Don't I know it.'

'What year is yours in?'

'They're both in Year Five. What about you?'

'Mine are in Year Six. Twins.' The woman rolled her eyes playfully. 'I mean, I love them to bits but mum to two ten-year-old boys? It's guerrilla warfare.'

Makayla smiled again. 'Believe it or not, I've got twin boys too.'

'Really?'

'Yeah. A year younger than yours but, you know, same rules apply.'

'Wow,' the woman said, chuckling to herself. 'I'm surprised we never crossed paths before. I've been looking for someone else to share the horror with for ages.' The woman laughed again and then paused, eyeing Makayla for a moment. 'Look, I know this is a really weird thing to say, but do I know you from somewhere?'

Makayla shook her head. 'I don't think so.'

'Were you on TV?'

'Oh,' Makayla said. 'For a time, a couple of years back.' She didn't say anything else, but then felt bad: the woman looked thrown. 'I work for the police. I had a case.'

'Ah, right,' the woman responded, and it was like the clouds had cleared in her face. 'Right. That's where I remember you from. The girls in the dunes.'

Makayla eyed her. 'That's right, yeah.'

'Don't be disconcerted,' the woman explained. 'I have a thing for faces.'

Just then, the school doors swung open and a tidal wave of kids poured out – a wall of bodies and noise, which carried out both her sons. Joshua came sprinting towards her first and then – a few seconds later, slower, more gingerly – Isaiah trudged across. 'Hey, Mum!' Joshua said, handing her his Batman bag.

'Hey, big man,' Makayla said, and kissed her son. When Isaiah arrived, she bent down and kissed the top of his head too. 'You two ready to rumble?'

When Makayla turned, the woman had gone. She looked around the school playground for any sign of her or her twins, but it was busy now, a sea of faces.

They headed back to the Sierra and got in.

'Guess what, Mum?' Joshua said, beaming, as they got in. 'Robert Kelvin said the F-word today. He called Nancy Kim an "F-word B-word", and when she began crying he called her "a whiny B-word".'

Makayla turned in her seat and looked at Isaiah. 'Is this true?' It was a routine they'd got into, an attempt to include Isaiah in conversations that his brother was leading, which was most of them. Sometimes, in quiet moments alone, she worried that there might be a problem with Isaiah. He was smart as hell but he was socially awkward – often just completely silent.

'It's true,' he said softly.

Makayla told Joshua to sit back and put his belt on, and then – as she pulled away from the school – caught his eye in the mirror. 'Did Mr Greenwall tell him off?'

'Yeah,' Joshua said frantically, pushing against his belt again, trying to get the story out. 'Robert went to Mr Quinlan's office and he didn't come back again.'

'No?'

'No. We reckon he got shot into space.'

Makayla smiled. 'That seems the most likely scenario.'

'Tied to a rocket and whoosh,' Joshua said, using his arm to gesture towards the roof of the car and the vastness of the universe beyond. 'You know how you always told us to be honest with you, Mum? Can I be really honest about Robert?'

'Are you going to say something mean?'

'No.'

'He is,' Isaiah said.

'I'm not, Zi, shut up.'

'Hey, hey, hey,' Makayla said. 'Be kind, rewind, remember?'

Joshua nodded. 'Sorry, Zi.'

Isaiah shrugged.

Joshua pushed forward for a third time, locked against his belt, trying to get Makayla's attention in the front seat. 'Can I, Mum? Can I be honest about him?'

She nodded. 'Let's hear it, then.'

'I liked it when Robert wasn't there.'

She glanced at him in the mirror. 'That's not nice, Josh.'

'But it's true. He's mean.'

'Is he mean to you?'

'He's mean to everyone.'

'Is he mean to you, Zi?'

Isaiah had been looking out of the window, but now he turned to meet his mum's eye in the mirror. He shrugged again. 'Yes,' he said. 'He's mean to everyone.'

Makayla tried to think of the right answer, the correct response to your sons wishing that a bully be shot into space and never come back down. Maybe there wasn't one. Makayla learned a long time ago, perhaps in her first weeks at the Met, before they moved north for Tyler's work, that some questions didn't have answers.

She thought about the three women in the dunes.

About the killer they'd never found.

In the end, some questions just led to more questions.

Makayla left the boys in the living room watching TV while she prepared dinner. They lived in Whitley Bay, a couple of streets in from the beach, and Tyler worked in Newcastle as a director at an international accountancy firm.

Normally, his hours were pretty fixed, but he was at an event tonight he'd had in the diary for six months, so Makayla had reminded her DCI that she was going to have to leave the office a couple of hours early. She'd told him that she'd bring the paperwork for the hit-and-run home with her – and, as always, she'd brought her own personal copy of the Murders too. That was what she called what was in the file now. The Murders.

Not the Dune Murders.

Not the surnames of the women.

Just the Murders, capital M.

When she said that in the office, everyone knew what she was refer-ring to. Leon Coetzer had started referring to it in the same way. They were the only two members of the original investigation still active on the case, so – just in terms of the sheer amount of information they held in their heads, and how many man hours they'd ploughed into it – the case had become more personal to them than to anyone else.

Not that they'd ever found a killer.

Some days it felt like they'd never even come close.

After dinner was over and the plates had all been washed, she told the twins to get ready for bed and poured herself some wine. Quietly, glass in hand, she sat at the table and leafed through the Murders again, trying to force herself to focus.

Just after 7 p.m., the phone rang.

She got up and went to the kitchen, expecting it to be Tyler – he said he would call about seven. 'Hullo,' she said in the slightly comical style she and Tyler always used when answering each other's calls.

'Mrs Jennings?'

Makayla straightened. 'Uh, yeah.'

It was a woman.

'Sorry to be calling so late – we're running a little behind schedule here, so I'm playing catch-up this week. My name's Natalie Dover. I'm Dr Ramsey's secretary.'

Makayla's chest squeezed shut.

You denied it, she thought, but now it's here.

'Oh,' Makayla said. 'Hi. What can I do for you?'

She asked the question like she had no idea what was coming.

But she did.

In every part of her she knew.

17

I wrote down the name *Makayla Jennings* next to *Leon Coetzer* and *Tom Swainswick* in my notebook – but as I read the last few paragraphs of Swainswick's article, I started to realize that Makayla Jennings was already a dead end.

She found out she had a brain tumour.

'When Mak got ill, the wheels just completely came off that whole investigation,' one member of Operation Red recalls. 'We were done, basically. Mak was the glue that held it all together.'

Only forty-four at the time, and popular among the rank and file, the news hit the team hard – especially when Jennings had to take extended leave from the force and then early retirement. Many insiders believe her departure put paid to any realistic chance of the case being solved – short of a freak occurrence or an outrageous slice of good fortune. And, as has been well documented already, neither of those things happened here.

Unfortunately, the tragedy didn't end there for Jennings.

After four operations her long battle against the brain tumour was finally won – but then, in a second heart-rending twist, nine years ago – aged only 63 – she was diagnosed with dementia.

I kept reading, making notes the whole time, but the rest of the article seemed simply to be a roll call of failure, of how things had gone wrong, or could have been done better, or weren't done at all. From the outside looking in it didn't appear as if those things were necessarily down to failures on the part of the task force – although there were likely to have been some; there always were in every manhunt on this sort of scale – more the lack of available evidence. Actual, usable leads were the oxygen that kept a case breathing; without them it was inevitable it began dying.

There were two obvious questions I could see.

First, was *this* the 'dunes' reference that Georgia had overheard Cate talking about on the phone? If it was – and, to me, it now felt hugely unlikely that it wouldn't be – why was Cate interested in the case in the first place?

Could that interest have led to her own disappearance?

It was the call to Coetzer that gave me pause. She'd contacted Swainswick first on 4 November and *then* Coetzer, so it was possible that Swainswick may have given Cate the number for Coetzer. It was possible that Swainswick was simply a go-between, a call she made in order to try and get to who she *really* wanted: Coetzer. I looked down at the photograph albums, at the pages of notes that I'd made during the course of the day. Even if that was true and she *did* speak to him, where was the evidence of that in her work? Where were the pictures she'd taken while she was up north?

Bamburgh.

The dunes.

Coetzer. Swainswick.

There were too many connections now to the Dune Murders for me to write this off as just another trip Cate had made to take pictures.

It was something more.

Now I had to find out what.

18

At 3.30 a.m., I was still awake.

I lay in bed, looking up at the ceiling, feeling the light touch of the night as a breeze danced across my body. I thought about Healy, about the possibility that Connor McCaskell might have somehow connected the dots, but then I tried to talk myself back. As far as the rest of the world was concerned, Healy had been dead for seven years, his body in a cemetery in St Albans under six feet of earth. We'd been careful, we'd been precise; there was no reason why even a journalist like McCaskell – who spent his entire life in the gutter, digging around in people's private lives – should find anything that could give us trouble. Even so, it was still a hum in my head, a pressure building.

And when my thoughts shifted back to Cate and Aiden Gascoigne, the pressure became more intense.

I stared out of the bedroom window, across the darkness of the lawn, semi-lit by solar lights, but against the blackness of everything else all I could see when I blinked were the photographs I'd found online of the Dune Murders: the sweep of the sand and prickle of the beach grass; the bleakness of the weather at the time the bodies were discovered. I saw granite skies, and washed-out colours, and then the white forensic tents erected over the three young women's bodies.

I rolled over again, listening to the soft moans of the house as it contracted under the coolness of the stars, and I pictured the three faces from the photographs that the families had given the cops to distribute.

They were so young, people who the world deserved to know better than just as a series of names in a newspaper story. They were at the beginning of a trail that should have gone on for decades, one through which they should have walked unscathed and undamaged. Instead, they were a footnote in history, forgotten apart from by the family members that were still alive, who remembered, and who even now would still be bound to the memory of what had happened in 1992.

And yet, awful as the thought was, there had been so many women who had suffered in so many equally appalling ways, so what was it that resonated with Cate about those three?

Lilly. Felicity. Maggie.

I began to wonder if it might have been part of some wider project. Maybe Cate was documenting exactly what I'd just been turning over in my head – forgotten women, the many victims of violence, trying to ensure they weren't just an afterthought. So often it was the killer that was remembered, sometimes perversely, their acts lionized, even exalted, and it shouldn't have been like that. Perhaps Cate had been trying to put that right and it had ended up leading her somewhere dangerous.

Perhaps the finale was what happened on Gatton Hill.

I got up and padded through to the living room where I'd left the photograph albums that Martin and Sue had given me. Putting on a lamp, I made myself some tea and started going through the pictures again. I'd been through all seven of the albums so many times now, but I went back over them again, looking for anything that might connect with the idea of Cate taking an interest in the victims of violence, or even women in general – life stories, moments in time that captured them as people and not just some statistic.

I couldn't see anything.

I pulled my notebook towards me and looked at the names of the four people I needed to chase down in my hunt for answers: the cop and the journalist who Cate called two months before she and her husband vanished into thin air; and two witnesses who might have lied about what they saw the day of the crash.

What was going on with you, Cate?

What was your interest in those murders?

Why might two witnesses lie to the police about you?

I lingered, looking at the pictures that Cate had taken, turning page after page in a search for answers, and returned to bed and tried to sleep.

By the time the sun came up, I was still awake.

19

I got up before 8 a.m., my head throbbing from the lack of sleep.

Taking some paracetamol, I washed out the exhaustion in the shower, letting the water pound my face and body, and then ate breakfast on the back deck and tried to soak up the sun. It was another hot day: blue skies, no clouds, the heat already dense and oppressive.

At 9 a.m., I called Leon Coetzer.

It went to the same voicemail message I'd heard the night before. I didn't have a mobile number for him, just a direct line at Northumbria Police, so as I listened to the same recorded message, I considered my options. I could go hunting for his mobile – get someone like Spike to dig it out for me – which would be a more direct route to him picking up, but I also didn't want to scare him off before we'd had the chance to talk. If I called on his mobile, and especially if it was a number that he didn't hand out very often, there was a good chance it would paint a negative picture of me and the tactics I was prepared to use to get hold of information not in the public domain. For now, it was easier to follow the route Cate had taken. So, after the tone, I left a message of my own: 'Superintendent Coetzer, my name's David Raker. I'm looking into the disappearance of Cate Gascoigne. I was hoping we could speak.' I left him my number and hung up.

Next, I tried Tom Swainswick at the *Star*.

This time I didn't have to wait long for an answer.

'This is Tom.'

'Mr Swainswick, my name's David Raker. I'm a missing

persons investigator in London and, at the moment, I'm looking into Cate Gascoigne.'

A brief pause on the line. 'Okay.'

'Do you remember Cate?'

'Yeah, of course.'

I heard the tap of a keyboard. He was probably googling me.

'Well, I've been going through her phone records and, in the November before she disappeared, it looks like she called you.' I had my laptop open in front of me and zoomed in on the entry for Swainswick. 'According to this, the call lasted thirty-one minutes.'

Swainswick was quiet.

'Mr Swainswick?'

'I thought I'd heard your name before,' he said. His Google search had clearly been successful. 'You were the guy who found out what went on down at Black Gale.'

Black Gale was a tiny village in Yorkshire. All nine residents had disappeared one night and I was asked by their families to find out what had happened. That had been the last case of mine to really blow up big. In fact, Black Gale was a major reason why Connor McCaskell was sniffing around my life.

'That was impressive,' Swainswick added.

I paused for a moment, seeing for the first time the risk in calling Swainswick. Maybe he wasn't the type of journalist that Connor McCaskell was, but he was still a journalist. Even without knowing him, I could almost hear the cogs turning, the first kernel of an idea forming. I'd been there once, just like Swainswick, so I knew how it was when you started to smell a story. What I had to do now was try and head him off.

'Could I ask why Cate called you?'

'She was phoning to catch up.'

'Catch up?'

'I'd met her before,' Swainswick explained. 'She'd shot

some images for the tourist board up here – ooh, maybe six or seven years ago – and, before I worked on the crime desk, I was a bit of a jack-of-all-trades. They used to send me out to do all sorts of boring old crap. One of those things was covering this multimillion-pound marketing campaign that Visit Northumberland had come up with. Cate was there on the day I went to interview the chief exec, and we just got chatting. Being completely honest, she was the sole reason I even remember covering the story. I've done tons of other shit like that and I've forgotten all of it. But I never forgot that one.'

I dragged my notebook towards me. 'Did you keep in touch after that?'

'Not really, but when she called that day, I was pleased to hear from her.'

'So what did you two talk about – do you remember?'

This time he took a long breath, the sound crackling down the line, and that was when I knew for sure: he wanted to try to turn this into a negotiation. We were barely a couple of minutes in and he already saw the mileage in my story.

Or perhaps in the story I was yet to write.

'She was just interested in some of the things I've done.'

'Do you remember which pieces specifically?'

'Why is this important?'

I considered my options, and then lied. 'It probably isn't. I'm just chasing down all the angles I possibly can – and this happens to be one of them.'

No reply this time. I could sense he was trying to get ahead of me, and maybe didn't fully believe me, but that he also couldn't see through the cracks.

'I think I talked her through a story I did about our local MP not paying taxes on a second property,' he said. 'There was another about a husband and wife in Blyth. Basically, she poisoned him.'

He paused, trying to remember some of the others he'd told her about, but instinctively it didn't feel like either of the ones he'd mentioned would be relevant to Cate and Aiden going missing. As he talked me through a few more – cut from the same cloth – I waited patiently for him to get to the one I wanted.

'I guess we probably talked about the Dune Murders too.'

Bingo. 'The Dune Murders?'

He filled me in on all the details I was already familiar with, but I just stayed silent. When he was done, in order to disguise where my real interests lay, I went back and asked questions about the other stories he'd mentioned, before working my way back around to the murders again. 'And these so-called "Dune Murders". Same question again. Do you remember what Cate wanted to know?'

'Not really,' he said. 'It was – what? – getting on for three years ago.'

'You don't remember anything at all?'

He sighed. 'I think she mostly asked about Jennings and Coetzer.'

'Jennings and Coetzer?'

'They were the kind of figureheads on the task force.'

'What did she ask about them?'

'I honestly don't remember.'

It was frustrating but I didn't blame him. In my experience witnesses often failed to recall exact details an hour after something happened, let alone nearly three years down the line.

'And you'd only met that one time before she called in the November?'

'Yes,' he said.

I could hear the doubts in his voice this time.

The more he was thinking about it, the less transparent Cate's call seemed. Why *would* she get in touch with him after only meeting him once? Why would she start asking about the stories he was writing? In some of the things he'd said to me – *She was the sole reason I even remember covering the story*; *I was pleased to hear from her* – it felt very possible that Swainswick had taken a real liking to Cate. I realized too – and perhaps he did as well now – that she might have subtly used that to her advantage – not just to get the answers she needed from Swainswick, but to create some fog if he happened to recollect the call later on down the line. In the days and weeks after, even when he read about Cate disappearing, he might still have been thinking about the catch-up part of it, the bit of their call that he'd enjoyed the most. And if he thought about the other part at all, about what her real intentions might have been, he was less likely to have connected the dots.

Not to the Dune Murders.

And not from there to any potential link to the Gascoignes' car crash.

If those two things intersected at all.

But increasingly it felt like they might, and if that was the case, I had to make sure that Swainswick wasn't stalking my shadow, so he and I talked some more, mostly so I could sow a few more seeds: dead ends, things that were going to ensure he didn't make me part of some story he might want to write – or, worse, start looking into Cate himself.

After the call was over, I went back over my notes – and as I did, I felt a flutter of alarm. It wasn't just that Cate had called Swainswick after not speaking to him for years, and seemed to have fed him what felt like a half-truth about wanting a catch-up. It wasn't just that she seemed to have used the fact he appeared to like her, had maybe even fancied her, to get what she needed. It was that the whole call might have just been a Trojan Horse.

I wasn't convinced she had any interest in the other stories he'd written.

It felt like she only cared about the Dune Murders.

PART TWO

The Witnesses

20

Audrey Calvert lived in a maze of flats off Streatham High Street.

I parked up and headed to a concrete spiral of stairs. It was stiflingly hot already, even though it was only mid-morning, but hardly any light or heat made it into the stairwell. Instead, the ascent was dark, cool and enclosed, the sound of leaking water and smell of stale urine keeping me company all the way up.

Emerging out of the stairs on the fifth floor, I found a long walkway with the doors to the flats on the left. Calvert's was at the other end. The views out from the walkway were decent: a play park, the next block of flats, identical to this one except for the angle at which it had been built, and then the sprawl of the city.

I knocked on Calvert's door.

A few moments later, I heard a chain slide across.

The door opened a fraction and a man in his early fifties appeared, bald, unshaven, in a white vest and blue shorts. He had some scarring near his shoulder, but it had faded over time.

'Yeah?' he said.

'I was looking for Audrey.'

There was a blank expression on his face.

'Audrey Calvert,' I said.

'Yeah, I know who she is. Why you looking for her?'

I held out a business card. He reached through the gap in the door with a thin arm, his skin mottled with a parade of pale bruises, and took the card. After eyeing it for a second, he looked at me again, his eyes moving between the card and my face, and said, 'Missing persons investigator. What would one of those want with her?'

'That's what I plan to tell Audrey.'

'Oh, you plan to tell her, do you?'

He seemed to revel in my confusion.

'You're a bit late, pal.' He finally pulled the door open, revealing more of himself and the flat behind him. The smell of cigarette smoke and fried food drifted out to the walkway. 'Audrey left two years ago.'

Shit. 'This is still listed as her address.'

In response he just shrugged.

'Have you got any idea where I could find her now?'

'Nope.'

'She never mentioned where she was going?'

'No.'

'But you two were living together?'

He nodded. 'Yeah.'

'For how long?'

'Eight months.'

'So one day she just – what? – ups and leaves?'

'Pretty much,' he muttered. 'I went to work one morning, kissed her goodbye; I got home later in the day and she was gone. She hadn't even cleared her stuff out.'

'She'd left all her belongings here?'

'Everything. Even her phone.'

I felt the first stirring of disquiet.

There was something else too, written plainly in the man's face: whatever had gone on between him and Audrey Calvert, it lingered, *hurt*, even two years on.

'Can I take *your* name?' I asked.

'No.'

116

I looked at him, staring him down. 'I was just being polite. If you choose not to give me your name, it's inconvenient, but it won't prevent me from finding it.'

He must have seen I wasn't playing him.

'Stanley Gray,' he said quietly. 'Stan.'

'Okay, Stan. So, just to be clear, Audrey left when?'

'The middle of June 2020.'

Mid June was nearly six months after the crash.

'And you haven't seen her at all since?'

'No.'

'Did you report her disappearance to the police?'

'I don't know if she disappeared.'

'She walked out and didn't even take her phone with her.'

But he shook his head, as if I didn't understand.

'She was complicated,' he said.

'In what way?'

'I don't even *know* you. Why would I get into all this shit with a total stranger?'

It was a fair enough point, but I wasn't leaving without answers, so I gave him a moment and tried to imagine why Audrey would up and leave a guy she'd been dating for eight months. Not even a goodbye. If she'd taken her stuff with her, maybe it could have been explained away – she could have been unhappy with him, had maybe met someone else, or it could have been something to do with her son. She'd mentioned him in the police interview, when she'd given this flat as her home address, and had said he was twenty-seven at the time of the crash. Kids, however old they were, were a pretty powerful incentive to make quick life-changing decisions. Maybe her son had been in trouble. Maybe he'd been sick, or was in a desperate situation somewhere. Except she hadn't taken any of her stuff, even her phone, and never got in touch again.

I asked him again: 'You said she was complicated?'

He eyed me and didn't say anything.

'In what ways was she complicated?'

Again, he didn't answer. Was it possible that Gray himself had something to do with her going missing? I couldn't write it off, but the look in his face as he'd talked about her leaving seemed to be one marked with a genuine anguish. So, if he was confused and had questions about where Audrey went, why not go to the cops?

'Have you heard of Cate and Aiden Gascoigne?' I asked, changing tack.

He squinted, the sun coming into his flat from over my right shoulder. Shifting to his left, he looked at my card again and said, 'That was the car-crash couple, right?'

'That's right.'

'That happened a couple of months after we started going out.'

'Do you remember what Audrey said about that day?'

'Not really.'

But then he paused, his gaze suddenly distant. When he finally looked at me again, I saw the same thing I'd glimpsed earlier: he was hurting. And even though it was obvious he was still conflicted about sharing his life with the total stranger on his doorstep, the hurt had been festering since the day Audrey left without any explanation – and after so long, a part of him desperately needed to let it out.

'She got quiet after that crash,' he said softly.

I took a step closer. 'What do you mean?'

'I mean, she changed after that car went off the road.'

I thought of Zoe Simmons, of what her mother had told me.

'How did she change?'

He shrugged. 'Before, she always had an opinion about

something. You could wind her up really easily, which I loved. Aud always hated being wrong. Sometimes if you decided to bring her up on something you *knew* she was wrong about . . . well, all hell would break loose.' He was chuckling, though. These were good memories for him. 'I didn't mind. Actually, I liked it. She was fun. We always had a laugh about it.'

'But not after the crash?'

'You had to work harder at everything. She didn't smile as much, or as often. When you tried to wind her up, she didn't rise to the bait. There was a . . .' He paused. 'I don't know, a sadness, I guess. Like I say, she got quiet. Maybe it was watching that car burn, thinking those people were being barbecued inside. Aud was like that; deep down, she was a kind person. What she saw that day, that sort of shit would have stayed with her. That's why I say she changed.'

Except this behaviour was exactly what had happened with Zoe Simmons, and it was too convenient that both witnesses were different after the crash, too convenient they both became quieter, sadder, more insular, as if part of them had become lost.

Something had got to them.

Or some*one*.

If I'd had worries about Audrey Calvert before, those worries were even more intense now. Because she and Zoe Simmons didn't feel like suspects any more.

They felt more like victims.

I felt another stir of disquiet.

'Would you have a picture of Audrey in there, Stan?'

He lingered, as if he wasn't sure whether this was a trap or not, and then told me to give him a minute. He disappeared back inside the flat and then returned with a photograph.

I took it from him and got my first look at Audrey Calvert.

It was a shot of her and Gray, taken in a pub garden. She was attractive, a little overweight, and had shoulder-length hair that she'd dyed white blonde, a fork of black roots showing through. Faint age lines formed like a mesh around the arc of her eyes, which were blue-grey. And, although it had faded over time, I could see that she had a tattoo on her upper right arm. It was small, but it looked like two written lines.

I took a camera-phone picture of the photo.

'What's her tattoo of?' I asked, pointing to it on the photo.

'It was her son's first and middle names.'

I made a note of it. 'Which are what?'

'Well, Michael was his first name,' he said straight away. 'His middle name . . .' He stopped, trying to cast his mind back two years. 'Pretty sure it was Christopher.'

'Did you get in touch with Michael after Audrey went missing?'

'Yeah, of course I did. He never heard from her again, same as me.'

Now it wasn't disquiet I was feeling.

It was genuine alarm.

'And did Michael report her missing?'

'No.'

'Why the hell not?'

Gray's eyes flicked away from me.

'Stan?'

'We tried to find her ourselves. Especially him. I used to phone him sometimes to see if he'd heard anything from her or found anything. He never had. But he was still looking for her earlier this year.'

'Why not just get the cops to look for her?'

He took a long breath. 'Because Audrey was a drug addict.'

I looked at him, completely thrown. I'd had no idea. That

information hadn't been anywhere in the paperwork I'd already seen.

And then I spotted something else.

A ripple in his expression.

'Was she using *before* the crash?'

He shook his head. 'I asked Michael if he'd ever seen her doing drugs growing up and he said no. Not ever. I guess she'd been clean for so long he didn't even remember that his mum used to be into that shit. Or she hid it from him so well he never noticed. But that's hard to do, hard to hide – even from kids – and she told me that wasn't how it was. She said it was an old problem. "Old demons", she called it. "Old demons coming back to haunt me".'

'But she was definitely using after the crash?'

He nodded. 'I found her gear hidden in the flat.'

'When?'

'I don't know. Couple of months before she left me.'

'When did you tell Michael?'

'After she left. She told me not to mention it to him when I found the gear; said she needed to tell him herself. But I guess she never did, because he didn't know.'

I rubbed at my face, trying to let the new information bed in. They didn't call the cops because neither of them trusted the police to take Audrey's disappearance seriously. And now, two years later, it was too late. She was long gone.

'You said you confronted Audrey about her drug use?'

'Yeah. I asked her why she'd started putting that crap in her veins again.'

'And what did she say?'

That same ripple in his expression. 'She said it was the only way she could escape.'

I found a space in a car park on Tooting Common and then got on the Tube from Tooting Bec. Taking the Northern Line to Leicester Square, I sat in an overheated carriage and used the time to go over everything Stanley Gray had told me about Audrey Calvert.

The same feeling of panic lingered in me.

Audrey had started using drugs again as a way to escape – but from what? Gray didn't know, but he – and presumably Audrey's son Michael – seemed to believe it was to do with what she saw the day of the crash, the trauma of the scene. But what if it wasn't that at all? What if someone was leaning on her? Threatening her?

What if that was what she was escaping from?

Given how Zoe Simmons had also behaved in the aftermath of the crash, drawing into her shell, becoming the antithesis of the boisterous twenty-year-old she'd been before, it wasn't hard to see how an addict in recovery, always teetering on the high wire, might fall and relapse. Simmons had become a shadow of herself; Audrey Calvert had returned to the only thing she thought could bring her comfort.

I exited the Tube at Leicester Square and made my way through the crowds to the Memorial gallery, using back alleys where I could in order to avoid the tourists.

Inside, it was air-conditioned, which was a big relief after the heat of the city, and I stood there for a moment under the vent, letting the cold air hit me as I took in the layout. It was one long room divided into three aisles, paintings – hanging from brass arms in the ceiling – operating as the dividing walls. At the front, to my right, was a counter with a till and what looked like some sort of guest book. At the rear – beyond the paintings – was another door into what appeared to be an event space.

'Can I help you?' a man said, emerging from the door. He was well spoken, in his early sixties, with wispy grey hair, a thick salt-and-pepper beard and, despite how hot it was outside, a smart fawn-coloured suit.

'I hope so,' I replied. 'I'm an investigator.'

He stiffened automatically. If you told people you were an investigator, some made a leap and assumed it meant you were with the police. I didn't correct him.

'Toby Platt,' he said.

'Mr Platt, I'm hoping you can help me. I'm looking into the disappearance of Cate Gascoigne.'

Platt recognized the name straight away. 'Are you reopening the case?'

'I'm picking up the search.' It wasn't a lie exactly – although, given that he probably thought I was with the Met, it wasn't really the truth either. 'Could I ask you a few questions?'

He nodded. 'Sure.'

He directed me through the door to the events room. It was much smaller than I'd imagined, although he'd laid some chairs out in tight rows of two. Three small windows looked out over a pretty mews. He offered me one of the chairs, and then I got out my notebook and flipped back to the shorthand notes on the interview I'd done with Martin and Sue. 'So, Mr Platt –'

'Toby.'

'Toby. I understand from Cate's parents that she exhibited here in June 2019 – which would have been, what, just over six months before she disappeared?'

Platt's eyes lit up. 'Yes, that's right.'

'"Tragic, Drawn".'

'A wonderful collection. We'd worked with Cate before – maybe late 2017 or early 2018; I can check my records if you need to know – on a series of photographs she shot of protests. She called it "All the Days Say the Same". That was good too, but "Tragic, Drawn", that was *seriously* good. It was socially important work as well.'

'In what way?'

'Well, it was showing the work of the police, the court system, the way prisons are – at its simplest it was a chronicle of how justice plays out in this country. But this was Cate, so it was obviously more subtle than that. The thing I always loved about her work – one of the reasons that I broke with tradition and decided to let a photographer exhibit here – was because there were always layers to her shots. It was like a painting in many ways. With most photographs you look at them and they tell an instant story. That's its job, right? It's overt, it needs to deliver a crystal-clear message because it's going to be running on the front pages of newspapers or on a billboard somewhere. With Cate there was that immediate hook, that initial story, which was why she *also* ended up on the front pages and the billboards – but there was always something else going on. Some lovely moment that only came to you after you'd spent some time in the photograph's company.' He shrugged. 'Cate was very gifted.'

'You said "Tragic, Drawn" was about the justice system?'

'Broadly, yes,' he responded. 'She toured the country, taking pictures of people involved in crimes at every level: the police, the victims, the perpetrators; and then she followed some of those people in their daily lives – in their homes, in the courts.'

'Do you know if she ever went to Northumberland as part of it?'

Platt considered it. 'I don't think so, no.'

Cate's phone calls to Leon Coetzer and Tom Swainswick happened five months after she'd exhibited in this gallery. I hadn't found anything to suggest she'd been up to Northumberland *before* November – so it seemed that the series on justice she'd shot for the 'Tragic, Drawn' exhibition and her interest in the Dune Murders were two separate things. But I was also wondering if her series on justice had ignited that interest. Could she have found out what happened to the three women while she was shooting 'Tragic, Drawn'?

'Did Cate ever say what she'd be working on next?'

'No,' Platt said, shaking his head. 'Not that I recall.'

I made a note to ask Martin, Sue and Georgia the same question. In the June, Cate had exhibited here. In the July, it was very possible she'd started thinking about what her next project was going to be, and had maybe even shared early ideas with her husband. Was it a coincidence that July was also around the time she and Aiden had their rough patch, and Aiden had googled the address of his local police station?

A fizz of adrenalin surged through me.

I felt more certain than ever that I was on to something. But what had Cate and Aiden fallen out about? What, in the Dune Murders, could have been a source of conflict between them? What had Cate wanted to photograph? And why would it lead Aiden to that Google search?

A second later, my phone buzzed in my hand. It was a message from a telephone number I didn't recognize. But, while I didn't know the number, the text was the one I'd been waiting for.

It's Zoe. Becky gave me your card.
I'll meet you in Covent Garden at 4.30.

Shelter

30 Years Ago

Amelia emerged from the hospital forty-five minutes later.

She felt panicked as she tried to recall everything she'd just been told. There had been so much information to take in, she wasn't even sure where to start. When she'd mentioned to the woman doing the ultra-sound that she hadn't told her parents yet, the woman grimaced – only very briefly, but as if Amelia really should.

'They'll go nuts,' she tried to explain.

'It's up to you, sweetheart,' the woman said. She said it as if she saw and heard this kind of thing every day of the week, which Amelia sup-posed she did. But then she looked at Amelia again, and said, 'You're going to need to tell someone, though.' She moved the transducer and the gel around Amelia's belly.

'Why?' Amelia had said. 'Is everything okay?'

'Yes. Everything's fine.'

And then she'd shown Amelia the image onscreen.

The rev of an engine, pulling into the hospital car park, brought her back to the present, and – feeling in a kind of daze – Amelia headed for the bus stop outside the main gates. The whole time her head replayed that same image on the monitor: the distorted grey and black of the baby moving around, then the technician putting a finger to the screen and saying, 'Look.' The woman had said it was too early to tell the sex – too early to tell much at all, in truth – but Amelia had been able to see one thing, blinking like a tiny light.

A heartbeat.

It had almost brought tears to her eyes.

As she sat down on the bench, inside the protection of the bus shelter, rain began to dot against the glass. That was when she made a decision.

She was going to tell Mum when she got home.

'Well, that was good timing.'

Amelia looked up as a woman in her thirties or forties – Amelia was never good with ages – ducked under the roof of the bus shelter and perched herself on the bench further along. She looked at Amelia, smiled, and then started to brush some of the rainwater from her sleeves. 'This weather,' the woman said, rolling her eyes.

Amelia smiled politely back and returned to thinking about how she was going to tell Mum. In her head she started to plan out what she was going to say, imagining the things that her mum might reply with. She imagined her dad coming in halfway through the conversation, and how he might react.

'You just come from the hospital?'

Amelia's thoughts were disturbed again by the woman. She looked at her. She was wearing a pair of glasses with big circular lenses and was close enough that Amelia could see the ghost of her own spectral reflection: her dark hair, her pale skin, eyes that looked like flecks of wood.

It's not really any of your business, Amelia thought.

But she just smiled and said, 'Yeah.'

'Not a fan of hospitals myself,' the woman responded.

'I don't think many people are.'

'Both my parents died in there, so this hospital I especially don't like.' But the woman said it with a hint of humour. 'Sorry. That's an awful habit of mine. I've always been a serial oversharer.'

Amelia smiled again, this time more genuinely and – as she studied the woman more closely for the first time – she had a vague sense of recognition.

'Do I know you?' she asked.

The woman frowned. 'No, honey, I don't think so.'

'We haven't met before?'

'No. I think I'd remember a face like yours,' the woman added. 'So, did you come to hospital on your own?'

'What?'

'I just mean, where are your parents?' The woman leaned forward a little and looked past Amelia, along the rest of the bench, as if Amelia's mum and dad might be hiding there. 'What are you? Sixteen? Seventeen?'

'Nineteen.'

The woman was clearly surprised. She studied Amelia for a moment, gaze fixed, tightening a scarf she had sitting around her neck. 'I didn't mean to offend.'

Amelia chose not to say anything.

'I'm jealous, that's all.'

Where was the bloody bus?

'You've got such beautiful skin.'

This time Amelia looked over.

'Wait, that sounded weird.' The woman frowned and became more serious. 'In actual fact, it sounded weird and creepy. I meant it to sound like a compliment.'

Amelia didn't know what to say.

'That's something else I'm not good at,' the woman said. 'Compliments. But I mean it. Your skin really is amazing. I expect you've broken a few hearts before.'

She'd never broken a single heart, barely seemed to even register with most boys. Amelia eyed the woman again and, for a second time, had a flicker of recognition. There was a familiarity in the woman's face that Amelia couldn't quite place. Did she just look like someone Amelia had met before?

Who did this woman remind Amelia of?

'I take it you haven't, then?' the woman said.

'Sorry?'

'Broken a few hearts. I've got to say, I'm surprised.'

Amelia shrugged. 'I think you might need better glasses.'

That made the woman roar with laughter.

Afterwards, the two of them sat there for a moment in silence, and then the woman's eyes went to Amelia's lap and she remembered that she was still holding a couple of leaflets they'd given her at the clinic. She'd rolled them all up into a tube as she'd left the hospital, but as she'd been sitting on the bench in the shelter, they'd slowly started to unfurl in her hand. Now it was possible to see some of the writing.

And one word in particular.

Pregnancy.

'Congratulations,' the woman said.

Amelia squeezed the leaflets tight, trying to conceal them. She didn't want the first person she discussed her pregnancy with to be some random woman at a bus stop.

'You don't have to be embarrassed,' the woman said.

'I'm not,' Amelia responded.

'I was your age when I had my first one.' That stopped Amelia. She turned on the bench, looking at the woman. 'I know. I probably seem really old to you, but I promise: when you get to my age, it won't seem old at all.'

Amelia didn't know what to say.

'Just don't make the mistake I did,' the woman said.

'What mistake?'

'I gave my baby up.' For the first time a sadness carried across the woman's face, an alteration in the light. She stared off into the middle distance for a moment, then seemed to realize she'd drifted far from here. 'Sorry. That was a mood-killer.'

'Are you okay?' Amelia asked, not knowing what else to say.

'Oh, bless you, sweetheart. Yes, I'm fine. But when I first found out I was pregnant, I was absolutely crapping myself. Actually, I think I was less worried by the pregnancy, or what would happen after the birth – you know, what I was going to do – and more worried about telling my parents, especially my dad.'

'I'm also worried about telling my dad.'

'I expect you are. But you know what dads are like. Always protective of their little girls – and we wouldn't have it any other way, would we?' She winked at Amelia. 'You'll be fine, sweetheart. I promise. It seems scary, I know, but if I could get through it, so can you. Just promise me: don't give that baby away. Keep him or her, and love them. Just give them all the love you can, and make sure the dad does too.'

'I don't even . . .' But then Amelia stopped herself.

'You don't even what?'

She was about to tell the woman she didn't even know who the father was. It was like she suddenly felt drawn to this stranger. 'I don't know what to say. To my parents, I mean.'

'You'll find the words, I promise.' The woman reached out and gently patted Amelia on the thigh. 'I know I can be an annoying so-and-so, but I do talk some sense sometimes – and I can tell you from experience that, in the moment, you'll definitely find the right words.'

Amelia smiled. 'Thank you.'

The woman returned her smile.

Their eyes stayed on one another for a second, and then the woman went to the inside pocket of her coat. She removed a small purse and opened it up.

'Here,' she said.

She gave her a business card.

'I know you don't know me from Adam,' the woman said, 'but if you ever find yourself struggling, you can always pick up the phone to me. I'm not perfect, I'm annoying, and I overshare – but I'm a good listener.'

Amelia looked at the card. 'You work for the police?'

'Yes,' the woman said. 'But don't let that put you off. I'm really nice, I promise.' She broke into a smile again. 'I won't make you call me by my official title.'

Amelia looked at the card a second time.

At the woman's name.

'You can just call me Makayla,' the woman said.

22

I waited for Zoe Simmons at a pub in Covent Garden.

With the sun beating down the air was thick, uncomfortable – the city choked by heat and exhaust fumes – but I managed to find a table out front in the shade.

Just as I was sitting down, my phone started buzzing. It was Ewan Tasker. I'd called him after leaving the gallery, sent him the photo of Audrey Calvert, and had asked if he could contact the Missing Persons Unit. That was the main UK agency for all unidentified bodies and remains.

'I hope I'm getting paid overtime for this,' he said when I answered.

'What, that lunch yesterday wasn't enough?'

'Not even close. Anyway, we'll work out your penance later.' He paused for a moment, and I heard him leafing through some papers. 'Okay, so I double-checked just in case but, as you already told me, no missing persons report was ever filed for Audrey Calvert. I did some digging around and the last address for her on the system is still the flat you've already been to, owned by a Stanley Gray. She doesn't have a car – her last one, the Fiat 500, she sold in February 2020 – and her record's clean in the time since the crash. It was clean before that as well. Basically, not a single red flag against her.'

'That all makes sense. What did you find at the MPU?'

'I spoke to the guy I know there and sent him the picture of Calvert that you messaged over to me. He put her personal details – or as much as we know, anyway – and physical description into the system.' Tasker halted. 'We may have something.'

'You got a hit?'

'Maybe. You know where Ruskin Park is?'

'Yeah, south London.'

It was only about four miles from the flat in Streatham.

'There's a series of railway arches down there, just off the north-west corner of the park. We're always finding dead bodies in that area. There are a lot of abandoned businesses in those arches, and the homeless get inside and use them to sleep in.'

'They found a body in one?'

'Yeah.'

'When?'

'Just under two years ago: end of July 2020.'

A month and a half after Audrey walked out on Stanley Gray.

'Obviously,' Tasker said, 'I'll preface this with the usual caveat that it *may* not be her – particularly as the body wasn't in great condition. I looked it up for you, and that week in London it was hotter than the sun.'

So decomp had been accelerated by the heat. The body would have liquified and swollen, then become so bloated it erupted and burst. 'Was there much left of her?'

'Enough,' Tasker replied. 'I'll send you over the picture in a sec. Her hair had begun to fall out, but there's still plenty there: it's definitely dyed blonde, and she definitely has the dark roots Calvert had as well. Same eyes too – blue-grey, same sort of shape. I mean, there's one shot to go off, but they look pretty similar to me. Plus, the body was the same build, same weight – or estimated to be, because obviously it had started to flatten due to the decomp – so that's another potential match. And she was approximately Calvert's age as well – late fifties, early sixties.'

'Any identifying marks on the body?'

'Uh . . .' I heard Tasker going through the paperwork. 'I guess you're thinking about the tattoo.'

'On her arm, yeah.'

A pause and then: 'Yeah, it's there.'

My heart dropped.

I got the photograph up on my laptop of Audrey Calvert. I studied her face, the dyed blonde hair, the blue-grey eyes, and the tattoo on the upper flank of her right arm.

Her son's first two names. *Michael Christopher.*

'Upper right arm?' I confirmed.

'Right arm, yeah.'

'Two lines? Two names?'

'A bit trickier to tell,' Tasker said, 'as the in situ photo-graph the MPU have has her lying on that side. But there's definitely a tattoo there. In the autopsy, before this got passed across to the MPU, the pathologist described it as "a quota-tion or a name", although the skin had deteriorated – but it sounds like we're in right ballpark.'

'Was there anything else that might help identify her?'

'No ID on her, no phone.'

'She left both of those at the flat.'

'So that explains that. The victim had a bracelet on her left wrist. Green and blue, braided. Like one of those friendship bracelets.'

I looked at Audrey again, pinch-zooming in on what I could see of her left wrist, her fingers laced together in her lap. It was there. A green and blue braided bracelet.

'Shit,' I muttered.

'She wore one of those?'

'She did, yeah.'

Dental records would have been a sure-fire way of confirming if the body was Audrey Calvert or not, except Audrey was never reported missing so the MPU were never able to start that process themselves. That meant starting it from scratch, as of now, which wasn't going to be quick. But, even without dental, the similarities were compelling.

Hearing my silence, Tasker caught up. 'You thinking dental?'

'Yeah, I was. I don't want to put you in a tight spot, though.'

'I can keep everything on the down-low, so from that side it's fine. But getting her dental records and *then* getting them compared to the body in those arches – I suspect you've already guessed that it won't be a fast turnaround. Three or four days at the *very* best. Maybe a week. More likely two or more.'

'Whatever you can do is a bonus, Task.'

'All right, leave it with me.'

'I really appreciate it.'

'You want to know how she died?'

I already knew the answer from the way he'd asked the question. 'Was it a drug overdose?'

'Correct.'

I heard more pages being turned.

'They found drug paraphernalia next to her: cooking equipment, a lighter, a needle. The needle had traces of heroin in it.'

I looked at Audrey again, at her face, her smile, at her bracelet and the tattoo of her son's name on her arm, and then googled *Michael Calvert*.

No social media. Nothing online about him at all.

'You at a desk, Task?'

'I can be.'

'Could you run a name for me?'

As I listened to Tasker moving between rooms, I checked

around me for any sign of Zoe Simmons. She'd said she wouldn't be with me until four thirty.

I checked the time.

It was four forty.

'What's the name?' Tasker asked me.

'Michael Christopher Calvert.'

I heard Task hit some keys. 'Michael Calvert. I don't have his middle name listed here, but his date of birth is the 3rd of September 1992. Clean record, as far as I can tell. I don't even see a speeding ticket.'

'Is there an address listed there?'

'Yeah, it's 14 Havant Gardens. That's Camberwell.'

That was the one Stanley Gray had given me too.

'You got a photo you can send me?'

'Sure,' Tasker said. 'I've got one from his driving licence. I'll shoot it over to you in a bit, along with the photo of the body in the arches.'

I thanked Task and, once the call was over, checked my messages.

Nothing from Zoe Simmons.

I texted her but got no response, so went to a Tube app on my phone to see if there were any major delays on the route she was taking.

There weren't.

The trains were all clear.

So where the hell was she?

More time passed with no sign of her. After forty-five minutes, I texted her once again, but – just as before – got no response. I tried to figure out why she might decide not to turn up and then glanced up and out at the crowds.

That was when I caught someone looking at me.

23

The pub was on the western flank of the market, facing St Paul's Church, and the man was in the shadows of its portico, half obscured between the pillars. The second we made eye contact, he dropped further behind the first pillar so that only an arm was still visible.

After that, he didn't move back into view, didn't show his face and the longer it went on like that, the less certain I became.

Had he been looking at me?

A group of Spanish schoolkids started to gather in the spaces between us, all of them with matching backpacks, their leader – shouting instructions – trying to organize them into some sort of order. The pillars of the church drifted in and out of view beyond the kids, the man more difficult to see now, and then I felt my phone buzz again in my pocket.

I took it out, hoping it would be Zoe Simmons.

But it wasn't. Tasker had emailed me the photographs of Michael Calvert and the body in the arches. As I opened my Inbox, I glanced in the direction of the man again. I couldn't see him now, not because the tourists were in the way – they'd all started to move, heading off in a line towards the market – but because he was no longer there.

I waited, just in case, my gaze lingering on the pillars, double-checking for any sign of the man – but he was definitely gone. Once I was certain of that, I switched to the message from Tasker, and tapped on the first attachment. It was a .png.

The shot of the body was decent quality, allowing me to

zoom in and move around, although the lighting in the railway arch was subdued, which meant I had to turn up the brightness on my phone. The woman was on her right side, in what looked like a corner, a syringe close by. One of her shoes had come off. All the other things Tasker had mentioned already I could see were true: she had dyed blonde hair, black roots, her eyes – one of them open – a clear match for Audrey Calvert's. She'd flattened during decomp, the frill of her ribs exposed, but it was possible – via her hips, her legs and the span of her shoulders – to get an idea of what physical size she'd been before her death, and it looked to be very similar to Calvert. I could see the bracelet on her wrist, and although the tattoo, as Tasker had said, was partly obscured – partly under her, in fact – it looked exactly as the pathologist had described: a quotation or a name.

Or two names.

I zoomed in. It was still fuzzy, but it was a good fit for the design of the tattoo that Audrey Calvert had had inked on her. And while it still might not have been her in the photo, equally, it was very possible that it was.

I closed the attachment and went to the next one, and an image of Michael Calvert filled my screen. It was the photograph from his driving licence.

He didn't look anything like Audrey. His mother had blue-grey eyes and black hair beneath the blonde dye; Michael's eyes were green and his hair blond-brown. I looked at his age: twenty-nine; twenty-four at the time the licence had been issued.

I closed my email and went to Maps on my phone, and then put in the address I had for Michael. It was just off Denmark Hill, a small cul-de-sac in a sprawl of terraced houses and flats. I pinch-zoomed in and saw that Calvert's house was at the end. It backed on to a long row of council garages.

I closed Maps and checked the time again.

It was half five now and it seemed pretty obvious that Zoe Simmons wasn't coming. She was an hour late.

I got to my feet, thinking about my next moves.

And that was when I spotted him again.

He'd moved across the street, to the entrance to the market. He was wearing tailored shorts and a plain white T-shirt, and had a red baseball cap pulled down over his eyes, the shadows it created masking everything above his chin.

But it was him.

And, despite how little I could see of his face, I knew he was looking right at me. His body shape was a giveaway.

I started walking towards him and he immediately stiffened.

Turning on his heel, he disappeared inside the market hall.

I headed after him.

24

For a second I lost him in the crowds.

I looked ahead of me, trying to pick him out. The market hall was packed, the shop-lined walkways full; so was the café in the middle, its boundaries marked out by Perspex walls.

Where the hell did you go?

I moved forward, eyes everywhere. There were so many routes for him to use, so many ways to disappear. As I danced around groups of tourists, forced to drop my pace, I wondered if I was already too late. Maybe he'd used one of the tiny corridors that knotted the market hall together. Maybe he'd already double-backed on me and returned along the same route I'd just come in on.

But then I spotted him.

He was there and gone again – but I saw the red cap, heading in the direction of the East Piazza, out the other side towards Russell Street. Upping my pace, I crossed from one side of the hall to the other so that if he glanced back over his shoulder, I wouldn't be where he expected.

I saw him look, his face still shadowed by the baseball cap. I still couldn't see enough to identify him, but I could see the panic in his movements. He didn't know where I was. He didn't know if he'd lost me or been outsmarted by me. I rounded a family taking pictures of each other, and then I was back outside again, next to the pillars by the east entrance – hot, the sun in my eyes.

His red cap flickered in and out at the periphery of my vision, and I zeroed in on him. I'd expected him to head out along Russell Street – where it was quieter and easier to get up a head of steam – but he was going south now instead, past the Transport Museum. I didn't know if he had a destination in mind, or if he was simply trying to lose me in all the tourists. One thing I *did* know was that the red cap was a bad idea: it might have covered his face, but it made it much simpler to find him. He was eighty feet ahead of me, and the place was absolutely heaving – but because he was tall and, because of that red cap, it was easy to put a marker on him.

I watched him glance back in my direction, but he couldn't see me now. There were too many people in the way. I kept to the edge of the market hall and then followed him at a distance down towards the Strand. It was clear now that he'd simply been trying to lose me in the crowds because he'd almost double-backed on himself and was heading towards Charing Cross Tube station.

Again, I dropped away, careful not to drift too close, then followed him down the steps, into the Underground. He made a beeline for the Bakerloo line. I wasn't as worried about him briefly vanishing from sight here because there were only two ways he could go – north or south.

He went for the northbound platform.

I waited out on the concourse until the train slid into the station, not wanting him to see me on the platform, then quickly moved as the carriages came to a halt. He was as far up the platform as it was possible to get – almost as if he were about to jump the barrier and get down on to the line. He'd grabbed a phone from his pocket and his head was down, his body turned away from me.

As soon as he boarded the train, I hurried along the platform and got on to the next carriage.

I headed to the end that butted up against the car he was in and glanced through the doors. He was on the far side of the next carriage, leaning against a glass panel, his back to me. His head was still in his phone, thumb working the screen, scrolling. I tried to figure out if I knew him from somewhere. I could see he had black hair, a straggly tangle of it poking out from under the back of the cap. He was skinny, his shorts baggy around his legs, his T-shirt badly fitted, a dark grey sweat stain in an inverse V stretching from his neck to the middle of his spine. I waited there as the train took off, hoping that he would move – but he just stayed exactly where he was, head down, looking at his screen.

Even so, I felt a flicker of recognition.

This was the first time that I'd been able to lock eyes on him properly, and – despite the fact that I didn't have a great angle – something about him stirred a memory. I couldn't grasp at it, couldn't bring it into the light, but I knew I was right.

I know him.

But from where?

I swapped sides so I could look in at him from a slightly different perspective, but it didn't make much difference.

Who was he?

A second later, I got my answer.

The train began to slow as it entered Piccadilly Circus, the brakes squealing, darkness turning to light as we edged along the platform – and, as we did, he turned and looked out at the station.

And, finally, I saw who it was.

Healy

He knocked on her door and waited.

He had the morning off because the father and son whose boat he worked on had had to attend a funeral in Bangor. As he waited for her to answer, a warm breeze washed in off the Irish Sea and he looked out and thought to himself, *If I never went out on the water again in my entire life, it would be too soon.* He'd loved the sea once, especially when the kids were small, but now it just made him morose.

As he waited, Healy looked through a window, into a low-lit living room, with a stone fireplace, a TV on a cabinet, a bookcase and two sofas. It looked neat in there, modern. Before long, he saw Paula's silhouette form behind the frosted glass of the front door, and when she opened it, she looked surprised, and then the surprise became a big smile. 'Oh,' she said, pulling the door back. 'Marcus. Are you okay?'

Except for last night, he'd barely said a word to her in over two years, so she obviously thought – for him to turn up out of the blue like this – it had to be some kind of emergency. He'd planned out what he was going to say in his head, but seeing her again – how she looked; that smile – had thrown him.

'I was just wondering, you know . . . uh . . .' He stopped himself. *Get it together.* 'I was just thinking about what you were saying about seeing someone up at my place.'

'Oh, yes,' she said. 'Is everything all right?'

'It's fine,' he responded, holding up a hand to her. 'Really, everything's fine. I was just thinking that, uh . . . Look,

I know this is a bit cheeky of me to even ask, but you mentioned that you worked from home, and obviously I'm out on the boat most days, so . . .' He paused. He felt oddly nervous, but wasn't sure if it was the favour he was having to ask, or just being this close to someone, being part of a real conversation, with a real person – especially someone who looked like Paula did. 'I'm sorry,' he said. 'What I'm trying to say is, do you think it might be possible for you t–'

'Yes,' she said, smiling. 'You want me to keep an eye on your house for you?'

Healy returned her smile. 'If that's okay.'

'Of course. My office is actually at the back here,' she said, gesturing over her shoulder, 'so that gives me a really good view of things. That was how I was able to see that guy the other day. There's a little gap in your laurel bush.' But then she stopped, eyeing Healy. 'Are you worried about him?'

'No, not really,' Healy lied. 'It's just I've had some experience in the past with burglaries. I don't want to fall victim to that again.'

She nodded, seemed convinced. 'Shall I take your number then?' she asked.

'I, uh . . . I don't actually have a phone.'

'Really?'

'Really.' He tried to make light of it.

'Are you a technophobe, Marcus?'

For a second he was so caught up in how she looked that he completely forgot that he was living here under the alias Marcus Savage.

The name *Marcus* didn't even register.

'Marcus?' Paula repeated.

'Oh, sorry.' He shook his head. 'I was miles away. I had a phone, but I lost it out on the boat a couple of weeks back.' He forced another smile and had the sudden thought that he hadn't smiled this much in months. Maybe years. 'I had it in my hand,' he said to her, 'then – *boom* – this monster wave crashes over the side of the boat and it was gone.'

'Do you have a landline then?'

'No. I don't have one of those either.'

She laughed a little, and the sound of it gave Healy a minor buzz. 'So how do you get in contact with people? Smoke signals?' She winked playfully.

'Carrier pigeon.'

She laughed again. 'Okay, then, mystery man. I'll just walk up the hill and knock on your door if I see anyone acting suspiciously, shall I?'

'Until I get my phone, that would be great.'

They stood there for a moment.

'I've got some coffee on,' she said. 'Did you want to come in?'

Healy looked along the hallway, into the living room. He could see she had the back doors open and a laptop on a table.

No, he thought. *You definitely shouldn't go in.*

'Only if you're sure,' he found himself saying.

And then he was following her through to the kitchen.

As she poured them both coffee and cut them a slice of apple cake she'd made from more of the Bramleys in her garden, Paula did most of the talking. She told Healy how her husband had left her four years earlier for someone he worked with. 'We had this great place, on the coast near Llandudno,' she said. 'To be honest, I was more upset about putting the house on the market than Terry leaving.'

If she harboured any resentment towards her ex, she didn't show it.

Just then, Healy recalled the female detectives he'd worked alongside at the Met. He'd got to know a few of them well, run cases with them, but they'd always been cautious, rarely talking with this kind of freedom. At the time, he'd never really given it much thought, but it seemed so clear now: in order not to concede ground to male colleagues, they'd been forced to shut part of themselves off. Their lives outside the station, what *really* mattered to them – it all just got buried.

'Marcus?'

He startled, turning back to Paula, realizing he'd allowed himself to drift again. *I don't want you to find out who I am*, he thought. *I like the way you talk to me like a person.*

I like being someone else.

'I thought I'd talked you into an early coma,' she said.

'No, not at all. So you moved here after the split?'

'Yes. But it's okay. I love it here.'

'It's very quiet.'

'I know. That's what I love. I don't ever see myself moving.'

Paula studied him.

'You don't say much,' she said, a smile tracing the corner of her lips. 'I hope it's not because I'm taking over the conversation. I have a habit of doing that, I'm afraid. I think it might be the Yorkshire lass in me.' A full smile bloomed in her face. 'As hard as it is to imagine, my mum was even worse. She could talk the hind leg off a donkey.'

'It's nice to have company,' he said quietly.

'What about you? When did you come over from Ireland?'

'A long time ago,' he said. 'Back in my twenties.'

'You said you're from Galway, right?'

Dublin. 'Cork.'

'Cork, yes, that's it. It's lovely there. When my son Joe was still young – he's eighteen now – my ex-husband took us over to that part of the world for a few weeks. It's so beautiful.'

Healy glanced out of the kitchen window, the sky darker, rain clouds forming, trying to remember all the details that he and Raker had set out: his name, his age, his date of birth, his career, the reason he originally went to London, where he'd lived after that, what jobs he'd had and why he'd moved around. In this new life he was divorced, same as always, but Marcus Savage didn't have kids. No daughter. No sons.

Not like Healy had.

As long as you keep your head down, Raker had said to him after it had all been thrashed out, *you won't have to worry about trying to spin a consistent story.*

'Are you okay?'

'I'm fine,' he said.

'Why don't you let me cook you dinner, Marcus?'

She touched his arm gently, and he could feel her fingers against him, their skin only separated by the thin cotton of his top. No woman other than his wife had taken an interest in him for as long as he could remember. He'd hardly *spoken* to anyone in two years. He'd grown used to being alone, but that didn't mean it was easy. He was in his mid-fifties. What happened if he lived to ninety? How could he go another thirty years living like this?

'Marcus?'

He thought of Raker. He thought about all the reasons to say no, everything they'd talked about – including the threat of that tabloid hack Connor McCaskell.

'No pressure,' Paula said.

But then he found himself smiling yet again.

'Dinner would be nice.'

25

I waited for the doors to open and then switched carriages.

He'd turned around again already, his back to me, his nose in his phone. I could see, over his shoulder, that he was reading through emails. I stood there for a moment, just taking him in, thinking about what I was going to say, and then the doors closed, the train started moving, and he looked up from his screen.

I perched myself on a seat across from him.

His expression dissolved for a second and then, just as quickly, he recovered his composure. He switched off his phone, pocketed it and turned in his seat.

'This is a surprise,' Connor McCaskell said.

I looked him up and down. The sweat stain on his T-shirt had begun to fade a little, but he still looked a mess: the few times we'd come face-to-face, he was always untidy – not dishevelled exactly, but badly dressed, his clothes not cut for his frame. He took off his cap, his thinning hair damp and matted to his scalp. He swiped it back from his face.

'The red cap was a mistake,' I said.

A smile lingered at the corner of his lips and then he opened his hands out. 'I only put it on an hour ago. Needed to protect the old head from the sun.' His eyes searched me. 'Until I did, you never even knew I was there.' The implication was obvious: he'd been following me for a while.

He'd probably been waiting outside my house this morning.

The question was, had he been outside *another* house

yesterday? I thought of what Healy's neighbour had said she'd seen at the place in north Wales.

'So what were you hoping to find out today?' I asked.

He just stared at me for a moment. I assumed he was giving himself a second to think about what he should say. He was a tabloid journalist, but first and foremost he was an agitator. He liked to unsettle the people he was going after because, when they were rattled, their discretion fractured and they made mistakes. Eventually, he said, 'I just wanted to see what you were up to. It was fact-finding, David.'

'Is that what you call it?'

'I think, deep down, you enjoy all the to and fro.'

'I don't enjoy anything about you. This is harassment.'

This time he laughed. 'How am I harassing you, David?'

'I had to block your number you were calling me so often.'

'Well, there you go,' he said. 'Now you know why I've had to resort to following you around. It would have been so much easier if you'd just returned a few of my calls. I'm sure we could have worked something out.' He winked at me. He was from Essex, but I'd noted a small quirk over the time he'd been pursuing me: he'd always start out talking a little differently, as if he were trying to lose his accent or suppress it. But as the conversation went on, and especially as it became more of a game to him, he'd forget and his real accent would start to leak through. At the start, I couldn't figure out why he did it – other than, perhaps, not liking the way he sounded. But over time I began to realize it was something else: he tried to soften his accent because it made it harder for someone to get a handle on him. McCaskell was the sort of man who would like that; it gave him just the sort of unpredictability he needed. He tilted his head. 'Huh, David? Why didn't you just pick up the phone to me? We could have avoided all this run—'

'No,' I said, cutting him off. 'We've done this dance before. We're not doing it again. I mean, you've been at this how long now? Three years? Four? This is an obsession over *nothing*. There's no story here to tell. Everything I've ever done – any case, anything remotely important – is *in* the public domain already. I'm not hiding who I am and what I do. And yet you're *still* pulling crap like this. You've tried to sneak into my life by lying to my daughter about who you are. You've turned up at my house and threatened to ruin me. Now you're following me around like some amateur-hour detective. Why do you care so much about hurting me? I don't have a story. There's no dark secret to reveal.'

I thought of Healy again. But I didn't let my expression slip. I needed to find out if McCaskell was the man that the neighbour had seen at the cottage – or perhaps someone he'd employed to snoop around – but would have to find a route around to the answer.

'The thing with you, Raker,' McCaskell said, leaning forward, his expression suddenly more serious, more dangerous, 'is that your life, these wonderful things you do for people out of the goodness of your heart –'

'I get paid. I'm not doing it for free.'

'Yeah, but you're just a little *too* perfect, aren't you? The lengths you go to for the families you help, the risks you take, it's not normal. You must get something out of it. Something more, something you're not telling everyone. That's why I'm still on this thing. Because I *know* you've lied to the police in the past. I might not be able to prove it yet but there are little things in your cases that don't add up. Tiny things, but they're there. And the cops might have swallowed all these stories you've told them, but I haven't. I'm not swayed by how charismatic and handsome you are. I just see a whole lot of question marks that have been squared off a little *too* neatly.'

'So now you're going to follow me around for ever?'

He leaned back. 'Not for ever.'

'Until when?'

'Until you make a mistake.' His forefinger and thumb rubbed together, as if he were desperate for a cigarette. 'Maybe it'll take me years to get there, but I know there's a story here. I *know* it. And when I break it – when you finally slip up – this is going to create an earthquake with the public. All these big investigations, all the lies you've told to protect yourself, all the lies the cops have swallowed. They'll be handing me a fucking Pulitzer.'

The light of another station filled the carriage.

'The public don't give a shit about me. If anyone out there cared who I was, or even knew my name, you wouldn't be the only journalist in the world trying to magic up a story out of nothing. It's been *years* of you spouting this crap and you've still got zero evidence. You're a conspiracy theorist, nothing else. Just let it go.'

He was slowly nodding to himself now, his eyes still on me.

'You remember that case you had in Yorkshire?' he asked me.

Now I knew where we were going.

'A whole village disappears and of *course* David Raker has the answers.' He eyed me. 'Do you remember there were a few days there – right at the end of that case – where you were missing in action? Well, before you turned up safe and well, the cops were busy trying to tie everything together – and they received an anonymous call.'

The anonymous caller had been Healy.

He'd called to point the cops in the right direction, because we'd worked part of that case together. But mostly he'd called because he, like everyone else, thought that I was dead and wanted the police to find me.

Basically, it had been an act of kindness.

But it had put him on the map.

'Who's your Irish friend, David?' McCaskell asked.

I just looked at him. 'I don't know what you're –'

'Talking about, yeah, I know. The anonymous caller had an Irish accent. So who in your life comes from Ireland?' He was looking for chinks in my armour. I gave him nothing. 'Like I say: tiny little things that don't add up.'

We looked at each other, a silence settling between us, and – as the train emerged from the dark into Baker Street – I saw the first flash of frustration in his face. And in that moment I knew I was safe for now. McCaskell was familiar with my background and had studied my career, so he must have found Healy somewhere in my history, even if only in passing. But he hadn't made a connection from there to the Irish accent – and why would he? Healy had been gone seven years and his 'body' was six feet under the earth in Hertfordshire – or, at least, that was what the forensic evidence said. It meant McCaskell hadn't been the man snooping around Healy's place the day before.

So who was?

The doors to the carriage opened.

'I'll see you around, Connor,' I said, standing.

'Raker,' he responded, and when I looked back at him, he'd recovered his poise, his arrogance, his threat. 'Just remember: I'm a patient man.'

26

It took me another hour to get all the way back down to my car at Tooting – and, as soon as I did, I tried calling Zoe Simmons. Her mobile just rang, unanswered, until it hit voicemail. I left a message: 'Zoe, it's David Raker. You need to give me a call.'

From Tooting I drove four and a half miles east to her flat in Dulwich. No one was home. I buzzed a couple of times, and then tried calling Simmons again when I returned to the car. Still no answer. I felt a turbulent mix of frustration and unease now. I was pissed off by Simmons's no-show, but I was concerned by it too. For a second, I thought about calling her mum, to see if she'd heard from Zoe, but I didn't want to concern her for now, not least because she already seemed worried about her daughter's well-being.

I checked the time – it was just before eight – and then fired up the Audi again. Making my way back along Dulwich Common towards Brixton Hill, I headed to Michael Calvert's house. There was still a chance the body in the railway arch wasn't Audrey, but it was hard to deny that it was beginning to look likely. So as I drove, I tried to work out what the best approach was if Michael was at home. Should I tell him about the woman they'd found in the railway arch, only a few miles from where he was living?

I decided to put off the decision for now.

Just let it play out.

The evening was still bright as I pulled into his road, the sky blue, the air thick with the heat of the day. Michael

Calvert's house was at the end of the cul-de-sac, and as I parked at the kerb, I spotted an alleyway leading to the long row of council garages I'd seen online. His property, and the one opposite, were either side of the alley.

I got out and wandered down to the house.

The front garden had been paved over, but the slabs had begun sinking in the middle and some of the pointing had started to crumble away. Two red ceramic pots sat either side of the front door, but there was nothing in them, just twigs and earth.

I knocked on the door.

To my right was a bay window, a pair of pale net curtains half pulled across the glass. I knocked again and, when I got no response, headed for the alleyway that connected the road to the garages. Eventually, I entered a path with high brick walls on one side and high fences on the other; the fences were the boundary for the row of homes that Calvert lived in.

I got on to tiptoes and looked over into his back garden. Like the front, it had been paved over – except for a square of unmowed grass at my end – and there were two old-fashioned patio doors. Next to them was a kitchen which looked small and dated, decorated in floral wallpaper and lined with old appliances. I felt fairly certain no one was home so headed back around to the front. As I got there, I heard a door being opened.

It was Calvert's neighbour.

A guy in his late seventies appeared – very thin, grey-haired, but bright-eyed – and looked out at me, still partly hidden by the door frame. 'Can I help you, son?'

I could hear his wife talking somewhere else in the house, a one-way conversation that sounded like a phone call.

I introduced myself and handed him a card. 'I was hoping

to talk to your neighbour, Michael,' I said. 'I don't know if you're friendly with him?'

He finished reading the card. 'Missing persons, eh?'

I nodded.

'Is Michael missing?'

'No,' I said, although, in truth, I wasn't sure. 'I just need to talk to him about something.' I could see he didn't entirely believe me, or knew there was more to the story than just that, so I quickly pushed on. 'Do you chat to him much?'

'On and off,' the man replied. 'We see him from time to time, but you know . . .' He edged out, on to the front step, glancing across the fence. 'Actually, now you come to mention it, it's been a while since we've seen him around. I mean, he's pretty quiet but . . .' The man looked out at the other houses. 'I guess it's not unusual. Me and the missus have been in this house forty-one years and, when we first moved in, we knew every person in the street. These days, I couldn't tell you very much about anyone.'

'Any idea how long Michael's been living here?'

'Must be four years, I reckon. Could be five, actually.'

'So when was the last time you remember seeing him?'

The man sucked in a breath. 'Ooh, I don't know.' He glanced behind him, into the living room. 'Vera?' His wife didn't hear him: she was still on the phone. '*Vera.*'

'What?' came a reply.

'Come here.'

His wife appeared a few moments later.

'This is David,' her husband responded. 'He finds missing people.' Vera's attention had been snagged. 'He was asking about Michael next door, when we last saw him.'

'*Really?*' she said. 'Is he missing? Is he in some kind of trouble?' She shuffled past her husband to the front step, and looked right to Calvert's property.

'No,' I replied. 'I just want to speak to him is all.'

They looked at one another.

'I reckon it must be at least two months,' Vera said. 'At least. It could easily be three or four.'

Stanley Gray had told me that, earlier in the year, Michael was still looking for answers about where his mother went, long after Gray himself had stopped. Now I was wondering if he'd found something.

Something that had led to him disappearing too.

The starkness of the situation was now impossible to ignore: there was every possibility that Audrey was dead; her son had been desperately looking for her in the first part of the year and hadn't been seen by his immediate neighbours for two months, possibly more; and I couldn't find, or contact, Zoe Simmons. And all of them were connected to the same event.

The disappearance of Cate and Aiden.

'Did you ever meet Audrey, Michael's mum?' I asked.

'A few times, yes,' Vera said. 'She used to visit him here.'

'So when was the last time you think you saw *her*?'

Vera let out a long breath, looking at her husband again, the answer clear in her face already. It had been a long time, so long they were struggling to even remember.

'Honestly?' she said finally. 'It must be a good few years.'

Another little piece snapped into place. It was just under two years since the body, matching Audrey Calvert, had been found in the railway arch.

'Did you ever talk to her?' I asked.

'Oh yes,' Vera said, 'quite a few times. She was always nice. She isn't much younger than us, is she, Barry?' Her husband nodded in agreement. 'I don't want to give you the wrong impression. We weren't best mates or anything. I just used to pass her sometimes, out front here, when she came to see Michael. We'd stop and chat.'

'Do you know what Michael did for a living?'

'Plumber,' Barry replied. 'Self-employed. But he was also a bit of a handyman. He's helped us out once or twice with things – hasn't he, love?'

Vera nodded. 'It's useful having him next door.'

'Have you ever seen anyone else at the house?'

They both seemed confused.

'I mean, has anyone else been knocking on the door like me?' I glanced in through their living-room window and could see a plump armchair facing me. It was in a prime position to see people as they came and went from Calvert's door – and it was obviously how Barry had managed to spot me out here in the first place.

'No,' Vera started, 'I don't think we've seen –'

'Wait a minute, love,' Barry interrupted. 'Wait a minute . . . There *was* that one fella who came here.' He turned back to me, frowning, his mind clearly trying to grab at the memory. 'I don't know when it was exactly. A couple of weeks back. Maybe a month.' He looked at his wife again. 'The guy with the, uh, arm. You remember?'

Vera made an *oh* with her mouth.

'"The guy with the arm"?' I repeated.

'Yeah.' He pulled up the sleeve of his cardigan, showing me his own arm. 'There was scarring here. The skin was all mottled and that.'

'He looked like he'd been burned?'

'Yeah. It was a big patch of it too, all along the top of his forearm, from wrist to elbow. I could see him from the window here, trying to get into Michael's house, and I thought it looked suspicious, so I went out to see what was going on. He had a set of keys and was trying some on the door – so obviously I asked him what he was doing.'

'And what did he say?'

156

'He said he was a friend of Michael's. A friend who had no idea which key was for the front door. I thought it was damned suspicious, which is why I remember him. Well, that and the scar. When I asked him who he was, he told me he must have brought the wrong set of keys – and then, just like that, he was out of here.'

'What did he look like, do you remember?'

'I don't know . . . thirties maybe, six foot, well built.'

'Hair colour?'

'Brown, although he had a cap on. He had a thick beard, though.'

'Eye colour?'

'Dark. Brown too maybe. To be honest, when I first saw him out there, I thought it was Michael. You know, they had a similar sort of build – tall, muscly and that. But then, when I came out, I could see it wasn't.'

'Did you ever see this guy come back?' I asked.

'No.'

Which didn't mean he hadn't; he might have just waited until Barry and Vera weren't around.

I tried to process everything I'd just found out but my mind was already skipping back to what the couple had said about the man's scarring – and, as it did, an image of Cate and Aiden's Land Rover formed. I pictured it on its roof in the ravine, its frame crunched, the flames tearing through it.

Because that was one way you might scar your arm like that.

By pulling people out of a burning car.

The Phone Call

30 Years Ago

The talk with her parents went better than Amelia had expected.

Her mum, as she'd predicted, had stayed relatively calm, even when Amelia had admitted to going to the early-assessment clinic by herself. She'd simply asked Amelia if she wanted to keep the baby. Amelia had said she didn't really know and, in response, her mum had said that it wasn't the baby's fault that Amelia had gone out and had drunken sex with some guy whose name she didn't remember. That last part had made both of them a little emotional, perhaps because, like with the scan, Amelia was forced to think about the baby as an actual person — growing and shifting inside her — not just a subject to discuss.

After that, her mum had given her a long, unbroken hug.

Amelia's dad hadn't offered much of an opinion either way, which was a better outcome than Amelia had expected. After all the talking was done, he said, 'I really think you need to figure out who this "Phil" guy is, Mee.' He always called her Mee; she'd told him for a while in her mid-teens that she didn't like it any more, but as she got older, she began to change her mind. She recognized that her father hadn't always been a great husband — but he'd always been a loving dad.

'I don't know who he is, Dad.'

'What did he look like?'

She glanced at her mum, both of them still a little tearful, and said, 'I told you: I was drunk.' She swallowed, hated having to admit it, especially to her dad.

Her dad just nodded.

He was hurt, she could tell; not just because Amelia didn't remember who Phil was, or what he looked like, but about how careless she'd been.

158

It was the antithesis of everything they'd taught her. They'd always been open with her about relationships and sex – Amelia's mum had even gone with her to the doctor when, aged sixteen, Amelia had wanted to go on the pill. Her mum had never asked her if she was planning to have sex – she wasn't; in fact, Amelia had never even had a long-term boyfriend before – she'd just heard the girls at school talking about being on the pill and didn't want to be the odd one out. After she picked up her first prescription, her mum said to her, 'Just promise me you'll be careful – and never, ever do something you're uncomfortable with.' But although Amelia had had sex a couple of times with a boy she'd gone to school with – just to get it out of the way more than anything – she stopped taking the pill about a year ago because there didn't really seem any point any more. There was no boyfriend. There weren't even any prospects. So Amelia understood why her dad was hurting, why her mum was too, despite doing her best to disguise it: Amelia may not have done something that she was uncomfortable with, but she hadn't been careful.

'I think we need to find out who this guy is,' her dad said again.

'Just be quiet, Ian,' her mum said, squeezing Amelia tighter.

'You don't think we should know who he is?'

'Let's cross that bridge when we come to it.'

'We've crossed that bridge. She's already pregnant.'

Her parents looked at each other.

And then her dad backed down, just as he always had in the months since her mum had found out about his affair. He looked at Amelia and, with just one glance, she could see how much he loved her. He smiled, winked at her, then got up and came across, putting a hand to her head. 'I think a cuppa is the order of the day,' he said.

After he was gone, Amelia's mum said, 'He's right, you know, about finding out who this guy is. He deserves to know, for one thing. But it's really about more than that, hon. If you keep it, the baby is his responsibility, as much as yours.'

'I know.'

'So are you going to find out who he is?'

Amelia nodded. 'I'll ask around.'

But asking around didn't get her very far.

She didn't tell her best – in fact, only real – friend, Coralie, who'd she'd gone to the party with, that she was pregnant; she just made up a story about really liking the evening she'd spent with Phil and wanting to know more about him. Coralie believed the lie, but no one she asked on Amelia's behalf seemed to know who Phil was. One person thought Phil had come to the party with another guy's brother; a second said he was part of a larger group that no one knew because they'd been there on a stag weekend. Someone else told Coralie that she wasn't even convinced the guy's name was Phil, and she thought she heard someone else calling him Paul. And then, after a while, Amelia had to stop talking about it altogether when Coralie began getting suspicious about the type of questions Amelia was asking.

Over the following week, her mum organized a midwife appointment for her, and then a week after that, Amelia got through a letter confirming her twelve-week scan. The whole time she and her parents, especially her dad, tried to track down Phil. They got nowhere.

In truth, they had no real idea where to begin.

But then, the day before the scan, Amelia was at home looking through the job sections of the newspaper, at roles she was never going to be able to take unless she lied about her pregnancy, when she noticed something. It was poking out of a Stephen King novel she was reading, being used as a makeshift bookmark.

A business card.

It was the one that the lady at the bus stop had given her a few weeks before. Amelia studied the woman's name and title: Detective Inspector Makayla Jennings. Taking the card downstairs to the phone in the living room, she paused. Was this really a good idea? The woman would probably be pissed off about her time being wasted – or just laugh in Amelia's face. But then she looked across at the table, at a notepad her dad had been writing in, trying to fill it with whatever information they had about Phil – which was basically nothing – and she thought, *What the hell?*

She punched in the woman's number.

'Hello?'

'Oh, hi,' Amelia said. 'Is that . . .' She faded out. What was she supposed to call her? Detective Inspector? Makayla? 'Uh, this is Amelia Robbins. You probably won't remember me, but we talked outside the hospital a week ago at the bus stop.'

'Oh, sure. Hello there. How are you?'

The woman seemed pleased to hear from her.

Amelia relaxed. 'I'm sorry to call you out of the blue like this,' she said, 'but I was wondering if you . . .' She stopped; didn't know how to phrase it. 'I was wondering if you could help me.'

'Help you?'

'Yes. I'm, uh . . . I'm trying to . . .'

'Trying to what?'

The woman sounded confused now, or suspicious.

'This is really embarrassing but . . .' Again, Amelia stopped. For some reason her heart rate was climbing. She wasn't sure if this had been a good idea after all.

'It's okay, love,' the woman said. 'What's up?'

Amelia cleared her throat. 'I was wondering if you could help me find someone.'

27

I headed back to the car from Michael Calvert's house.

As I slid in at the wheel, my phone started buzzing, and then, immediately, the Bluetooth kicked in and the dashboard screen lit up. I tapped Answer. 'David Raker.'

'Mr Raker,' a voice said. 'This is Leon Coetzer.'

Surprised, I said, 'Detective Superintendent Coetzer,' using his full title deliberately. Over the years I'd come to realize that some cops needed to have their egos massaged, and sounding like you believed you were subordinate to them, even in civilian life, could make it easier to get them onside. 'I really appreciate you calling me back.'

'What do you want?'

Business-like; straight to the point.

'It's about Cate Gascoigne.'

Silence. It could have meant anything, but I felt certain it meant he remembered her.

'I'm an investigator,' I said. 'I find missing people.'

Again, he didn't respond, but I doubted he'd have been unaware of that. Most likely – before phoning – he'd found out all that he could about me.

'Do you remember Cate Gascoigne?'

'Yes,' he said, his voice tight. I wasn't an expert on dialects, but I knew from the background that I'd done on Coetzer already that he was from Sunderland – born to South African parents, which explained his surname – and I could hear the Mackem accent coming through when his hackles were up. It didn't bother me that he'd started fully on the defensive – if anything, I'd been expecting this kind of fight.

'So I've been going through Cate's phone records,' I said to him, 'and I can see that back in November 2019 – two months before she disappeared – she called you.'

'Did she?'

'I think you know that she did.'

Another pause on the line.

I pushed again. 'She called you on your landline at work. The investigators on her case only went back a month when they were looking at her phone records. That was how they missed her call to you. I went back three.'

'Are you looking for a pat on the back?'

I didn't say anything this time.

He was just venting, probably frustrated at being on the other side of the table; in all his years as a cop I doubted he'd had to sit through many moments like this, where it wasn't him asking the questions. I waited him out for a while, and then he said, 'Hold on a second.' I could hear a door being opened, then the dull sound of an empty room. He'd gone somewhere quieter, out of earshot. 'I haven't got time to play games with you, Raker,' he said, voice hushed.

'I wasn't aware this *was* a game.'

'I've read about you. I know who you are.'

'Then you'll know I'm serious.'

'You're not a friend of police officers, that much I *do* know.'

'Cops tend to get prickly when you solve their cases for them.'

To him it probably sounded arrogant, but it wasn't meant that way. It wasn't ego speaking, just a statement of fact. I'd been finding missing people for twelve years and if it had been possible to work with the cops, if – for even a second – any of

163

them had ever expressed any interest in pooling resources, I'd have done it in a heartbeat. It would have made my life a million times easier. I wouldn't have had to dance around the edges of police investigations, trying to understand how they worked and why they failed while being fought by the very people who had stalled the case.

'What am I missing here?' Coetzer said. 'What does Cate's disappearance have to do with me?'

I flipped open my notebook and made him wait. 'That's what I'm trying to figure out,' I said. 'Do you remember what you and Cate talked about?'

'It was over two and a half years ago.'

'Even just the bare bones.'

'I don't remember. And even if I did, why would I tell you?'

'Was it about the Dune Murders?'

I felt a shift on the line, and then I heard a chair being moved, its legs dragging across a hard floor. 'What do you know about the Dune Murders?'

Not as much as I'd like, I thought.

Instead, I replied, 'I've done a little digging around.'

'And Cate's family asked you to look into all this?'

'Yes,' I said.

'I read about how she went missing.'

I didn't offer anything in return. I wanted to see what he said.

'No one knows why they weren't in that car?'

'Not so far, no.'

I heard a gentle *tap-tap-tap* and imagined him in a meeting room, somewhere in the Northumbria Police HQ, using his fingers as a backdrop to his thoughts. 'Yes,' he said, 'she called me about the murders.'

'What did she want to know?'

'Like I said, it was two and a half years ago.' There was still an edge to his voice – but now his answers were woven with something else. Interest. Intrigue.

He wanted to find out what I had.

'You don't remember *anything* she asked?' I prompted.

'She just wanted to talk about the case.'

'Did you only talk to her on the phone?'

'As opposed to what?'

'As opposed to actually meeting her in person sometime after.'

He was quiet. I imagined he was giving himself a moment to try and figure out what he lost by telling me. 'Yes,' he said. 'I met her in person as well.'

'When she came up to Northumberland?'

'Yes. A few days after her call.' He paused, and I could hear the same finger beat on the same tabletop. 'Normally, someone phoning me up out of the blue like that, I'd just hang up on them. But I suppose I was inclined to hear her out.'

I frowned. 'Inclined? Why?'

'Because Cate and I knew each other.'

28

'You knew each other?' I paused, brain firing. 'How?'

'*Sort of* knew each other, I should say. I'd met her once before – way back – via someone I used to work with.'

'Who?'

'Makayla Jennings.'

'How did *she* meet Cate?'

'Mak used to work down in London before she moved up here. Her husband got a big job with an accountancy firm in Newcastle, so they all shifted north in the late eighties. But she did a year as a detective down at the Met before all that.'

'So she got to know Cate down here, in London? How? Cate would only have been a kid back then.'

'I think Makayla's children went to the same school as Cate for a while.'

I stopped, pen hovering above my pad. So did that mean that it was Martin and Sue that knew Makayla Jennings originally? Given that there was a thirty-year age gap, it seemed unlikely Jennings would have met Cate any other way than through the school the kids had gone to. And if Cate had met Jennings again, later on in life, and been introduced to Coetzer, it meant the two families had kept in touch.

'Do you remember when you first met Cate?'

'I don't know . . .' He faded out. 'Early 2000s maybe.'

That would have made Cate late teens, maybe twenty at the time.

'How did you meet her?'

'She was up here for a while – a few weeks – taking

photographs of landscapes. I think it was something to do with her university course. Way I remember it is that she met Mak for a coffee, then I ran into them both. When Cate called me up two and a half years ago, I didn't remember it, but she jogged my memory. Like I say, I felt inclined to at least hear her out, because she was a friend of Mak's.'

I'd have to ask Martin and Sue about Makayla Jennings, but it wasn't much of a leap from here to the idea that one of the reasons Cate was drawn to the Dune Murders case might have been because her family had known the SIO on it.

'So what questions did Cate ask you?'

'I just told you: it's hard to remember.'

'You can remember you met her two decades ago when she was a student, but you can't remember what she asked about when she called two and a half years ago?'

I didn't have time for a game of cat and mouse. I completely believed that someone – even cops, who tended to have a natural proclivity for recalling fine detail – might have trouble remembering conversations or events that occurred a long time ago. I just didn't believe this was one of those times. He was playing coy because he wanted to see if I had anything he might want in return.

I looked out at the street, waiting for Coetzer. I'd almost completely forgotten I was in my car, still parked in Michael Calvert's road. The sun was starting to bleed across the sky, the light dwindling a little. And then Coetzer pulled me back into the conversation. 'We spent a while talking about Makayla. She's . . .' He stopped. 'She's not well. Late-stage dementia. It's a bloody travesty after everything she went through before.' For the first time there seemed to be some genuine emotion in Coetzer's voice. 'Anyway,' he said, 'eventually, we talked about the case. It was top-line stuff. She'd been reading about it and wanted to know more. I asked her where the sudden interest had come from, and she said it wasn't sudden; it was something she'd been interested in for a long time: unsolved crimes, the justice system generally. I think she said her intention had always been to do an exhibition on victims, not just justice generally – but it had never quite panned out.'

I'd wondered whether Cate's interests may have lain in the victims of crimes. It looked like I hadn't been far off.

'So she'd been gathering information on unsolved crimes?'

'That's what she told me.'

'And – what? – the Dune Murders had become her main focus?'

'It sounded like that was what she was zeroing in on, yeah.'

'Do you think it was because she knew Makayla?'

'That would be the assumption.'

'So what about when she then came up to Northumberland a few days after the call she made to you?'

'Same sort of stuff,' he said, 'but in much more detail. And she recorded it.'

That stopped me. 'She recorded your conversation?'

'Yes. On her phone.'

So where was the recording? Her phone had burned up in the car wreck, but everything on it had been downloaded from the Cloud – except I didn't recall seeing any mention in the police investigation of forensics finding audio files.

'She definitely recorded your conversation on her phone?' I asked.

'As opposed to what?'

'Something like a Dictaphone.'

'Yes,' Coetzer said, 'it was definitely on her phone.'

I thought of what Georgia had told me, about how Cate would sometimes write an accompanying paragraph of text – to sit next to her photographs when they were on display – as a way of providing some context to the picture.

'So her plan was to quote you in her next exhibition?'

'No, no,' Coetzer said, as if I didn't understand.

I heard him shifting, a chair scraping.

'It wasn't for an exhibition.'

I frowned. 'Then what was it for?'

'She said she was writing a book.'

Captive: Part 1

2 Years and 7 Months Ago

The room was somewhere on the left.

She moved slowly along the corridor, passing other residents. She didn't have any recent photographs of Makayla, but she figured she'd recognize her once she found her.

Almost at the end of the corridor, she stopped at the room she'd been directed to. It was small but tidy, a bathroom off to the right, the living area divided by a wooden railing that split the bed and a tiny two-seat sofa.

Makayla was sitting on the sofa.

She was shocked at how different the former detective looked – not just older, but smaller and more fragile. The TV was on but it was hard to tell if Makayla was watching it. She was perched at the edge of her seat, as if about to get to her feet, her hands on her knees. Her hair was white, a scattering of snow on her scalp, and she was in a pretty dress with daisy chains on the collar. On the seat beside her was an old CD player, cases, most still open but untouched, stacked in a small pile.

She knocked on Makayla's door.

Makayla didn't look up.

She knocked a second time.

Nothing again, so she took a step into the room. Initially, it smelled nice, of bed linen, and when she looked down she could see a plug-in air freshener. But then, slowly, another odour began to gather in its wake. It wasn't unbearable but it wasn't particularly pleasant either. It was the smell of someone who'd spent a long time in the same space – the smell of inactivity, of stasis. She took another step and looked around the room. Was that what this place felt like to Makayla? Captivity?

Or did it feel like nothing?

Did Makayla even know she was here?

'Hello,' she said, and – after another small step – she took her notebook from her pocket. Her fountain pen was clipped inside the spiral binding, in the same place she always kept it. She'd had the same style of notebook for years – all the way back to her school days – and the fountain pen had been a birthday gift from her sister. She started fiddling with the lid, shifting it back and forth with her thumb.

Makayla still hadn't responded.

'Hello,' she said again, even softer this time, as if trying to stir someone from a dream, and this time Makayla flinched, turning her head, seeking her visitor out.

'Oh, hello.' Makayla smiled, suddenly cheerful, her colour brightening, her eyes coming alive. 'I was wondering what time you would be here.'

She returned Makayla's smile and said, 'Oh, you knew I was coming? I didn't think you . . .' She stopped, stumbling over her words. 'There was a lot of traffic on –'

'Oh, don't worry,' Makayla said.

They looked at each other for a moment.

'I was hoping we could have a little chat.'

'Yes, I thought so,' Makayla responded.

'Would that be all right?'

But this time Makayla said nothing. Something had changed.

'Can we have a chat, do you think?'

Again, Makayla didn't respond.

'Would that be okay?'

Makayla turned her attention back to the television.

'Makayla, would it be okay to ask you some questions?'

Makayla Jennings wasn't listening any more. It was like she was in another room, on another sofa, in another place.

Suddenly, this felt hopeless.

She looked at Makayla, at the ghost of the woman she'd known once, her thumb working the lid of the fountain pen, then tried one last time.

'Makayla?'

Nothing.

'I wanted to talk to you about a case you had back in 1992. The Dune Murders. I expect you remember it.' But then she paused, realizing how absurd that statement was, how pointless the drive here had been, how much time she'd wasted pursuing a desperate idea that she knew all along would only ever end in failure. The Makayla she'd read about — and known — was gone. This woman was all that was left of her.

'I wish we could talk,' she said softly.

She stared at the hollow image of the former detective.

'You and I, we know each other, Makayla.'

Makayla turned to her.

For a second she felt a tremor of excitement. Had she finally managed to punch through the fog? Had Makayla latched on to something she'd said? But then, slowly, defeatedly, she realized the truth: the movement was like a weathervane in the wind, its swivel — its change of direction, its vitality — just a fleeting illusion.

'I really wanted to be able to talk to you.'

But Makayla had turned away already, her gaze fixed on the TV screen again. Lingering there for a second longer, watching, pitying, she reclipped her pen to her notebook and headed to the door. Outside, in the over-lit sterile blue of the corridor, a nurse was walking her way.

'Is everything okay?' he asked as he approached.

She nodded. 'Fine.'

He paused at the door, looking beyond her. 'She's getting more bad days than good now,' he said, his Australian accent soft. The way he spoke it was clear he'd really warmed to Makayla. 'Her son said she used to be some sort of detective.'

'She did, yeah.'

'Did you work with her?'

'No. But I knew her a little a long time ago.'

The nurse looked into the room again. 'It doesn't happen as often these days, but sometimes she has flashes of clarity. I can tell her you dropped by if she does.'

She looked in at Makayla. 'Yes, okay. Thank you.'

'Who shall I tell her visited?'

'Cate,' she said. 'Tell her Cate Gascoigne came to see her.'

Cate headed out of the building into the cold of the day.

It was raining softly but she didn't mind. The cool tingle of the drizzle on her skin was a relief after the warmth of the nursing home. She stood there for a moment at the edge of the car park, looking at the notebook in her hands; the latest page she'd turned to, in preparation for her visit to Makayla, was still blank, filled with nothing but unwritten question marks. She wondered what exactly she'd hoped to achieve. She'd known Makayla's condition, had heard how bad it had become. So had she really expected to just walk in there and get answers from a woman with no memory? Deep down, she'd always known it was never going to be that easy – but part of her had hoped. Because somewhere in Makayla's head, buried in the decay and murk of a ruined brain, were answers.

About the three women in the dunes.

And maybe something even worse.

29

'Cate was writing a book?' I asked Coetzer.

'That's what she said.'

'About the Dune Murders?'

'That's what it sounded like. She wanted me to talk her through everything again, from the moment Mak and I arrived on that beach to the point, a couple of years down the line, when we were suddenly the only people left on the case.' He paused, as if the revelation – and him having to admit that the case had gradually been wound up – still stung as badly now as it did back then. 'I asked her what she was planning on doing with all that information, and that was when she said she was hoping to write a book about unsolved crimes. It would have photographs in it as well, obviously, but she said the focus would be on the victims. She said the girls were a big part of it.'

There could have been something patronizing in the way Coetzer had said *the girls* rather than *the women*, even though *the girls* was how the media had constantly referred to the three victims. But there was such an obvious and genuine attachment to the women in his voice, as if he'd known them – and cared for them – in life, not just in death, which was impossible to ignore. It was clear that was how Cate had managed to get him to talk about the Dune Murders and open up about its failures. The victims in this case – in fact, victims in unsolved crimes more generally – had obviously become important to her. And they were important to Coetzer too. When the two of them had sat down, perhaps they saw their mirror images.

Two people who wanted answers.

Two people who cared deeply about the truth.

'Were there any suspects at all?' I asked.

'There were suspects,' he replied, 'but none of them went anywhere. There were too many question marks, way too many solid alibis, and nowhere near enough hard evidence. We became desperate. It was hard telling the families of those girls, over and over, that we had nothing new; hard to admit to them the whole case was a failure.'

I gave him a moment and then moved the conversation on.

'Did Cate ever show you any of her book?'

'No.'

'Any of the photographs she planned to put in it?'

'No.'

'Did she say how many words she'd written?'

'No, nothing like that.'

Coetzer was adamant she'd used her phone as a recording device so where were the files she'd had on there? Where were the photographs she'd taken for inclusion in the book? Where were the notes from that day? If she was writing a book, particularly a non-fiction book, she should have had reams of research. But I'd found nothing like that at the house. Nothing left with Martin and Sue, with Georgia.

No notes. No transcripts. No recordings.

Which, to me, meant one of two things: either she'd lied to Coetzer and wasn't writing a book at all, which didn't make much sense and didn't feel at all likely.

Or, for some reason, her research had disappeared.

Captive: Part 2

2 Years and 7 Months Ago

As she was getting into the car, Cate's phone started going.

It was Aiden.

'Hey, sweetheart.'

'Hey,' her husband replied. 'What are you up to?'

She looked at the front of the nursing home, dreary under cloudy autumnal skies, a semicircular roof fanning out over the doors where some smokers had gathered.

'I've just been taking some pictures,' she lied.

'Cool,' Aiden said. 'Have you called your mum?'

'No. Why?'

'It's her birthday, Cate.'

'Oh, of course,' she said. 'I forgot.'

She was struggling to think about anything else but the book. It was consuming her thoughts, from the second she woke to the instant her head hit the pillow at night. It felt like she was constantly processing everything – all the answers she'd found, and the many more she was still searching for. She glanced towards the nursing home again. Most of those missing answers are inside these walls, she thought.

Lost inside Makayla Jennings's head.

'Cate?'

'Yeah,' she said, stirring from her thoughts. 'I'll call her now.'

'Are you all right?'

'Yeah, I'm fine.'

'Okay, I'll speak to you later.'

'Yeah, speak to you later, honey.'

She hung up the phone and then paused there, holding it in her hand, feeling guilty about lying to Aiden. But when she'd tried to tell him what she was doing a few months ago, that there was a story she wanted to tell – and not just with photographs this time – he took one look at the subject matter, at the reams of notes she'd made already, at some of the things she'd found out, and balked.

Right now, they were navigating the aftermath of a rough patch, the first of their marriage. Cate had initially refused to let go of what she was doing and Aiden had fought her on it, not liking the direction she was taking. She remembered Georgia asking her what the matter was, and why she and Aiden were arguing, and she had told her it was nothing to worry about, that it would soon blow over. And it had. Because, eventually, to make things right between them, Cate had told Aiden that she'd let go of the idea of writing the book. She'd forget about it, put all her research in a drawer and go back to just taking photographs. But that wasn't really the truth. She hadn't forgotten about it at all.

Cate was still writing her book.

She was still trying to find a killer.

30

When I got home, I purposely didn't think about Cate and Aiden Gascoigne for an hour in an effort to unclutter my thoughts. But then, after dinner, I put on a pot of coffee and grabbed my phone and, still having no luck with Zoe's mobile, tried the sports centre in Croydon that she worked at. Immediately, I hit another dead end. It was her day off.

Where the hell are you, Zoe?

My anger with her had long dissipated, and in its place had grown something much worse: an anxious knot, a horrible inevitability. I thought of Audrey Calvert, and then the fact that her son hadn't been seen by his neighbours in months. It felt like events were slowly and inescapably gelling together, with answers that were impossible to avoid.

Audrey Calvert killed herself to escape.

Michael got too close to finding out why.

And now Zoe Simmons had been silenced too.

I called Martin and Sue at home, and it was Sue that answered.

She put me on speakerphone.

'I'm just trying to figure out what Cate was working on next,' I said to them both. 'Did she ever discuss her next project with you, even if only vaguely?'

A blank silence.

'It's okay if you don't know.'

'We're just trying to think,' Sue explained.

I heard them discussing it, but it was obvious that they

didn't know, so I changed direction. 'Do you know someone called Makayla Jennings?'

'Yes, of course,' Sue said. She seemed thrown by the question.

'What's she got to do with this?' Martin asked.

'I've been running down some of Cate's phone activity in the months before she went missing and one of the calls she made was to a police officer in the north-east who worked alongside Makayla in the nineties. At the moment, I'm just trying to figure out all the connections that are going on here.'

'You're saying Cate talked to Makayla before the crash?'

'All I know,' I said, 'is that in the time before she went missing she *definitely* talked to a guy who worked with Makayla back in the nineties. Did you know her well?'

'We were neighbours,' Sue told me, 'when we all used to live in Islington, and things just developed from there. Her husband, Tyler, was really nice too. Once her boys started at the same school as Cate and Georgia we'd chat at school socials, do each other favours at pick-ups and drop-offs, and then, after that, we had them round for barbecues, or dinners, and vice versa.'

'So how long were you friendly for before they moved up north?'

Sue asked Martin what he thought. He said he didn't know. 'I'm not sure, to be honest,' she said. 'We were in that place in Islington for the best part of five years, and we got friendly with Makayla and Tyler quite early on. So, four years maybe, give or take. I remember that Makayla had only been a police officer for a year or two when we first met – and then, about twelve months before they moved, she became a detective.'

'And you kept in touch after they moved?'

'Yes, Makayla and I would call each other a few times every year, on certain dates – her birthday, mine, Christmas, that sort of thing. We always enjoyed a catch-up. And after mobile phones came along, we used to text.' Sue paused. 'But then it got more difficult for a while in the . . . I guess it must have been the mid-nineties.'

'Because of the brain tumour.'

'Yes, it was absolutely tragic.'

From what I'd read, and the information I'd garnered from Coetzer, Jennings was diagnosed in 1994, had undergone four operations over the course of five years, and then was given the all-clear. In 2000 she rejoined Northumbria Police as a consultant. It was a year or two later, when Cate travelled up to the north-east as part of her degree, that Makayla met her for a coffee and introduced her to Coetzer.

'As I understand it, Cate met up with Makayla in the early 2000s.'

'Yes,' Sue replied, 'she did, that's right. Cate was up in that area doing this huge thing for her degree where she wanted to map out – in photographs – every fifth mile of Hadrian's Wall. Anyway, she mentioned she'd be up that way and I told her it would be nice, if she had the opportunity, to look Makayla up, because obviously Makayla had had a tough time.'

It was hard to imagine that Cate's coffee with Jennings was anything other than a favour to her mum, but it may have unwittingly laid the groundwork for what came after. Not only did she end up meeting Coetzer, who became important two decades later, but maybe Makayla Jennings had mentioned the Dune Murders at that meeting, sparking the first tiny flames of interest in Cate.

'Of course Makayla's even worse now,' Sue said, pulling me out of my thoughts. 'She's got dementia. We hear occasionally via her boy, Joshua. I think it's, you know . . .'

Sue faded out.

But it was obvious what she was saying.

I think it's almost the end.

A New Memory

28 Years Ago

Makayla kissed the twins goodnight and then lay between them for a long time as they slowly drifted off to sleep. Tears filled her eyes as their breathing changed, as she imagined the time ahead of them all, scenes playing out in her head, some too painful to bring to life in full – but in all of them the tethers binding her to her boys had been shredded. If she managed to beat the tumour, maybe Josh and Zi would still be exactly the same as they were now – as innocent, as sweet, as invested in her; maybe she would feel the same, almost overwhelming sense of love for them as she did now. Or maybe once she left the operating table, every-thing in her life would change. Maybe she would come back to them wired differently.

Maybe it would feel to them, to her, like they'd lost each other.

Eventually, she slid out from between them, turning on their night light, and returned to the living room. She could see the back doors were both open. It was a warm night, the sun only just starting to go down, and outside on the patio, partly lit by the glow from the house, she could see Tyler at a table, a can of beer in hand.

He was facing away from her, looking out at their garden, but Makayla was able to see a partial reflection of him in a mirror – its edges an elaborate mosaic – that they'd mounted on a wall to his left. Fractured as the image of him was there, she could see the tears on his cheeks. She could see that the entire time she'd been in with the boys – hugging them harder than ever before – he'd been out here crying.

She stepped out on to the patio and, without saying anything, slid her arms down his chest, placing her cheek on to the dome of his head. They stayed like that, saying nothing – just her head on his, and his hand on her one arm – and although she didn't bring attention to it, she knew Tyler was crying again. She couldn't hear it, but she could feel it: the slow, rhythmic movement of his shoulders; the way he would occasionally reach for her cheek, touching it as if he never wanted to let go.

When they finally broke off, the sun had vanished beyond the horizon and the sky had coloured a bruised mauve. Makayla pulled a chair out from the table and sat next to Tyler, and after she took a swig of his beer, he reached for her hand.

'You okay?' she asked softly.

He smiled a little. 'I should be asking you that, not the other way around.' He squeezed her hand gently, and his eyes started to fill up again. 'Sorry. This isn't right.'

'Which part?'

She returned his smile, and they both understood. Tyler had meant it wasn't right that he was the one doing the crying. But nothing about this was right.

Not him doing the crying.

Not the news Makayla had got today about her brain.

Not the stopwatch that was now their time together.

'Everything's going to be okay,' Tyler said – and, this time, it set them both off, because now he was just trying to be brave. He was trying to reassume the role of her husband, her support, the pillar against which she could lean for however long it was going to take. The tears came again, and when the moment had finally passed, Tyler got to his feet and said he was going to put the kettle on.

Makayla sat there, enjoying the quiet of their road, the sky darkening every second until, eventually, the little solar lights at the bottom of the garden came on, winking in the dusk like jewels. For some reason the sight of them – the memory of installing them with Tyler, of creating this entire garden from scratch out of the patch of dirt that had been here when they'd first moved in – set her off again. She let the tears fall, wondering if this would be her new normal: looking at the small things in her life, the things she just glanced at every day, and suddenly seeing the importance of them, the meaning they had, the memories they carried. She saw death every day in her work, but the death most of her victims suffered was sudden and unexpected. Hers, if this didn't go the way she and Tyler wanted, would be signposted. The tumour would grow, and the doctors wouldn't be able to stop it, and the whole time all Makayla would be able to do was stare into the certainty of what was coming. She would be leaving her boys, her husband, the home she shared with them, the garden she'd created; even insignificant things like the lights were going to feel like a loss, because they too glowed with the recollection of time together with Tyler, of the two of them on their hands and knees digging out the mud, the radio on, the sound of their laughter. She'd spend her last months on this earth looking at her family, at every tiny component of her life, and seeing the value in it. So was this death worse than the ones visited upon the countless victims she'd stood over down the years? She thought of the girls in the dunes two years ago.

Was it better not to know it was coming?

Tyler returned to the patio with a cup of tea and put it down in front of her. They sat for a moment, perfectly comfortable, enjoying the silence, then her husband looked at her and said, 'I can work overtime. If we can get enough money together, maybe we can go private. We can get it looked at by a doctor much more quickly –'

'It's okay,' Makayla said, cutting him off gently.

'Mak, we need to –'

'It's okay, Ty. It's okay.'

She reached for his hand, smiling at him, studying the face she knew so well. He was so handsome, always had been; his eyes were dark, but they were so soft, a tenderness written into them that had drawn her in immediately when they'd first met. She'd often wondered if one of the reasons she'd been attracted to Tyler was because he represented the exact opposite of everything she saw in her work: with him there was assurance, and safety, and kindness; in her work, in places like the dunes, there was nothing except instability and pain.

'Mak,' he said quietly.

'It's all right, Ty.' She squeezed his hand gently. 'I know you will do whatever it takes to make this better. I know that. But is it okay if we're just quiet for a while?'

She saw a shimmer in his eyes again but he nodded, and they sat there for a long time, listening to the sound of the sea. The house was only a quarter of a mile from the beach at Whitley Bay, so – on a still night – they could hear the waves turning over. Makayla had grown up in London and had only ever been to the beach when her parents had been able to afford a week away in a caravan, so the sea still felt special to her. She didn't know if there would ever be a time when she grew tired of its noise. But then, as that thought settled, she looked out at the garden again, at the lights she'd fixated on earlier, and she saw the truth: that there may soon be a time when she wouldn't be able to hear the waves or smell the salt on the breeze, that there may soon be a time when this house and this garden made another memory.

And that memory would be her.

31

After finishing up with Martin and Sue, I called Georgia. She was on a shift at the pub and said she'd call me back, so I started to ring around some of Cate's friends to see if she'd mentioned her next project to any of them. It was a dead end; if Cate hadn't discussed it with her family, it was unlikely she'd have discussed it with anyone else.

That in itself raised a question mark: why *not* discuss it? Maybe she *had* talked to Georgia, her closest confidante, about it, and I'd find out for sure once I caught up with her. But somehow, given that Cate had kept all the Dune Murders stuff back from her sister, I doubted it. More likely, if she'd talked to anyone, it was Aiden. And while I had no way of knowing if her doing so was the spark that ignited their rough patch, it wasn't a ridiculous leap to make. Could a conversation he'd had with Cate have sparked that search for police stations? What, if anything, in Cate's work could have led him to do that? Certainly there was nothing in Cate and Aiden's file that remotely suggested Aiden had actually talked to the cops at any time before the crash. But, still, that Internet search was an anomaly I didn't like.

I let it go for now and reset – thinking instead about where the research Cate would have gathered might be – and then locked up the house and headed to bed. Grabbing my laptop and my notes on the way through, I wrote out a timeline of events, of things I knew for certain.

- **28 April 1992** | Three bodies discovered
- **May 1994** | Makayla Jennings finds brain tumour
- **2000** | Jennings rejoins Northumbria Police
- **2001/02** | Cate (19/20) meets Jennings / Coetzer
- **2013** | Jennings diagnosed with dementia
- **June/July 2019** | Cate and Aiden have rough patch
- **4 November 2019** | Cate calls Leon Coetzer
- **5–8 November 2019** | Cate visits Northumberland
- **6 or 7 November 2019** | Cate interviews Coetzer
- **3 January 2020** | Cate and Aiden disappear
- **Mid June 2020** | Audrey Calvert leaves boyfriend
- **End of July 2020** | Body (Audrey?) found in arches
- **April (ish) 2022** | Last time Michael Calvert is seen
- **Today** | Zoe fails to turn up for our meeting

I zeroed in on Michael for a moment. Weren't people missing him? Audrey appeared to be his only family, and he was a self-employed plumber according to his neighbours, so work colleagues weren't going to be asking after him. But there must have been friends who were now wondering where he was and customers, perhaps, who he'd failed to turn up for. I pictured the man with the burn scars who'd been trying to get into Michael's house. I didn't know for certain if he was even involved in any of this; all I knew was that he arrived at a place that clearly wasn't his and had tried to gain access to it. What was he looking for? Did he know where Michael was?

In my head I placed the man with the scars at the scene of the crash.

There were immediate questions, none of which I had answers to. Firstly, why would he have been at the crash site at all? What connection did he have to the Gascoignes? Why might he have been involved in their disappearance? I'd started off thinking the two witnesses might be in on this – but now I wasn't convinced of that at all. Plus, their behaviour in the weeks and months after the crash didn't make me suspicious of them. It made me concerned for their safety.

Maybe that concern also came from my own part in what might have happened to Zoe Simmons. I'd backed her into a corner, forced her to meet. In demanding she meet me, what if I'd painted a target on her back?

To distract myself I added a question to the chronology.

Who is the man with the burns?

I was tired, my thoughts starting to drag, so I didn't try to think too hard about the answer for now. It would be something to look at again in the morning. Instead, I set the notebook aside and took my laptop through to the living room, putting it on to charge. As I did, my mobile started to buzz across the table.

Georgia.

I thought about just letting it go to voicemail and giving her a call first thing in the morning as it was now almost eleven thirty, but I figured the conversation probably wouldn't last very long anyway – because if I was right, Cate wouldn't have told her a thing about the book.

'Hi, Georgia.'

'Hi, David. Sorry it's so late. I've just got off work.'

'No problem,' I said, and asked her if her sister had ever talked about her next project. As I suspected, she hadn't. Georgia had mentioned her sister had been almost as good a writer as a photographer when we'd met, and if Georgia had known anything about a book, that would have been the time to mention it to me.

'Okay, well, I appreciate it,' I said, wrapping things up.

'Look, David, this might be nothing . . .' She faded out.

I heard her take a breath, as if about to speak, then she stopped again. I sensed she was doubting her instincts about something – but I couldn't imagine what.

'What's going on?' I said, trying to reassure her.

'Like I say, it might be nothing, but it's been kicking around at the back of my head for a few weeks.' She paused again. 'Basically, there's this guy, and he's been . . .'

Again, she faltered.

I waited her out.

'He started coming into the pub a few weeks back . . .'

'Okay,' I prompted.

'It's really subtle but . . .'

'But what?'

I pulled my laptop towards me and flipped open the lid.

'He's been asking questions about Cate's disappearance.'

32

I felt a flutter of alarm in my throat.

'Someone's been asking questions about Cate?'

'Yes,' Georgia said. 'But it's taken a while for it to click with me. Everything he asks, he asks in this roundabout sort of a way, which is why I didn't think to bring it up before. But tonight he started asking about you.'

'What does this guy look like?'

'Thirties maybe. It's hard to tell. But he's big.'

'Big, as in overweight? Or big, as in well built?'

'Big, as in well built.'

'Is he about six foot? Brown hair? A thick beard?'

'Yes,' Georgia said, clearly thrown.

'Any scarring on his arms?'

A confused pause. 'Scarring?'

So she hadn't seen any – or he'd kept the scars hidden.

'Do you know who he is then?' Georgia asked.

'No,' I said, looking closely at the physical description that Michael Calvert's neighbours gave me, 'but someone matching all those details is on my radar. You said he's been coming into the pub for a while?'

'Yeah, maybe three weeks, maybe a little more.'

I'd only been on the case two days; he'd been going to Georgia's pub for nearly a month. What had instigated his visit?

'So what sort of questions does he ask?'

'My manager let me put a poster with Cate and Aiden's photographs up on the wall of the pub – basically, it says to ask inside for me if you have any information. Anyway, he said he'd seen the poster and gone away and read about Cate online, and then next time he was at the pub he asked me about her. It didn't feel creepy. I've never felt threatened by him. It's just felt like he was asking out of concern.'

'Does he ever ask for specific details about the case?'

'No. Over time it's become more about how the case is progressing.'

'He wants to know if there have been any breakthroughs?'

'Right. But it's always felt genuine, never forced or inappropriate.'

'And you said he came in again tonight?'

'Yeah. He asked about you, about how you were getting on, and I told him a little bit and went off and served other people. And then, later, I thought to myself: "I'm not sure I'd ever mentioned that you'd taken on Cate's case."'

'So how would he know about me?'

'Exactly.'

'When did he first come in?'

'I think it was around the time Mum and Dad began talking about finding someone to look for Cate.'

'So at the same time your mum and dad were looking for an investigator, this guy just appears out of the blue and starts asking questions?'

'Yes.'

As if he knew what the family was thinking.

And there were only really two ways he'd know what they were thinking. Either he was a good friend of the Clarks', the type of friend they might confide in – and that seemed unlikely given that Georgia didn't recognize him and he'd never mentioned to her about knowing her parents. *Or* the man had somehow been listening to Martin and Sue. So could Martin and Sue's phones have been tapped? Their emails and Internet activity watched? Might their home have been bugged too?

'Has he ever given you his name?' I asked.

'Harper.'

'That's his first name?'

'I don't know.'

'You've never seen his name on the card he pays with?'

'He never pays by card, always cash.'

'Do you have CCTV at the pub?'

'Yes,' Georgia said, 'but it doesn't cover the end of the bar where he always sits.'

'Does he have to walk past *any* of the cameras to exit the pub?'

'No. We have another door on that side.'

'Any external cameras?'

'No.'

None of that was surprising. He'd spent almost a month talking to Georgia about the disappearance of her sister and she didn't even really notice until tonight. He may have been watching Martin and Sue for weeks before they picked up the phone to me. Whoever he was, he was organized and he was exceptionally careful.

Except tonight he'd made a mistake.

He'd asked Georgia how I was getting on.

Had he been distracted by something?

I thought about his pleasantness in front of Georgia being a mask of some kind, a way to fit in. At best, it was the behaviour of a confident liar; at worst, the symptoms of a psychopath. And then my thinking shifted to Zoe Simmons, to her no-show, and the fact that I hadn't been able to get hold of her since – and a swirl of panic hit the pit of my stomach. Was Zoe on his mind?

Or what he'd done to her?

'David?'

'Yeah, I'm still here. How often does he come in?'

'A couple of times a week. Three at the most.'

'So if he was in tonight, when is he likely to be in again?'

'Probably Thursday.'

'I'll be there.'

I thanked Georgia and told her I'd be back in touch.

This *had* to be the same guy who was at Michael Calvert's house.

This had to be the man with the burns.

But if I had a hope of trying to find out who he was, I needed to recharge, to be able to think clearly and lucidly – and that meant calling it a day.

I headed through to the bedroom, undressed and crashed out.

When I stirred next, it felt like I'd been out for hours.

But then I checked the time and it was only 2.03.

Rolling over, I closed my eyes, listening to the intermittent sound of traffic on Uxbridge Road. But just as I felt myself drifting again, I heard a noise.

Click.

I looked across the bedroom, into the darkness of the hallway. Silence. Turning on to my back, I lay there, the cool of the night wafting in through the open window.

Click.

The same noise a second time.

It was coming from inside the house.

Search

30 Years Ago

The scan was scheduled for 3 p.m., so Amelia told her mum, who she'd asked to go with her to the hospital, that she needed to pop out for a couple of hours in the morning.

'Don't be late,' her mum said.

'I won't.'

'Where are you going?'

'I might know someone who can find the guy.'

The guy. That was what her and her mum had started to refer to Phil as, at least when it was only the two of them at home. Around Dad they still called him Phil, because it sounded better – but the more time that passed, the less certain Amelia was that the man she'd slept with was even called Phil. When she tried to recollect that night – trying to piece it together – she couldn't remember a single moment when anyone – even the guy himself – had used the name Phil. It was just a name that someone at the party thought that they'd heard, and because it was the only name Amelia had to work with, it had stuck.

'Is it one of your friends who might be able to help?' her mum asked.

She'd never told her mum that she only really had one friend, and that was Coralie. It would just make her worry.

'It's fine, Mum, I'll explain later.' Her mum seemed more confused than ever, but Amelia didn't want to get into it all now. She didn't have time for twenty questions, but also her parents, and especially her dad, had only just got used to the idea of her being pregnant and she didn't want to load anything else on to them for now. 'It probably won't come to anything,' Amelia summed up, and then kissed her mum, hugged her and told her she would be back for lunch.

As her bus wound its way through clogged Wednesday morning streets, Amelia wrote in her diary and listened to music on her Walkman. Her mum and dad had bought her a Discman for her last birthday, but she got frustrated with the way it kept skipping – especially on the bus, where the seats creaked and shifted the whole time – so she'd switched back to the Walkman. She preferred making mix tapes anyway and, as 'Charly' by The Prodigy throbbed in her ears, she realized her hand was resting on her belly. She wondered what the music sounded like to her baby.

As the chorus kicked back in again, Amelia let her mind wander: she pictured herself in a couple of years, when her baby was walking, and she was playing this song on the stereo and the two of them were dancing along to it, a pair of tiny hands in hers. She still felt scared, was still nervous about telling Coralie; she was scared about what it might mean for her future and the things she'd always wanted to do. But as the bus snapped back into focus around her, she felt a fizz of excitement. Maybe this wasn't exactly how she imagined her life turning out. Maybe she would start to wobble and feel overwhelmed. But, for now, she just wrote in her diary and listened to her music, and imagined her baby listening too.

And in that moment nothing else mattered.

Makayla was waiting at a coffee shop, close to where she said she worked.

As soon as Amelia walked in, she broke into a smile, and stood up at the table she'd grabbed for them both. 'Hello again, sweetheart,' she said warmly, and touched a hand to Amelia's arm. Makayla asked her what she wanted to drink, then told Amelia to sit while she went and ordered.

'So, how have you been?' she asked when she got back to the table.

'Good,' Amelia said. 'I told Mum and Dad.'

'You did? How did that go?'

'Actually, better than I expected.'

Makayla had her tea in her hand. She made a cheers gesture with it. 'See, I told you it's never as bad as you think it's going to be. It'll be the same for everything else too.' She gestured to Amelia's belly. 'So you said I might be able to help you find someone?'

Amelia nodded. She brought her own mug of tea closer, putting both hands on it. 'I, uh . . .' She stopped. 'It's a bit embarrassing, but basically . . .' She stopped for a second time. 'Basically, I don't know who the dad is.'

Makayla made a soft 'oh'.

'Exactly,' Amelia said.

'What was it, a one-night stand?'

'Not even that, really. Just a . . .'

A drunken mistake, she thought.

'Well, you need to stop thinking about it as a mistake,' Makayla said, as if she'd read Amelia's mind, and in that moment Amelia felt herself drawing closer to this woman. She remembered the story Makayla had told her at the bus stop outside the hospital: how Makayla had also had a baby at nineteen; how she'd given the child up for adoption; and how she'd regretted it ever since.

Makayla reached over and took her hand. Amelia felt a little awkward, but she didn't withdraw, even as Makayla leaned closer, her bright eyes fixed on Amelia's. For a second Amelia got that same sense of recognition that she'd had the first time she met Makayla at the bus stop.

Why did she feel like she recognized Makayla?

Makayla withdrew her hand and got out a notepad. It was small, pocket-sized, but when she opened it up Amelia could see there was nothing in it. Makayla noticed her looking. 'I like to begin a brand-new notepad when I start a brand-new case.'

Amelia hadn't even considered the idea of this being a 'case', but it gave her a momentary buzz; if Makayla saw it that way, she was taking it seriously.

Maybe they really could find this guy.

'Right,' Makayla said, 'tell me what you remember about that night . . .'

33

I sat up, eyes pinging to the hallway.

The noise was coming from inside the house.

Standing, dressed only in my boxers, I quietly moved to the bedroom door and looked in the direction of the living room. Small squares of moonlight leaked into the hall from the spare bedrooms on either side, creating a flare of ivory in the middle. Beyond that, in the living room itself, the only thing I could see were the vague shapes of furniture. I moved along the hallway, carefully checking the bedrooms as I passed, and then took in the living room and the doors that opened out on to the deck. Everything appeared normal. Nothing was out of place. I double-checked that the doors were still locked, looked in the toilet, then went through to the kitchen.

Beyond the slatted blinds at the windows, I could see out to the front garden, and – via a side door – on to the driveway. I stepped up to the side door, looking in both directions. To my left, my Audi was parked, boot facing me; to my right, a little further down, was the garage and, next to that, the side gate leading to the back garden.

Everything was fine.

I tried the handle on the side door, just in case.

It was unlocked.

I paused, my heart instantly beating faster. Had I forgotten to lock it before bed? I thought I'd gone around the house checking all the doors like I normally did last thing at night. But maybe I hadn't. Was I so tired I'd forgotten to check this one?

I pushed the door open and went outside, looking both ways again, the night air ghosting past me. My skin tingled in the cold, goosebumps forming, as I glanced towards the side gate. It remained closed. The garage was shut as well, the door pulled all the way down. Because it was separate from the house, I'd installed an alarm on it, so even if the garage had been opened then closed again at some point, I would have known about it.

I went back inside, grabbed a T-shirt and looked around a second time. The bedrooms were clear, the living room too. I then returned to the driveway, doing a half-circuit of the house, front to back. The gate was still locked from the garden side, nothing looked disturbed on the porch and none of the locks had been tampered with. Heading back inside, I went out through the rear doors on to the deck, and checked everything there.

It was exactly as it should have been.

I locked up again, double-checking entrances and exits at both ends of the house, and as I was passing a mirror in the living room, I noticed something.

There was a mark on the side of my throat.

It looked like I'd nicked the skin, although I couldn't imagine on what. I hadn't shaved in three days, so it wasn't razor damage, and I didn't remember knocking against anything. I tilted my head slightly, picking at the dried blood with a nail. It flaked away easily enough, leaving a red dot in its wake, small, like a pinprick.

I leaned into the glass.

What the hell is –

But I never finished my thought.

Suddenly, everything started to blur.

My vision, my image in the mirror.

It came so quickly I was barely ready for it: a rush of dizziness so unexpected and violent, I felt like I'd been ripped from dry land and thrown to the sea by a wave.

I reached for the wall, missing it completely.

And then I hit the floor and blacked out.

PART THREE
The Fugitive

34

I stirred, head banging, nausea bubbling at the back of my throat.

My muscles were sore, my bones ached.

And I was freezing cold.

When I rolled over, the ground felt as hard as a rock, and as I opened my eyes, I saw why: I was on the floor of my living room, still dressed in a T-shirt and boxers.

I forced myself up, into a seated position.

Pain throbbed behind my eyes as I looked around me. Sunlight was pouring in through the windows at the back and I could hear the sounds of summer outside: birds, the kids a few doors down playing, the far-off tinkle of an ice-cream van. Hauling myself to my feet, I flipped my laptop open, still charging on the living-room table. As it woke from its slumber, I looked at the time.

9.22.

And then my gaze fell on the date just next to that: Thursday 7 July. I'd been woken up by the sound of clicking in the house just after 2 a.m. on Wednesday 6 July.

Thirty hours ago.

I hurried across to the mirror in the living room that I'd been in front of before I'd blacked out. I looked awful. My skin was pale, my hair a mess, the whites of my eyes crazed with thick blood vessels.

But it was the bruise on my throat that I saw first.

And the needle mark at its centre.

I reached up and touched the bruise with a finger. It was

sensitive, inflamed, a dark violet pool. The dot of dried blood fell away as I touched it. Again, I thought of the noise that had woken me thirty hours ago.

And then horror washed over me.

It had been the side door closing.

Someone had got into my house, they came all the way into my bedroom, they injected me – and I never even heard them until they left.

The realization was like ice on my skin.

My head started thumping again and then I felt like I might throw up. Rushing through to the bathroom, I leaned over the toilet and was sick. It just kept coming, like a flood, and when it was finally over, all I could do was stay there for a while, dizzy, struggling for breath, my throat burning.

Eventually, I hauled myself up and wandered back through to the living room, my gaze landing on my laptop again, on the phone next to it. They were still charging on the table, *exactly* where I'd left them.

Something about that felt too perfect.

Someone breaks in, but doesn't go through my things?

I opened my laptop. Going to the Activity Log, I typed *wake reason* into the search bar. A long list of times the laptop had been woken up appeared. The last entry was a minute before, when I'd opened the lid. The entry above that should have been well over thirty hours ago, when I'd been using the MacBook just before bed.

But it wasn't.

According to the log, it had been woken five times across a period of sixteen hours, all of them the day before.

When I'd been out cold.

Using the trackpad, I closed the logs and went to Recent Items, looking for an idea of exactly what applications and activity had taken place. It had been cleared. I opened Chrome, but if it had been used, that evidence had been erased too.

I went through my emails, but there was nothing, through my photos, my calendar, my Dropbox. None of it looked like it had been touched. I wondered for a moment if software could have been loaded *on* to the laptop – specifically spyware – but, although I was no IT expert, after a search, I couldn't see any indication of that.

Not that it brought me any comfort.

Because *someone* had been using my laptop.

I moved through to the kitchen, my head still thumping, and filled a glass with water. As I did, I heard a car pull up outside.

A white Skoda with two people in it.

To begin with I thought they were going to my neighbours' place: they bumped the car up on to the kerb and left it only a few yards from next door's driveway.

But then one of them – a woman in her mid-thirties – got out and, straight away, looked at my house. Automatically, like an animal sensing a threat, I stepped back, into the shadows, trying to conceal myself from view as a man got out of the passenger side.

This time the nausea burned in my throat.

I didn't know her, but I definitely knew him.

35

His name was Davidson.

He was a cop.

I tried to imagine why the police were here – but it was all happening way too fast and my head was hammering hard. It was just relentless, a thudding rhythm behind my eyes that made it difficult for me to even see clearly, let alone focus. As quickly as possible, I found some ibuprofen, filled a glass with water and grabbed the nearest food available: a banana. Even the smell of it made me wretch – but I needed to line my stomach, to try and settle myself. I needed energy, clarity. I forced the banana down, then swallowed the pills with another glass of water. I then went back to the side door, peering along the driveway. The two of them were standing beside my car and the woman seemed to be pointing towards the registration plate.

Davidson glanced at the house.

Twice in the past, he and I had had major run-ins with each other, and the second time it had ended up with him being put through a disciplinary procedure. That was years ago – maybe getting on for a decade – but a man like David-son was never going to forget something like that. The last time I'd seen him was at Healy's funeral – or what everybody had believed was his funeral. Even there, Davidson had come at me, on the attack because he believed I'd cost him a career as a high-ranking detective. So there was just no way that he'd appeared here by accident – he must have heard my name come up and requested he be part of this.

Whatever *this* was.

I could see the two of them following the path to the front door. I glanced around the living room and spotted my laptop, my phone next to it, and my heart rate began to rise. What if they *had* been tampered with somehow? What if something had been put on to them that could compromise me and I just hadn't found it yet?

I didn't feel prepared for this.

I didn't know who had got inside my house. I didn't know what they'd put in my neck. I didn't know what had happened in the thirty hours I was out. I felt completely unmoored.

A knock at the front door.

I paused for a moment, closing my eyes, trying to steel myself for what was coming – and just as I was heading to the front door, my phone buzzed.

Ewan Tasker.

It was his burner phone.

What the hell's going on?

I grabbed the phone and texted him back.

What do you mean?

Another knock at the door.

'Mr Raker?' The female cop. 'Are you there?'

Phone in hand, I retreated into the shadows of the hallway. Softly, almost in a whisper, I could hear the female cop saying something.

Tasker's reply buzzed once in my hand.

feedme.com/news/cops-twelve-trees-road

I tapped on the link.

'Mr Raker, if you're in there, I need you to open up.'

I kept my eyes on my mobile as the story that Tasker had

sent me loaded. *Come on, come on.* I glanced at the front door. I could only see the crest of their heads – there was one small window, high up and frosted – and they couldn't see me at all. But that didn't settle my nerves even slightly. The cops were at my house – and I didn't know why.

Onscreen the story appeared.

It had been uploaded in the early hours of the morning. At the top was a picture, fuzzy, bleached, taken from a CCTV camera: it was a shot of a car on a London street. I pinch-zoomed in on the image.

It was my car.

And below the image of it was a headline:

COPS SEEK DRIVER IN HIT-AND-RUN

36

It felt like my legs were about to give way.

Breathe.

Just breathe.

'Go and check around the back,' the female cop said and, for a second, I had a panic about the side gate. Had I definitely locked it? My head was on fire. I couldn't remember. But then I heard the handle on the side gate being turned – and a padlock rattling.

They couldn't get through.

For now.

I switched my attention to the phone again and swiped to the next photo in the story. The readout in the corner showed exactly the same date and time as before: 20.33, 6 July. This whole section had been recorded during the hours I was knocked out, prone on the floor of my living room – but it was definitely my car. In the second still from the CCTV video, it was clearer than ever: the Audi was approaching a zebra crossing.

Except it wasn't stopping.

It was accelerating towards it, the car beginning to blur, a man halfway across the road. Now I recognized the street that the car and the man were on. It was where the *Daily Trib-une* building was.

And Connor McCaskell was the man on the crossing.

Fuck.

Davidson had returned to the front of the house and was

saying something to the female cop – and then there was yet another loud knock at the front door.

'Mr Raker?' She was sounding tense, frustrated.

This time she tried the front door.

'Go and ask the neighbours if they've seen him,' she ordered Davidson, and then banged on the door again.

But I couldn't rip my eyes away from the picture of McCaskell.

His head was turned towards the car, realizing too late that it wasn't going to slow down for him. He had a hand out, as if his outstretched arm could somehow prevent what was about to happen. And as I swiped to the next shot, I saw McCaskell on the ground, almost in the gutter, the Audi accelerating away.

I felt overwhelmed, frightened, but all I could see behind my eyes was the picture of McCaskell's pixelated body at the side of the road. Was he dead? I skim-read the story, trying to find the answer – but it just said the victim had been taken to University College Hospital with life-threatening injuries.

The female cop stepped away from the door, her shoes crunching against the path outside, and I started to panic again. Shit, where was she going now?

I could hardly think straight. My head was pounding like a drill. Whatever had knocked me out had been strong, maybe stronger than it had needed to be. Now I was dealing with the after-effects – nausea, dizziness, confusion. An image came back to me from Tuesday, of being on a Tube train, opposite McCaskell.

Now he might be dead.

And my car was the weapon.

The cop appeared at the side door.

Automatically, I backed up, even deeper into the shadows – and for one awful moment I thought she'd seen the movement.

As she mounted the second step at the door, cupping her hands to the glass, her gaze instantly went beyond the kitchen to a space in the hallway, about three feet from where I was. I froze, not daring to move, hardly breathing. But then her eyes shifted again, back to the kitchen, settling on the key rack just inside the door, where the Audi fob was hanging.

I watched her, trying to think.

If I opened the door and told her the truth, my story would sound impossibly convenient. I thought someone had broken into my house but I had no evidence of it. Most likely, whoever had injected me would make certain there was nothing left of it in my bloodstream. All I had was a needle mark on my neck but no idea who had put it there, no memory of the last thirty hours, and the knowledge that my car was recorded on CCTV ploughing into someone I loathed. Worse, now it was back on my driveway, and I realized that the cops at my door hadn't been looking at my registration plate. They'd been examining the damage to the front.

Any story I tried to spin out from here would sound like a lie. There was no way I could let them in. I was too exposed and knew far too little.

Davidson rejoined his colleague at the side door.

'Anything?' she asked.

'The neighbours aren't home.'

'What about across the road?'

'Same story. What do you want to do?'

'We put a trace on his phone and his phone says he's here,' the woman replied quietly, and I looked down, to the mobile in my hand. 'So he could be inside, hiding from us, but . . .' She glanced at my car.

'But what?'

'Why stay here with the car that implicates him parked on

the driveway like that?' She cupped her hands to the glass again, her attention landing on the key fob for a second time. 'More likely, he's long gone.'

'He knew we'd use his phone to find him,' Davidson said. 'Exactly.'

I looked at my phone again. If they'd already put a trace on it, I couldn't take it with me. It wouldn't be long before they were pulling all my information out of the Cloud either. I began scrolling through the messages I'd missed, the numbers that had called me, and apart from Tasker's text from the burner, there was nothing that couldn't wait. I'd have to get in touch with Tasker at some point and warn him to be even more careful than usual.

My laptop was a problem too. It was connected to the same account, and even if I untethered the device, it was only going to be a temporary inconvenience to forensic teams. They'd soon locate the laptop, know it was mine, and use it to find me. I had no choice but to pull everything off the laptop and the mobile that I needed, then leave them both behind.

Just like, right now, I had no choice but to run.

'Yeah, it's DI Parkes.' The female cop was on her phone now. *Parkes.* I made a mental note of it. 'Where the hell's my forensic team?'

Shit. Forensics were on their way.

My head started banging again, another wave of nausea hitting me. What the hell had I been given? I felt terrible.

Even so, I knew what I had to do.

I quietly moved back through to the bedroom, grabbing a bag from one of the wardrobes. Hurriedly packing enough clothes for a week, I then dug out a mobile phone and SIM card from a box in one of the wardrobes. I always kept spare ones at home. I kept an old laptop in the same box for the same purpose, so I took that too, some money I kept stashed for emergencies, plus anything else I thought I might need. Pulling on some clothes, I swung the bag over my shoulder and crept back along the hallway. Parkes and Davidson were further down the driveway now, Parkes still on her phone, Davidson knocking on more doors on the other side of the street.

As quickly as I could, I transferred everything I needed on my phone and laptop across to the new devices, and then – once I was done – rushed to the rear doors. As I was letting myself out on to the deck, I heard footsteps beyond the side gate. I froze halfway out of the door, not daring to move.

The clatter of a wheelie bin.

Either Parkes or Davidson was going through my rubbish.

The side gate was solid, no see-through panels, but the deck was elevated and now I could see the dome of Davidson's head. I slowly lowered myself on to my haunches, pushing the door closed behind me. It made a soft click.

I paused, waiting.

Heart hammering hard in my chest.

Davidson was still at the bin, looking through it. I had no idea what he thought he might discover but I couldn't afford to hang around and find out. Quietly locking the back door, I headed to the gate at the bottom of the garden.

I was starting to sweat, to feel dizzy, but I tried to push it away, and as I opened the gate, I paused for a moment, looking back at the house, at the place that was supposed to be my sanctuary.

But there was no sanctuary now.

Because now I was a fugitive.

37

I used alleyways and back roads and headed straight into Ealing, looking over my shoulder the whole time. I had to get out of London and planned to head to the north-east – and in order to do what I wanted up there, I needed a car. There was a rental place at the eastern end of The Mall, so that part was easy. The real issue was that I'd have to use a credit card to put down as a deposit – and, as soon as I did that, I'd be back on the map.

I paused outside the rental place, considering the alternatives. I could use the Tube to take care of some things in London first, and then jump on a train up to Newcastle – but trains were only going to take me so far. Eventually, I'd need to get out into the countryside and it would make me more predictable and much less agile if I was having to rely on timetables and taxis to get me places. I briefly considered hiring the car in Newcastle instead of here, but that brought its own problems. If I picked up the car here, the cops were playing catch-up, trying to find out where I was headed; if I hired it in Newcastle, they'd instantly know where I'd gone.

Or I could stay put.

The trouble was, if I stayed put, I had nothing to fight *with*. If my plan was to go toe to toe with the cops, I needed to bring something big with me. I needed to bring them the truth about Cate and Aiden and their connection to the hit-and-run.

I needed proof that I'd been set up.

I went inside, asked for something mid-range but still felt

a flutter of disquiet as I watched the woman swipe my card. Afterwards, as I stood outside waiting for the vehicle, another, overwhelming wave of panic hit me. My head was banging. Nausea was bubbling at the back of my throat. What the hell was I doing?

Should I have stayed and fought the battle here?

The car arrived, ripping me from my thoughts. As soon as I was behind the wheel, I turned up the A/C and let the cool air hit my face before heading east into Hammersmith. I was being set up because, somehow, at some point, I'd drifted close to the truth. The hit-and-run on McCaskell was an attempt to derail me, and it was an easy win. The cops would hardly have to dig at all to find out what sort of history McCaskell and I shared. Worse, CCTV footage from the Tube would show we last spoke two days ago. Everything pointed in my direction – and whoever was behind this knew it too.

Whoever was behind this.

I thought of the man with the burns and then grabbed my phone and tried Zoe Simmons's number again. Nothing. I sank half a bottle of water I'd picked up on the walk from the house, my head still thumping behind my eyes, and then finished the rest. Despite being out for so long, I felt tired: my bones ached, my muscles hurt, I wanted to sleep.

Next, I dialled the sports centre in Croydon that Simmons worked at. A woman answered after a couple of rings.

'Is Zoe Simmons around?' I asked.

'Zoe isn't in today,' the woman replied.

'Is it her day off again?'

'No.'

'So she called in sick?'

'No. That's the thing. We haven't heard from her at all.'

I paused, trying to get my thoughts into some sort of order.

'Can I ask who's calling?'

I thanked her without giving my name and hung up, then remembered Zoe's mother telling me that Zoe's girlfriend worked at a Holiday Inn near Waterloo. Googling the number, I phoned through, and – after a few redirects – managed to get put through to the back office in which she worked.

The second she picked up, I knew something was wrong.

'Becky, it's David Raker. We talked the other day.'

It sounded like she'd been crying.

'Is everything okay?'

No answer. Just sobs.

'Is it something to do with Zoe?'

'Yes,' she managed a couple of seconds later.

'Is she okay?'

'No. No, she's not okay.'

'What's happened to her?'

More sobbing, her words unable to form.

'Becky, what's happened to her?'

And then, barely audibly, she said, 'Zoe's dead.'

38

'Zoe's dead? How did she die?'

I could hear Becky's movements, desk drawers opening. She must have been getting ready to leave. 'She took some pills.'

'She overdosed?'

'Sleeping pills,' she said by way of an answer.

I thought of Audrey Calvert.

Two witnesses.

Two overdoses.

'She never even *took* sleeping pills before,' Becky said, the first swell of anger in her voice. 'Why would she take them now? Why would she do something so reckless?'

I thought about Audrey again. I'd always assumed she'd overdosed because she'd been searching for an escape – from something or, more likely, from some*one*. But maybe she hadn't overdosed deliberately. Maybe someone just made it look like she did. And maybe that person had done exactly the same thing to Simmons.

The man with the burns.

Harper.

Was he the one that did this? A killer that made two murders look like two suicides?

'Where was Zoe found?' I asked Becky.

'In her car at Wanstead Flats.'

That was as good a location as any to fake a suicide. Lots of rugged open space and few cameras.

'Zoe's mum got a call from the police,' she sobbed.

'Did they say how long Zoe had been there?'

'They think since yesterday morning.'

'You didn't think it was odd that she didn't come home last night?'

'I was working the night shift.' She burst into tears again, long, uncontrollable moans that were terrible to listen to. 'I didn't even know . . .'

As I listened to her cry, I thought of Zoe Simmons's mother, of the concern she'd already had for her daughter, the ways in which Zoe never quite returned to her after the crash, and my heart ached for her.

The three women in the dunes.

Zoe Simmons. Cate.

All children lost to parents who'd loved them.

Becky said she had to go. I desperately needed to get out of London – but I also needed to try and find out more about the man with the burns while I still had a head start. I swallowed some more ibuprofen and hit the accelerator, heading south, back to Michael Calvert's house.

That was the place Harper had been trying to get into with a set of keys that clearly hadn't been his. Maybe, inside, there was some clue about what he wanted.

Halfway there, my phone started buzzing in my pocket.

I fumbled around for it, wondering who could possibly know the number of my back-up mobile, thinking of the credit card I'd used to rent the car. Had the cops picked up my trail already? But then I looked at the display – saw it said WITHHELD – and felt relief. There *was* one person I'd given this number to, months back – but, in doing so, I'd told him it was only to be used in emergencies.

I hit Answer.

'Why are you on this phone?' Healy asked.

'It's a long story.'

And then I thought, *It's a weekday. He should be working.*

'Shouldn't you be out on the boat?'

'I phoned in sick.'

'Why?'

'Because I needed to call you.'

'This isn't a good time, Healy.'

'Yeah, well, believe me: you're going to want to hear this.'

Healy

He saw it as he waited at the bus stop.

He was in the next town along the coast, arms straining under the weight of the shopping bags he was carrying. It didn't help that the Co-op was right at the bottom of a long hill, and the bus stop right at the top. Of all the things Healy hated most about starting over, not having a car was definitely up there.

Once he got to the top, he checked the times on the board, and then laid the shopping bags down outside a nearby estate agency. It was hot, his T-shirt wet, his face a sheen of sweat. He shuffled into a sliver of shade provided by an overhang above the estate agency's window, and tried to cool off, watching a clump of kids – no more than ten years old – sitting on a roundabout in a park across the road. He thought of his own kids at that age and something twinged inside him: Ciaran, Leanne, Liam – they were just memories to him now, only ever alive in his head, or in the briefest glimpses of them he caught in other children.

The wheeze of an approaching bus stirred him from his thoughts.

That was when he spotted it.

It was in the window of the estate agency, among a cluster of others for sale. Set back from the road and partially hidden behind a bank of fir trees, it had a slate roof, white walls, dark blue sills and a matching front door, and was built on the incline of a hill. He could picture what laid just off camera as well, how the road continued winding up, tracing the contours of the hill until it reached the next house.

His house.

Later that night, as planned, he went around to Paula's for dinner.

He knocked on her door, his thoughts rewinding to her telling him that she'd moved here, to the village, after she'd split with her husband. *I love it here*, she'd said to Healy. *I don't ever see myself moving.* He lingered on that last sentence.

So why was her house for sale?

Why would she lie to him?

She answered the door dressed in a red dress and a white apron, with a picture of three chillies on it and *Super spicy – and the food's good too!* written underneath.

'Good evening,' she said, beaming.

'Hey.' Healy forced a smile.

'Come in, come in. I hope you like lamb, because I forgot to check whether you were a veggie or not.'

'No, you're safe,' Healy said, and followed her inside.

They stood in the kitchen chatting as she finished off the lamb chops, although Paula did most of the talking. Healy kept waiting for her to bring up the house sale – or, at least, mention it in passing – but she didn't. Once the meal was ready, they moved to the garden, the sun slipping from the sky, and if there were silences, they never seemed awkward. In the quiet the two of them would listen to the sea, or to the squawk of the gulls drifting across the still of the evening. From the patio at the back of Paula's house, Healy could see all the way down to the beach, and there was a boy there with his dad. After a while, Healy caught Paula watching him.

'Are you okay?' she asked him.

He looked along the slate pathway that ran down the side of the house, to where a FOR SALE sign should have been standing out front. He tried to reason with himself. What did it matter if she'd put the house on the market? They'd had one meal together. They weren't even really friends, so she didn't owe him an explanation. She wasn't obliged to tell him a single thing about herself or her life. And yet, even so, it felt weird that she hadn't mentioned the sale of her house, weirder that she claimed to love living here so much. The fact that she might have lied to him hurt for some reason; deeper down, it concerned him.

He thought of Raker.

'Marcus? Are you okay?'

'Sorry,' he said, forcing another smile, 'I'm fine.' But there was a tautness to his voice he hadn't been expecting. As she heard that, she almost seemed to flinch, and he became annoyed that he'd let his guard down so easily and so quickly. This was the man he used to be.

This was the man he'd come here to hide.

'I'm sorry,' he said quickly. 'Long day on the water.'

'It's okay.'

'No, it's not.'

'Honestly,' she said, eyes sparking, that same smile on her face again, 'don't worry about it. Being up so early, five days a week, would make me pretty tired too.'

He returned the smile. 'Thank you.'

'You won't be thanking me once you taste my crumble.' She started chuckling to herself. 'And, no, that's not a euphemism.'

She giggled again, and then they both watched as a seagull rode thermals up the lane towards them, eventually landing on the A-frame of her roof. It took in the view, head inching jerkily from side to side. Paula, collecting their plates, wagged a finger at it and said, 'If you take a dump on my roof, I *will* hunt you down.'

'Are you moving house?'

It was out of his mouth before he could stop it. He swallowed and cleared his throat, as if trying to will the words back in. But the moment had gone. He'd said it automatically, instinctively, a temporary loss of control.

Why was he even bothered about any of this?

Because you've let someone get too close to you, he thought. He barely knew her – and that was still too close.

'Am I moving house?'

He looked at her. *Shit*. Swallowing again, he took a long breath. 'It's, uh . . . it's none of my business. But I was in town earlier today, and I, uh . . .' He shrugged. 'I saw that your house was for sale. I didn't know you were selling up.'

Raker would hit the roof if he was here now.

'Why would I sell the house?' she said. 'I love this place.'

'I know you do. That's why I was surprised.'

'I'm not selling,' she assured him. 'I'm happy here. What estate agency was it? I'd better call them in the morning.'

He told her and then looked out over the edge of the garden, up the slope towards his house. He had left the lights off – and as day began to crawl towards night, it was disappearing.

'Marcus? Are you sure you're okay?'

'I'm sorry,' he said. 'I must be confused.'

'If I was putting my house on the market, I would definitely tell you. But I'm not. I don't *want* to move. I never *have* wanted to move. I absolutely love it here.'

She reached out and gently touched his hand.

He felt a charge of electricity.

'I guess I'm more tired than I thought,' he said.

Her eyes lingered on him, confused, concerned, and then

she gestured to the house. 'Do you fancy going in, warming up a bit, and eating a bang-average crumble?'

He followed her inside, and – as they moved from the patio on to the cool flagstone floor of the kitchen – he started trying to figure out what had happened. He'd been working longer hours on the trawler the past few weeks – trying to earn more money – but it wasn't like he'd been overdoing it. He'd been sleeping okay too. Not great, because he never slept well these days, but good enough. The hot weather could be exhausting but it wouldn't make him see something that wasn't there.

I know what I saw.

'Take a seat,' Paula said, gesturing to the sofas in the living room. He padded through, perching himself on the edge of the nearest one. The house was small – much smaller than the one he was in – but it was beautifully finished. Paula had an old fireplace on one side, a cast-iron wood burner in it, and a set of floor-to-ceiling windows with majestic views across her garden and the sea. In between were the sofas and an oak TV cabinet, a TV on top, a farmhouse dresser and a white bookcase.

Paula kept talking to him from the kitchen, and Healy listened, but then a minute later, something caught his attention. The early evening breeze had picked up, coming in off the water, and outside something had been blown out on to the lawn, landing with a dull thud.

He'd been around to that side of the house the previous evening, when Paula had given him a tour of the downstairs. That was where she kept the firewood. In contrast to the rest of her home, it was a mess: an old stable, small, crumbling, its roof rusted red, only its back wall still standing. As well as firewood, Paula dumped things there that were no longer of use: broken tools, cracked kitchenware, old shelving and furniture.

And other things.

Things she wanted to hide.

Paula returned with the crumble. 'Well, I may have lied. I gave the crumble a taste in the kitchen – and I think average is overdoing it a bit.'

Healy smiled and glanced out at the garden again.

To what had fallen on to the grass.

A FOR SALE sign.

39

'So let me get this straight: she lied to you about her house being for sale?'

'Yeah.'

I'd arrived at Michael Calvert's road. The hot sun was beating hard against my window, the temperature in the car unbearable, and I didn't know if it was that, or the headache, or the nausea, but I was finding it hard to see what exactly Healy was trying to tell me.

'She said she *wasn't* selling?'

'Right. She said the house wasn't on the market. Denied it to my face. She'd hidden the FOR SALE sign.'

'So do you think she's also lying about seeing a guy at the house?'

'I don't know,' he said again. 'Could be. I can't think why she would lie about it, though.' Healy was silent for a moment. 'Are you all right?'

'No, not really.'

'What's happened?'

I thought about all the reasons not to get into it over the phone – not here, not now, not when I was working against the clock, with the cops on my tail. The longer I stayed in London, the smaller their search area, the easier I was to find. I needed to finish up here fast and then put some distance between me and the city. But I also knew Healy might be able to help me. He might be able to see something I wasn't. So I told him about the case and about my car mowing down Connor McCaskell.

'Shit,' he said quietly.

I kept the engine running, redirecting one of the vents, trying to get as much cool air on me as possible. I didn't just feel ill, I was on edge, constantly on the lookout for signs I was being watched or followed. What was it going to be like in a day's time? In two? Was it still going to be like this in a week, or would I have been caught and arrested by then? If this whole thing ended with my arrest, I had to make sure I had something to fight with – and the best weapon to defend myself with was going to be the truth about what had happened to Cate and Aiden Gascoigne.

'Do you think McCaskell's dead?' Healy asked.

'I have no idea,' I said, rubbing my forehead.

I thought back to the photo I'd seen on FeedMe, the way my car had started to blur as it approached the zebra crossing. The driver had hit the accelerator as soon as he'd seen McCaskell. It *had* to have been doing more than forty-five miles per hour, and if it was fifty or fifty-five, the chances of survival were slim. As I processed that, I squeezed my eyes shut, not just trying to rid myself of the headache and the nausea but the perverse and inappropriate sense of relief. If he was dead, he couldn't write about me in his shitty tabloid. If he was dead, all of it was over. No more threats. No story. But then I buried the thoughts as deep as I could, knowing they were profane. Much as I'd grown to hate McCaskell, it wasn't right that he'd been attacked like this. And his death, if it happened, wouldn't be a source of relief; it would just make things worse.

'This neighbour thing,' I said. 'Maybe it's safer if you leave the village for a few days.'

'And go where?'

'I don't know,' I said, and closed my eyes again. Every thump was agony. It hurt behind my eyes, in my ears, in my throat. 'Get on a train, maybe go to the other side of the country for a couple of weeks.'

Healy was quiet.

'I know you don't want to,' I said, 'but if, for even a second, you think you're at risk there, it's the only real option. If she's lying to you, we first need to get you out of there and *then* figure out why. People lie for all sorts of reasons, but it's rarely good.'

Another long pause.

And then, finally, he said, 'Okay.'

He sounded sad, resigned.

'Have you got enough money?' I asked him.

'Yeah. For a few days. A week maybe.'

'Good.' I took a breath. 'This will be over by then.'

But I sounded more confident than I felt.

'Give me a call at some point to let me know where you are,' I said.

'I will.'

I hung up. It had taken me fifty minutes to get down here and I'd just spent ten minutes on the phone to Healy. What I was about to do, I had to do fast.

Getting out of the car, I looked at Michael Calvert's house again, then popped the boot. There was the holdall inside that I'd packed at the house, with everything I might need in an emergency.

One of those things was a pair of gloves.

Another was a set of lockpicks.

40

I went to the front door and knocked, just in case.

As I stood there, waiting for an answer I knew wasn't coming, I began feeling woozy again. The sun was intense, unrelenting against my back.

I placed a hand on the wall.

Squeezed my eyes shut.

Let it pass.

Once it had, I checked the place next door – it didn't look as if anyone was there this time – and then the rest of the road. The advantage I had was that this was an end of terrace, which meant I only had to worry about being seen from one side. Using the porch as cover, I snapped on the gloves and shifted closer to the door.

I set to work on the lock.

My headache was so bad it was like my vision was warping, a discordant pulse of static that made it hard to focus. The lock shouldn't have presented too much of a challenge, but it took me a full five minutes before I felt it click.

Making sure I was still in the clear and not being watched, I pushed at the door with the toe of my boot, letting it swing back into the house. Everything was shadowed, semi-lit, the sun behind me only making it part of the way in.

'Michael?'

Nothing.

'Michael?' I paused, listening. 'I wanted to talk to you about your mum.' Nothing again. Just the silent reply of an empty house.

I moved inside.

Pushing the door all the way closed behind me, the hum from the city outside vanished and the sounds of the house faded in. A fridge. The tick of a clock. The faint gurgle of a water tank somewhere.

Apart from that, the house was quiet as a tomb.

The living room was narrow, long, with sofas and a TV at one end and some French doors at the other. A bookcase too but it had no books in it at all and it appeared to have mostly been used as a dumping ground for old DVDs, charging cables and a series of cardboard boxes. Next to the bookcase, set in a kind of alcove, was a table, and under the table were some more boxes.

I went upstairs to the bedrooms.

There were two of them, small, poky, dominated by floor-to-ceiling fitted wardrobes. The beds were made, everything tidy. One of them looked like the room that Michael Calvert had been staying in; on one of the side tables was an empty glass, on another an alarm clock and a potted plant. The plant was dead, its leaves frail and brown. The whole place had the feeling of abandonment.

I checked over the wardrobes and then went back downstairs.

In the living room I pulled the boxes out from the bookcase. They were full of junk. I took everything out anyway and went through it, doing the same with the three boxes under the table. In the first was a tangle of leads, instruction manuals, an old mobile phone, a broken modem. I tried to power up the mobile phone, but it was completely dead. In a second box I found more of the same, as well as some old paperwork. I emptied the third box.

More junk.

Until I got to the bottom.

Under a mess of wires and plastic debris was an old Ordnance Survey map. I unfolded it and immediately saw that part of it had been circled with red pen.

Next to the circle was an address.

Next to that, someone – presumably Michael Calvert – had written *What really happened here?*

41

I crossed London, south-west to the north-east, thinking the whole time about how far behind me the police might be. They'd put a trace on my phone and had managed to get that up and running fast, but gaining access to my financial records was more complicated, requiring more sign-off, and would probably take them longer. I felt like I was still ahead of the curve – just – but this detour wasn't going to help.

I didn't have a choice, though.

Not after finding the map at Calvert's house.

As I arrived in Epping Forest, I felt worse than ever, but tried to push everything into the background. I finished a sandwich I'd started back in Camberwell and then got out of the car. The approach had been busy, a hot day in July bringing families in to cycle and walk, but this stretch of road was quiet. There were also no exercise trails, no paths to follow on foot or on bike – it was just a strip of tarmac, flanked by huge trees, except for a single clearing.

I looked at the address Michael Calvert had written on the map.

Slade Youth Hostel
Saxon Lane
Epping Forest

I made my way along a loose stone path towards the compact building in the clearing, the words YOUTH HOSTEL emblazoned on the front. The T of YOUTH had dislodged and swung one-eighty degrees, but my focus was already on something else.

All the windows were boarded.

And judging by the state of the paintwork, the graffiti on the boards, the height of the grass and the avalanche of circling weeds, it had been like this for a long time.

Shit.

This drive – this detour – had been worthless.

'You all right there, son?'

I started, turning round.

An elderly man was standing behind me, a cane in one hand, a dog on a leash in the other. It was a retriever, jet black, but it barely seemed interested in me; instead, it was sniffing around in the long grass off the track, gently parting it with its nose. The man let her go, the lead unfurling from his hand. 'Most of the kids I see hanging around here are a bit younger than you,' he said and then broke into a smile. 'No offence, obviously. You're still a spring chicken compared to me.'

'I didn't see you hiding in the grass.'

He chuckled at the joke. 'I like to walk past most days and try to keep an eye on things. I work as a layman at the church down the road, and y'know . . .' He shrugged. 'If kids start hanging around here – doing drugs or whatever – the church is going to be next.'

'So how long has this place been shut?'

'Oooh.' The man let out a breath. 'I think it was July 2012.'

I looked at the youth hostel again and another wave of pain flared behind my eyes – and then the panic really hit. I'd wasted over two hours on this. I'd followed a literal trail on a map and now it was just as possible that it was completely unrelated to the death of Audrey Calvert, the disappearance of her son and the overdose of Zoe Simmons.

'What brings you here?' the old man asked.

'Just a bad hunch,' I said.

'Oh. I've had a few of those in my time.'

'Do you know why this place closed?'

'They had a fire.'

I thought of the man with the burns.

Harper.

'Was anyone hurt?'

'No. It was some electrical thing. The place was empty at the time.'

I looked at the building more closely and could see the hint of scorch marks at the windows, some blackened roof tiles too – but if there had been a fire, most of the damage must have been inside.

'You ever hear of anyone getting in?' I asked.

'You mean, like squatters or something?'

'Anyone, really.'

I was thinking about missing people.

About where they could have ended up.

'I don't think so,' the man replied. 'I mean, it doesn't look all that easy, even if you wanted to.' He meant the boards were as thick as concrete blocks and all secured into the masonry with rivets. No one was getting them off with a crowbar and elbow grease. The whole structure was on one floor, which was presumably why the boards had been made so immovable: the windows, and charred interior, would have been easy to gain access to otherwise. 'Anyway,' the man continued, 'like I say, there was a fire here, so the inside will be a mess, even if you did manage to get those bloody great boards off. How come you're interested?'

I thought of Michael's note on the map. *What really happened here?*

'I'm just trying to find someone,' I said.

He frowned. 'What, are you like a copper or something?'

'An investigator, yeah.'

I really was feeling terrible again now, the relief of the shade slowly wearing off – but I tried to concentrate, tried to keep going for a little longer.

'Do you know who used to run this place before it closed?' I asked.

'His name was Slade. Hence the name of the place.'

'Was that a first or second name?'

'Second.' The man's face scrunched up. 'He had some weird first name. You know, unusual. Like, Jasper or Jenson. I'm sure it was something with a J, anyway. He was a nice guy, though. I didn't speak to him a lot, but when I did, we had a good chat. This place always seemed busy – plenty of back-packers, tourists and all of that. I think he did pretty well out of it. But then I think he was doing all right already.'

'You mean financially?'

'I just heard his father was loaded and, after he died, he left the boy a ton of money.' The old man shrugged. 'That's just what I heard. Not that that really makes any difference to any-thing. Everyone seemed happy here, that was the main thing. That was why we were so surprised when he just took off.'

'He just left?'

'Yeah, literally straight after the fire.'

'No one saw him again?'

'Nope, not a dicky bird.'

'And he never mentioned where he was going?'

'No, nothing,' the man replied. 'I just figured he probably went back.'

'Went back?'

'To where he was from originally.'

'Which was where?'

The man pulled his dog back towards him. 'He was from somewhere up in Northumberland.'

Names

30 Years Ago

After they left the coffee shop, Makayla offered to give Amelia a lift home and they headed to a car park a few streets away. Makayla talked on the way about the things she was going to set in motion in the search for 'the mysterious Phil'.

When they got to the car, Makayla apologized for the mess on the back seat. The car was a red Astra that looked like it had seen better days a decade ago, and Makayla was soon apologizing for that too. 'It's a real bus, I know, but, trust me, this thing goes and goes.' She started up the engine and, after an initial tick-tick-tick, it fired into life. 'We've got a fleet of new Volvos at work, but the thing I like about this old girl is that it's got all my music in it. Music helps me see clearly.'

Amelia nodded. 'Me too.'

'Really? Are you a music fan?'

'Yeah.'

'What are you listening to at the moment?'

'The Prodigy.'

Makayla frowned. 'I must be getting old.'

'It's dance music.'

'As in, Abba?' But she winked at Amelia.

Amelia smiled. 'No. Not quite.'

'Well, I'll have to check out The Prodigy, then. I've got to be completely honest, I'm not much of an expert when it comes to modern music. I'm stuck in a time loop, where it's always the seventies and eighties.' Makayla pulled out of the car park, joining the main road, then reached down and fumbled around in a tray under the radio, where there was a pile of cassettes. She picked a few of them up, checked the labels

234

and put them back, then eventually found the one she wanted and slotted it into the stereo. 'Now this is the kind of tune that gets this old girl going.'

It was the Bee Gees.

'You know this one?' she asked Amelia.

'Everyone knows "Stayin' Alive".'

'That's because it's a timeless classic.'

They drove for a few minutes – just listening to the song – and then out of the corner of her eye, Amelia caught Makayla watching her.

'Is everything okay?' Amelia asked.

'Sorry,' Makayla said, her eyes pinging back to the road. But then she glanced at Amelia again. 'Sorry, sweetheart. I don't mean to be weird. It's just you, uh . . .'

Amelia frowned. 'I what?'

'You remind me so much of someone else.'

'Really? Who?'

'She was about your age. And she loved music like you.'

Amelia didn't know what to say.

'Her name was Lilly Andrews.'

'Lilly's a really nice name,' Amelia responded, just for something to say, but then a light went on at the back of her head. 'Wait a second. Lilly Andrews. Isn't that the name of one of the girls that they found in those dunes yesterday?'

Makayla nodded. 'It is.'

Amelia studied her – and then a second realization sparked. 'Shit, is that one of your cases?' For some reason she hadn't expected Makayla to be in charge of a case like that. She wasn't sure why. Maybe because Makayla wasn't how she imagined a murder detective to be. Not that Amelia knew all that much about the girls or the case. She didn't really watch much TV, and definitely didn't read newspapers, but she remembered news reports that her parents were watching.

'Yes,' Makayla said. 'That one's mine.'

The Bee Gees became Bonnie Tyler, and then Makayla turned to

235

Amelia again and said, 'So have you given your parents the good news, then?'

'The good news?'

'That Makayla Jennings is on the case for you.'

'Oh.' Amelia smiled. 'No, not yet. I hope you don't mind. I just wanted to see how far we got before telling them. My mum and dad . . .' She paused. 'All the baby stuff has been a shock for them and I don't want to throw all this at them yet. They worry about stuff, you know? I think they'd worry I was wasting your time.'

'We'll give them the good news when I find the mysterious Phil.'

'Okay, cool.'

'So, have you thought about names?'

'For the baby?' Amelia shook her head.

'Not even once?'

'Not really. It's all still sinking in.'

'Of course it is,' Makayla said, and put her hand on Amelia's arm again. 'But let's just play the game. What names do you like? Tell me.'

Gradually, Amelia started to smile again.

'See?' Makayla said. 'This is the fun bit. What about if it's a girl?'

Amelia took a second to think. 'I like Hope.'

'Hope,' Makayla echoed. 'That's cute. And if it's a boy?'

'Boys are harder.'

'They are. I have two boys, so I should know.'

Amelia felt thrown. 'I didn't know that.'

Makayla had talked about giving her child up for adoption when she was still in her teens, and so Amelia had assumed that the sadness that lingered was because she'd never had kids.

Makayla seemed to second-guess her again. 'Just because I went on to have other children doesn't mean I've forgotten what it was like to give up that first one.'

'No,' Amelia said, flushing. 'No, of course not.'

But Makayla held up a hand. 'I wasn't telling you off, sweetheart. It's just you never forget the things in life that have hurt you. They always stick with you.' She was distant for a second, and then pinged back into focus. 'Anyway, yeah, boys. Twins.'

'Wow.'

'They're a handful.'

Amelia looked out through the window. Then for some reason she thought of her Grampy, her mum's father; he and Amelia had always been close. He'd been so tall but incredibly gentle, patient, kind – all things that Amelia had loved.

'I do have one name I like,' Amelia said.

'Ooooh, what is it?'

'It was my grandfather's name.'

Makayla nodded. 'That's lovely. What was he called?'

'Dylan,' Amelia said. 'You know, like the poet.'

'Such a nice name.'

And then Makayla paused, and when she finally looked across at Amelia again, there was a faint shimmer in her eyes. 'Do you know what I called him?'

Amelia frowned. 'Who?'

'The boy I gave up for adoption.'

'Oh. No, what?'

Makayla swallowed. Another flash of sadness.

'I called him Michael,' she said.

PART FOUR
True Crime

42

I finally headed north.

My plan had been to get the whole way to Newcastle in one go if I could manage it – but it only took ninety minutes for reality to hit. The longer I spent driving, the harder it was to concentrate and, west of Peterborough, I dropped off at the wheel for a split second and drifted across to the next lane. The blare of a car horn startled me back into consciousness.

If I got into an accident, I'd be in hospital or in handcuffs as soon as I woke up – *if* I was lucky enough to wake up at all – so I pulled into the services and found a corner of the car park in the shade. I paid for a two-hour ticket, crawled on to the back seat, and – with a faint breeze escaping through the partly open windows – closed my eyes.

I went out like a light.

When I stirred next, my head was still fuzzy, but some of the pain had finally subsided. I noticed something else too: outside, it was getting dark.

What the hell . . .?

I checked my watch – and, instantly, my stomach coiled. I'd been out for almost six hours. It was now after eight thirty in the evening.

I grabbed a bottle of water from the front and sank what was left of it, then hurried into the service station and bought another. I bought a sandwich as well, feeling hungry for the first time, and, as I exited, kept my eyes on my surroundings. I looked for cops and security guards, and when I didn't see any, I switched my attention to members of the public, to anyone whose gaze lingered on me for too long. My name hadn't been released yet – at least as far as I knew – but that didn't make me any less cautious.

There wasn't anyone.

As I ate, I quickly checked the newsfeeds for stories about Connor McCaskell. There was no update on his condition, and I got confirmation that my name still hadn't been put out to the public. But it was only a matter of time now.

I'd lost any head start I might have had.

I got back on to the motorway and put my foot down. I knew I was going too fast, knew it only increased the chances of me alerting the police, but I had so much time to make up. As I drove, it felt like my head was on fire, as much from the noise of my thoughts as the pain, but I tried to focus. At this moment my car was probably being worked on in a forensic lab, and that meant my neighbours and the people in my road would have seen it being removed from my driveway. So even if my name wasn't out there on the newsfeeds right now, it would be being discussed already. And soon everyone would know for sure that I was a prime suspect in a hit-and-run – and that included Martin, Sue and Georgia.

I came back to the same question: why try to frame me?

And had the man who'd done it been Harper?

Whoever it was, I could see one obvious reason for setting me up like this and not just killing me. If I was dead, McCaskell would have followed a trail even deeper still, and along that trail there was always the chance that he might discover the truth about what had happened to Cate and Aiden. But if *McCaskell* was the victim, and I was fitted for the crime, neither of those things happened – because I looked guilty as hell, and McCaskell was no longer capable of following *any* trail, let alone Cate and Aiden's.

I called Ewan Tasker's burner.

He answered quickly. 'Raker?'

'I'm all right, Task.'

'What the hell's going on?' He sounded concerned, fearful.

'I don't know,' I said.

'Someone took your car?'

'Yeah. And put it back on my driveway.'

'And – what? – you never even realized?'

'I was out cold at the time. Drugged.'

'Shit,' he said eventually, almost to himself, and then ground to a halt again, as if processing everything. 'It's still locked down tight where the press is concerned, but there's a ton of chat about you internally at the Met. I'm trying to keep my ears open, but there's only so many times I can log into the database or ask people questions before it starts to look suspicious.'

'Please don't take any risks for me.'

'I won't. But I'll do what I can.'

'Thanks, old man. That means a lot.'

We shared a moment's silence, and then Tasker said, 'I looked into how long it would take to process dental work for that body in the arches.'

'Let me guess: weeks?'

'At least two, even if I got a rush on it. Probably more, though.'

It meant I wasn't going to get confirmation that the body belonged to Audrey Calvert any time soon. Not that it changed much. I was pretty convinced, given what else I'd found out in the time since I last spoke to Tasker, that it was Audrey's body and, like Zoe Simmons, she'd been killed for what she knew.

I said to Tasker, 'Could you do one quick favour for me?'

'Sure. What do you need?'

'Can you do a search for a Jasper or Jenson Slade for me? The last address I have for him is . . .' I paused, checking my notes, and told him about the youth hostel.

'I'll do it for you now,' Tasker said. 'Hold on.'

I looked down and saw I was doing almost a hundred, so eased off the accelerator. There was making up time and there was being reckless.

'Got a Jasper Slade here,' Tasker said.

'Does he have a record?'

'No, it's just his driving licence. Do you want me to send this to you?'

'Only if it's not going to put you at risk.'

'It won't. Where shall I send it?'

I gave him my back-up email address.

Afterwards, I called directory enquiries and got them to redirect me to the Coast Inn, the hotel that Cate had stayed at when she'd visited Northumberland in the November before she vanished. When someone picked up, I asked if they had any rooms available tonight. The woman I spoke to confirmed that they did.

I told her I'd be there after midnight.

43

The Coast Inn was just off the A1, thirty-three miles north of Newcastle.

I pulled into the car park, the night dark, almost absolute. This far up the country big towns were just a memory, the scattered villages of Northumberland existing only as tiny lights dispersed among the gloom.

The main doors of the hotel were locked, so I pushed a buzzer on the wall. It was much cooler here than in London, the wind carrying a chill in from the North Sea.

As I waited, I took in the exterior of the hotel.

It was a double-storey building built in an L-shape that looked a little like a US roadside motel. The doors all faced out on to the car park, and the first floor was accessed via stairwells at either side. There were two vending machines at the end of a row of doors on the bottom floor, although one was out of order, and the signage for the hotel – mounted atop a huge pole at the edge of the road – was flickering, the bulbs inside on the blink. It wasn't that the hotel was run-down exactly, it was just past its sell-by date, the paint a little dull on the walls and doors, the decor I could see in the reception old-fashioned.

I'd arrived wearing a cap, so I pulled it down a little further, covering my face from view of the camera inside, and pushed the buzzer again. A moment later, a man in his thirties emerged from a door. He was fair-haired and blue-eyed, and looked like he might have spent a good proportion of his life on a sunbed.

The reception smelled of furniture polish and fried food, the evidence for the second in a small room behind the counter where I could see some half-eaten chips and a thin cheeseburger in a polystyrene carton. He pulled the door closed, then woke a computer from its slumber. I leaned against the counter, my back to the CCTV camera, pretending to study some flyers for the local tourist attractions.

'Long drive?' he asked.

'Long enough, yeah.'

'It's Mr Kennedy, right?'

'That's right.'

I seriously doubted I had to worry about a night manager at a hotel over three hundred miles from home – not yet, anyway – but sooner or later the cops were going to pick up a trail, so it was better to try and insulate myself from the start. It was why I was being so cautious around the camera. It was also why I was using the name Kennedy. It was an old ID I'd had made for Healy. When the manager gave me a form, I put in a fake address, a fake email, and then put down my first name as *Bryan*. I'd booked for two nights and it was £50 a night, so I paid him the lot in cash.

'Can I take a contact number, sir?'

I looked at him. 'A contact number?'

'It's just for emergencies.'

'Such as?'

'It's nothing to worry about,' he said. 'It's just, say we have a fire alarm and guests congregate out front, we may need to phone around to account for everyone.'

'Sure,' I said. I didn't want to make a big deal of it because if I did, he'd definitely remember me, so I wrote a fake number on the form, took my key and headed back outside.

The room was on the first floor, right at the end. Most of the others were dark, the occupants presumably already asleep. As I unlocked my door, I looked out across the car park in the direction of the North Sea. It was far too dark to see anything, other than spots of light between here and the water, but I could picture what awaited me in the early morning further up the ragged coastline.

Photographs of the dunes were seared into my mind, but not the tourist board shots of big skies, swirling patterns in the sand and lime-green beach grass. The portraits I saw were older, spotted by age, taken on a freezing day in late April 1992. They were of white tents, buffeted by the wind; serious expressions; cameramen and journalists bunched together behind a line of police tape as it snapped and twisted in the breeze.

They were of three faces I could never unsee.

Three women Cate Gascoigne had tried to find answers for.

Three women that might have cost her her own life.

44

I let myself into the room, still thinking of Cate and the book she'd been writing. As I dumped my bag on to the bed, I eyed an old desk pushed up against the opposite wall, and imagined Cate hunched over it, her laptop open, furiously writing. I saw the spaces either side of her filled with research notes, folders of paper, pictures.

None of which I can find.

Was it possible that, in the days preceding the crash, she'd realized she was in danger and found a hiding place for all the material she'd gathered? Did she know who was making her feel threatened enough to do that? Or was she just aware of a shadow in her wake?

If she knew someone was on her trail, I tried to imagine why she would have looked so relaxed and apparently happy on the CCTV recording taken on Gatton Hill ten seconds before the crash. Was it just a show for Aiden? Did he know what she was working on? Or had she not felt troubled at all and the crash really had come out of nowhere?

The same questions continued playing in my head as I unpacked. Even though I'd slept for so long in the car, and been out for almost an entire day before that, I still felt tired. I guessed it was the after-effects of whatever I'd been jabbed with; a residual exhaustion lingered in my bones and muscles, and behind my eyes, like a physical weight.

I pulled my notebook towards me.

Slowly turning the pages, I started rereading everything I'd written down over the course of the last four days. It felt like there were still so many untethered strands: not just Cate and her book, not just what happened to her and Aiden that day – and who else might have been there – but other threads that I felt like I needed to solve in order to arrive at the answers I sought about the Gascoignes.

Grabbing a pen, I wrote:

Q. Is Harper the man with the burns?

I stared at the question I'd posed. I didn't have definitive proof but, in my gut, it felt like he must be. The physical description Georgia had given me matched the one I had from Michael's neighbours of the man trying to get into the house. Georgia hadn't seen evidence of burns, but everything else aligned. The bigger question was how exactly he fitted into the narrative. Could he have been in the ravine that day? One thing I knew for sure was that Georgia and the neighbour had estimated Harper to be in his thirties, or in his forties at most, so in 1992 he would only have been a kid. That meant, whatever else was true, there was no way he could be the Dune Murderer.

Q. Did Harper kill Audrey & Michael Calvert & Zoe Simmons?

Both eyewitnesses were dead and Michael Calvert seemed to be missing – for two months, probably more – which now made it more likely than not that, eventually, his body was going to turn up somewhere. Audrey may have been a lapsed addict, but with Zoe Simmons having had no history of drug addiction or pill-taking of any kind, I was willing to bet her death wasn't self-inflicted. The question was, why silence them? And why not do it at the same time?

Just then, my phone started ringing.

It was the number for the payphone in north Wales that Healy used.

249

I pushed Answer. 'Is everything okay?'

'Yeah,' he said in response. 'Why?'

'Well, it's twelve thirty, for one. And this number is for emergencies.'

'I know. I couldn't sleep and I thought I'd check in.'

We shouldn't really have been talking outside the times we'd agreed upon – it was just safer that way – but I allowed myself to relax a little. And, emotionally, I understood; Healy was about to move on again, from another place he'd started to call home. It was going to unsettle him. He was going to feel lonely.

'I expected to leave a message,' he said. 'What are you still doing up?'

'I only just got to Northumberland.' I called him back and put him on speaker. 'I thought we agreed you were leaving.'

'We did. I'm out of here first thing in the morning. I'll probably head to the east coast somewhere. You know, a real glamour spot like Grimsby or Skegness. Another leg on the world's shittiest national tour.' He said it like a joke but it was meant. He hated having to move around, hated having to run at the first sign of something even remotely out of kilter. He'd probably spent the entire afternoon wondering if a lie about a house sale from a woman he barely knew even remotely mattered, let alone mattered enough to run in the opposite direction. And I didn't blame him; compared to what I was dealing with, what we'd dealt with together before, it felt so small.

'You making sure the house is clean?' I asked.

'I'm assuming you don't mean giving it a hoover?'

I smiled.

'Yeah, that's why I thought I'd go in the morning. I've spent the whole evening going room to room, making sure there's nothing here that can be a problem for us. What have you been up to?'

'I'm still the fugitive you last spoke to.'

'So how are you going to fight back?'

I looked at the time – not certain that I wanted to get into it now – but then I found myself telling him more about the case, about what I'd found out even in the short time since we'd last talked, and then I was filling him in on everything. And the more I talked, the more I liked it; it helped me see clearly, laid a path for me.

'So do you *still* think the witnesses were lying?' he asked.

'Maybe, but under duress. I mean, this is just a theory at this point, but I'm thinking they saw what was *really* happening in the ravine – and who was *really* there. And so our suspect starts turning the screw on Audrey and Zoe.'

'And it's this Harper guy?'

I dragged my notebook towards me. 'I've been thinking about this ever since I started, this question of how two people – both likely to be severely injured – could vanish from that ravine so quickly. And, really, at this point, I can only see one way that happens.'

'And what's that?'

'We're dealing with more than one killer.'

45

Healy was quiet for a moment, taking in the idea.

'Whichever way I look at it,' I said, 'I just can't see Harper enacting some disappearing act entirely on his own. There's way too many moving parts, too many things to consider and sort in that ravine. He's got to take care of the witnesses up top and he's got to take care of Cate and Aiden at the crash site. And it's all a race against time. As soon as the 999 call goes out, the clock's ticking.'

'Then why let Audrey and Zoe call emergency services at all?'

'Zoe had dialled 999 before she'd even got out of her car, so the call was already made. So, from that point, he's got eleven minutes to threaten and then coach two witnesses on exactly what to tell the police *and* get Cate and Aiden clear of the ravine. I've gone over and over in my head the ways it *could* have happened, and basically none of them hold up. I mean, let's say he leaves a car parked down on the access road, on the other side of that sustainable forest there. It took me six minutes to walk from the ravine to the access road, which means twelve minutes both ways. And that's without a body on my back. So if he takes Cate to the car first, by the time he comes back for Aiden, the cops and fire crews are already at the scene. It's just not happening.'

'Even if what you're saying is true,' Healy responded, 'why coach Calvert and Simmons, *then* kill them off, anyway? Dead bodies just mean bigger problems.'

'I would guess killing them wasn't in the original plan. But Audrey began using again in the months after the crash. Maybe the heroin made her more unpredictable, more difficult to manage, maybe she threatened to confess. So Harper and whoever he's working with take her to the railway arch, and dress it up like she overdosed.'

'And then her boy starts looking for her.'

'Right. Audrey's ex told me that Michael didn't ever *stop* looking for her. He was still going eighteen months later, at the beginning of this year. And then he disappears.'

'Maybe because he finally found something.'

I remembered the map of Epping Forest I'd come across in Michael Calvert's home and the question he'd posed: *What really happened here?* But how was a hostel that had been shut for a decade, and on the other side of the city, connected to Audrey's death?

'I wonder if Michael is waiting to be found, just like his mum,' I said, and made a note to call Ewan Tasker again and have his contact at the Missing Persons Unit chase down any remains bearing a resemblance to Michael Calvert.

'And now Zoe Simmons is dead too,' Healy replied.

His voice was sombre because he could sense how much this one stung me, how much of it I'd put on myself. If I'd never boxed Simmons in, she wouldn't have agreed to meet me, and it wouldn't have forced Harper to target her before I got the truth out. Simmons would just have carried on as before: a normal, decent kid who'd been terrorized into silence.

'I'd better get to bed, Healy.'

'Yeah, me too. I'll call you tomorrow.'

I hung up and looked at my notebook, at the pages of shorthand I'd added – and then my gaze drifted to the end, to a question I'd added just before hanging up.

I thought of the person who'd run it, Jasper Slade, how the elderly man I'd talked to at the hostel had said Slade had originally been from Northumberland.

And then I thought of Slade's driving licence.

Ewan Tasker had mailed it to me.

I went to my back-up account and opened the attachment. It was in black and white and half disguised by a security mark, but I could see enough of him. Ten years ago – when the youth hostel had shut down – he would have been forty-eight. It was impossible to tell his hair colour, although it seemed dark, as was his moustache, and he was weighty around the face, the jawline a little doughy. He had a covering of stubble as well, darkening the lower half of his profile, but it was easy to see that he might have been handsome once, and may have had some Mediterranean ancestry in his family tree.

He had no middle name and his address was listed as Saxon Lane in Epping Forest, the road that the youth hostel was on. Other than that, Jasper Slade was a blank. In a Google search for him the only thing I could find was an old reference in a local directory from 1998, which listed places to stay in the boroughs of Waltham Forest, Redbridge, Barking and Havering. When I followed the link, I found a brief description of the hostel itself – twenty rooms, twelve shared, six doubles, two singles – and a low-res photo of Slade at the front entrance of the hostel.

I clicked on the picture.

As soon as I did, I realized something.

The Jasper Slade in *this* picture and the Jasper Slade on the driving licence weren't the same person.

46

The Jasper Slade in the 1998 press photo was paler, a little sunken around the eyes; the Jasper Slade on the driving licence was tanned, with a very different set of cheekbones. He had a similar moustache – but the more I looked at this version of the man, at his face, his expression, at the moustache, the more I saw all of it for what it was: mimicry. The driving-licence version of Jasper Slade wasn't the real one.

So if that man had *become* Jasper Slade, where was the *actual* Slade?

I felt a murmur of unease, and then remembered something the old man in Epping Forest had told me. *I heard his father was loaded and, after he died, he left the boy a ton of money.* Did the man on the driving licence kill the real Jasper Slade for his money, and then take on his life and identity, including the hostel?

And what did it have to do with Cate and Aiden?

I looked at the clock. One fifteen.

I showered and climbed into bed, setting my alarm for seven, knowing I needed to get some sleep but be up early. Except I couldn't get this new information out of my head. My thoughts were racing. As they did, my gaze briefly flicked to the hotel information folder, open on the bed next to me. I'd gone through it earlier, seeing if the hotel did room service. I hadn't really taken in more than the menu at the time, but now I looked at the last page more closely.

It was a potted history of the hotel with an old photograph of when it had opened back in 1951. I'd been right about its design: the original owner, a guy called Griffith Pardew, had spent the late forties living in Massachusetts and had modelled the Coast Inn on some of the US roadside motels he'd seen.

The hotel had been sold by Pardew in 1964, then sold again by the subsequent owner in 1967, and again in 1972, and 1983, and 1988. The folder didn't go into why the hotel had changed hands so often over the years, but as I googled the hotel I soon found out: a storm had ravaged it back in the 1950s. But it wasn't just one storm that had coloured the history of the hotel, it was a succession of terrible events: another storm in 1966 that had torn part of the roof off; yet another storm in 1971 that ripped a telegraph pole from the ground and speared it through a window, severely injuring a guest; a murder-suicide in 1982, when a husband had killed his wife and himself.

And then, finally, a fire.

Instantly, I thought of the youth hostel in Epping Forest, and of Harper, of his burns. But while the fire at the hostel appeared to have been contained, and most of the damage internalized, the one that had ripped through the Coast Inn in the nineties had been far more damaging. According to the Internet, it had gutted part of the hotel that had since been knocked down.

The account in the information brochure glossed over it. But it didn't take me long to find an old post – over thirteen years old now – on a website about local history:

To some, the hotel will always be tainted somehow, its history plagued by catastrophe, almost as if it were a magnet for tragedy.

I scrolled further down and, at the bottom, found a photograph. It was of the hotel after the fire. Although it wasn't the best quality, it showed a whole flank of the Coast Inn reduced to little more than a charred skeleton. The top floor had collapsed and part of it was hanging diagonally, having fallen through the ceilings of the rooms below. It was all a broken, blackened memory.

Under the picture was a short caption.

Something in it stopped me dead.

The aftermath of the fire on 30 April 1992.

The date.

The 30th was two days after the women were found in the dunes.

So was the fire – and the timing of it – purely coincidental? Or could it be connected to what had happened on that beach seventeen miles further up the coast? When I tried to think laterally, realistically, I was aware of what a stretch it was, given the lack of evidence. What could possibly link three murders to a fire at a hotel two days later? I thought of the one at the hostel in Epping Forest and the lack of links there too – to Cate and Aiden, to the witnesses at the ravine, to basically anything in this case at all, except perhaps Michael Calvert, who'd written the note on the map that had led me there. But a lack of links didn't necessarily mean it was a dead end. It just meant the links hadn't been found yet.

I put in a Google search for 'Coast Inn fire 1992' and found the hotel owner straight away. His name was Dean King. There were no local media stories about him or the fire at his hotel, presumably because everything that happened had been in the papers and on TV pre-Internet. Instead, the top hit was for the same local history website I'd already been looking at. The site had been created by a journalist called Alexander Weathers, and on it he said that authorities had ruled the fire as an accident and that King had been a suspect the cops at Northumbria Police had looked at – and dismissed – internally in relation to the Dune Murders.

I lingered on that last part. How did Weathers know that the cops had looked at Dean King? Had he talked to someone involved in the case?

Could Weathers have talked to Makayla Jennings?

It was hard to see the answers clearly now. I was finally starting to flag, all the questions becoming too much, so I decided it was time to call it a night and come at it fresh in the morning. But as I turned out the lights and closed my eyes, I kept seeing Cate.

Because one thing remained obvious.

She'd been writing a book about the Dune Murders, and in the months before she'd vanished – weeks, in fact – of all the hotels and B & Bs up here that she could have chosen to stay in, she'd slept at the Coast Inn.

It was clearly deliberate.

Like she thought the answers she needed were here.

Faces: Part 1

20 Years Ago

The two of them were in a tiny café in Ponteland, a small town about twelve miles north-west of Newcastle. Their table was in a corner, under an umbrella, with views across the street to a vine-covered pub. It was warm for April – the sun a perfect white disc in a clear blue sky – and Makayla was glad for the shady spot that Cate had chosen. Since coming back to work, although she would never admit it to anyone in the office – sometimes she didn't even admit it to Tyler – she found herself tiring easily, her muscles fatigued, a fuzz behind her eyes. Makayla tried not to think too hard about the fuzz – not after five years of operations, of heartache and pain and doubts about whether she would ever beat the tumour – because thinking too hard about it might bring all those emotions back. It might make her believe that something was wrong again. In her most recent check-up, the specialist told her it was all looking good, but still an echo of fear remained. Perhaps it always would. But one thing she knew for sure was that the warm weather made everything seem worse: she flushed more easily, she moved more slowly, she got sluggish and jaded.

She never thought she'd pine for winters up north.

'So you said the headquarters are close by?'

Cate's voice brought her back into the moment, and Makayla refocused on the woman next to her. The last time she'd seen Cate Clark, she'd still been a little girl; now she was twenty years old, blonde, blue-eyed, slender and tall. She'd developed into a beautiful young woman, and although it had been a long time since Makayla had seen Sue Clark in the flesh, she remembered enough to know that Cate was very much like her mother. She smiled at Cate and said, 'Yeah, Northumbria Police

HQ *is just down the road here. I really appreciate you coming all this way just to see me.'*

'*Oh, it's no problem at all.'*

Makayla could see she was being polite. '*You forget I used to be a detective, Cate,' she said.* '*I know your mum and dad forced you to do this.'*

Cate returned her smile. '*I think they just wanted me to see how you were.'*

'*Us parents are so annoying, aren't we?'*

'*Honestly, I don't mind.'*

Makayla nodded. '*You always were a lovely kid, sweetheart.'*

The two of them talked easily for a while about Martin and Sue, about Georgia, and about what the Clark family had been up to in the almost twelve years since Makayla, Tyler and the boys had moved up to the north-east. After that, Makayla switched to talking about her own life, to how Tyler was now the MD of the accountancy firm he'd been working for, and to how the twins – seventeen now – were doing at school. She glossed over some of it, because it just felt too exhausting to explain, especially the stuff about how she and Tyler had struggled for so long to get Isaiah statemented, and then she did the same when it came to her illness. She felt like she'd spent every day of the last eight years talking about her brain, every day feeling boxed in and terrified by her own mortality, and she couldn't face talking about it again. So, instead, she told Cate that she was doing brilliantly. It was a lie, but it was a lie that shifted the conversation on again to Cate's photography degree.

'*How's that going?' she asked.*

'*Oh, it's great,' Cate replied.* '*I love it.'*

'*You're up here taking pictures of Hadrian's Wall, right?'*

'*That's right, yeah. For the visual part of my dissertation, I'm going to try to do a three-hundred-and-sixty-degree display with a photo of every fifth mile of the wall.'*

'*Wow.'*

'*It's seventy-three miles, so that's only fourteen or fifteen photographs,* but I want each shot to be a different season, with different weather – so it's going to take a bit of luck, I think.'

'That's amazing, Cate.'

'Only if I pull it off.'

'I think you will. You always seemed to be a determined person.'

Cate shrugged self-consciously.

'Did you always want to do photography?' Makayla asked.

'I love words too,' she replied, slowly turning her teacup in its saucer, 'so it was a toss-up between this and maybe taking something like creative writing. But I think I'm probably a better photographer than I am a writer.' She shrugged for a second time – an attractive mix of humility and bashfulness – and Makayla warmed to her some more. It had been so long that she'd forgotten a lot of fine detail about Cate Clark. She still talked to Sue once or twice a year on the phone, and got all the latest news, but it was different to seeing someone in the flesh. Here, now, she remembered the little girl Cate had been – pretty, kind, but always laser-focused on whatever task lay in front of her – and this adult version of her didn't seem to have altered too much. Makayla could still see that determination in Cate, hidden behind the picture-book looks. She could still see that fire.

'So what made you choose Hadrian's Wall?'

'I just remembered coming up here on a school trip three or four years ago, and it had this amazing atmosphere. But actually, it wasn't my first choice. The thing I was really passionate about doing, it just never came together.'

'So what was that going to be?'

'It was where the three-sixty-degree idea started. I wanted to do a room full of portraits – a circle of faces – of women who were victims of unsolved crimes.'

Makayla couldn't hide her surprise. 'Really?'

'Yes. The concept was pretty solid – you'd basically have these victims, all of them facing in at you, surrounding you completely, so that you had no choice but to look at them and hear their story. Not the story

261

of how they died either, or the man that killed them, but the story of who they were before their death — you know, the things they loved doing, the things they were good at, if they had families, all that kind of thing. I'd then have a small biography of them next to each photograph.'

Makayla stared at Cate, unsure what to say, taken aback by the vision, compassion and drive of this twenty-year-old kid. It reminded Makayla of herself at that age, of the reasons she'd been so determined to join the Met, the fight she was burning to have on behalf of victims. But she'd never met anyone else who seemed to share that same absolute desire to try to fix, even in the most perfunctory way, every wrong visited upon the innocent, to give a voice to the victim, even after they may have been nothing but bones and dust.

'I love that,' Makayla said. 'It's incredible, Cate.'

'Thank you. It's a shame that it never came together.'

'Why didn't it?'

'My lecturer absolutely loved the idea but it was just too hard to organize. I put in tons of calls to different people, in the police, the justice system generally, journalists. It all went nowhere. No one was really interested in collaborating with a student, and maybe they didn't believe I would treat the subject seriously, or with the respect it deserved. But I definitely would have done.'

Makayla looked up to see Leon Coetzer approaching them.

'You slacking off, Jennings?' he joked.

He'd been to the supermarket and was now armed with a sandwich, a bag of prawn cocktail crisps and a bottle of Dr Pepper. For as long as Makayla had known Coetzer, he always tried to get out of the office for an hour, to walk and clear his head — and always came back armed with prawn cocktail crisps and Dr Pepper.

She smiled. 'I'm a consultant these days, Coetz.'

'I need to get me some of that consultancy work if this is what it involves.' He glanced at Cate and winked at her.

'Leon Coetzer, this is Cate Clark.'

Cate and Coetzer shook hands.

'Nice to meet you, Cate.'

'I used to order Coetz around a few years ago,' Makayla said to Cate, 'and he's still pining for those days, which is why he secretly sought me out here today.'

Coetzer laughed, and Makayla enjoyed the sound. She enjoyed it more that it was here, in these circumstances, and not Coetz trying to be brave and say the right thing on a hospital ward, or when he used to come and visit her in the evenings. He had checked up on her all the way through the five years of operations and seen some of the pain up close, the tumult of emotions.

The three of them talked politely for a while, mostly about Cate's degree, then Coetzer said he would have to head off, so he shook Cate's hand again and told Makayla he'd see her back at the office. As they watched him go, Cate said, 'He seems nice.'

'Yeah, he's a good guy.'

'You used to be his boss?'

'Before I got sick, yeah.'

They'd both finished their drinks and the conversation felt like it was almost at its end. Makayla reached into her pocket and wriggled out a business card, then pushed it across the table towards Cate. 'If you ever decide to do that thing again.'

'Thing?'

'The thing with the portraits of the victims.'

Cate frowned. 'You'd help me?'

'One hundred per cent.'

'Damn,' Cate said. 'I wish I'd thought of you. Until Mum and Dad suggested I give you a call while I was up here, I kind of forgot you even worked for the police.'

'Well, now you won't forget.'

Makayla tapped the business card. It had her landline at work, as well as an email address. Under her name, it just said CONSULTANT.

'It's definitely something I'd really love to come back to,' Cate said. 'I mean, who knows where things go from here? Maybe I won't be able to make a career out of this and I'll end up working in an office some-where, doing paperwork.' She paused, smiled again, and Makayla smiled back, because she imagined being stuck in an office doing paper-work was probably just about the worst thing a woman of twenty, with ambition and a little naivety, could imagine doing with her life. Cate put the business card into her purse and said, 'Do you get many unsolved crimes here?'

Makayla paused for a moment, tracing her finger through a scatter-ing of spilt sugar. The truth was, no, they didn't get a huge number of unsolved crimes up here. Certainly not unsolved murders.

But she could think of one.

Three women, a single crime scene.

'Put it this way,' she said to Cate, 'if you ever decide to do this por-trait thing — if you ever decide to pick up the phone to me — I know exactly where we can start.'

47

The alarm woke me from a dead sleep at seven.

I got up and checked the newsfeeds, but there were no updates to the stories about the hit-and-run, so I showered, got changed and headed out.

It was a bright morning, the skies unmarked by clouds, but the oppressive heat of London felt a long way away. I made my way back on to the A1 and started arrowing north towards Bamburgh. A couple of miles in, I called Georgia. It was early but she had a young daughter so I figured she was likely to be up. I was supposed to have met her at the pub the previous evening in the hope that Harper would be back in. But on the run, with the police in my wake, there was no way I could have risked it.

I wasn't calling from my usual number so – when she answered – it was with a cautious hello. 'Georgia, it's David.'

'David,' she said, 'hi.'

'Listen, I'm sorry about last night. Something came up.'

'I did try and give you a call.'

I could already tell she was disappointed, because it probably felt to her like the sort of thing the investigators on Cate's case had repeatedly done over the past two and a half years: not delivered on a promise, not followed up, not been there when they said they would. 'So did this Harper guy come to the pub last night?'

'He did, yeah.'

'Did he ask you about the case?'

'Not really, to be honest.'

What did that mean? That he realized Georgia had begun to suspect him? That he thought she may have said something to me? It was a pretty good bet that he was the one who'd broken into my house and stuck me with a needle, and then driven a car into Connor McCaskell – and if he had, then he must have thought I was getting too close to finding out whatever he was hiding. Not that I had a clear view of what that might be.

'I took a picture when he wasn't looking,' Georgia said.

I tuned back in, my pulse quickening.

'You did? That's great work. Can you send it to me now?'

Thirty seconds later, my phone buzzed.

It was taken from the opposite end of the bar, and Georgia had zoomed in, decreasing the quality slightly. But it was decent. He was square on to her, looking at a newspaper laid out on the counter in front of him. He was exactly as Georgia and Michael Calvert's neighbours had described: well built, dark hair, a thick beard that covered his jaw, his neck, and was busy climbing its way up towards his cheekbones. I knew for sure that I didn't recognize him and hadn't come across him until now – and yet something about him set me off, a feeling that I couldn't shake. It was almost like a memory had flared in the dark of my head – but I couldn't imagine why I'd have a memory of a man I'd never met.

I studied his photograph a while longer, even after I'd said goodbye to Georgia, but the answer wouldn't come. Whatever it was about him, it was out of reach for now.

But only for now.

I knew it would come to the surface eventually.

The truth always did.

48

As I drove, I called Alexander Weathers, whose website about local history I'd found the previous night. The section he'd written about the Coast Inn was over thirteen years old, but he'd kept other sections updated and had his number listed, offering his services to local TV and radio stations as an expert on the area. He referenced a couple of appearances on BBC Radio Newcastle, but as his website seemed to be a weird mix of overwritten, incredibly dry historical essays, and – as was the case with his article on the hotel – more salacious stuff that felt like low-rent tabloid journalism, it was hard to say how successful he'd been.

He answered after four rings.

Again, I introduced myself as Bryan Kennedy. As much as possible, I needed to limit the trail I was leaving behind me, needed to try and stay ahead of the police, so I pretended that I was a journalist working on a story about unsolved crimes, including the Dune Murders.

'So what newspaper do you work for?' he asked.

'I'm freelance.'

'I'm still spending my days selling household insurance, but I hope one day I'll be doing what you do. I've always wanted to. History. True crime.' He sighed, as if it were a dream that felt miles off. 'So what did you want to talk about?'

'I was reading about the Coast Inn on your website.'

'The Cursed Inn?'

'Is that what people call it?'

'That's what *I* call it. I mean, storms, murders, suicides, it's all happened there down the years. The fire, though – that was the biggie.'

'What do you mean?'

I knew exactly what he meant. I just wanted him to give me everything he had or had heard – and that was going to be best achieved by pretending I knew nothing.

'Basically, forty-eight hours after the cops found the bodies, the hotel went up in flames. One whole wing burned down. From the outside looking in it probably seemed like a coincidence, but I've done some digging on this, and I'm telling you it's anything but. No way was it accidental. It was only called that because they couldn't find any evidence of arson.'

'But you still think it was?'

'I'm convinced,' Weathers said. 'I think it was Dean King.'

As signs for Bamburgh appeared up ahead, I pulled off the A1 on to a B-road flanked by flat green farmland, and said, 'The owner of the hotel.'

'Correct,' Weathers said.

'Why would King burn down his own hotel?'

'I think the more pertinent question is, why would he burn down that *wing* of the hotel? Do you know what was in that wing?'

'No. What?'

'That was where he stayed. He and, from what I hear, whatever young woman he happened to be dating at the time. That was the wing where the cheaper rooms were. I talked to this lady who used to work for King, cleaning rooms there, and she said that King used to offer those rooms dirt cheap, and would basically let the guests have free rein. You know, booze, drugs, partying, whatever. And the reason he did that was so that he could attract a certain ... *type* of guest.'

'You mean, young women?'

'I mean, young people generally, but women especially. They'd all come up the A1 from Newcastle and Sunderland, from other places up here too, and then just spend the weekend in that wing getting stoned, or hammered, or both. So, you know, maybe the reason there's no evidence of wrongdoing at the hotel, or by King himself, is because – two days after those three women were found on the dunes – that entire wing of the hotel burned down. Maybe any evidence went up in flames.'

I gave myself a moment to think. 'Let's say King *did* kill those women and there *was* some evidence of his guilt at the hotel. I can see why he'd want to dispose of those things but why gut an entire wing to do it? All those rooms, all that money, when he could have just physically removed whatever evidence was there. It's overkill.'

'I still think he's the best fit for this.'

'But did the cops ever find a concrete forensic connection from King to the three women in the dunes? I mean, was there a DNA match, or fingerprints?'

Weathers didn't respond this time.

Obviously the answer was no.

'What did King himself have to say about it?'

'Well, that's the whole point. He didn't.'

I frowned. 'No one spoke to him?'

'No one got a chance to.'

'Why?'

'Because no one could find him,' Weathers said. 'Straight after the fire, he just disappeared.' *Exactly like Jasper Slade did twenty years later in Epping Forest.* Different times, different places, but the same set-up: a roadside hotel in 1992, a youth hostel in 2012; a fire in both; and then an owner who went missing.

'How old was Dean King in 1992?' I asked.

'Late twenties.'

I felt a surge of adrenalin.

What if it was the same man? It would fit: two decades later, at the time of the hostel fire, the man who stole the identity of Jasper Slade was listed as forty-eight.

I saw a layby up ahead and pulled off the road. Telling Weathers to give me a second, I grabbed my phone and put in a search for *Dean King Coast Inn*. There was only one image and it wasn't great quality: King was standing in front of the hotel on the day he'd become the owner in 1988. He appeared dark-haired, tanned, the T-shirt showing off what seemed to be a muscular frame. The Jasper Slade in the driving-licence photo had been overweight, bloated, but I'd wondered if perhaps he'd had Mediterranean heritage: it made me wonder if the tan colour of Dean King's skin wasn't down to the sun at all.

I couldn't be one hundred per cent sure because twenty years of ageing and weight gain, plus the poor quality of the King image, made it hard to be unequivocal. But the arc of the eyebrows were the same; the amount of space between the nose and top lip; the shape of the ears, the one on the right more protrusive than the left.

If they really *were* the same person, that meant that at some point after the fire had ripped through the Coast Inn in 1992, Dean King had ended up in Epping Forest, running the youth hostel there, stealing the identity and life of Jasper Slade, as well as the financial resources that Slade had been left by his father. So was that what Michael Calvert was looking into when he wrote, *What really happened here?*

And what about Cate?

Could she have made the same connections as me, from the fire at the Coast Inn to the fire at the Slade Youth Hostel?

Did she work out that King and Slade – or, at least, the man *purporting* to be Jasper Slade in 2012 – were one and the same?

'They didn't have DNA,' Weathers said, replying to the question I'd asked earlier but which he hadn't answered. He sounded a little stung now. 'But that doesn't mean King didn't do it. And it's not just me that thinks that. The police did too.'

I glanced at the image of Dean King again. 'But in your article you said the cops looked at King and dismissed him.'

'Most of them did, yeah.'

'But not all of them?'

'No. There was one cop who always believed King was the killer.'

Faces: Part 2

10 Years Ago

The hotel was on Gallowgate, opposite St James's Park.

Cate walked the half-mile from Newcastle Central Station, umbrella up. Even though it was the middle of May, the weather was cold, the city shrouded in a cloak of mist and rain, the temperature barely in double figures. When she'd left London that morning, it had been cool but the sun had been out; now, if there was a sun, it felt like it was lost for ever, thick cloud knitted together over the rooftops of the city.

She got to the revolving doors at the front of the hotel, popped her umbrella down and shook off the rain, then passed through to the foyer. It was busy, people in suits milling around, and for a moment she was unsure where to go. But then she spotted a sign to the left of the large reception desk, with an arrow pointing right: POLICE AND FOREN-SICS CONFERENCE.

Cate followed the arrow along a corridor, deeper into the hotel, eventually entering a glass-domed conference hall with a stage at the front. On the stage was a huge projector screen and a lectern. A group of people were up there talking, two of them police officers in uniform, but the rest of the room were already seated in the rows of chairs that had been laid out. Cate grabbed a cup of tea and slipped into an empty seat at the back. There were more uniformed officers in her row, but she knew this conference was likely to have attracted a wide range of people from all sorts of professions.

Her phone buzzed in her pocket.

She took it out and saw that it was Aiden.

Did you arrive okay? x

She smiled to herself.

It was a year since they'd first gone out – and Cate's thirtieth birthday – in a couple of weeks, and the time had flown. She loved him so much, and knew he felt the same about her. Before she'd left for King's Cross this morning, he'd got up early and made her breakfast. And they talked about what they hoped lay ahead of them: Aiden's progression at the design agency he worked for; and Cate's emergence as a respected and sought-after photographer. It was already, quietly, happening for her: pictures she had taken had appeared in advertising campaigns, then on magazine covers, and were now becoming regular fixtures in national newspapers. She told Aiden that the next step for her was to do something really important, a project that actually mattered and made a difference. And that was why she'd got the 6.55 to Newcastle: because she was finally going to do what she'd been thinking about for ten years.

A three-hundred-and-sixty-degree display of faces.

All of them the victims of unsolved crimes.

And she'd travelled three hours on a train this morning to meet the woman she hoped would now make it a reality, a woman she'd last seen over a decade ago.

Around her, the conversations slowly died out as, onstage, the small crowd that had gathered there started to disperse and one of the uniformed officers shuffled to the lectern. He adjusted the microphone. Behind him, Cate read the words that had appeared on the projector screen.

MAKAYLA JENNINGS
RETIRED DETECTIVE INSPECTOR
20 YEARS ON: A RETROSPECTIVE ON
'THE DUNE MURDERS'

The police officer at the lectern started to speak, welcoming everyone to the morning session, and then he gestured to the projector screen and said, 'It's my absolute pleasure to introduce the next speaker. I know her well from her time with us at Northumbria Police, where she joined us from the Met in 1989. She worked in major crime and major incident teams in the north-east for five years, then took a career break, before coming back to us in 2000 in a consultancy role. In 2006, after working alongside Northumbria on some of the region's biggest and most significant investigations, she moved into police training and education.'

The officer glanced down into the front row of the audience and Cate lifted herself out of her seat a little and managed to pick out the back of Makayla's head. 'It's with great pleasure,' the officer said, 'that I get to introduce her today, as she offers a re-evaluation of one of our hardest and most painful murder investigations. Please give a warm welcome to Makayla Jennings.'

A ripple of applause went across the hall as Makayla made her way from her seat to the stage. Cate took her in. She was sixty-two now, looked older and moved a little slower, but she still had the same sense of poise about her, a stature, despite the fact she wasn't physically tall. She ascended the stairs at the side of the stage, and then shook the hand of the officer who'd introduced her. She was dressed in a black skirt and jacket with a pale blouse, and Cate thought how elegant she looked.

She adjusted the microphone. 'Good morning.'

Cate had chosen a seat at the back, close to a speaker, so she took out her phone and set her audio recorder running.

Makayla started talking, her soft London accent audible even after so many years living in the north-east, and gave a potted history of cases she'd worked. Eventually, she wound her way back around to what she'd come here to talk about today.

The Dune Murders.

She began by talking about the disappearance of Lilly Andrews, and then – using a clicker to move the projector screen to the next slide – brought up images of all three victims: Lilly, Felicity Sykes and Maggie Wilkins. It struck Cate how young all three women looked, which they were: Lilly and Felicity were both still teenagers at the time they *vanished. Makayla talked about them as people – about what the families had told her of their interests, personalities – and Cate felt an instant connection: Makayla wasn't talking about the women as elements of an investigation, or as a name on the front page of a file, she was talking about them as human beings who should still have been with us.*

This was what Cate wanted her project to look like, to feel like.

Makayla's voice brought her back to the room.

Cate hadn't called ahead to let Makayla know she was coming. The first reason was that Cate hadn't been certain if, ten years on, Makayla's offer still stood. Would Makayla still be willing to help her? If the answer was no, Cate had figured that she'd stand a better chance of talking Makayla around if they were face-to-face – and, although cynical, she figured her chances doubled if Makayla realized that she'd travelled three hours to be here.

The other reason was that Cate had wanted to see how Makayla talked about the Dune Murders. The idea for the exhibition of faces had been with Cate for a long time, but she'd only seriously started to think about it again over the last six months, as her work began to take off. Only now might she have the reputation and draw to do this thing justice. Because of that, it was only in the last few months that she'd started to properly read about the murders that were the subject of Makayla's talk today. Cate had come here wanting to know how Makayla saw the three women, to listen to how she described them, witness how hard the sense of injustice still burned in her – and it was obvious, even from the short time Makayla had been speaking, that these women mattered to her now as much as they had back in 1992.

Slowly, Makayla started moving on to the major lines of enquiry, and how they'd approached each of them. Although she was no expert, to Cate the evidence seemed thin on the ground from the start: a collection of leads that were already going nowhere a second after they landed. But then Makayla started talking about some additional work she'd done on the case, pro bono and in her own time, a few years after she went into police training and education. 'Of particular interest to me,' she said, 'were the hessian sacks that the women were found in.'

She used the clicker to bring up an image of a hessian sack. In the front row Cate noticed that a couple of the uniformed officers, including the one that had introduced Makayla, were saying something to one another, frowns on their faces.

'This is the make of sack that the women were wrapped in,' she said. 'Between 2008 and 2012, I spent months of my own time looking into these. It was painful and it was tedious and it felt like I was never going to get anywhere. A lot of people become experts in extremely useful subjects – I became an expert in hessian sacks.' A murmur of laughter. But Cate noticed that the men at the front, the cops, weren't laughing. Was something wrong? Makayla didn't seem to notice as she said, 'To cut a long story short, I eventually discovered that the plain unmarked sack you see here uses a very specific and completely bespoke weave.'

She used the clicker again. A photograph appeared of a pinboard with six long rows of pages pinned up. There must have been eighty sheets of A4, and on each sheet of paper were tens of lines, too small to make out, but filling the entire page top to bottom.

'Now one of the advantages of cooperating with small local family-owned companies of the sort that make these hessian sacks is that they tend to work the old-fashioned way. They keep records and don't get rid of them quickly. So this is a record of every customer who bought one of these specific hessian sacks across the entire fifteen-year period that the company made them this way.' She directed the laser at the end of her clicker to the first sheet of A4 on the pinboard. 'This is November 1986. And this' – she directed the laser to the last sheet on the pinboard – 'is July 2001.'

Makayla paused for effect and looked out at the audience. This time she noticed the cops talking in the front row. Something passed across her face, as if she'd maybe been expecting it. And there was something else in her expression too.

Was it defiance?

'Basically,' Makayla went on, 'it took me almost five years of working this in my spare time, of driving all over the place, of being on the phone to textile experts at universities in every corner of the country, of having to collate information I barely even understood, before I finally came full circle and found the answer I sought. And it was right here in the north-east the whole time. Because it turns out that the only place that our killer could have got those particular hessian sacks was from a company just up the road from here, in Alnwick.'

Makayla used the clicker.

On the projector screen, four faces appeared. Three had been partly covered by a black rectangle, presumably to protect their identity, and there were no names either. 'I started off with over six thousand names and now, after almost five years, I've whittled it down to four.' Makayla had one hand on the lectern, her body turned towards the screen. One of the cops was now getting up and heading for the exit, a mobile phone in his hand. 'We never interviewed any of these men at the time. Three of them were never on our radar at all, despite them having criminal records which included crimes that could be relevant. But as best as I've been able to ascertain over the past few months, they all had alibis for the dates on which the women went missing, anyway.' She paused, using the laser again. She waved it across the face of the fourth man. He was in his late twenties, with a mane of thick hair and tanned skin. His was the only face that hadn't been covered up. 'This man has no criminal record.'

Makayla pushed her thumb to the clicker again.

A bigger photograph of the same man appeared.

'And two days after we found the three women, this happened.'

Another click.

Another picture.

On the projector screen was an image of a raging fire. It was tearing through what looked like a hotel, the roof half collapsed, the walls of the first floor crumbling. Windows had blown out. Doors had warped and twisted. The place was an inferno.

'This is the Coast Inn on the A1,' Makayla said. 'And this man' – another click and the same photograph appeared – 'was the owner, Dean King. Unlike the others, we looked at him back in 1992. Well, I did. I never liked the timing of the fire versus the discovery of the women, but with no evidence connecting King to the crimes, despite – in my opinion – him acting extremely suspiciously by disappearing after the fire, my commanding officer told me to drop it.'

Another click.

The pinboards full of paper appeared again.

At the lectern, Makayla turned and directed her laser pointer to one of the pages about a fifth of the way along. 'In November 1991, five months before we found those three women in the dunes, Dean King bought ten hessian sacks from the company in Alnwick. It's right there in black and white.'

She looked out at the audience again.

And then at the cops still left in the front row.

'Twenty years ago, I was told Dean King wasn't worth pursuing,' she said. 'But today, with this new evidence, we mustn't make that same mistake again . . .'

49

'I was in the audience that day,' Weathers said.

Suddenly, all of this had become much more than just a blogger throwing around accusations built on vague whispers. If Weathers was right – if Makayla Jennings had stood on that stage ten years ago and announced that Dean King had purchased those hessian sacks – it tilted the entire axis of the case. But why was this the first time I was hearing about it? Why hadn't it ever come up in a Google search for the Coast Inn or Dean King?

'Did the police reopen the case?' I asked.

'No.'

'Why not?'

'From what I heard there were a few reasons.'

'Such as?'

'Well, I think mainly they were worried about optics.'

Immediately, I understood. Everyone had bypassed the hessian-sack angle the first time – in fact, no one had even looked into it. Then, twenty years later, a retired cop, who'd refused to let unanswered questions lay dormant, had spent almost five years of her own time connecting the dots back to a suspect she'd liked the look of – and been told to stop looking into – two decades before. The optics, for Northumbria Police, were awful. Whatever happened, even if it ended up with a conviction, there were going to be big questions with difficult answers about why it had taken so long for the force to get to the truth. Most likely, heads were going to roll at the top.

'And no one in the media picked up on any of this? Not a single newspaper or journalist was there that day? This should have been all over the news, surely?'

'There were a few local journalists there but anyone who attended that conference had completed an NDA at sign-up. If you bothered to read the small print – which I did – it said it was to do with the conference covering "sensitive material" on "active investigations". The upshot was that if you wanted to print something, or put something on TV, you had to get the written permission of Northumbria Police. Do anything without their say-so and you were liable for prosecution. It's unusual but, from what I've been able to find out, not unprecedented. I think the difference is that in most other examples of similar arrangements at similar events, approval of media requests seems commonplace and relatively straightforward.'

'But not this time?'

'No. It's why you can't find anything online about Jennings's talk.'

'Because Northumbria never agreed to any requests.'

'Exactly.'

'So why even let her stand up there in the first place?'

'Because, basically, I don't think they had a clue about how much work she'd actually done and how far forward she'd pushed the case. I spoke to her after the conference and it sounded like Northumbria Police didn't know anything about the stuff with the hessian sacks. They had no idea she'd been working the case – on the quiet – for so long. They invited her to do a segment at the conference, and she told them she wanted to talk about the Dune Murders, and I think they expected her to just stand up there and recount everything that happened in 1992. I don't know, maybe they were hoping it would be some kind of PR exercise – Jennings talking about how hard the force worked the investigation back in the day, how many leads they chased down, and how the girls hadn't ever been forgotten, even twenty years on. I mean, there are still quite a lot of people locally who bear a grudge against the police for not solving those murders. Maybe they thought Jennings could massage it all somehow.'

'And afterwards?'

'I spoke to her again about six months later.'

'In person?'

'No. I emailed her and she responded.'

'What did she say?'

'Not much. I think she was being deliberately cautious. I mean, I could be speculating here, but it sounded to me, from what she *did* say, like she faced immediate resistance after the talk from people high up in the force. They didn't like the fact that she'd gone rogue, didn't like her digging everything up again, and they said the hessian-sack stuff was circumstantial, which I suppose it was. That's basically what they briefed – off the record – to journalists who came asking afterwards.'

'Her own bosses briefed *against* her after the conference?'

'I don't know. I just heard a few things and Jennings seemed to hint at it too. Northumbria didn't sign off on any media requests as far as I know – hence no stories – but, from what I can work out, they had plenty of off-the-record conversations with journalists. At best, they said Jennings's theories didn't represent the findings of the official investigation. At worst, they outright discredited her entire talk.'

'That's crazy. Why wouldn't they want to find King?'

'I don't think it was necessarily to do with King; I think it was more to do with how Jennings dropped everything on them out of the blue and, perhaps more likely, the stage all that stuff was at.'

'The stage it was at? What does that mean?'

'Before she did that talk, the families of those three women hadn't moved on exactly – but they'd made some sort of peace with the girls' deaths after twenty years. Like I said, some locals – including what's left of those families – are still annoyed that the police never found the killer, but a lot of that generation are old, or they're dead, and the families aren't fighting every day for answers any more. For the vast majority of people that ship has long since sailed. So maybe it would have been different if Jennings had prints for King, or even better a DNA match – but all she had were those hessian sacks. And I think the force basically shut her down because they didn't want the full glare of the media focused on a suspect who had no forensic connection to the victims, was dismissed as irrelevant first time around, and who they would probably have to sink mountains of money and manpower into even *finding* – let alone interviewing and charging – because he'd been in the wind for twenty years by then. For them I guess it was just a monumental lose–lose. The media would tear them apart again, just like they had in 1992, if they came up with nothing for a second time.'

'So the case just got buried?'

'Yes. When I emailed her and she sent me that message, it basically sounded like the entire thing was back in cold storage.'

I took in the new information, trying to process it, and wondered if there was anyone else I could use to help me try and find Dean King. And then I had a thought. 'You told me earlier that King liked hanging around with young women, but did he ever have a serious relationship?'

'Oh, I'm sure he must have.'

'Any you know about?'

'From what I heard he was with a woman called Mariet at

the time of the fire. The cleaner from the hotel told me Mariet was more serious than most of the others.'

'You got a second name?'

'No. Just Mariet.'

'Any idea what happened to her?'

'No,' he said, 'no clue. Given his history, it's not out of the question that he might have killed her too.'

The name was unusual, so I quickly went to my phone and googled her in relation to King. I got nothing.

'If you want to read more about the hotel side of things, try the City Library,' Weathers said.

'In Newcastle?'

'Yeah. The fire coverage that the *Northumberland Star* did is all still on microfiche. If you dig around in there, you'll find a few old photographs of King in those articles that you won't find anywhere else.'

'Can't I access those articles online?'

'No, only by physically going to the library.'

'Okay, I appreciate the tip.'

'Sure. Do you think you'll try and speak to Jennings?'

'I think it's probably a bit late for that.'

'Yeah, I heard she has dementia.'

I started up the car again.

'Maybe her son, then,' Weathers said.

'Her son?'

'Joshua. Did you know he ended up marrying the brother of Lilly Andrews?'

I frowned. 'As in, *the* Lilly Andrews?'

'Yeah,' Weathers said. 'The two of them run a café in Bamburgh.'

I looked at my notebook and went back all the way to the genesis of the search, to the details I'd written down about the receipt I'd found in Cate's records.

'Do you mean the Castle View Café?' I asked.

'Yeah, that's the one.'

I thanked Weathers and killed the call, then pulled out of the layby, following the winding B-road in the direction of the sea. My mind was going, buzzing, trying to fit all the pieces together. I wondered if there was any value in trying to see Makayla Jennings after all. I'd basically written it off after Sue had insinuated that Jennings's battle with dementia was almost at an end, so she was unlikely to be capable of remembering anything. But even if Jennings herself was a dead end, her son was still in play. The fact that he was married to the brother of Lilly Andrews was interesting too. How did the son of the SIO on the Dune Murders end up with the brother of the first victim?

And then my thoughts circled back around to Cate.

Was it possible she might have found out some of the details about Jennings's talk at that conference? Was it even possible that she might have been in the audience that day? She had an established relationship with Jennings, so reading about – or even actively being at – the conference that day was a definite possibility.

And then my phone burst into life.

It was Ewan Tasker's burner again.

'Task. Is everything okay?'

'You haven't seen the news yet, have you?' A pause. 'You're all over it.'

50

After getting off the phone to Tasker, I pulled in and went through my newsfeeds.

Thirty-six hours after my car first struck Connor McCaskell, the cops had now done what I'd expected them to do: they'd named me as the person they were seeking 'in connection with the hit-and-run of a newspaper journalist'. That revelation didn't just prep members of the public to be on the lookout for me; it made my story instantly attractive to other journalists. I knew this was coming but it didn't make it less disquieting. With the media and public on high alert, the pressure on me was cranked up even more.

I'd always known my hire car would put me on the map, especially once the cops had access to my financial records, and now they would use automatic number-plate recognition to trace my direction of travel. Trying to coordinate a response with Northumbria Police was going to take the Met a little time, but it wouldn't be long before they were working together, a joint task force charged with the job of tracking down a suspect.

Skim-reading some of the news stories, I saw knowledge gaps were being filled with barely concealed speculation: the police couldn't find me, so I must have been on the run – and if I was on the run, I was guilty. I didn't like that – not least because my daughter would be seeing these lies; maybe not believing them but trying to make sense of them all the same. There was absolutely nothing I could do about that for the time being, because I couldn't contact her and didn't want her involved, and for a second I saw the irony in my situation. Only minutes ago I'd been thinking that Dean King had vanished because he'd committed three murders.

A fugitive killer who had disappeared because he'd done it.

Now that was what people were thinking about me.

I arrived in Bamburgh twenty minutes later.

It was another two weeks before the school holidays started, but the town was already heaving with tourists. I came in from the west, right through the centre, the castle ahead of me the whole time, perched like a moored ship on an emerald beach.

Winding around to the right, I followed the road to a car park and managed to find one of the last spaces. As I switched off the engine, I watched some French kids filing off a bus, directed by their teacher, and wondered if the crowds were a help or a hindrance. The more people there were, the more chance there was that someone might identify me. But the more people there were, the more I could try and blend in. It was harder to be anonymous in a place when no one was around.

I grabbed a ticket for the car and headed into the town. The main street was picturesque, flowers everywhere, the whole thing built on a gradual slope, with period buildings on either side and a tree-dotted green in the middle. I didn't know exactly where the café was but most of the places serving food seemed to be on the left, so I followed the path up until I came to some tables set on a flagstone patio.

The entrance was in a little side street.

Above the door was a sign saying CASTLE VIEW CAFÉ.

Just below that was another one with PROPRIETORS: LIAM ANDREWS AND JOSHUA JENNINGS on it. And, finally, in an adjacent window was a wooden heart hanging from a nail, twisting gently in the light wind escaping inside.

As it twisted, I saw there was an inscription on it.

LILLY ANDREWS

GONE BUT NEVER FORGOTTEN

51

Inside, it was small but quaint, a quintessentially English café that the tourists were absolutely lapping up. At the back, a guy in his late forties – tall and sinewy, his cheeks flushed red – was behind a counter making hot drinks.

I weaved between the tables. He looked up, gave me a smile, and said, 'I'll be with you in a second, sir.'

As I waited, I spotted a series of photos on a wall to the left of me.

A few of them showed the Castle View Café, presumably before it had been taken over: a bare, empty room, no carpet, stray wires dangling from light fixtures.

But most of the others were of people.

Two men – including the one behind the counter – either side of a well-known comedian from the north-east. The man behind the counter had to be Liam Andrews. There was another photo of a much younger version of him with his arm around the shoulder of a teenaged girl I recognized as Lilly. The other man was Joshua Jennings, who I recognized from a second picture of him with his parents and his brother. And there was another of Joshua with Makayla Jennings taken recently, her hair grey, her eyes unfocused. As I looked at her, I thought of all the knowledge that was lost to her now, the intricacies of the case she'd come to know so well, and the things that would have mattered to her even more than her work – her boys, her husband, her family life.

'Are you okay there, sir?' Liam Andrews had appeared at my shoulder. 'We're full right now but I can offer you takeaway.'

'It's okay,' I said. 'I'm actually here to talk to you.'

He frowned. 'Me?'

'I'm trying to find out what happened to your sister.'

He looked completely thrown.

'Your sister, Lilly. I'm trying to find out what –'

'I heard you. What are you, a journalist?'

'No.' I handed him a card. 'I find missing people.'

I'd been wavering over whether to continue using the Kennedy alias, but now I was here, looking at these photographs, it didn't feel right any more. As he glanced at the card, at my name on it, I waited for a spark of recognition, a realization that I was the person being sought in connection with the hit-and-run on the news. But there was nothing at all in his face. He didn't know who I was.

'I'm David,' I said, holding out a hand to him.

'Liam,' he replied. 'I don't understand why you're here.'

'I'm trying to find a couple called Cate and Aiden Gascoigne.' I paused, seeing if either of those names, particularly Cate's, meant anything to him, but there was no shift in his expression. 'I believe – before she disappeared – that Cate had started to take an interest in what happened to Lilly and the other two women.'

'An interest?'

'I think she might have been writing a book about them.'

This time there was a spark in his eyes.

'Does that ring a bell with you?'

'Yes, it does.' He shook his head again, like he was trying to loosen something, an old memory clinging on like a limpet. 'I remember Cate now.'

'She came in here, I think.'

'Yes.'

I got out a picture of her. 'Was this her?'

He took the photograph from me and then started

nodding. 'That's her. This was a good while ago, though. I couldn't honestly tell you how long ago it was.'

'It would have been just over two and a half years back.'

I could see his mind still ticking over. 'Actually, I remember Josh – that's my husband – telling me she disappeared. He saw something about it online, I think. He knew the family.'

'He did, yeah.'

I looked around the café; at least two tables were waiting on their bills, and at the door there was a queue of five or six people. I wanted to talk to Liam, but I didn't want to do it while he was trying to juggle table service.

'Is there anyone else who can take over from you?' I asked.

'No. I've only got one other person out back helping with breakfasts.'

I leaned a little, looking through a partly open door to a small kitchen, but there was no sign of Joshua Jennings – just a lady in her sixties busy buttering toast.

'What time do you close?'

'Not until five.'

It wasn't even ten o'clock. I couldn't afford to wait until closing time. That would be seven lost hours – and seven hours closer to the police locating me.

'Can I quickly ask you a couple of things?'

'It will have to be quick,' he said, looking around the café.

'Do you remember anything specific Cate asked when she came in?'

He glanced at her photograph again, his eyes working over her face. 'No, not really. I mean, it was a long time ago. I definitely remember that the three of us sat out there, though' – he gestured to the front – 'and she asked questions about what happened.' He looked up at me from the photograph again.

About what happened. It was only three words – but all of them carried the torment of thirty years of unanswered questions.

'I really am going to have to go,' Liam said.

'Okay, I understand. Just one final thing.'

He looked out at the café, then back to me, then to the wall of photographs he and Joshua had mounted.

'I'm assuming you and Joshua met through Makayla?'

'Right. Makayla used to come up here to see my parents from time to time to update us on the case. That went on for years. Anyway, she introduced Josh to me, we got talking and, well . . .' He smiled; these memories were a little better.

'Did Makayla ever mention a Dean King to you?'

'Uh, excuse me,' a pissed-off voice said behind us.

'Sorry, sir,' Liam replied, then moved behind the counter again, looking for the guy's bill. I followed Liam over and, as he was totting everything up, he said, 'I really am going to have to get back to it. But, yes, Dean King was the one Makayla was convinced had done it.'

'Did Makayla or Cate ever mention the name Jasper Slade to you?'

'No.'

'What about the name Harper?'

'No, I don't think so. With Makayla, it was Dean King or nothing. I think she felt haunted by it.' He paused, looking up at me. 'I think we all did. Lilly, Felicity, Maggie – I mean, it's not right, is it? It's not right that it's been thirty years and they've had no justice. It's not right that Dean King got away with it.' Liam stopped a second time, his eyes shimmering. 'If Dean King's dead, I hope he's burning in hell.'

Liam went across to deliver the bill, and collected up some plates, bringing all of them back to a sink behind the counter. I watched him for a moment, the grief and anger of those last few sentences lingering. As he returned to where I was, he said, 'That really is going to have to be it. I'm rushed off my feet here.'

I nodded. 'Is Joshua around today?'

Something passed across Liam's face like a shadow.

'He and his brother are kind of out of action,' he said, his gaze straying to the wall of portraits. And then I realized which photograph he'd landed on.

'Is it because of their mum?' I asked.

He looked at me, not sure how I'd made the leap.

'Yes,' he replied quietly. 'Makayla died yesterday.'

Faces: Part 3

10 Years Ago

Makayla's talk lasted forty-five minutes and then she started taking questions from the audience. The first few were from serving police officers, more interested in her history as a detective. Cate found herself drifting, checking her phone, the discussion descending into a bland conversation about rules and regulations and how they were interpreted – or even bent – in the pursuit of a suspect. Then a man – who barely looked in his twenties – put his hand up and someone brought a microphone over to him.

'Hi,' he said, the microphone feeding back. 'My name's Alexander Weathers. I'm a freelance journalist.' The man paused, swallowed, and Cate was unsure if that was simply because he was nervous, or because his line about being a journalist was an inflation of the facts, which – like half-truths often did – got stuck in his throat.

Onstage, Makayla smiled and nodded.

'I was just wondering,' Weathers went on, 'what about DNA? I mean, I know when the women were found it was still in its infancy, but could you now go back and use DNA to find Dean King? Do you have a way to extract King's DNA?'

Makayla nodded again. 'DNA is obviously an avenue we explored at the time, but there are a couple of issues specific to this case. One is that the women were out on those dunes for at least two months – in the case of Maggie and Felicity even more. The weather was appalling during that period, and decomp was advanced; the bodies had been picked at by animals . . .' She faded out, swallowed, and again Cate could see how deep this case ran for Makayla. 'We extracted DNA samples from the girls' bodies but any foreign DNA – especially anything on them that might have belonged to the killer – was less successful. My colleague, Leon Coetzer, went back three years later, about twelve months after I'd had to go out on long-term sickness, and had a forensic team swab absolutely everything. I literally mean everything. I spoke to Coetz most days and they were unbelievably exhaustive.' Another pause, and it was obvious what was coming. 'Anyway, you can probably guess the rest. Even though we worked that thing hard, even though we swabbed everything we possibly could, we didn't get a match for any potential suspect on the national database.'

A hush fell across the auditorium. It seemed like the only significant thing connecting Dean King to the crime was his purchase of a set of hessian sacks. And then the silence was shattered by a mobile phone.

Everyone looked around.

Cate did as well.

But then she felt the buzzing against her leg, the vibration in her pocket, and realized it was her. She tried to be casual about it – didn't want to be the one person who'd forgotten to turn their phone off – and slowly reached to her trouser leg. Through her jeans, she found the edge of the phone and killed the call.

'Any more questions?' Makayla said from the stage.

As people started putting their hands up again, Cate wriggled the phone out of her pocket and checked who had called. It was Mum. She switched the phone to vibration only and then listened as someone in the audience asked about training.

A text buzzed through.

Cate saw her mum's name pop up.

Flipping open the phone, she went to Messages.

CATE! PLEASE ANSWER YOUR PHONE!

Feeling a flutter of alarm, Cate grabbed her coat and ducked out of the hall, heading back to reception while dialling her mum's number.

Her mum answered after three rings. 'Cate?'

'What's going on, Mum?'

'Where are you?'

'I'm in Newcastle,' Cate said. 'I'm on a work thing.'

She heard her mum make a sound, somewhere between a sigh and a cry for help. This time the alarm Cate felt wasn't just a passing flutter, it was a tidal wave.

'What's happened?' she said.

On the other end of the line, she could hear sobbing.

'Mum? What's wrong?'

'It's your dad. He's had a heart attack.'

Makayla exited the stage twelve minutes after Cate had left the hotel, running for a train that would take her back to London – and to the hospital Martin Clark was in, fighting for his life. As Makayla made her way to the rear of the hall, where coffee was being served, she had no idea that Cate Clark had been watching her for most of her talk – even that she had been in the room at all – and was completely oblivious to what the Clark family were going through.

Instead, after asking for a coffee, she got into a conversation with the journalist in the crowd who'd asked about DNA. He talked to her about the NDA they'd all had to sign and whether she might be able to help him get approval from the force so he could write something, and Makayla said that was a question he'd have to take up with Northumbria Police directly. She then drifted from one handshake to the next, people telling her how interesting the talk had been, and by the end of it Makayla just wanted some time to herself. She felt drained, mentally and physically exhausted from thinking about the three women she'd failed to bring justice to. And she knew, at some point, her old bosses at the force were going to find her and demand to know why she dropped the hessian-sack stuff on them out of the blue onstage – and the thought of that exhausted her even more. She'd steeled herself already for that fight, and was going to tell them that it felt like – until now – they'd seemed too content to leave the entire case in a filing cabinet, and that she'd simply been attempting to get this thing going again. But she knew that wouldn't douse their rage. She'd dropped this on them as a way to shock them into action – but whether it worked, or it didn't, they were still going to be angry.

Eventually, she managed to find a quiet corridor, away from anyone else, and after finding a seat she started going through her phone. There were tons of work emails, all of which could wait, so she focused on the texts she'd got from Tyler – asking her how the talk had gone – and then one from Josh.

Is it okay if we get there for 7 tonight, Mum? x

She'd forgotten that Josh and Liam were supposed to be coming for dinner, and while she remembered inviting Isaiah too, she couldn't remember if Zi had confirmed whether he would be there or not. She started scrolling back through her last conversation with Zi, and then the one before that, and the one before that, but she couldn't find a reply where he actually said he would be there. That didn't mean he wouldn't be. Sometimes – often, in fact – he would just turn up. Makayla never minded. She loved her sons with everything she had – and she knew every part of them, every characteristic, Zi especially. His social anxiety had got even worse as he'd got older, and he'd become more focused than ever on his computer coding. He'd been okay for a while when Josh had split with his first boyfriend – would come to the house more, have dinners as a four with Makayla, Tyler and Josh – but since his brother had met Liam, Zi had retreated into his shell. It wasn't Liam, because he was lovely; it was that Zi had become disordered by the change.

Makayla fired off a text to Zi, not necessarily expecting a reply – and then her mind wandered back to Liam.

He really was a nice guy. He made Josh so happy, and that was all Makayla wanted. But sometimes, much as she hated herself for thinking it, she found it hard to be around him. There were too many echoes in his face of Lilly, too many reminders of the way Makayla had failed his sister and their parents. Liam never made her uncomfortable, never brought up the subject of his sister unless Makayla brought it up first, but the spectre was there the whole time.

Why couldn't she find Dean King?

'That was a hell of a speech.'

Makayla looked up.

A man in his mid-forties was standing over her, smiling, a scattering of grey stubble on his face, his belly poking out between the lines of a smart navy-blue suit jacket. 'I imagine you've set the cat among the pigeons there,' the man said with a laugh.

When Makayla didn't respond, his smile gradually faded and a frown started to form, a look of concern.

Tilting his head slightly, he said, 'Are you okay?' He was examining her, the look almost intimate, as if they knew each other. Makayla tried to work out if she recognized him or had met him before.

'I'm fine,' she said.

A flitter in the man's face.

And then, barely a second later, it was like a torch cutting through the dark, the realization of who he was crashing against her. A tremble passed through her throat, all the way into her mouth, and emerged as the small, frightened sound of an animal.

'Are you okay, Mak?' Leon Coetzer asked.

Except she couldn't reply.

She'd forgotten the face of a man she'd known for twenty-one years, and now the fear was like a hand on her throat. Because this had happened before, not as bad as this, not as stark, but over the last few months she'd been forgetting details that she never should have. Names of people she knew. What she'd driven to the shops for. Places she needed to be. It was another reason why she'd done this talk: she needed to get the information out there before she started forgetting the women too. Worse, she knew it wasn't the tumour this time. She felt certain of that.

It was something far worse.

Something she couldn't bear to even name.

She was losing the tether that not only connected her to the family she loved, to her boys, to her husband, but to the women she still, even twenty years on, needed to save. She was losing the very things that had always made her such a good cop.

Her speed of thought. Her logic.

Her memory.

52

The dunes unfurled in a vague crescent along the coast between Bamburgh and Holy Island. It was why they'd gained the nickname 'The Hook', their shape an arc of white sand and grass sweeping inwards and then outwards from Bamburgh's northern tip. From the air it probably didn't seem like much – just a quarter of a mile in width – but from the ground, as I arrived from the south, it was a labyrinth.

Sandy trails weaved in and out of tall beach grass, snaking back and forth as if they were patterns carved by hand. The grass itself swayed and bobbed, an almost perpetual dance in this part of the world, where the breeze from the North Sea rarely ceased. In places the greenery was as opaque as concrete, thick clumps of it gathered in dense knots. It was easy to see how the three women had remained hidden for so long.

I got out of the car and headed along the nearest trail I could find. It undulated immediately, dropping away into a cleft full of beach grass, before climbing steeply back up to a mound. It went on like that, up and down, left and right, and the longer I walked, the more the wind seemed to pick up. Grey cloud scudded across the sky, swallowing the sunlight, and all of a sudden it could have been a freezing cold morning at the tail end of April, just like that morning thirty years ago.

I reached the middle section of the dunes about fifteen minutes later, unsure now why I'd come all this way out or what I'd expected to find here. The topography had altered so much over the last three decades – grass receding in one place before growing in another, sand remoulded by thirty winters and hundreds of gales – that, even though it felt like I'd committed to memory every photograph from 28 April 1992, it still felt like a place I didn't recognize. It took me a long time to even find the area in which Lilly Andrews had lain for so long. I walked on another quarter of a mile but couldn't identify the narrow tangle of greenery where both Maggie Wilkins and Felicity Sykes had been left only six feet apart. I stood there, my skin rinsed pink from the wind, and thought of Makayla Jennings. I imagined her here, in these dunes, thirty years ago, and then her dying – with her sons beside her – only a day ago.

There was something wrong about all of this, about me not being able to find or recognize the final resting places of Lilly, Maggie and Felicity, about three women being taken so young, so violently. I hated the idea that the man who'd killed them had got away with it. I hated the idea that, of all the endings that Makayla Jennings could have had, it was this one: a finale where she lost every memory she'd ever formed of the women, and died without ever having tracked down the man responsible. I barely knew anything about her, and would never get to know her now, but that didn't stop me feeling a strange kind of connection to her.

As it started to spit with rain, I went back to the car and, by the time I left the dunes and hit the sand-dusted edges of the car park, it had turned into something heavier, clouds gnarled, the rain whipped up by the wind. I hurried across the last few yards, sliding in at the wheel, and thought about whether I could risk calling in at the Coast Inn on the way down to the library in Newcastle. Had the cops found out I'd stayed there the night before? Had they been in touch with the hotel to tell them to be on the lookout for me? I needed to try and find out. I wasn't going to spend another night there but I'd left behind clothes and other things I needed to pick up.

I grabbed my phone and called reception.

'Good afternoon, this is the Coast Inn.' I recognized the voice instantly. It was the guy who'd been working the late shift the previous night.

'Hi, this is Bryan Kennedy. I'm in Room 47. I was just –'

'Oh, Mr Kennedy, hi. I've actually been trying to get in contact with you, but I haven't been able to get through on the number you provided.' He paused for a second and I heard a faint tapping, like fingers on a keyboard. 'I wanted to let you know that there's been a problem in your room. Unfortunately, one of the cleaners informed us this morning that there's a leak in there.'

I frowned. 'A leak?'

'Yes, sir.'

I felt myself tense. *This doesn't feel right.*

'Um, we'd really like it if you could come back now, just so we can sort out this problem. We, of course, will fully reimburse you for the cost of any damage to your belongings –'

I hung up.

I'd been able to hear something else in the background of the call. It was faint, only audible between the gaps in the receptionist's sentences – but it had been there: static from a radio.

He was being told what to say.

Which meant the police hadn't just been in touch with the hotel.

They were already there.

53

I switched off my phone, took out the SIM card and the battery, and put all three in the glove compartment of the car.

Crouching at the tail end of the vehicle, I found a puddle, scooped up a fistful of mud and smeared it across the number plate. I did the same on the front one too, disguising letters and digits enough that it wouldn't look deliberate but would make it hard to read the registration from more than a couple of feet away.

By the time I was back in front of the wheel, I was soaked through, but the rain was easing off. I figured the mist that had started to settle in its place could give me a small advantage, as visibility was reducing all the time. But whatever tiny win I could find didn't make up for the bigger picture: I was on the run, the cops were further ahead than I thought they'd be, and I couldn't go back to the hotel. I couldn't collect my clothes or my belongings. All I had was my laptop and what I was dressed in.

And all I could do was keep moving.

I got to Newcastle in under an hour.

Parking at the Sage in Gateshead, I crossed the Tyne on the Swing Bridge, then hurried up Sandhill, then Side, then Dean Street. At the bottom of Dean Street, I paused for a moment as the rain started to fall again, spattering off my coat and filling the gutters. Here, on a small roundabout under the shadow of a looming railway arch, was a gift shop.

In 1992, it had been T-Bridge Records.

The place Lilly Andrews had worked.

I pushed on, in the direction of the City Library. On the way, I grabbed a sandwich and a bottle of water and wolfed them down, and by the time I was done the glass-and-grey-brick library building had come into view.

I headed through the main doors.

At the front desk, a woman greeted me with a smile. 'This weather,' she said, looking at my coat and hair. 'Can I help you with something?'

I explained what I needed.

'Our newspaper archive is all on computer,' she said, and then came out from behind the desk and walked me over to a bank of PCs, most of which were in use. '*Unless*,' she added, 'the articles that you're after were published prior to 1995.'

'They were,' I said.

'In that case we'll have to do this the old-fashioned way.'

She led me to a separate part of the library, talking about the weather again as she did. I made polite conversation but was concentrating more on what was around me. The immediate risks to me weren't high here, but it didn't mean I was going to be safe for long. On one of the far walls a television was playing BBC News 24 on mute.

Pretty soon my face would be on it.

We arrived in a smaller area, surrounded on three sides by floor-to-ceiling bookshelves. Against the fourth wall was a table with two microfiche readers.

Neither were occupied.

'Do you know how to use one of these?' the woman asked.

'I do, yeah.'

'Great.' Another smile. 'Now what can I get you?'

'I'm looking for an issue of the *Northumberland Star* from the 30th of April 1992, and then maybe every issue available over the week that followed.'

'A week's worth of *Star*'s?'

'Correct.'

'I'll see what I can find.'

I thanked her and took a seat, my eyes drifting back to the television. Tapping out a nervous beat on the table, I watched one story finish, then another one begin. Neither were about me, but I couldn't see the news ticker at the bottom of the screen from where I was, so felt no sense of relief. For a minute I wondered whether to call Martin and Sue, or maybe Georgia – maybe my daughter Annabel too – and try to explain my side of it all, but I couldn't figure out if it would make it better or worse and soon the woman had returned. In her arms were two boxes full of white-paper sleeves. She set them down on the table and said, 'It was just easier to bring you across the whole of April and May 1992.'

'I really appreciate this.'

I watched her go, then switched my attention to the box marked *April*, flicking through until I got to a tab marked *30/04*. I took out the film, flipped up the glass lid under the reader, and slid it on to the bed. Snapping the lid back in place and pushing it forward, under the microscope, I started using the dial on the reader to navigate the film. It was the entire issue of the *Northumberland Star* from that day.

The murders were on the front page.

I briefly read the article, just to double-check that there wasn't any information I didn't have, and then moved on to 1 May. Now the fire at the Coast Inn had made it on to the front page too. It was a column on the right rather than the main story, the Dune Murders still the central focus. I magnified the hotel story.

The headline was LOCAL HOTEL DESTROYED IN FIRE.

Under that was a subhead: *Owner may have been inside.*

That wasn't true, otherwise they would have found a

body, but the assumption had been a solid one in the first twenty-four hours: Dean King couldn't be located, so it stood to reason that he was a victim of the fire. I read the story from start to finish, but there was nothing I didn't already know.

I moved on to 2 May.

The headline had been revised down from the entire hotel being destroyed to just a wing, but – after confirmation no body had been found among the debris – now the subhead was more accusatory: *Where is the owner?* The story was still playing second fiddle to the Dune Murders, because the murders were probably the worst crime the county of Northumberland had seen for as long as anyone could remember. But there was also more detail on the damage done, a little on King, and some quotes from a source in the local fire department who claimed that it may have been arson. I knew that the fire had been ruled an accident, but the arson angle made it a much juicier read in these early days.

I switched films to the 3rd.

There were some vague hints about how Northumbria Police might have been looking at the timing of the fire in relation to the discovery of the three women, but it was half-hearted and never really followed up on, which suggested that the journalist who'd written the piece had been unable to corroborate it. Under that was a photograph of Dean King, different to the single blurry Google image I'd found of him. It was better quality for a start, clearer, his thick black hair swept back from his tanned face, his eyes dark, his body lean. He was a strong, tall, good-looking guy in his late twenties.

In the picture he was smiling, pointing to a sign next to the A1 that had COAST INN written on it. I made a note of the page and date in order to come back to it – and also to get the librarian to print a copy of his picture for me – then grabbed my laptop, went to my email and tapped on the scan of Jasper Slade's driving licence. I zoomed in on Slade's picture, holding it up next to the monitor. For the first time I had a high-quality shot of King to match the one I had of Slade.

It told me exactly what I'd suspected.

He'd aged, of course, but had also grown bigger, his face bloated, his body too, the combination of the two hiding the echo of Dean King that existed beneath. I wondered if the weight gain had been a deliberate act, camouflage he'd pulled on.

Either way, it was definitely him.

Dean King and the Jasper Slade of 2012 were the same man.

I pushed on, switching films to 4 May. The stories were shorter now and, on the 5th, the fire was sharing space with a story about a family who had taken a boat out into the North Sea and drowned. By the 6th, the *Star* had stopped talking about the hotel fire at all. I loaded in the 7, 8 and 9 May, but the only other story I found on the fire was on the 10th. Northumbria Fire and Rescue said, 'It was a miracle no guests were in that wing of the hotel at the time,' and the cause of the fire was given as an electrical heater whose plug socket had been overloaded.

An electrical fire.

The same as at the youth hostel twenty years later.

The newspaper seemed to conclude that that was why Dean King had disappeared: although no one had died, he would most likely have been prosecuted by the authorities for a major health and safety violation. In fact, the *Star* said they had looked into it, and found that King had forged a safety certificate a year before the fire. They had printed the safety certificate and then, towards the bottom of the article, printed a second photo of King taken in the weeks before he vanished.

I hadn't seen this one anywhere else before.

A caption under the picture said it was *an example of the kind of parties that Mr King used to throw regularly at the hotel before his disappearance.* In the centre was Dean King himself, smiling, a few stray streamers draped over his shoulders. In the background were a clutch of young people in party hats, holding beer cans or glasses of wine. On the sofa with King were two more young women.

I went over to the librarian and asked her to print out a copy.

As I waited, I went through the rest of May, checking for any other updates, but the last one of any significance had been on the 10th. Once I was done, I packed the microfilm away and glanced across the library, to the news playing out on the TV.

A face was staring at me.

It was mine.

Healy

He got up early, just after the sun came up.

He'd crawled out of bed at this time every weekday for the last two years and three months and his body still fought against it even now. Healy wasn't sure if it was middle age or the thought of spending seven hours on a trawler with the father and son, but today he wasn't going to the boat, and he wasn't going to be seeing the father and son either – maybe ever again, depending on what happened from here. And yet he still ached. *Maybe it's this shitty mattress*, he thought, pressing it with his fingers.

A spring pinged in response.

He glanced around the bedroom and pictured himself beneath the covers at night, the room lit by a single lamp, reading the books Raker brought for him every three months. He went downstairs and fixed himself some breakfast, looking in at the living room, and imagined himself there, watching old movies. He sat at the table in the kitchen, beside the window that overlooked the beach, and had a cup of tea and a bowl of cereal, and remembered all the times he'd done this. And, in that moment, he realized, terrible as the mattress was, much as he hated working on the trawler, despite how boring his routine was here, part of him was going to miss it all. Maybe he would be back if everything with Paula turned out to be fine, but there was more of a chance that he wouldn't. Raker was distracted with his case – with having to deal with the fact that his name would soon be all over the news – but after it was over, he would see clearly, just as Healy did that they weren't going to return here. Small as his doubts were about Paula, much as he thought her reasons for lying about the house sale were likely to be perfunctory, they couldn't one hundred per cent trust her. Because if she'd lied once, she might do it again.

He finished his breakfast, washed up the bowl, and then showered. After that, he did one last sweep of the house, making sure that there was nothing he'd missed that was going to compromise him or Raker. He checked his holdall to see if he had everything he needed and, as he looked at what amounted to his life packed into a bag no bigger than a doormat, he was hit by a sudden sadness.

This was all he was now.

Just a single bag.

Burying the feeling, he carried the bag to the front door, pausing at the table he'd sat at for so long, at the views out across the beach and the bay, his attention settling on Paula's house. He looked at its windows, the ones on this side of the property cast into shadow because of the position of the sun.

It looked as if Paula wasn't home.

Her car wasn't on the driveway.

He glanced at his watch – 6.36 a.m. – and figured Paula must have left early for a meeting. One day a week she said she had to drive to the main office in Chester. As he saw the empty driveway, a thought came to him, one which he instantly dismissed. Instead, he went to the front door and locked up. At the gate, he glanced back at the house and then started making his way down the slope, the road snaking gently to the beach. On his right Paula's house drew closer – and he had the same idea again.

This time he let it in, let it form and settle.

And, as it did, it morphed into a rational argument. *If you got inside her house, and you found something, some reason she lied, at least then you'd know.*

This is all probably nothing, anyway.

But when you know for sure, you can move on.

He stopped at the bottom of her driveway and looked along it. She definitely wasn't home. It wasn't just the lack of a car that was a giveaway; whenever she was at home, she always kept the bathroom window open upstairs, because she'd told Healy that there was a moisture problem in there. So the only time the window got locked was when she was out.

He looked up and down the road, wavering there at the edge of the driveway – and then he moved, heading along it, holdall slung over his shoulder.

At the front door he knocked once.

He glanced down the slope again, into the town, and the payphone he always called Raker from drifted into view. It was partly obscured by the branches of a pine tree, but they were moving now in the wind.

Through the glass on the front door he had a distorted view of the hallway. It was obvious no one was going to answer, but he knocked a second time and said, 'Paula? Are you home?' He waited. 'It's Marcus. Are you there?'

Marcus.

It probably wasn't just the house and this village he was about to leave behind. Wherever he ended up, Raker would have to organize another ID for him.

Another name.

Another life that wasn't his own.

When there was no response again, he hauled the holdall off his shoulders, left it at the front door and headed around the side of the house, following a slate path to the back garden. There was a side gate but it didn't take much to get past it.

'Paula?' he said again.

He wasn't expecting a reply and didn't get one.

At the back, he wandered to the patio doors, cupped his hands to the glass and looked into the living room. No sign of her in there, or in the adjacent kitchen. He knocked on the glass anyway and waited, but after a minute he moved to the next window along.

This one was the kitchen.

He looked through the glass, confirmed she wasn't there, and then wandered to the back door. It led into a utility room. To his right, on the opposite flank of the house, was the woodshed. That was where the FOR SALE sign had fallen out from when he'd come for dinner. He checked it again, the piles of firewood, the old broken tools, cracked kitchenware, and discovered that the sign was still there. She'd obviously found it out on the lawn at some point and put it back, wedging it into a tighter space that it wouldn't escape from again.

He glanced along the rear of the house to the utility-room door. It was the best potential entrance with the fewest sight lines. There were no surrounding houses and no windows overlooking this part of her home.

Stepping under the roof of the shed, Healy began looking around. It took him a couple of minutes, but then he found a rusting hacksaw. He levered off the blade and discarded the rest, dumping the handle and frame back into the pile of old tools, and then crouched next to the old kitchenware and started going through that. Eventually, he found a fork. Pinching one of the tines between thumb and finger, he bent it over.

Now he had a pick and torsion wrench.

Within a minute he was inside.

He stepped into the house and pushed the door shut behind him. He went into the kitchen, looked around, then into the living room and did the same in there. He wasn't sure what exactly he was expecting to find, but he kept going anyway, and as quickly as he could. He didn't know how long Paula was going to be away for. It would be most of the day if she really *was* on her way to Chester. But she could just have easily gone somewhere else, somewhere local, and already be on her way back – even if he couldn't imagine why she would have left home so early.

He took the stairs up.

He hadn't been to the first floor yet, only the rooms on the ground floor. It was as attractively decorated up here as it was everywhere else, but even so, something immediately felt off.

In Paula's bedroom there was a suitcase with clothes in it on top of a chest of drawers, the things that had obviously been on the chest – photographs, a pot plant, some toiletries – pushed off on to the floor. The suitcase was already almost full, clothes spilling out of it.

In the other bedroom to his left – identical in size, but not as lived in – there were two big wardrobes, and both sets of doors were open, revealing clothes on hangers.

She was packing to go somewhere.

Or she was doing something else.

Escaping.

54

I tore out of the library and walk-ran back to my car in Gateshead.

Once inside, I paused for a moment, taking a breath, trying to calm myself. I stared ahead at the wave-like roof of the Sage, drumming my fingers against the wheel, and then reached into my back pocket and pulled out the photograph the librarian had printed from the microfiche: Dean King – on a sofa in his wing of the Coast Inn, a wing that he'd set fire to and destroyed – surrounded by men and women, none of whom were much older than their early twenties.

I speed-read my notes, trying to think how it all tied up. I felt certain that Cate had come to the Coast Inn to speak to Liam and Joshua at the Castle View Café, to walk the dunes – maybe even to attempt to talk to Makayla at the nursing home she'd been in – because she thought Dean King was responsible for the Dune Murders.

But what then?

Had she tied Dean King to the man who'd stolen the identity of – and presumably murdered – the real Jasper Slade? Did she know they were one and the same? The only reason I'd been able to tie the two men together was because I'd broken into Michael Calvert's home and found his note on the Ordnance Survey map.

So how would Cate have put it together?

How did the man called Harper tie into it all?

And how did it lead to the events on Gatton Hill?

I thought about Aiden's Google search – six months before they disappeared – for his nearest police station. *Maybe he'd told her to go to the police.* So why *hadn't* she if that was the case? And why did they then stop arguing? How did they resolve things if they were on opposite sides of the dispute? Again, all I could do was speculate, but I could think of one answer right off the bat: Cate stopped whatever she was doing and ceased writing the book.

Or at least that was the story she told Aiden.

I grabbed my phone, put it back together, and called Joshua Jennings. I'd got his mobile from Liam Andrews and he answered after a couple of rings. I explained who I was, told him I was sorry to hear about his mother, and then said I was looking into the Dune Murders. It was cynical and I felt bad for dangling bait in front of him the day after he'd had to say goodbye to Makayla, but I didn't have a choice now.

'I'm really so sorry to do this today,' I said to him. 'I promise I wouldn't call if it wasn't important. I'm trying to find out what happened to Cate Gascoigne.'

A long pause. For a second I wondered if he'd seen my face on TV, had maybe recognized my name, and was trying to figure out what to do. But then he said, 'What does Cate have to do with me?'

'I think it's got more to do with your mum,' I replied, and then I gave him the briefest of backgrounds; I also made sure to carefully avoid why I was so pressed for time. I didn't know him, so I was pretty sure he'd start to clam up if I told him the cops were on my trail. 'Did your mum ever retain old files or case notes? I'm thinking specifically of the Dune Murders.' I was also thinking about information she might have gathered as prep for the talk she did at the conference a decade ago. She had publicly called out Dean King as her prime suspect and gone deep on the hessian-sack lead – and, therefore, a cop as good as Makayla Jennings was likely to have had a reliably sourced paper trail.

'I'm not sure,' Joshua said. 'She's been in a nursing home for five years. If she had anything like that, she'd have left it behind.'

'Behind?'

'At the house in Whitley Bay.'

'Where your dad lives?'

'No, my dad died three years ago. It's just my brother, Isaiah, who lives there now.'

'I'm sorry to hear about your dad,' I said.

'Thanks. Look, Isaiah and I are heading to the nursing home now to clear out Mum's stuff. If you wanted to meet us there, we can go to the house after.'

I was three hundred miles from home, and unlikely to get another chance to search through Makayla's belongings. The only thing that worried me was that I might be in for a long wait at the nursing home while the Jennings brothers cleared everything out – and by wasting time I was making the target on my back even bigger.

'So do you and the other guy work together?' Joshua said.

I stopped; felt a stab of alarm.

'The "other guy"?'

'He was asking exactly the same questions as you.'

'Someone else came to see you?'

'Yeah, a couple of weeks ago.'

'Did he tell you his name?'

'Uh . . .' A beat. 'Yeah, I think he said his name was Harper.'

55

I messaged Joshua the picture I had of Harper.

'I know it's not great quality,' I said, once he'd received the shot that Georgia had taken the night before, 'but does that look like the man who came to see you?'

'Yeah, that looks like him.'

So I'd been right. A couple of weeks ago would have been at least eight or nine days before I'd started working for Martin and Sue, possibly more – and Harper was already up here asking questions. I'd suspected that Martin's and Sue's phones were being tapped, or their emails and Internet activity were being monitored. Now I felt more certain than ever that it was. Harper had travelled to the north-east, and then returned on repeat to the pub that Georgia worked in, and he'd only do those things if he was trying to stay ahead of the curve. And he'd only need to stay ahead of the curve if he felt like he'd been compromised.

But compromised how?

I looked at the photograph Georgia had taken of him and, for the second time, something set me off. I'd never seen him before, I was absolutely convinced of that, but even so – as I stared at the image of him – a part of me couldn't settle.

What is it about you?

'Do you remember what you talked about?' I asked Joshua. 'Was he just asking about the Dune Murders?'

'Yes. He also asked if Mum had any old case files and all that sort of stuff, and I told him the same as I told you – if there *are* any, they're at the house.'

'So did Harper go to the house?'

'He did, yeah.'

I rubbed at my face. *Shit.* That meant there were two possible outcomes and neither of them were good. The first was that he'd found nothing; the second was that he'd found evidence that might point in his direction – and removed it. In either scenario if I'd planned to go out to the house, it was probably worthless now.

'So you two don't know each other?' Joshua asked.

'We're interested in the same things,' I said, trying to muddy the waters. I didn't want him to worry, or derail our momentum. 'Did Harper go to the nursing home?'

'No. There wouldn't have been any point.'

'Your mum was too sick by then?'

'Way too sick. She was sleeping most of the time.'

I paused, thinking again.

'What does all of this have to do with Cate?' he asked. But before I could answer, he said, 'Hold on a sec, it's my brother.' He covered the mouthpiece with his hand, obscuring the conversation he was having with Isaiah. I heard a rustle on the line. 'Sorry about that. Isaiah says Cate came to the nursing home.'

I frowned. 'Does he remember when?'

Joshua put us on speakerphone.

'*Two years, seven months, thirty days ago,*' came the reply.

I didn't know much about Isaiah Jennings – about either of them, really – but his exact recollection of how much time had passed, the incredible precision of his memory, and the unique cadence of his speech filled in a lot of detail about him. 'So that would have been November 2019?' I asked.

'*The 8th of November.*'

'How did you know about Cate's visit?' I heard Joshua ask his brother.

316

'*Jason told me.*'

'Who's Jason?' I interjected.

'He was Mum's nurse for years until he went back to Australia last summer,' Joshua explained.

'*He promised to tell Mum about Cate. If Mum had a moment.*'

Joshua took a long breath and I could almost hear his pain, almost feel it along the phone line, as he expanded on what his brother had just said. 'Sometimes Mum would get these periods of clarity. They never lasted long, and they stopped coming so often the worse she got, but – when they did – it was like . . .' He faltered, a tremor in his voice, and I remembered again that it had only been a day since his mother had died. 'It was like part of her came back to us.'

'She could remember things?'

'In a very limited way, for a very short period of time, yes. The doctors said it was unusual, but not unheard of.'

I wondered if the nurse, Jason, had ended up telling Makayla about Cate's visit, if – like Joshua had articulated – Makayla had come back for a flicker of time. And then I wondered, if she had, how she might have reacted to the news about Cate coming to see her.

Joshua said, 'I don't know if that's any help to y–'

'*Two years, six months, eight days.*' Isaiah again in the background.

It took me a few moments to realize that the time frame he'd given was different: this one was at least a month and a half afterwards.

'*Two years, six months, eight days,*' Isaiah repeated.

'When's that, Zi?' Joshua said.

'*The 31st of December 2019,*' Isaiah replied instantly.

That was only three days before Cate and Aiden disappeared.

'What happened then?' Joshua said.

'*The present from Cate arrived.*'

'Cate sent Mum a present?' Joshua asked.

'*Yes. Two years, six months, eight days.*'

This was leading somewhere. *Somewhere big.*

'*It was in brown paper.*'

'How do you know all of this?' Joshua asked his brother.

'*I was there when Jason brought it in.*'

In the silence I could almost picture the conversation that was playing out on their faces. Joshua saying, *And you didn't think to mention this?* and Isaiah replying matter-of-factly, *You never asked.* In Isaiah's head this whole thing was black and white: Joshua had never enquired about Cate, her visit or the present she had sent to Makayla, so why *would* he ever mention it?

'Does Isaiah know what the present was?' I asked.

'*I took off the brown paper for her.*'

'What was under the paper?'

Quiet.

'What was under the paper, Zi?' Joshua repeated for me.

'*A shoebox.*'

'Okay,' Joshua replied calmly. 'What happened to the shoebox?'

'*I put it under Mum's bed,*' Isaiah said.

'You hid it at the nursing home? Why did you hide it?'

'*I wanted to help Cate.*'

'Why?'

There was a long pause.

And then Isaiah said, '*Because Cate was in danger.*'

56

The nursing home was at the south-eastern tip of Tyne-mouth. It was a cavernous Victorian house that had – over time – been extended further, a glass-and-wood entrance the newest addition, with a matching two-storey wing at the back.

The car park was almost full, and it was easy enough to find Joshua Jennings's vehicle: there was a *Castle View Café* sticker in the rear window of a sand-speckled Renault Cap-tur. As I hurried past it, I could see empty boxes in the boot, presumably waiting to be filled.

At the front desk, I asked for Joshua.

After I signed in, a nurse accompanied me into a long cor-ridor. We went all the way down, the building smelling of boiled food and antiseptic, of furniture polish and women's perfume, to one of the last doors on the left.

As soon as I saw them, I recognized both Jennings brothers from the photographs in the Castle View Café. Joshua was closest to me: a strapping, handsome 37-year-old, who looked like he spent every day in the gym. At the back of the room was Isaiah. They had the same brown eyes, the same contours on the same parts of the face, and were the same basic build, but it was still hard to tell they were twins: Isaiah looked about three inches shorter than his brother, his posture bent, as if he were slowly deflating. Unlike Joshua, he hadn't added to his natural bulk but gone the other way, his clothes hanging off him, his frame slim-mer, more sinewy.

I shook hands with Joshua and he told me to call him Josh. I was hoping he hadn't yet seen my face on the news, was banking on the fact that he'd have been too consumed with the aftermath of his mother's death – and I could see from his eyes that I was still safe for now.

His brother didn't look at me or say anything. He was standing at a wardrobe on the left, both its doors open, and when I greeted him he shuffled into the space, as if trying to disappear inside. The rest of the room was split in two, a wooden railing dividing the bathroom, the bed and two side tables from the wardrobe, a two-seater sofa and a TV cabinet with drawers. It was small but it was homely, the walls decorated with photographs of Makayla, Tyler and their boys.

On the bed, almost at the centre, was a shoebox.

The lid was still on.

'That's the present Cate sent your mum?' I asked.

'It appears so,' Joshua replied.

He had no idea what was going on, what the shoebox was for, or even that it was there in the first place, and – fresh from saying goodbye to Makayla – I could see he was emotional. The shoebox was a small thing, but it felt big in the midst of grief.

'Have you looked inside?' I asked.

'I thought it was best to wait for you,' Joshua said.

'I appreciate that.'

He just nodded.

I looked at his brother. 'You said Cate was in danger, Isaiah?'

He was still partially hidden behind one of the wardrobe doors, still moving the hangers along the rail. I waited but he didn't reply.

Eventually, Joshua moved closer to his twin and said, 'Zi, why don't you tell David what you've told me?'

It took a moment and then, from behind the wardrobe door, Isaiah started to speak. 'She wrote it in the letter.' He took a minor step back, half his face visible to me behind the open door of the wardrobe. 'She wrote it in the letter she put in there.'

And then he pointed at the shoebox.

57

I lifted the lid off and set it down on the bed.

On top was a letter. It was short, only a few lines, and was written in what I recognized as Cate's hand. I felt a rush as I lifted it out, another as I saw what lay beneath it: portraits of Lilly Andrews, Felicity Sykes and Maggie Wilkins; more photographs; a roll of photocopies secured with an elastic band; a memory stick; a VHS tape with *Dune Murders news reports* written on the label; then a spiral-bound notebook with a fountain pen clipped to it.

I smoothed out the letter.

Makayla – I don't know if you will remember me, or if sending this to you is even the right thing to do. All I know is that I need this stuff to be somewhere else now, with someone who will look after it. If something happens to me, I hope it can be of use . . . Cate x

I returned to the last sentence again, and then the rest of the letter, and with every read my blood ran colder. I'd always wondered if Cate had felt like she was being shadowed in the days before the crash, whether – when the CCTV image of her on Gatton Hill had been captured, smiling – it was all an act.

Now I knew for sure that it was.

She'd sent this to Makayla Jennings, despite knowing that Makayla would in all likelihood no longer remember her or the case that she'd once been the lead detective on.

I need this stuff to be somewhere else now.

Whatever she'd dug up, whatever she had planned to put in the book, it had placed her at risk. The things she'd found out – the things in *here* – were too dangerous to keep close to her – and not just too dangerous for her, but for Aiden too, for her family, for anyone she cared about.

I set the letter aside and the photographs of the three women. They were high-resolution scans, taken from the original newspaper articles about the murders and then cut out. The other photographs were a mix: pictures of Makayla, Leon Coetzer and others that had worked on the case; shots of the beach that day, which she must have sourced from newspaper archives; portraits of the Coast Inn, before and after the fire; of Dean King, all of which had run in the *Star*; and then another shot I'd also found on the microfilm and had printed out: King at a party, two women beside him on a sofa, his shoulders draped in streamers.

I moved on.

There was nothing I could do with the VHS tape for now, but the writing on the front – *Dune Murders news reports* – seemed to be self-explanatory. My laptop was in the car so I set aside the memory stick for the time being and switched my focus to the photocopies and the notebook.

Cate had got through about half the notebook, filling pages with what looked like shorthand, but then, when I looked more closely, I saw that it was some kind of system she must have developed herself. I'd learned shorthand as a journalist – Pitman, when I'd trained in the UK, then Gregg during my time in the States – and also knew enough about Teeline, which was now used by journalists in the UK, to be sure that it wasn't any of them. I traced the spirals, curves and straight lines of her writing with my finger, trying to recognize any words. I didn't. Whatever this was, it was bespoke, created by Cate, and it was obvious why.

No one but her could understand it.

I looked at the memory stick again. Was Cate's book on here? Her research? Could there be some sort of key, a way to interpret what she'd written in the notebook, because why send this to Makayla – why send it to *anyone* – if there was no hope of the recipient translating any of it?

I switched my attention to the photocopies.

Snapping off the elastic band, I unrolled them and set them down on the bed. There were five pages, and they were all full of names of what looked like businesses. Cate had put a line through about three-quarters of them – and there were about fifty left to check off. But then, a second later, I realized they were all a specific *type* of business.

Hotels.

I felt a charge of electricity.

Had Cate been trying to do the same thing as me? Had she been trying to chart Dean King's path after he vanished in the aftermath of the Coast Inn fire? If she had, she'd got further than me.

I needed to look more closely at them, needed to see what was on the memory stick too, so I thanked Joshua and Isaiah for their help and started packing everything up. As I did, one of the photographs escaped and fluttered to the floor.

It was the picture of Dean King with the women on the sofa that I already had myself. But then I bent down, picked it up and realized that the photo Cate had wasn't *exactly* the same as the one I'd printed out from the microfiche. It was larger and wider, with more people visible in the background and at the sides of the shot, as well as an additional woman on the arm of the sofa, close to Dean King. In the newspaper she'd been cropped out. This must have been the original version of the photograph, not the one that had run in the *Star* that day.

I became aware of Isaiah moving hangers, of Joshua off to my left, waiting, his back against the wall. I'd almost forgotten they were in the room with me. But I didn't look up at them, just kept my attention focused on the photograph, because now I'd noticed something else.

Cate's version had been marked, gently, in pencil.

A circle had been drawn around Dean King's face. I hadn't seen it at first. A second was around the face of the woman on the arm of the sofa.

I studied her, trying to work out if I knew her.

She must have been only eighteen or nineteen, petite, sweet-looking, with dark hair. She had a can of beer in her hand – but it hadn't been opened yet, the ring pull still secure – and she wore a necklace, the colour of the jewellery easy to see against the pale crescent of her throat.

Hanging from the necklace was a letter.

It was an *A*.

Photograph

30 Years Ago

As Amelia waited on the bench for Makayla to arrive, her thoughts returned to the twelve-week scan two days before. She was still buzzing from it, still excited and surprised by what the ultrasound had shown, her guts a weird twist of elation and nerves. It had brought everything home to her seeing it all again, how real this was now, how there was no escaping the reality: in six months she was going to be a mother.

No, not a mother. A mum.

'Mother' was what you got called if your kids hated you, Amelia thought to herself, and – however many she had – hers weren't going to hate her. They were going to love her every bit as much as she loved them. Seeing what she was carrying in her, on the screen in black and white, watching the heart beat again, the flicker of a hand, an arm, a leg, a head – it had all been too much. Amelia had started crying, then so too had her mum.

Happy tears, her mum had called them after.

The wind picked up, bringing her back into the moment. She'd taken the bus from home to the Metrocentre and was now waiting on a bench on the east side of the mall, where the Marks & Spencer's entrance was. It was 1 May but there was still an unseasonable chill in the air, and the longer she waited, the colder she started to feel. Makayla had asked to meet here because she said it was on her way home. It didn't seem all that convenient for Whitley Bay but, in the end, it was up to Makayla how far she was prepared to travel, and Amelia didn't suggest an alternative because the Metrocentre was close for her. Plus, she was grateful to Makayla: not only had she called Amelia to see how the scan had gone, she'd also said she had found out some information about Phil.

The wind picked up again and – shivering, even inside the winter coat she was wearing – Amelia decided to wait inside the entrance of Marks & Spencer. She could still see out through the windows, still see when Makayla pulled up in her trademark red Astra – and at least she would feel a little warmer.

She retreated indoors.

Five minutes passed, and then ten, and then Makayla was officially twenty minutes late. Amelia was starting to feel pissed off. She'd promised Coralie that they would go out for a glass of wine this afternoon – or, in Amelia's case, a lemonade – and if she had to wait any longer here, she was going to be cutting it fine. Amelia planned on telling Coralie about her pregnancy. It had felt weird waiting this long to tell her as she and Coralie had been mates since juniors. In fact, Coralie was the one who'd suggested going to the party at the Coast Inn the night Amelia had slept with No Surname Phil. She said the place was run by a friend of a friend and that they were always having parties up there. And it was true: the hotel had been packed with people her age, all crammed into a single wing. It had been fun, though, from what Amelia could remember of it. Which was just the problem: she couldn't remember enough about the second half of the night. She'd woken up the next morning and – although she recalled being in one of the rooms with the man she thought of as Phil – she'd woken up alone, with him already gone, and Coralie, and some of the other girls, had about as much of a memory of their evening as Amelia did. Amelia would normally have just laughed the whole thing off, but that blank space mattered to her now, because in that blank space somewhere was her baby's father – his surname, his address, his whole life.

She checked her watch again.

Makayla was twenty-five minutes late.

On the other side of the glass, she watched an old couple stop, the man trying to find his car keys while juggling a shopping bag and what looked like a well-read newspaper. The wife was talking to him gently, a half-smile on her face, as if him not remembering where he put his car keys *was something which happened a lot and never failed to amuse her. He returned her smile, got rid of the newspaper on the bench Amelia had been sitting on a few minutes before, and then eventually produced the keys, holding them up for his wife like he'd just pulled off the world's greatest magic trick. The two of them smiled at each other, then the wife threaded her hand through the crook of her husband's arm, and as they headed off to their car, Amelia experienced an odd, unexpected stab of jealousy. She wasn't going to have any of that – not that warmth, not that support and companionship, not now, not any time soon – even if Makayla found out who Phil was. She was all alone, except for Mum and Dad. And, good as her parents were, it wasn't the same.*

But then her attention switched to the newspaper that the old man had left on the bench, its front page fluttering up, like wings in a breeze, before settling again.

She turned her head slightly, trying to get a better, straighter angle on one of the headlines. It wasn't the main story – the main story was still about the three women they'd found on Bamburgh dunes three days ago, Makayla's case – but a column at the side, with a picture underneath it.

LOCAL HOTEL DESTROYED IN FIRE
Owner may have been inside

The image printed beneath the headline instantly looked familiar and, as she moved from the relative warmth of the entrance back out to the cool of the day, she saw it more clearly: it was the Coast Inn. And, not just that, it was the actual wing of the hotel that she'd been partying in with Coralie only a few months ago – except now it had been reduced to little more than a blackened husk.

A car horn sounded.

She looked up from the newspaper and saw that Makayla's red Astra was waiting for her at the kerb. From the driver's seat Makayla waved at her, her face apologetic. Amelia hurried across, letting herself in.

'Afternoon, honey,' Makayla said. 'Sorry I'm late.'

Amelia pulled her door closed and realized she still had the newspaper with her, so she dumped it into the footwell and yanked her seat belt out. 'It's okay.'

'Something came up at work,' Makayla added, and then her eyes switched to the newspaper at Amelia's feet, which had been rolled up and had now unfurled to reveal the front page. 'Keeping up on current events?'

'I was just reading it while I was waiting,' Amelia said.

Makayla nodded and pulled out, heading for the exit at the southeast corner of the car park. 'What were you reading about?' she asked, and looked at the paper again. 'All that stuff on the beach?' She paused for a second, glancing at Amelia as they looped back around the outskirts of the vast car park in the direction of the A1.

Amelia shrugged. 'I was just flicking through.'

But Makayla seemed different today and something about the last thing she'd said – 'All that stuff on the beach' – had stuck with Amelia. It was weird, but Makayla made it sound like she wasn't really connected to what had happened out on those dunes just a few days ago – and yet she'd said herself that it was her case.

And then, as she looked at Makayla again and the two of them locked eyes, something lodged with Amelia. It took her a couple of seconds to work out what it was, before it pinged back into focus. It was that same sense of recognition that Amelia had had the first time at the bus stop, that certainty that she'd met Makayla before.

'You okay, sweetheart?' Makayla asked.

'Yes,' Amelia lied. 'Yes, I'm fine.'

Makayla nodded. 'So I've managed to find the address of your friend Phil.'

'Really?'

'Yes. It wasn't so hard for a woman of my means.' She winked at Amelia playfully and then pulled out on to the A1, heading north. 'His name's Phil Ellory.'

'I didn't expect you to find him so quickly.'

'Well, I wouldn't be a very good detective if I didn't.'

Makayla glanced at Amelia and, this time, Amelia asked her outright. 'I know this is weird to go on about, but I really do feel like we've met before.'

Makayla broke into a smile. 'This again?'

'Before the other day at the bus stop, I mean.'

'We haven't, honey. I promise.'

Amelia nodded. 'Okay.'

But the doubts didn't leave her.

They stuck, festered.

And for the first time Amelia wondered if Makayla was lying to her.

58

Back at the car, I grabbed my laptop from the boot and inserted the memory stick that Cate had left in the shoebox. Its icon appeared on the desktop.

But it was an instant dead end.

It was encrypted, asking for a password.

Burying my frustration for now, I switched my attention back to the photograph of Dean King and the woman with the *A* necklace.

Who are you?

I attempted a Google search, knowing it was unlikely to get me anywhere, and I got exactly what I expected. I needed a full first name or something else to hang a search for her on – so I switched my attention to Cate's list of hotels instead.

Googling a few of them, I started to realize they were actually a mix of hotels and B & Bs. But no youth hostels. The Slade Youth Hostel wasn't on here, neither were any others as far as I could see. So did that mean that Cate hadn't connected Dean King to what happened in Epping Forest?

I kept going, looking at every name that Cate had printed out, and as I did, I started noticing a pattern: it became clear that all of them had opened or been majorly refurbished since 1992. It must have taken her hours – probably days and weeks – to collate all this information, but it appeared to confirm that she'd been trying to find out where Dean King went after the Coast Inn. She'd been working the theory – correctly, it seemed – that he'd stick to a pattern, to something that had worked before. That meant installing himself in a place where young people willingly congregated.

As I worked my way down the list of hotels and B & Bs that Cate had found, I attempted to zero in on the identity of the owner in each case. I couldn't always find the answer – and I put an asterisk next to those entries – but most proprietors were easy to find and, once I'd got visual confirmation that it wasn't Dean King – using another identity, as he'd done with Jasper Slade – I moved on to the next. I had to assume that this was exactly what Cate had done too, which would explain why a lot of the entries were already ticked off. It was slow, painstaking work and I was conscious of the clock ticking the whole time.

On the last page, I noticed that a couple of hotels and B & Bs had question marks next to them. They were all in London. Had she singled them out because they were local to her? Perhaps she'd had the idea that she might physically go there to ask questions, rather than just use Google. I worked through them, just as I had with the others, until I got to the final London hotel.

It was called the Fir Grove.

From its website I could see that it was a small boutique operation near Borough Market, which had closed in order to be refurbished in 2014. That was two years after the fire at the youth hostel in Epping Forest. On the website, it didn't list any information about the owner – but when I looked at a few of the other Google results, I found a story on the *Southwark News* website from the month the Fir Grove reopened. In it was an old photograph of the owner, Nolan Winter. He was listed as fifty-five years old, even though the picture of him must have been taken when he was in his forties, and he was described as a 'secretive multimillionaire property magnate' and 'notoriously publicity-shy'. When

I went looking for more background on Winter, I found a small profile of him in *Forbes* – with the same photograph; it appeared to be the *only* photograph of him the public had ever got to see – and confirmation that he had no siblings and was unmarried.

There was something else too.

He'd inherited a fortune from his father.

Alarm bells started ringing. *Secretive. Publicity-shy. Rich.* Nolan Winter didn't get seen in public, didn't have family, wasn't married and was sitting on a fortune. The last – and only – photo most people would have seen of him was taken some time in the early 2000s. Those were perfect conditions for a man like Dean King, not least because Winter was olive-skinned and had the same colour eyes as King did. There were definitely a lot of minor differences between them, areas of their face where they weren't the same – but not enough to stop Dean King. He could have moved in, assimilated himself, become Nolan Winter – and most people would never have realized.

I kept moving through the hotel's website. It was simple and elegant, with a high-class kind of feel, a tagline under the hotel name stating *5-Star Service, 3-Star Prices*, in a clear attempt to widen the potential guest pool. And the longer I spent on the site, the more I started to notice small anomalous details: a sentence in the *Rates* section that said the Fir Grove would give *up to 50% discount* to solo travellers; then something else, something worse given what I already knew about Dean King: a special, discounted rate for UK and foreign students.

It was an animal trap.

If this really *was* him – and the reason the Fir Grove had closed to refurbish in 2014 was because Dean King had killed off Nolan Winter and become him – he was luring young people in with the promise of reasonable rates at the type of hotel they'd never be able to afford in London normally.

And then my gaze fell on a customer notice at the bottom of the homepage.

It said the Fir Grove was now closed again, this time for 'essential repair work'. It didn't say when it would reopen, but the update was only a day old, posted on Thursday 7 July at 9 a.m. At 9.22 that same morning, I'd woken up on the floor of my living room, drugged, sick, having lost thirty hours. And while I was out – and then after, while I was on the run, distracted and under pressure, trying to prove my innocence – he'd shut the Fir Grove down to get ready.

Because Dean King was about to vanish again.

And I might already have been too late to stop him.

PART FIVE
The Blackbird

59

The Fir Grove was small: three storeys high and five windows wide, with a single large red door. It was in the middle of a row of other businesses and had a back entrance – accessed via an alleyway to the south – that employees must have used. It was 11 a.m. and Borough Market was packed, but the hotel itself was like a mausoleum.

I stood under the sign at the Stoney Street entrance, watching the place, going back over the last eighteen hours. I'd headed to London straight from the nursing home, except for a two-hour stop-off in a layby off the motorway, where I'd parked up and tried to catch up on some sleep in the back of the car.

The first thing I did once I got back home to Ealing was dump everything I had – except for the phone, which I'd taken apart again, separating the handset, battery and SIM card – into a locker at a gym I used on Broadway. There wasn't much because most of my clothes were still in the north-east, in the room I'd had at the Coast Inn. I then drove on to the car rental place on The Mall, which had a 24-hour drop-off, via a secure garage beneath the street. I used a key fob to access the garage, left the car there and headed for the Tube. I rode the District Line to Blackfriars and walked the rest.

The whole time I was thinking of Martin and Sue, of how they'd probably seen me on the news and been trying to call me on the mobile that the police now had. I tried not to think too hard about what the cops would have told them about me, what sort of picture had been painted. I knew that what they were seeing would feel like a betrayal, and that answers about their daughter and son-in-law would feel further away than ever. They were probably wondering what sort of man they'd given their money to, what sort of monster was capable of the hit-and-run that was described in the papers and on TV. But, in reality, there was only one monster, and I believed he was hiding behind the walls of the Fir Grove.

Or he was already in the wind.

I'd been at Borough Market since 7 a.m. In that time no one had left or gone in through the front of the hotel – and no one had used the alleyway to the south either, which meant no one had exited out of the back of the hotel.

It was time to make my move.

I tilted the peak on my cap a little lower, trying to cover more of my face, and headed south down Park Street to the alleyway at the end that led around to the rear entrance of the Fir Grove. The alleyway passed under an enclosed walkway and then opened out into a narrow cobbled space that was being used as a car park for hotel guests and the other businesses in the row.

I took in the rear of the hotel as I approached. There appeared to be five floors on this side: not only ground, first and second, as there was at the front of the building, but a third floor in the roof, with dormers, and a basement level with a STAFF ONLY sign next to its entrance. Down the bottom of a set of steps was a door, and through an adjacent window I could see a kitchen.

I made a beeline for it.

Keeping my eyes on the hotel – its doors, its windows – I unzipped a pocket on the front of my jacket and took out my lockpicks. There was a camera mounted above the door, but it was facing downward, as if deactivated, so I didn't have to worry about being seen. I imagined, at this point, all the cameras inside were off.

At the bottom of the stairs, I paused, checking my surroundings – the windows above and either side of me; the cars in the parking bays – and then dropped to my haunches at the lock. Another reason I'd chosen the kitchen door was because the lock was a lot simpler, and within a minute I had it ajar.

The kitchen was silent.

Surfaces clean, everything packed away.

I moved inside and pulled the door shut behind me.

I glanced around, searching for something I could use to protect myself with and spotted a knife rack on the wall. Selecting one, I headed towards three doors on the other side of the room.

The first was a staffroom: circular tables, lots of chairs, a counter with a kettle and microwave on it.

The second door went through to a staff staircase.

The third opened out into the hotel restaurant. Another staircase – running parallel to the staff one but separated by a wall – was at the far end, but these stairs were much grander: they corkscrewed up to reception on the ground floor, with design flourishes at every turn.

I backed out and moved towards the staff staircase, taking the steps two at a time, ensuring I kept any noise to a minimum. On the next floor up was a door with a push-bar on it. It opened out into the reception. No one was behind the desk. The hotel was basically silent; I could hear some traffic but nothing from the market. Both were suppressed by thick concrete walls.

I folded a piece of card and propped the door open, then hurried across to the reception desk, checking the office behind it. In one of the drawers I found a key card on a chain. It was blank, white with a black strip, maybe some sort of master.

I pocketed it, headed back to the stairs, closing the door behind me, and then padded up to the first floor. Another push-bar, another door; this one opened out on to the rooms. There were five on either side, a lift and guest stairs at the far end.

And then I heard something.

A noise.

It was coming from above me.

60

I backed up, into the stairwell, and looked up through its spiral to the second-floor door. Leaning against the railing, I tried to get a better angle.

And then I heard the noise again.

This time I could tell what it was: a door softly shutting.

I hurried up to the second floor.

This was as high as I could go, which meant whatever was behind the third-floor dormers that I'd seen from the hotel car park was only accessible using the guest staircase on the opposite side of the hotel. That meant it was probably a suite.

Clicking in the push-bar, I gently eased the second-floor door back.

Something was different here.

Halfway down the corridor, a socket was hanging off the wall.

Wires snaked out from inside the wall cavity. Some were connected – fused – to other wires inside the wall, others were connected to wiring that ran off along the corridor and under the doors of the rooms.

A dawning horror gripped me.

This place – just like the ones before – was wired to go up in flames.

And I was right in the middle of it.

I followed the path of one of the wires, quietly using the master key to open a door to a room on my left. The socket in the room had been completely overloaded: two bedside lamps, a standalone heater, a radio, a fan, the television. An electrical fire would be how it started, like in every other place King had run.

But knowing it and seeing it were two different things.

Frozen for a moment, I tried to clear my head.

This whole thing felt like a trap. Back out in the corridor, I looked at the rooms on either side of me, to the staircase at the other end that led up to the third floor. Was he waiting for me up there, drawing me deeper and deeper – higher and higher – into this place? Or was he simply going to gut the hotel and run?

I thought about cutting the wires, but would that disable them? Could he have created some sort of a failsafe?

Grabbing my handset from my pocket, the battery, the SIM card, I flirted with the idea of calling the cops. I didn't have what I needed to clear my name – but I had a little, something I could build on, and if I made the call, I had more of a chance of being alive at the end. But as I put the phone together again and powered it on, I noticed something.

I couldn't get a signal.

I was in the middle of London and didn't even have a single bar. Something sparked at the back of my head – a memory of another time, on another case, where something similar had happened to me. And that was why, straight away, I knew what was happening.

King was using a signal jammer.

It made perfect sense: without a phone signal guests had to rely on Wi-Fi – and because King had set up the Wi-Fi network himself, because he knew the access codes, because he would have been the administrator, it made it much easier for him to access their devices. And it meant something even worse: he was watching them – finding out about them – from the second they checked in.

Above me, softly, a floorboard creaked.

He's up on the third floor.

I used the key card to access the room opposite the one I'd already been in, checking it over – its sockets had been overloaded too – and then the next, and the next, and the next, switching between rooms on both sides. I needed to make sure that no one was going to come at me – behind or in front – from inside them.

As I did, I started to notice a pattern.

The rooms on my left all had windows that looked out over Park Street and, to the north, Borough Market, and were bright, airy. The ones to my right didn't have any windows at all, save for a small skylight in the bathroom, and felt dark and closed in.

Something slowly started to pulse at the back of my head, a gut feeling – an instinct – that something wasn't right about the design. I inched inside one of the rooms on the right, letting the door soft-close behind me. As soon as it did, the entire room descended into shadow. It was sunny outside, hot, but the only light in here was dappled, faint, formed from the skylight in the bathroom, and reflecting dully off a mirror in the bedroom.

I looked at the red windowless walls, the grey carpet, at the bed, the desk, a lamp. I dropped my gaze to the wires as they snaked between my legs, from the plug in the corridor to the plug in here. He'd rigged this entire floor to burn first.

But why?

Suddenly, a memory came to me. When I'd been on the phone to Alexander Weathers, I'd wondered aloud why King would burn down one entire wing of a hotel just to get rid of some evidence. Weathers had believed that King had set the fire to dispose of weapons, trophies. But, as I thought about the design of the hotel on this floor, I was starting to wonder if he might have been getting rid of something far worse.

Please don't let me be right.

I headed back out to the corridor and spotted a door marked HOUSEKEEPING at the end of the rooms on the right. Another wire was snaking through to there too. I held the master key to a reader on the wall and let the door bump out towards me. Immediately inside were shelves full of linen, soaps and toiletries. Cleaning products. A bottle of Brasso. In a box of random junk I found candles, matches, a set of spare key cards and spare parts for what looked like a tumble dryer. Beyond that I found the tumble dryers themselves and washing machines, all double-stacked. And then, finally, a metal cabinet with DANGER! ELECTRICITY on it.

One of its doors was ajar.

I gripped the knife I'd taken from the kitchen and pulled the cabinet door open. It should have been full of circuits, a generator, *something.*

But it wasn't.

Inside the electrical cabinet was a wooden door.

61

I pulled open the door.

Immediately inside was an extended wall cavity, running behind the rooms like a narrow corridor. I stepped past the door into the space. Now I realized why there were no windows in the rooms on this side of the hotel: they were all in here. This whole section had originally been part of the rooms – but, at some point, the rooms had been reduced in size in order to create this space behind them. On my left – the exterior wall – the windows looked out at the car park; on my right was the new internal wall, the remodelled bedrooms on the other side of it.

I inched further along the narrow space.

There was a cupboard at the far end but I hardly took it in. All I could think about was why my instinct had kicked in, what I'd felt in my gut as I'd entered the rooms along this side of the building. This was why I felt as if something was wrong: instead of windows like the rooms on the other side of the hotel, the rooms on this side had all had large mirrors.

My blood pulsed in my ears as I thought again about the theory that Dean King had burned down an entire wing of the Coast Inn so he could destroy evidence.

Now I knew what sort of evidence it was likely to be. Not weapons or trophies, but the building itself.

I was now level with the first of the rooms.

I shouldn't have been able to see anything of it from in here, just the internal wall. Instead, I could see the whole room: the bed, the desk, into the bathroom, where the shower and bath were.

It was because the mirror in the room was one-way glass.

Dean King was spying on his guests.

He'd done it here since 2014, so it wasn't hard to imagine he'd done it at the Coast Inn until 1992. He'd probably done it at the Slade Youth Hostel too. As my skin crawled, I saw something under the mirror for the room furthest down from me.

A video camera on a tripod.

The legs of the tripod had been collapsed and it was leaning against the wall, the camera fixed to the top, a lens cap on. It was an old-fashioned JVC, maybe fifteen years old, the tape slot open. There was no tape inside, but I could guess why King was still using analogue technology. It didn't leave a data trail. What he recorded didn't sit on a server somewhere. The only footage was on a DV tape.

Along with the camera, I could now see a signal jammer mounted on the wall above the cupboard, a multitude of antennas poking out of the top like charred blades of grass. I reached up and switched it off, then turned my attention to the cupboard. It was unlocked, one door partly open, and there was an unzipped holdall just inside. The holdall was filled with DV tapes.

At least fifty of them.

I dropped to my haunches and scooped one of the tapes up. The plastic case had a strip of masking tape on it with a name and a date written.

I swallowed, nausea bubbling in my throat.

March 2011, Eleanor. That was when King had stolen the life of Jasper Slade. This would have been recorded at the youth hostel in Epping Forest.

I picked out some more.

November 2019, *Gregory*, when King was Nolan Winter and firmly embedded here. *January 1997*, *Harry* – I didn't know *where* King was in 1997, or what hotel he was running, but it was in between the Coast Inn and the youth hostel. It went on and on – more dates, more names – until I picked a tape out that stopped me dead.

September 1991. Lilly.

Lilly Andrews.

It had to be.

So she'd gone to the Coast Inn the year before she'd been murdered, almost certainly for one of King's parties. I looked for the names *Maggie* and *Felicity*, convinced that they'd be here, and I soon found them. *July 1991, Maggie. March 1991, Felicity.* They'd all been to the Coast Inn – Lilly, seven months before her body was discovered; Maggie, nine months; Felicity, just over a year. They'd been murdered at different times but it had all started the same way: King had watched them in his hotel, stalked them for months – and then moved in for the kill.

I looked for tapes with female names beginning with *A*, thinking of the girl in the photograph Cate had, her face circled in pencil.

But there weren't any.

I dumped all the tapes back into the holdall.

I didn't know if most of these young men and women had simply been watched – studied from the other side of a mirror – rather than suffered the fate of Lilly, Maggie and Felicity. But it hardly seemed to matter.

This man was exactly the monster I'd imagined.

He'd filled the holdall with all his tapes, which meant before he started the fire on this floor and left this place for good, he was planning to come back for them. Maybe he was going to destroy them. More likely, he was going to take them with him.

Because *these* were his trophies.

These were what were important to him.

And, as that landed with me, so did something else.

I looked at the signal jammer on the wall, and then down at my phone, where all four bars had filled in now I'd flicked the switch off on the box.

I thought about the products I'd spotted on my way into the laundry room, including the bottle of Brasso and the box of matches.

Then my eyes went back to the holdall, to the tapes, to the trophies Dean King had collected over three decades.

And in my head a plan quickly formed.

And, suddenly, I knew what I had to do.

62

Heart thumping against my ribs, I crept up the guest staircase, my hand pressed hard to the holdall, trying to limit the
soft clinking sound the DV tape cases were making as they
shifted around. Above me I couldn't hear anything at all – no
movement, not even a hint of it. It was completely silent.
With every new step the same thought kept returning: what
if this really *was* a trap?

When I was almost at the third and final floor, the stairs
twisted right. I paused at the turn, looking ahead of me. A single door had been propped open with a fire extinguisher. I
could see a lounge area with a sofa and a coffee table, and a big
window – one of the dormers – looking down at the car park.

Beyond the lounge, the room split into two: a corridor on
the left, which must have gone through to the bedroom, and
a door on the right through to the bathroom.

The bathroom light was on.

There was an L-shaped kink to the design, making it impossible to see who was in there. But it was clear someone was: I
could see a shadow dancing across one of the bathroom
walls, the brief outline of a head, an arm, a body. I heard a tap
being run, a sudden gush of water, and then it snapped off
again with a clunk. More shadows, indecipherable, difficult to
pinpoint. And then the person started to move.

It wasn't Dean King.

It was someone else; someone whose role in all this I'd
never quite figured out. I hadn't seen him in the flesh before
now, but he looked exactly like the photograph that Georgia

had taken. Six feet, early thirties. Broad, well built, with brown hair and a thick beard. It was untidy and I could see it for exactly what it was: a mask, a way to make it harder for people to get a handle on who he was.

Harper.

He stopped in the doorway of the bathroom, looking off to a corner of the suite that I couldn't see. As he did, he rubbed his hands together, trying to get the last of the water off. He had a T-shirt on, no jacket, nothing to cover his arm.

The burn marks were exposed.

They were angry, mottled pink, stretching from his wrist to the crook of his left elbow. There were more on his biceps, smaller trails of them, clinging to the arc of his muscles. Despite his injuries, I saw again how strong he appeared, how powerful.

'I'll be back in a second,' he said.

Someone else is here.

I removed the kitchen knife from a side pocket on the holdall. Harper moved off along the corridor leading to the bedroom. As soon as he was gone, I edged closer to the suite door and peered around the frame to see who the second person was.

It was a man, his back to me – slumped, frail – in a wheelchair.

He'd been positioned at the edge of the window. Sun was pouring into the room, but he was in the shade, greyed by it, dulled.

As I came around on him from his right, emerging at his shoulder, I could see him twitch; suddenly he noticed me, reacted to me being there.

But he didn't call for Harper.

He couldn't.

Dean King was incapable of doing anything now.

63

His gaze was on me – dark, unyielding – but he didn't move an inch. He made a sound instead, a slight suck of breath and then blinked a couple of times, his eyes watering, his mouth sloped.

He'd had a stroke.

I studied him, this shadow of a killer: his black hair had greyed and thinned; his bulk had gone, the skin hanging off his bones; his lower half was even smaller, the lack of exercise and movement withering him from the waist down. His eyes were still that same dark chocolate brown, but the colour of his skin had started to wane. It was almost yellow now, a jaundiced hue that had begun to infect the whites of his eyes as well.

He was staring at me, the intensity of the look recalling the person his broken body hid. I grabbed his wheelchair, released the brake, and manoeuvred him across the room, towards the door I'd come in through. Dumping the holdall in his lap, I opened the zip. There was enough of a gap for King to see what was inside.

All his DV tapes.

I came around him, watching him, his eyes moving from the bag to me, a mix of anger and panic in them. His expression gave me a moment of satisfaction, knowing that there was nothing he could do now but watch and suffer whatever was coming, then removed the bottle of Brasso and the box of matches I'd grabbed from among the housekeeping items.

'I hear you like fire,' I whispered to him.

Anger in his eyes.

The sucking sound in his angled mouth again.

I emptied most of the Brasso into the bag. All King could do was watch. I didn't have any intention of setting light to the tapes – I knew they were going to be crucial evidence if I made it out of here – and knew as well that the cases would protect the tapes, even doused in liquid. But Harper needed to believe that I was serious.

He needed to believe all that mattered to me was survival.

Once I was done, I snapped the brake on again. I could hear Harper: the soft creak of a floorboard as he moved around in the other room; drawers opening and closing as he got ready to leave this place behind for good. Once he came out, I'd still have more than enough distance between myself and the corridor: if he tried to launch himself at me, tried to stop me, he'd be too slow.

One strike of a match and he'd believe the bag was about to go up.

And King along with it.

A noise in the bedroom, more movement, and then Harper said something. I craned my neck, trying to hear, but his voice was soft, intermittent; it sounded like he was on the phone. And then his side of the conversation stopped.

I took a match out of the box.

A second later, I heard footsteps padding along the corridor.

He was coming.

I straightened, readying myself. Harper slowed again, his footsteps stuttering to a halt. He must have been looking at the empty space where he'd left King.

I expected a reaction.

I expected Harper to hurry now.

But he didn't.

Instead, I heard him take another couple of careful steps, a shadow forming on the wall as if it was reaching out to us ahead of Harper himself.

And then, very quietly, he said, 'Dad?'

64

I had about a second to process what I'd heard before Harper emerged.

'Dad will be fine as long as you don't do anything stupid,' I said.

I thought of that vague, unexplained sense of recognition I'd had when looking at the photo of Harper. But he and King didn't look especially alike, and I'd seen Harper's picture before I ever saw Dean King's, so what was it about the way Harper looked? I started to wonder if it was something much simpler: I didn't recognize him, I just recognized what he was.

The darkness inside him.

'What do you want?'

His accent was soft, generic, hard to place. It was probably deliberate. I didn't get the sense anything he or his father did was by chance. Everything was some sort of act, a part to play, a mask to wear.

'How long's your dad been like this?'

He didn't answer.

'How long?' I said, threatening to light the match.

'Eleven months.'

I glanced down at King. 'That's unfortunate.'

'Fuck you,' Harper spat back.

'So here's how it's going to work,' I said. 'You're going to tell me exactly what I need to know, or I set these tapes alight – and your old man goes with them.'

Harper glanced at his father.

'You're not going to burn the tapes,' he said to me.

'Why not?'

'They're evidence.'

'If it's me or these tapes, you'd better believe I'll burn them.' I tilted the bag in King's lap, letting Harper see the Brasso running off the cases.

'You think I give a shit about those tapes? If you burn them, that just helps us.'

I'd saved some of the Brasso for just this moment. I emptied the rest over King – the back of his head, his shoulders, his chest – and then quickly pressed the match to the striking plate on the matchbox.

Harper flinched.

'I *do* believe you don't give a shit about the tapes,' I said to him. 'But you definitely give a shit about your old man.'

He took a step forward.

'Take another step and I light him up.' We eyed each other as I tossed the empty bottle of Brasso across the room towards him. 'I swear. I couldn't give a damn if he lives or dies. All the people he's killed, all the lives he's violated with these tapes, all the damage he's done: I'd be doing the world a favour.'

'You're not a killer.'

'You have no idea who I am.'

Harper swallowed. 'I should have cut your throat when I had the chance,' he said. His voice was little more than a whisper, but there was so much rage in it, the words were almost tremoring through his teeth. 'It would have been so easy to do it. You were fast asleep.'

'So why didn't you?'

'It didn't seem like the right choice at the time.'

'And this place? Why isn't it already burning? It's been three days since you stuck me with that needle. I thought

both of you would be in the wind by now. What are you waiting for?'

I tried to get a read on him, but it was impossible.

'You're going to tell me what I want to know.'

He smiled. 'I'd rather talk about them.'

Them. Cate and Aiden.

I eyed him for a moment. 'So let's talk.'

He looked like he was toying with me. I didn't like it. Even
though we were at least ten feet apart and I was one strike of
a match away from setting his father alight, it no longer felt
like I had control.

'Are they dead?' I said again, trying to keep my voice even.

'What do you think?'

'I want to hear you say it.'

'Yes,' he said. 'That bitch is dead.'

Part of me caved in, but I tried not to show it. I'd suspected it was coming, hadn't really believed – two and a half
years down the line – that Cate and Aiden would be alive, but
the news still hit as hard as a punch. I thought of Martin and
Sue, and of Georgia, imagined them getting the news, and
then I refocused on Harper.

'Where are their bodies?'

'Not far.'

I moved the match closer to the strike plate. 'Where are
the bodies?'

Harper looked at his father, then at me. 'Beneath the
basement.'

I studied him. 'They're *here*?'

'Under about twenty tons of concrete.'

'You buried them under the hotel?'

He nodded. 'Them, some others.'

My stomach turned.

I stole a look at the tapes, knowing that the other bodies

would belong to the people who'd been recorded in their rooms here, never knowing they were being watched, studied, hunted. And then I realized that King was looking at me too through his peripheral vision. There was no expression in his face – not even a hint of what he was feeling – because he couldn't control anything in his body. But his eyes were alive, moving, communicating. They were saying, *You're too late. Too late for Cate and Aiden. Too late for all of them.*

The full weight of it hit me.

King hadn't just been a killer.

He hadn't just been a serial killer.

He'd been a serial killer no one had even known was still active.

'How did you make Cate and Aiden disappear?'

When he didn't answer, I lit the match and put it to the side of Dean King's face, where Brasso was leaking from his hairline. King didn't react, maybe didn't even feel it, but Harper stepped towards me, reaching out automatically. We stood like that, watching each other and then I said again, 'How did you make them disappear?'

No response.

Instead, something else happened: the anger in his face, the concern for his father – the moment of fear that had been there as I'd lit the match – completely vanished. And in its place something else emerged: that hint of a smile.

That same malignant smirk.

Click.

A gun touched the back of my head.

65

I froze. I could just about make out my reflection in the window, a ghost of me; could see the gun at my head, the hand holding it, an arm extended. But the rest of whoever it was existed beyond the edge of the window, in a reflection that hadn't yet formed. All I knew was that they were shorter than me – the gun aimed slightly upward – and they were wearing a white shirt.

Harper came over, blew out the match and took the box from me.

He was still smiling, the smile so dangerous it was like an open wound on his face. He then grabbed the handles of his father's wheelchair, released the brake on it, and manoeuvred King away from me.

'I guess now you know why we're still here,' he said.

They were waiting for the person behind me.

I didn't say anything; it was taking all my concentration just to keep standing, my muscles tremoring, my heart pounding so hard in my chest it was like I could feel the vibrations in the carpet. When Harper looked away for a split second, I quickly took in the room again, searching for things that I could use or somehow get hold of – ideas, a plan, anything at all. But there was nothing.

'All this effort,' Harper said. 'For what?' He stopped about a foot and a half from me, so close now I could feel the warmth of his breath on my face. 'You never should have taken this case. You're just a speck of dust compared to us.'

'A speck of dust is worth more than your dad is right now.'

He grabbed me by the throat. 'You talk to *me* like that?' he screamed, his saliva flecking my face, my head lurching back, knocking the gun away. I heard the person behind me stagger backwards, but they recovered quickly.

The gun touched my skull again.

Harper released his hand. In his face there was a flash of guilt as he realized he'd lost control.

I looked at him, saw the flush in his cheeks, and then glanced at Dean King on the other side of the room to me, his entire body petrified in the wheelchair. But not his eyes. In them I could see an intelligence, a recognition – almost an admiration – for what I was doing. His son was a hothead. Maybe before the stroke, King had been able to keep Harper on a leash. But not any more.

'Where's her book?' Harper said, trying to keep his voice soft, contained.

I glanced between father and son, trying to give myself a moment. The book Cate had been writing was the only reason I was still alive. They'd figured out that I knew where her manuscript was – and that meant Cate didn't tell them.

Which meant she'd either held out.

Or she'd already been dead in the ravine by the time they got to her.

'You know where it is, Raker.'

I suspected it was on the memory stick, which was in the shoebox, and I definitely knew where that was: inside the locker at the gym in Ealing.

'Is the book about your father?' I asked.

'Where is it?'

'Is it about the people he killed?'

Harper didn't reply.

'Because here's what I think: Cate wasn't just writing about the Dune Murders. That's where she started – but that's not where she ended up. I think she caught a glimpse of exactly how big this goes, all those tapes in that bag, so you had to cut her off before she got a chance to finish what she'd started.'

Silence.

It was a quiet that instantly told me I was right. Cate might not have got to the point I had – but she'd seen more than enough. She'd caught a glimpse of displaced earth and had started digging – and, somewhere along the line, she'd begun to connect the dots. She'd been writing a book on unsolved murders.

But not just the three in Bamburgh.

She'd been trying to chart the whole history of Dean King.

'Where's the book?' Harper repeated.

Behind me, the gun pushed against my skull.

'You won't find it without me,' I said.

'So where is it?'

'I can take you to it.'

'It's a Word document, not a bank vault.'

'The document's on a memory stick.'

He eyed me.

'There's no other copy of it,' I said. I wasn't certain if that was true or not, but I was confident it was. If Cate had emailed it, or uploaded it to the Cloud, or just left it in some file-hosting software, they'd have found it. 'There's one copy and I have it.'

'Where is it?'

'As I said,' I replied calmly, 'I can take you to it.'

He was breathing hard – seething – his shoulders rising and falling. He tried to dial it back again and then, for the first time, he glanced at King, as if acquiescing to him, as if unsure what to do next. But King didn't return his son's gaze.

He just kept staring at me. Except gradually it dawned on me that King wasn't staring at me at all.

He was looking at whoever was behind me.

I glanced at the dormer window and, for the first time, something registered with me: the person's arm, what they were wearing. It wasn't a white shirt.

It was a white blouse.

It's a woman.

'Where's the fucking *book*?' Harper screamed in my face.

'Chris.'

One word, spoken from behind me.

But enough to stop Harper dead.

Chris. That was his real name.

Harper looked across me. '*What?*'

'Calm down.'

I tried to think if I recognized her voice, tried to think if there was a woman I'd come across in my search for Cate and Aiden who could have allied herself with Dean King. But then Harper, flushed with anger, stepped forward, his gaze still pinned on the woman behind me, and said, 'Oh, I didn't realize we were using our fucking *first* names. Well, why don't you ask the questions then, *Mariet*?'

Mariet.

Out of the grey of the conversation I'd had the day before with Alexander Weathers, the name came back to me. She'd been the girlfriend King had had at the time of the fire. Weathers speculated that it had been the most serious relationship Dean King had ever had. And when King had vanished, Mariet had disappeared too. Weathers had wondered if King had killed her.

But he hadn't killed her.

She'd made a life with him.

'Mariet,' I said to King. 'She went with you.'

361

'Shut up,' Harper responded.

'She's been there the whole time in the background.'

'Shut your fuc–'

'*Chris.*'

A tremor passed through the room.

I could hear the anger in her this time – and it stopped Harper dead. For a moment the gun inched away from my skull and, out of the corner of my eye, I saw part of her reflection in the dormer window: red hair, a hint of a profile. But part of me was still stuck on the way Mariet had spoken to Harper, the way she'd chastised him, shut him down, the way he'd seemed to shrink and retreat – and when I glanced at him, and then at King, the pieces clicked into place.

She'd spoken to him like a son.

And then the full horror of it hit me. A father, a mother, their son. A unit that had existed for thirty years in one form or another, bound by blood.

A family of killers.

Mariet moved in behind my shoulder, her face still not fully visible to me. When I glanced at our reflection, I couldn't see her: her head was hidden by my body.

'You're very clever, David,' she said quietly.

A blank impossible-to-trace accent, just like her son.

Her arm strayed into view, briefly allowing me to see more of the detail on the blouse: the sleeves were see-through up close, her skin visible.

'They were good boys waiting for me today,' she said. 'They've always been good boys.'

And then I saw her arm again, the skin under the sleeve of the blouse, and I noticed something high up, at the shoulder.

It took me a second to work out what it was.

A tattoo.

'That's the thing about me, David,' she said, coming further around again. 'I can always rely on my family.'

And as I saw more of the tattoo – two written lines inked on to her skin, one over the other – she finally allowed me to see her.

The whole room fell away.

'Family is absolutely everything,' Audrey Calvert said.

66

She moved around in an arc, so she was fully facing me, but kept the gun pointed at my head. Unlike her son, there was absolute stillness in her face – none of the anger, or the panic, or the hate.

She was in complete control.

She looked so different from the photograph that Stanley Gray had shown me. The blonde dye and black roots were gone, replaced by an autumnal red. Her hair wasn't shoulder-length any more and it lay halfway down her back, tied into a ponytail, the ponytail as thick as rope. A fringe sat at a slant, hiding the top corner of one side of her face. She was wearing contact lenses too, or maybe the blue-grey colour of her eyes in the picture that Gray had were the counterfeit, because now her eyes were a deep dark brown. But she'd lost so much weight it was hard to even square her with the version of Audrey that had existed two and a half years ago. Now she was barely more than ten stone – toned, even muscular.

For a second I couldn't take my eyes off her and then I looked at Harper and it came together in my head. Finally, I realized why it felt like I recognized him, despite *knowing* I'd never met him before in my entire life – because in his face I could see the echoes of someone else.

I could see his brother, Michael.

I'd only seen one photo of Michael, from his driving licence, but it was clear now that Harper, despite using the beard to disguise himself, was related. And as I glanced at the tattoo on Audrey's arm – *Michael*, with *Christopher* underneath – I remembered how Stanley Gray had thought those had been Michael Calvert's first and second names. Except they weren't.

They were two people.

Two brothers.

'You're going to take us to that memory stick,' Audrey said.

Her voice was quiet but it was steely, unnerving.

'Where's Michael?' I replied.

She barely reacted. But, behind her, Harper – *Christopher* – did. I couldn't be absolutely certain of what was in his face, but it looked like a mix of sadness and anger.

I thought of how the neighbours had seen Harper trying to get into Michael's house, using a set of keys which he didn't appear to be familiar with. It seemed clear that Michael hadn't been home that night. But as I looked at Harper's face now, I started wondering if it wasn't just that Michael was out.

Maybe he was already dead.

As that hit me, more of it began to form. 'Michael didn't want anything to do with you, did he?' A shift in Audrey's face told me I was right. 'He wasn't like you three. He was wired differently.' I thought about the Ordnance Survey map I'd found in his house. 'He didn't have the full picture about who you were, what the three of you had done and were capable of – not until recently, not until earlier in the year. I don't know how you kept it back from him, or how you explained it away, but the mirrors in the rooms, these tapes, the fires, the identities and lives you took on as you kept moving around, he either didn't know about them, or only knew a small part of what was really happening.'

Audrey smiled. 'You don't disappoint, David. Michael's my son. I love him and his brother with everything I have.

365

But he's not smart.' She was talking about him in the present tense. Did that mean he was alive? Or was it a refusal on her part to acknowledge what she'd done to her own flesh and blood? She shrugged, the gun shifting in front of my eyes. 'What do they call it? "Learning difficulties". He's a hell of a handyman, let me tell you. You give Michael something to fix and he fixes it. *Anything.* With his hands he's a genius. But his head, it's a wasteland.'

The air seemed to chill.

It was a cold, brutal assessment of someone she was supposed to love, but she barely missed a beat. 'So we've told him all sorts of things down the years: Dean had a job offer so we had to move, or we wanted to try something new, or we'd lost our money and needed to start over and part of starting over was changing our names. I mean, take your pick. He believed all of it. We've always kept his first name, so he's always been Michael. It helped his tiny brain accept the transitions.' It was all so emotionless, so dismissive of her son's naivety. 'A small part of him – maybe *more* than a small part – had moments, I'm sure, where he felt things weren't right. But it didn't really start properly until last year. My baby got it into that head of his that something was going on with us and he started digging into it, or trying to. But he was clumsy.'

'And your boyfriend, Stanley Gray?'

A twist of disgust in her face. 'He was just my cover story. Why else would I choose to live with a slob like him in a shit-hole like that? While we were prepping for Gatton Hill, I knew I'd need to put some distance between myself, Dean, Christopher and this hotel. And that became especially important afterwards, when it all went wrong. So Stanley Gray was just an eight-month insulation blanket. He was there so that, when the cops interviewed me in the time after the car crash, I was just a woman living with a guy who was completely, crushingly

366

uninteresting. That was another time Michael's simplicity paid off. I didn't want Stanley to know about Dean or Christopher, so I told Michael never to discuss them with Stan.'

'And Michael just went along with it?'

'He didn't really understand why, but, yeah, he went along with it. I told him it was a sensitive subject around Stanley and I needed to find the right time to bring all of that up. Michael was a good boy.'

'What did he think you were *doing* for eight months?'

'Living with Stanley. He thought Dean and I had broken up.' She glanced at King, at Harper, and then back to me. 'That was the worst eight months of my life. When Stan touched me, I wanted to puke. There were so many times I'd wake up in the middle of night, and he was lying next to me snoring, when I thought about just crushing his larynx. Sometimes I'd put my hand there, squeeze a little until he started to cough, just so I could see what it felt like.' She spoke with startling indifference. 'Anyway, the second I felt it was safe, I dropped Stanley Gray like a stone. But I must have made an impression on him, right, David?'

She knew Gray was still hung up on her, even now, and that he'd partnered with Michael in trying to find her, at least initially. But what Michael hadn't told Gray was that he wasn't searching *for* Audrey; she had been here, at the hotel. Rather, he was searching for the truth *about* her and the rest of his family. Maybe, as Audrey said, he was naive – but, just like Cate, he'd caught a glimpse of something more going on.

'So who was it really in that railway arch?'

'Who cares?' she said. 'Just some worthless piece of shit we found living on the streets. It took some searching – months, actually – to find the right person, someone with a similar build, similar features, a similar tattoo in the same place as me. But we got there in the end and, once we did, we took her out, fed her, smartened her up a bit with a bottle of dye, my clothes, that bracelet I used to wear, and then we took her to those arches and stuck a needle in her arm. No one was going into those arches except addicts and the homeless, and who among them was going to report a body just lying there? They were *all* just lying there. So we knew it would be a long time before she was found. We needed the decay to set in to muddy the waters. By the time she was eventually discovered, I imagine she was in a bit of a state and that was why it was easy for someone like you to make the connection between her and me, given the story I'd been feeding Stanley. All the times I "accidentally" left a needle lying around that flat . . .' She rolled her eyes. 'He bought the story, you clearly bought the story – and, by then, Audrey Calvert was just a name. Part of a history another woman had.'

'Like Mariet.'

She didn't say anything.

'And then you did the same to Zoe Simmons.'

'Well, Zoe was sleeping pills – but, you know, semantics.'

'You *killed* her.'

'*You* killed her, David.' Another smile. 'Zoe was doing just fine before you came along. We made it clear two and a half years ago that if she talked, she died. We never had any trouble with Zoe, ever, and then we contacted her a few days ago to tell her there was going to be someone asking questions, even told her what to say, but she went into a spiral – she was panicking, scared, an absolute mess.' She made a sound that, with anyone else, might have been regret. But not on her. It was simply another line in the sand: the bleak, calculated decision to take Simmons's life. 'In the end it just became easier with her dead, a neat little suicide. I mean, if she's in a six-foot box, there's zero chance of her talking to you about what happened on Gatton Hill.'

'And what *did* happen?'

Audrey smiled again. 'Nice try, David. We need that memory stick. So be a good boy and show us where you've hidden it.'

'Don't you feel *anything*?'

'With regard to what?'

It was frightening; she actually didn't know.

'*All* of this,' I said. 'Your *son*.'

'Like I say, Michael overstepped.'

'That was why the neighbours saw you, wasn't it?' I said to Harper. 'You went to the house to make sure Michael had nothing that could hurt the three of you. But you missed something . . .'

He shook his head. 'No, I didn't.'

'You did. How do you think I found the hostel in Epping Forest?'

Audrey glanced at Harper, and him back at her.

'My dear Michael,' she said quietly, as if deep in a thought she couldn't easily escape from. 'He never really believed in the same things as we did.'

'Which is what?'

'There are no boundaries, just the ones we're told are there.'

'What's that? Your mantra?'

'You can take what you want in this life, David. Most of us, we're drones. We drift through life doing whatever the hell we're told to do – what's *expected* of us – what's passed down to us from our parents and our grandparents, this perpetual, pathetic, worthless ideology. But what I realized a long time ago is that I'm dominant. I'm not a drone. I think for myself. I *do* for myself.' Something changed in her face then, a twisted shard of fury, as if a storm had appeared out of nowhere. 'I speak, I take, I fuck, I kill.'

And then the fury was gone.

Her face was a blank.

Yet something lingered: a tacit acknowledgement that in this family *she* was the power. Everything they'd done, they'd done because she'd wanted it.

'Nature versus nurture is absolutely real,' she said. 'I've experienced that with my sons. They both came from the same womb – but they turned out so differently. Chris, we nurtured into exactly what we wanted. But dear Michael . . .' She faded out.

I looked at Dean King, prone in the wheelchair, his eyes on me.

Then I looked at Harper: simmering, destructive.

Then I turned back to Audrey. She glanced at Harper for a split second and the look was enough to initiate a response. He nodded at her – and then headed towards the corridor that led down to the bedroom.

'Nature versus nurture,' Audrey repeated softly.

I looked between her and the corridor, wondering what was going on, trying to figure out their next move.

Footsteps.

And that was when I realized that, earlier, Harper hadn't been on the phone in the bedroom.

He'd been speaking to someone in person.

His brother.

Michael looked at me as Harper led him out into the living area, Harper's hand at the back of his neck like he was herding an animal. Michael was stooped, bent over, as if he'd been snapped in half. Harper stopped him next to his father, two broken bodies side by side: one, paralysed by his heart and his brain; the other, crippled by the people who were supposed to love him.

'Michael's a good boy now,' Audrey said, 'aren't you, honey?'

He nodded, almost imperceptibly.

'No more digging around or asking questions.'

He shook his head.

'Show David.'

Michael looked at his mother, then at me: reluctant, scared.

'*Show* him.'

Slowly, Michael opened his mouth.

Fuck.

They'd cut out his tongue.

'Sadly,' she said, 'Michael was too much like her.'

I could barely take my eyes off him.

But then what Audrey said registered with me. 'Her?'

She nodded. 'The one who gave birth to them.'

A Mum, Twice

30 Years Ago

'You sure you're all right?'

Makayla's voice brought Amelia back into the moment, into the car, as they wound their way north.

'I'm fine,' Amelia said. 'Where are we going?'

'To see the mysterious Phil, of course.'

'Where does he live?'

'Not too far from here,' Makayla responded, and then reached forward and started going through the tapes she had in a slot under the radio. 'Time for a bit of music.'

Amelia forced a smile and then looked out of the window, watching as they crossed the Tyne, a hint of sun winking on the surface of the steel-grey river. She was nervous at the idea of meeting Phil again, but as Roxy Music began playing through the Astra's tinny speakers, Amelia was more focused on her certainty that she knew Makayla from somewhere. But from where? School? Could she have come in to do a talk before Amelia left? It was possible. They had always had people from the police and the fire brigade doing talks in assembly.

And then Makayla started singing along to 'More Than This' and, as she did, Amelia had a sudden flash of déjà vu.

She closed her eyes, trying to grasp at the image in her head. Almost instantly, Amelia remembered: Makayla not just singing but dancing to the music, arms up in the air, slowly turning circles like a ballerina.

'You all right, love?' Makayla asked.

Amelia could hear her pulse thumping in her ears now.

'Yes, of course,' she said, forcing out a smile again, her hand automatically going to her belly, as if she — and what she was carrying — were

under attack. But Makayla seemed satisfied now, her attention back on the road. She took the turn-off for the A69. They were following signs for Hexham.

Heading out of the city.

Amelia looked out at the houses on either side of her. They were starting to thin, Gateshead fading from memory behind them, the scenery becoming trees, and fields, and sky. Amelia touched her belly for a second time, and then told herself everything was fine. Maybe she was mistaken, her memory false.

Maybe.

But then Amelia thought of her mum and dad and emotion formed in her throat. And after the emotion, fear. She pictured her mum's hand in hers at the scan a couple of days earlier, the two of them welling up as the sonographer told them that there wasn't one baby, but two, one behind the other. They'd missed it in the first scan she'd had at the early-assessment clinic, but there had been no mistaking it now. Amelia would be a mum twice over.

I want my own mum, she thought. I just want to be at home where I know it's safe. Safe for me, safe for my babies.

She hadn't told her mum where she was going, which seemed so stupid now, but she'd done it because she hadn't wanted to overload her or Dad, and because part of her had wanted to try and put this right. She knew initially her parents were distraught at the idea of her being pregnant, even if they'd covered it up, so Amelia had the thought that, by finding out who Phil was, by locating him, she could at least do something sensible. She could go back to Mum and Dad and tell them, and as she imagined them, she imagined them cuddling her, and her lip tremored.

'I don't feel very well,' she said.

Makayla looked at her. 'Is it morning sickness?'

'No.' She swallowed. 'I think I just want to go home.'

'You don't want to see Phil?'

'No,' Amelia said. 'I just want to go home.'

She could see Makayla studying her, gaze flicking back and forth *between Amelia and the road. And then, finally, Makayla said, 'Okay, whatever you want.'*

'Thank you,' Amelia said quietly.

She allowed herself a moment of relief.

And then she moved her feet, and heard something wrinkle, and she remembered that she'd dumped the newspaper she'd been reading, back at the Metrocentre, into the footwell. She glanced down at it. It had unfurled further, the front page almost fully open now, revealing the photograph used to accompany the latest story on the murder of the three girls in the dunes. It was an image of one of the parents of the girls standing in front of a nest of microphones, the mother crying, the father – tearful, face red – trying to speak.

She noticed something.

She leaned forward slightly, the belt locking into place, stopping her from going any further. But she could see enough. In the photograph, behind the parents of the girls, were two other people: a woman and a man, both of them in suits, both wearing identical lanyards with POLICE printed on them.

There was a caption under the photograph.

Roger and Sara Sykes, parents of Felicity Sykes, appeal for witnesses in the death of their daughter and two other women. Behind them: Detective Constable Leon Coetzer and Detective Inspector Makayla Jennings.

Amelia froze.

She stared at the woman named as Makayla on the right of the shot, part of her shoulder cropped out, the rest of her visible, her body turned in the direction of the parents, listening.

Except it wasn't Makayla.

Or, at least, it wasn't the woman beside her, not the woman driving her out of the city, away from her mum and dad.

Not the woman who –

Amelia felt a flash of pain in her neck.

She touched a hand to it and a tiny pinprick of blood sat against the pink of her fingers. She couldn't work out what had happened.

But then her head started to swim.

She glanced at the woman next to her and saw that, in her lap, was an empty syringe. 'Just give in to it, sweetheart,' she said to Amelia.

And then everything hit Amelia like a flood.

Again, she could visualize the woman singing, dancing, turning circles like a ballerina, but now Amelia could see more, the memory colouring like a film fading in. She could see the woman had a silver wig on; a short black dress with sequins; she could see the two of them in a room full of people: beer, joints, laughter, music.

This woman had been there that night at the Coast Inn.

That was why she'd always felt so familiar to Amelia, right from the start. And as Amelia finally made that connection, as she started to fade into unconsciousness, another final picture formed in her head: the woman coming over to them all, kissing the owner of the hotel – who'd been sitting with them – and introducing herself.

She'd had an unusual name too. Marian? Marcella?

No.

Mariet.

67

The one who gave birth to them.

'Amelia,' Audrey said.

I thought of the photograph Cate had hidden in the shoe-box, and the necklace – with the letter *A* hanging from it – that had been at the girl's throat in the picture. *Amelia.* I glanced from Audrey to Dean King and saw a look pass between them. But it was one that told me exactly what had happened.

'You used her as an incubator,' I said, barely able to form the words.

'She gave us what we wanted.'

'She was just a *kid.*'

'She was nineteen. And she was simple, and she was drunk.'

I swallowed, shaking with anger.

As the colour rinsed my cheeks, Audrey broke out into a smile, one that was so reminiscent of Harper's that it was hard to believe they didn't share the same DNA. 'Ooh,' she whispered, 'look at how *furious* you are. Do you want to hurt me, David?'

I stared her down, her eyes dark, dangerous.

And then the smile was gone and her face was another blank. The switch was so sudden it was terrifying – she was like two different people.

'What did you do to her?' I said.

'I'm sure you can guess.'

I shook my head. 'You're a fucking monster. Did no one look for her?'

'Not really.'

'What about her family?'

'They were the only people who were going to.'

The subtext was obvious. 'So you killed them too?'

'No, they had an accident, didn't you hear?' She was goading me now, wanting me to come at her. 'The three of them hired a boat, went out into the North Sea, and never came back.'

A memory flickered into life from when I'd been at the library: I'd glimpsed a story in the *Star* – from shortly after the bodies were discovered and the Coast Inn had burned down – about a family who had drowned in the North Sea. I hadn't even given it a second look. My focus had been firmly elsewhere.

'I guess they must have all fallen overboard,' Audrey went on, 'because the coastguard could never find them. All that was left of Amelia was the bag she left on the boat.'

Except Amelia had still been in whatever place this family had been keeping her.

'Of course, it didn't help that the police were a little pre-occupied. We knew the cops would sink everything they had into the Dune Murders, the media would be all over it; the more pressure, the more their focus slips.'

I could feel the emotion building in me, a heat behind my eyes. I'd never known Amelia in life but her death had got to me, the suffering she must have gone through.

I wanted to tear this family apart.

'Maybe, in another life,' Audrey said, her voice so serene we could have been talking about the weather, 'I'll share my sad story with you, the reason I did all that. But not in this life. In this life you're going to take us to the memory stick an–'

'You couldn't have kids of your own, is that it?'

She blinked. For the first time in what felt like hours, there was silence in the room.

'Let's go,' she said, and jabbed the gun into my chest.

Harper grabbed me by the arm, his grip like a vice and led me out of the room, back towards the stairs. I glanced behind me as we walked, saw Dean King one last time – hands dormant in his lap, his eyes watching – and Michael next to him, small, broken, and then it was just me, Harper, Audrey and the gun she was pointing at me.

'Do you know much about blackbirds, David?'

We reached the bottom of the stairs up to the suite, and I glanced left, into the second-floor corridor. I'd left the door ajar and could see the wires snaking off across the floor, rigged to go up within hours – to erase the evidence of the hidden cavity wall.

We started down the stairs to the first floor.

'I'll take that as a no,' she said. 'I've always been fascinated by them. They're so common in this country that a lot of us don't take a moment to appreciate them. Did you know that the majority of English blackbirds hardly ever move any distance from where they're hatched? They prefer to stay close to home . . .'

We were walking, and I was concentrating on where my feet were landing, but as the staircase bent around on itself, I looked up at her, and she said, 'That's like my boys, isn't it? I'm their home. Wherever I go, whatever I decide is best for us – whatever place I take them to, or life we start – they always stay close to me. Always.'

'You cut the tongue from one of your "boys",' I said.

'Shut your *mouth*,' Harper spat into my ear.

'It's okay, Chris,' Audrey said from behind me. We were at the first floor now. 'It's okay, dear.' Her eyes drilled into me. 'You really have no idea what you're capable of, David, do you? Your mind is so small. You're so constrained by what's expected of you. We can do anything we like, *take* whatever we like.'

'You're insane.'

'The opposite, actually. But, anyway, as I was saying, black-birds hardly move any distance from where they were hatched and, yet, do you know what's wonderful about them? Do you know what the key to their success is?' We got to the last turn in the staircase, and as I took the bend, the two of us were almost face-to-face. 'It's adaptability. They're astonishingly good at adjusting to new environments. Gardens, remote woodland, city parks, rooftops – they can establish a life any-where. They can survive wherever they are. In fact, they *flourish*. And do you know what the best bit is? Barely anyone even notices they're there.'

She was the blackbird.

She and her family of killers had acclimatized to different places for thirty years. They hadn't just stayed together, her kin wasn't just her home – they'd adapted and thrived under every new alias and in every new location.

'Cate should have called her book "The Blackbird".'

I stopped. Harper tried to yank me forward, but I stopped again, trying to shrug off his arm, turning to look at Audrey. 'How long did Cate live for after the crash?'

Harper let go of my arm two steps short of the door into the reception area, and allowed me to turn, to look up to where Audrey was standing. She eyed me for a second and then said, 'Cate was dying, and she knew it. She was bleeding, her body was broken, she was drifting in and out.' She paused. 'But we had some time together.'

There was so much in that one phrase, so much pain and suffering woven into it, it was hard to know where to start.

Unexpectedly, she handed the gun to Harper.

'Cate was clever,' she said. 'At another time, I might have even grudgingly admired her. You and her, you're similar. You're both fucking annoying.'

'What did she say to you?'

She glanced at Harper, back to me, and then shrugged. 'I guess it doesn't make much difference now.'

The finality of her words chilled my blood. She had no reason *not* to tell me because, after this, I was dead.

'Before she died, she told us a few things. She told us she zeroed in on Amelia early on. She said she was always going to include what went on in those dunes as part of her next project, but she was also interested in unsolved crimes more generally – murders, disappearances, whatever. And, as she was digging around about the murders, she got hold of that old photo of Amelia and Dean at the party. And *then*, when she started digging even deeper, she somehow managed to find out who Amelia was and read about what happened to her and her parents on that boat.' Audrey began nodding, almost to herself, as if, in her head, she was holding an image of Cate's last moments. 'Suddenly, she could draw a direct line between Dean, the hotel, the murders, Amelia and her disappearance.'

'And she realized the disappearance of Amelia and her parents was staged.'

'Well, she knew *something* was up. And she believed Dean was responsible for Amelia's disappearance. And from there she started trying to follow our trail.' Audrey took a breath. 'We had no idea for a while. But the alarm bells started going for us when she turned up here.'

'Cate came to the hotel?'

'Yes. She asked the staff questions; eventually the staff called me down.'

'You spoke to her before the crash?'

'Yes. This was September, early October time, I guess. She didn't know who I was, obviously. But she was asking questions, the *right* questions – just the same as you. After that, we found out she was planning a trip to the north-east, to talk to journalists and police officers there. It felt like she was moving the final pieces into place. So that was why I went to live with Stanley Gray and why we did what we did that day on Gatton Hill. Although, as you've already guessed, things went wrong. We wanted them both alive, unblemished, so we could find out what they knew, what Cate had discussed with Aiden. But Aiden was dead before we even got him back here, and while Cate hung on – she was a fighter – she didn't hang on for as long as we needed her to.'

I had so many questions it was like a high-pitched hum at the back of my head, but all I could think to ask was, 'What happened?'

It was as if she hadn't heard me, though; her gaze was on me, her mind somewhere else. 'When I got her back here, I kept asking her, "What are you *doing* this for? What are you hoping to achieve? You take pictures for a living. Are you hoping we'll sit here and pose for a fucking photograph?" But she wouldn't tell us. She wouldn't tell us why she'd been following all these leads and doing all this digging on us. Not until just before she died, anyway.'

I looked at her, and then smiled; I couldn't help it. 'She waited until then to tell you about the book.'

Instantly, I could see I was right: in the dying light of her final minutes, Cate – knowing there was no way out for her – had done something fierce, and fearless, and defiant. She'd told them she'd written a book about them. But not where she'd hidden it.

'That was the first time you knew about it,' I said.

'Yes,' Audrey confirmed, 'and for two and a half years we've been trying to find what she wrote. We've been watching her parents, listening to them, reading emails and texts. We've been talking to the sister. Believe it or not, we'd been waiting for them to enlist someone like you because then we might actually *find* it. And now that's exactly what we're going to do because you're going to take us to it.'

Before I got a chance to ask another question, she nodded towards her son and Harper grabbed me, forced the gun into my back and pushed me into the foyer door.

Sunlight was pouring in from outside, in across the marble floor in thick shafts of light, creating shadows at every corner and along every wall. Harper grabbed my arm again, digging his fingers in, his attention on the stairs leading down to the dining room. Audrey's eyes were fixed on me, nothing else.

Neither of them saw who was hiding in the shadows.

Neither of them knew that, in the cavity wall, when I'd disarmed the signal jammer, when I'd grabbed the Brasso and the matches to enact the first part of my plan, I'd used my phone to set into motion the second part.

In the end, it had been the lesser of two evils.

'*Stop!*' a female voice shouted from behind us. 'Armed police!'

I saw DI Parkes. Next to her was Davidson. And all around the room, black-clad and encamped in the shadows, their guns directed at the mother and son holding me hostage, was a Met armed response team.

There was a brief moment of calm, a lull where all sound and movement felt like it had been sucked out of the room. And then Harper swung the gun around and screamed to keep back. He tried to grab me and use me as a shield for both of them.

But I'd been expecting it.

I dived to the floor, his arm swiping at air, and as his body moved, like a coil retracting, the gun bounced up and it looked like he was about to start shooting.

A split-second of calm.

And then the room was filled with gunfire.

PART SIX
The Interview

68

We arrived at Walworth station forty-five minutes later.

For whatever reason DI Parkes had made the decision not to handcuff me in the car – something that had clearly upset Davidson – but when she let me out, she walked next to me, a hand firmly on my arm, guiding me across a gated car park filled with police vans, to a blue door at the rear of the building. Inside, at the front desk, Parkes told the duty sergeant she'd brought me in for questioning in relation to the hit-and-run involving Connor McCaskell, but it felt like everyone there – not just Parkes and Davidson – was fully aware that this was far bigger.

I hadn't brought much with me. My spare phone had been bagged and taken away as evidence, and I told them my laptop and Cate's shoebox were in a locker at the gym in Ealing, so all I had were a few coins to drop into a tray as well as my watch. I was given some clothes to change into, the clothes I was wearing were bagged too, and I was taken to an interview room in the bowels of the station.

After that, I was left to stew.

A couple of hours later, Parkes came back.

She was carrying a takeaway coffee and a pre-packaged sandwich. 'This was all we had,' she said apologetically and put it down in front of me. 'I hope you like ham.'

'Anything's fine at this point.'

She nodded. 'Sorry you've had to wait so long.'

I looked at her, removing the plastic film from the sandwich packet, trying to figure out if she was genuinely contrite and, for the first time, I had a moment to properly take her in. Mid-thirties, five-seven, slender, with blonde hair and green eyes: I'd seen all those things at my house the day she and Davidson had turned up, wanting to speak to me about McCaskell. But now I saw subtler things too: confidence, strength, the hint of someone who was smart and objective. It felt like Parkes would treat me fairly.

'Is McCaskell dead?' I asked.

'No,' she said. 'But he might as well be. He's on life support. Hasn't woken up since he was hit.' I felt her eyes on me, probably trying to get a sense of whether that news upset me or not. 'They don't expect him to wake up. And even if he does, his brain and body are destroyed.'

'And Harper?'

'Harper? Oh, you mean Christopher King? Well, he took twelve bullets to the face and chest, so he was dead before we even got him into the ambulance.'

McCaskell didn't deserve the ending he'd had, much as I'd disliked him. But it was harder for me to pretend that I cared that Harper had been shot dead by the armed response team. I wondered where Audrey was now and if she knew.

'Did you find the shoebox?' I asked.

'Yes. It was in the locker like you said.'

'Has anyone taken a look at the USB stick yet?'

'Give us a chance, Mr Raker.' From her pocket she took out a notebook. 'Can I be honest? I don't know what to make of you.'

She studied me as I took a second bite of the sandwich and a sip of the coffee. It had already become lukewarm, but it didn't bother me. It tasted good. I shrugged and said, 'If it makes any difference, you're not the only one here who feels that way.'

'No. So I understand from DC Davidson.' She watched me for a moment. 'So are you going to be honest with us when we start the interview?'

I frowned. 'Why wouldn't I be?'

'I don't know.'

'I'm being set up. It's in my interests to be honest.'

She flipped open the front of a pad. 'We're talking off the record here, right?'

I eyed her, trying to figure out what the game was. I'd never seen a cop work this way before; I knew for a fact that it went against everything they were trained to do. But, again, I didn't get the sense she was playing me. The only thing that seemed to matter to Parkes was the truth, and if she got to it via an unorthodox route then, to her, that didn't matter.

'Right?' she said again.

I allowed myself a smile.

'Something funny, Mr Raker?'

'David. No. It's just you're the cop I've been waiting for all my life.'

A hint of a smile. 'You can call me Martine when we're alone, seeing as we're first-name friends now.' She picked up her pen. 'Okay, so here's the thing. I believe we can help each other, David. You want to walk out of here a free man, and I want to make sure the right people go down for the right crimes. I mean, you pulled some shit up north – obstructing police, maybe a little perverting the course of justice; I'm sure we could find a few more things dotted around in the mix – so there's going to be a lot of noise once this starts. But, to me, this thing is about the bigger wins. I don't think you attempted to kill Connor McCaskell, but I need to find out who did, why they did it and what preceded it. And if what you told me in the car journey over here is true, this thing is big.'

'It is.' I paused. 'And it's worse than you can imagine.'

She waited a moment, paying silent respect to all the people who'd lost a life across thirty years of murder, and lies, and cover-ups, and then said, 'Okay, so before we do this officially, give me everything you have.'

69

The official interview started three hours later.

There was an immediate surprise. Davidson was kept out, replaced by another member of Parkes's team called Rosa Naughton. I appreciated the gesture, tried to say *thank you* to Parkes with a look, but she was in a different mode now – less personable, more professional, even down to her choice of clothes. When it had just been the two of us, she'd arrived in a hoodie. Now she'd swapped it for a blouse and jacket. I figured it was just how she did things, a visual sea change between the two sides of her police work. Or it could have been to do with who else was in the room alongside us.

Leon Coetzer.

He'd driven all the way from the north-east. I'd found the killers responsible for the deaths that had haunted him and Makayla Jennings. Now he wanted closure.

Slowly, meticulously, I walked them through the case, from the moment I'd been contacted by Martin and Sue Clark over a week before. It must have been at least an hour before anyone even asked me a question. After that, both Parkes and Naughton intermittently stopped me in order to clarify points, but mostly they just let me talk. Eventually, Coetzer was asked if he had any follow-ups, and he returned me to the Dune Murders, to ground I'd already covered. He was looking for things he and Makayla Jennings had missed, errors, the reasons they'd never found this themselves. He wanted to hear about Dean King – a man who'd been dismissed as a credible suspect by the bosses he and Jennings had worked under in 1992, and again after Jennings's conference speech twenty years later. He wanted to hear about that, about King's two sons, and then about the woman behind them all, the matriarch they were in deference to: Mariet, Audrey Calvert and probably twenty other names.

The Blackbird.

By the time we were done with that, and with everything to do with the hit-and-run, it was 10.32 at night. Parkes called it for the tape, switched it off and then we all sat there in silence for a moment, the only sound the scratch of my solicitor's pen as he made the last of his notes.

Finally, Parkes said, 'Sit tight, David.'

Forty minutes later, a uniformed officer brought me another sandwich and another lukewarm cup of coffee, and I asked if I could go to the bathroom. He escorted me into a long corridor with toilets at the end and waited outside.

As I was washing my hands, I heard voices beyond the door, and then a second later, the door opened.

It was Davidson.

We stared at each other, his eyes burning with anger, and then in the quietest voice he could muster, he said, 'So another cop falls under your spell.'

I didn't say anything.

'You're fucking unbelievable.' He pressed his lips together, as if he were trying to muzzle himself, and glanced over his shoulder into the corridor. 'I've got zero time for tabloid hacks but I've gotta give McCaskell his dues: he knew exactly what you were.'

And then he was gone, the door gently swinging back and forth in his wake. I dried my hands and exited, and the uniformed officer returned me to the interview room in silence. As I entered, Parkes was waiting.

She'd returned to her hoodie, but her face was serious, concerned. I went back to my seat and she pushed another takeaway coffee across the table towards me. 'This is fresh,' she said. 'And it's hot.' But something lingered in her expression.

'Is everything okay?'

'Not really.'

My body tightened. I tried to think what had changed.

'Have you ever met Mariet King before?'

I frowned. 'Before today? No. I didn't even know her by that name. Why do you ask?'

'Because she seems a little . . .' Parkes stopped, pen tapping against her pad.

'Seems a little what?'

'She seems a little obsessed with you.'

I brought my coffee towards me. 'Okay.'

'Why would that be the case?'

I looked at Parkes. Something was lying there dormant beneath the surface of what she was saying, waiting to be spoken. I just couldn't figure out what it was.

'My colleagues have been trying to interview her,' Parkes said. 'For five hours.'

'And what has she said?'

'The same thing, over and over.'

'Which is what?'

Again, Parkes paused; again, her pen tapped out a rhythm.

'She says she'll tell us absolutely everything we want to know,' Parkes replied. 'But only if you're in the room with us.'

70

Two hours later, I followed Parkes and Naughton to another interview suite. This one was deeper into the station, buried in the middle of the building behind a series of locked doors. On the way, all three of us were silent, probably trying to work out the same thing: why the woman I'd known as Audrey Calvert wasn't prepared to talk unless I was in the room.

I suspected it was a power play, some attempt to wrestle back the control she so craved: her husband was confined to a wheelchair, unable to speak, unable to even really move, the man he was – until a year ago – lost to her for ever; her favourite son was lying on a mortuary slab and her other one she'd already cast adrift. So with nothing else to fight with or fight for, she wanted to go out with a bang: dictate what happened, choose the direction of travel, spin everything out just because she could.

Parkes had passed Audrey's demand for me to be there up the chain. But I doubted anyone at the Met, including Parkes herself, would have liked the idea of a civilian being in an interview room at the suspect's request.

'Don't say anything to her,' Parkes had told me before we'd left the interview suite. 'She's going to try and bait you, I think we both know that – but this absolutely *cannot* turn into some circus. We ask the questions and you sit there and you listen.'

'And if she addresses me directly?'

'You ignore her.'

We reached a room at the end of another identical corridor and Parkes showed me inside. Waiting at a desk were Coetzer and another man in uniform, the epaulette on his shoulder confirming he was in charge.

'This is Chief Superintendent Akpan,' Parkes said.

We shook hands. He didn't offer any other greeting and there was even less of a clue in his expression about what he was thinking. I glanced at Coetzer, perched on the corner of a desk to my left, who was gently turning his mobile phone in his hand.

Akpan looked me up and down. 'Why would she want you in there?'

He phrased *you* like the putdown it was.

'I don't know,' I said.

'You'll forgive me if I don't entirely trust you, Mr Raker.'

Parkes flashed me a look, telling me not to respond. I didn't like the fact that Akpan had already written me off as a fraud, a liar, or both. It told me everything I needed to know about him: he valued what he'd heard about me from cops just like Davidson over actually talking to me and making his own mind up. I'd have put my house on him coming up through the ranks, not off the back of being a great cop, but on being outstanding at kissing the right arse at the right time.

'Are we ready to go?' Parkes said.

Naughton grabbed her notebook. 'Yes, boss.'

They led me out to a room two doors down. As we moved, I could feel my heart rate increase, and then a low thump in my ears. With every second that passed I worried a little more, a swell of dread beginning to build.

I didn't like the fact I couldn't say or ask anything.

Because Mariet King wasn't just a killer.

She was a master manipulator.

393

Parkes ran a card through a reader next to the door and it buzzed open. A uniformed officer stationed just inside took his cue to leave. And then across Naughton's shoulder I saw her facing us. Both her hands were flat to the table and they'd changed her into station-issue clothes, which made her look smaller somehow, less threatening, older. But I knew it was all a ruse.

She'd made herself that way.

This was part of the game.

As soon as I entered, she straightened at the table, brought her hands together so that her thumbs were touching, and her eyes found me. A smile twitched.

It was like no one else in the room existed.

Not Parkes. Not Naughton.

Only me and the Blackbird.

71

Parkes and Naughton settled at the table, opposite Audrey and her solicitor, while I went to a seat in the corner of the room, little more than a spectator. After a short pause, Parkes started the tape, announced those present, and read Audrey her rights.

'What would you prefer to be called?' Parkes said.

Audrey didn't take her eyes off me.

'Would you prefer "Mariet"? That's your real name, after all.'

'What would David prefer?' she said. She held my gaze with a long lingering stare. 'I think David would prefer "Audrey", as that's who he's always known me as, not "Mariet". So let's go with that. I always liked the name, anyway. It's homely, like me.'

This was exactly what I always knew it would be: a way for her to sow discord, to agitate and confuse. She knew the next time she was breathing fresh air was going to be when she was doing laps in a prison yard, so what did she have to lose? It was revenge – against me, against the cops that had killed her son, against anyone who'd played any part in her being here.

'Okay, Audrey,' Parkes continued, 'why don't we start at the beginning?'

Audrey pushed a strand of red hair away from her face, tucking it behind her ear, then her eyes flicked back to me.

'The beginning,' she muttered. 'Where's that?'

'I don't know. Why don't you tell us?'

She shrugged. 'I suppose it would be Michael.'

'Your son Michael?'

'In a sense.'

'"In a sense"?' Parkes paused. 'What does that mean?'

'This is the sad story I was telling you about, David.' Her eyes lingered on me again, as if she were trying to convince Parkes and Naughton there were some secret message passing between us. Finally, she looked at Naughton. 'Where's my medication? I told you already, I needed to take it at six.'

'We're getting your pills for you now,' Naughton responded.

'It's almost two in the morning.'

'They'll be here before long.'

'Do you want me to have a stroke?'

'No, of course not.'

'I've got severe hypertension and high cholesterol.'

'I know. We spoke to your doctor.'

'Then get me my fucking pills, you stupid bitch.'

Parkes held up a hand. 'Calm down, Audrey.'

'I'm calm,' she said, and her voice – raised an octave as she swore at Naughton – returned to normal, and she turned her head, looking into the corner at me. 'Why does he have to sit over there?' she asked. 'I want him to sit closer, so I can see him.'

'Mr Raker is fine where he is.'

'Bring him closer.'

Parkes took a long breath, her shoulders rising and falling. 'Audrey, I need you to concentrate on the matter at hand. You were going to tell us about Mic–'

'I want him closer.'

'Audrey, even having Mr Raker in the room is against –'

'Closer,' she said, 'or I don't talk.'

For a long time Parkes said nothing.

But then, finally, she gestured for me to bring my chair in a couple of feet. When I got to the midway point between the wall and the table, she held up her hand again.

'That's far enough,' she ordered.

I set my chair down.

'Much better,' Audrey said, looking at me. 'Now we can begin.'

72

'Let's talk about Michael, then,' Parkes prompted.

Audrey nodded, looking down at her hands, which had barely moved for the entire time I'd been in the room. They were flat to the table, spread like butterfly wings.

'You said that was where it started?'

'Yes. It started with my baby.'

'Michael wasn't yours, though, Audrey, was he?'

She flashed Parkes a look. 'I'm not talking about *that* Michael, you moron. I'm talking about the *first* Michael.'

'I'm not sure I follow.'

A beat. 'When I was nineteen, I had a baby. A little boy.'

'You had a baby? And you called him Michael as well?'

'Yes. I just always loved the name.'

'So what happened to the first Michael?'

'He died.' Her voice was small but it was composed, and without being able to see all her face, her eyes, it was hard to tell exactly what she was thinking.

'Who was the father?'

'Who cares?'

'Maybe the father would have done.'

'I doubt it. I shagged a lot of men in my teens.' Parkes didn't say anything, just waited. 'The Michael you know and Christopher, they were my second and third children.' The mention of Christopher – *Harper* – stopped her. A flash, there and gone. 'My other babies.'

'Except they weren't *your* babies.'

'They were.'

397

'Amelia Robbins was the mother.'

'She wouldn't have been able to take care of them.'

'You never gave her the chance.'

'She was just a kid.' Finally, she looked up, at Parkes, and then to me. It would have been hard to say she looked regretful, but there was an expression on her face that I hadn't seen before: a hint of sadness. To start with, I thought it was for Amelia – a girl she'd kidnapped and killed, whose parents she'd murdered, who she'd kept alive for six months and then stolen two new lives from – but then I saw it wasn't Amelia she felt something for. It was herself.

'I had cancer when I was six. The chemo screwed up my insides, basically ruined my ovaries. They told me I would never be able to get pregnant. My parents, they were a waste of space. For all intents and purposes I brought myself up; got through all of that shit pretty much on my own – my dad was always pissed, my mum was catatonic. I left home at fifteen, as soon as I could. Back then I thought even if it *was* possible for me to have a baby, I wouldn't want one. Why would I want to do to a kid what they'd done to me?'

She stopped, the room entirely silent except for a minor hum from the tape. Audrey had changed, drawn in on herself, the pain of these memories obvious. It was mesmeric; all the bravura was gone, stripped completely, and this was what was left.

'But then, somehow,' she said faintly, 'I *did* end up pregnant.'

'How did your baby die?'

'He was . . .' Her head dropped again. 'He was stillborn.'

'I'm sorry to hear that, Audrey.'

She looked up at Parkes, anger in her eyes. 'Are you? You're sorry to hear that? Are you really?' She paused, looking between Parkes and Naughton, then out – across the room – towards me. 'I bet you're all just so *sorry* to hear I suffered.'

'I mean it, Audrey,' Parkes said. 'Losing a baby –'

'Fuck off.'

Parkes stopped, chose not to respond.

'*You* know what it's like to lose someone, David,' she said, turning to me. Her eyes were wet – only a hint, but there. 'David has his own sad story – don't you?'

I glanced at Parkes, who looked back at me.

'Poor Derryn,' Audrey said, but the insincerity was obvious in her voice now. She was metamorphosizing back into what she'd been before: darker, angrier, cruel.

'Why did you and Dean target Amelia Robbins?' Parkes asked.

Audrey's attention lingered on me for a second and then she slowly turned her head towards Parkes again, as if she were hauling some great weight. 'She came to one of our parties and she seemed like an easy mark. It wasn't personal. I don't know how many parties like that she'd been to before, but I'm willing to bet it wasn't many. She came in wide-eyed, only seemed to have one friend. It was pretty obvious from the very beginning that she wasn't popular. So after we plied her with a few drinks and she'd smoked a few joints, she was stumbling around like a newborn foal.'

'So it was rape?'

'No.'

'You plied her with drinks. It sounds like rape.'

'We don't do that.'

'You just kill people, is that it?'

That made Audrey smile. 'Look at you, all righteous.'

'So how would you describe it?'

Audrey rubbed at her brow, a disinterested expression on her face. She'd totally altered now; whatever emotion had gathered on her as she'd talked about her baby was gone. 'I was older than Dean – he was twenty-eight; I was in my early thirties – and I wanted kids. By then I wanted them badly. The one time I got pregnant, it was . . .' She stopped. It felt like she was going to say *lucky* but nothing about how she lost her son was remotely lucky. 'My baby, he was a miracle. I wanted to feel it again. So Amelia, she was one of two girls there that we took to a private room in the back of the hotel and Dean did his thing with. We'd been trying it with other girls at other parties in the months before that too, all of them similar to her: young, naive, easily influenced. Amelia just happened to be the one who finally gave us what we wanted.'

She looked at us all indifferently, then started talking through what happened after that night: how King had made his escape from the north-east after the girls in the dunes were discovered; how Audrey had stayed behind to trail the two women, waiting to see if they were pregnant. 'I happened to follow Amelia to a library one day,' she said, 'and she went straight to the health section and picked out a book on pregnancy. I mean, there was a *chance* it might have meant nothing, but given what we knew had happened to Amelia, it seemed unlikely. We knew, finally, it had worked. And that was when I moved in and started befriending her.'

The whole thing was so horrific I could barely even process it.

'Why use the name "Makayla Jennings"?' Parkes asked.

'If I was a cop, Amelia would trust me. And I was interested in Makayla.'

'Because she was leading the Dune Murders task force?'

'In part.'

'You felt threatened by her,' I said.

'David,' Parkes responded.

'It speaks.' Audrey smiled at me. 'I actually went to see Makayla once. She was waiting for her kids outside their school, and I pretended mine went to the same place, and we got talking briefly. I wanted to see what she was like up close; get the measure of her. I thought it was kind of fun that she was trying to find me, I was trying not to let her, and at the same time we had something big in common.'

'Which was what?'

'Twins.'

'So what did you do with Amelia while she was pregnant?' Parkes asked.

'We took her to a rented house in Runcorn.'

'Runcorn? Why there?'

'Dean had spent some time there as a kid, so he knew the area a little – plus, who the hell goes to *Runcorn* out of choice? No one was going to come looking for us there.' Gently, she rubbed the tips of her thumbs together. 'No one knew us, we could exist below the radar for six months while everything died down in the north-east and we waited for the babies to arrive. It was perfect. We just put her in a back room there, fed her up, made sure she was healthy, then after Michael and Christopher were born . . .' She stopped and looked between us, face barren. She remembered it all and felt nothing. It was chilling. 'We hired another boat.'

'You dumped Amelia's body out to sea?' Parkes probed. 'You did the same to her that you did to her mum and dad six months prior?'

'Different sea, but yeah.'

'The Irish Sea?'

'Correct. Right out there.'

Parkes and Naughton did a good job of showing nothing. I didn't.

Almost instantly, Audrey picked up on the way I was looking at her, the disgust in my face, and she turned her body towards me. 'Does that make you angry, David?' But she wasn't baiting me now. The words were completely neutral.

'You should be angry at the fact that only her parents were ever going to care she was missing. Her friend? The people she went to school with? The *media*? Amelia was just a footnote to them. That's not right, is it? She was lost in all the furore over the "Dune Murders"' – she used air quotes, as if it was a moniker she loathed – 'but there was a deeper, societal reason why Amelia got lost: she was from a low-income working-class family; she wasn't pretty, let's all be honest about that, so she wouldn't look good out there on a front page; she was bang average at school, unemployed at the time; and she went and got herself pregnant at nineteen. These things aren't appealing to the press, who like their victims to be young and white, pretty and middle class, so it was –'

'Okay, Audrey,' Parkes said, cutting her off, 'thank you for the sociology lesson.'

Audrey stopped talking; a flash of ire in her face.

'You mentioned the Dune Murders.' Naughton this time. I could see the switch douse some of Audrey's rage, her brain firing up, trying to work out what tactic the two cops were using and why Naughton had now picked up the baton. 'Let's speak about that.'

'We only made that mistake the first time. Dumping bodies in the dunes like that, even when they were really well hidden . . . that was stupid.'

'So those three women were yours and Dean's first victims?'

'Depends what you mean by victims,' Audrey said flatly.

Naughton eyed her. 'Were they the first people you killed?'

'Together?'

'You mean you killed people before you met Dean?'

'When I was seventeen, I went home to pick up some things and my dad began shouting at me like he always did. So I calmed him down by offering him a drink. And then

402

I kept him drinking all night.' She sat back in her chair. 'He drank three bottles of vodka that night and died of alcohol poisoning. Could I have stopped topping him up? I guess I could have. Did I want to?' She shook her head. 'No. I hated that prick.'

'So between your dad dying and you and Dean killing those three women and dumping their bodies in the dunes, there wasn't anyone else that you killed, either on your own or as a pair?' Naughton paused, watching; Audrey's face was like a mask. After a while, Audrey shook her head again. 'For the tape the suspect has shaken her head.'

'How did you and Dean meet?' Parkes asked.

'At a nightclub in Bradford,' Audrey said, a finger tracing small circles on the table. 'That was where the two of us were living at the time. We bonded over our shitty families, then realized we had similar tastes.'

'You both liked to kill,' Naughton said. 'What is it you liked about it?'

'Now we're getting philosophical.' Audrey played with her hands, her fingers brushing her knuckles. 'It was the ultimate rush, I suppose.'

'That's it? You just did it for kicks?'

'No, not for kicks. To explore what I was capable of. To claim what was mine, my birthright. The act of extinguishing a life is what separates me from drones like you.' She looked between Parkes and Naughton. 'I mean, look at you both. You're the absolute dictionary *definition* of drones. You' – she gestured to Parkes – 'spend your days desperately trying to hide your looks by scraping back your hair and dressing in the dullest, most conventional clothes you can find, because perish the thought that *anyone* could deal with the fact you're attractive *and* doing a job in a male-dominated environment. But it's not the seventies any more,

403

sweetheart. Women are allowed to be police officers *and* wear make-up *and* dress in clothes that don't make them look like they just walked out of a Mormon temple. And you' – she nodded towards Naughton – 'well, I don't even know where to start with you. You spend your life in the gym, bulking up so you can look more like a man, probably for the same reasons *she* dresses like a nun. But you also do it to give yourself something to talk about because, otherwise, you're nothing. Zero. A mote of dust. You've made so little impact on the world, no one will remember you two minutes after you're dead.'

Silence.

I couldn't see the expressions on either Parkes's or Naughton's faces, but something must have flickered in one of them because, a couple of seconds later, Audrey cracked a smile that spoke of victory. She'd touched on some minor doubt they'd had about themselves, an insecurity of some kind, and all it did was make her more frightening.

'We are freeborn.'

'Freeborn?' Parkes echoed.

'We have the right to experience *everything*,' Audrey replied, her voice almost wistful. 'It's just society that tells us we can't. It's government. It's lawmakers. People think we live in a civilized culture, but we don't. A civilized culture doesn't try to pull the weak back on to the ship in a storm. It lets them go. It lets them all go. It lets them fall and watches the sea take them away. We'd create a firmer, more robust society that way because its foundations would be stronger.'

'So you were performing a public service?'

It was out of my mouth before I could stop it.

'Mr Raker,' Parkes warned me.

'Haven't you heard of Darwinism, David?' Audrey asked.

'You were killing kids.'

'That's *enough*,' Parkes said, turning in her chair to stare me down.

'They were never kids,' Audrey responded. 'They were always over eighteen.' She paused, using the silence to underline what she saw as the rationality of her moral code: no to rape, no to kids. 'We liked them at the age they were, because they're just so full of energy. Plus, of course, Amelia, Lilly, Felicity, Maggie, none of them were street-smart. They could all be led.'

A beat, as Parkes and Naughton reset the conversation.

Eventually, Naughton asked, 'You said you followed Amelia after she came to the Coast Inn. Did you do the same to Lilly, Felicity and Maggie too?'

'Yes. Inside and outside.'

'Inside? You mean, the mirrors in your hotels?'

'We didn't just leap into things. We took our time. Dean and I, we loved watching them from behind those mirrors. Sex has got nothing on the rush you get from that. There's something so exciting about a person not knowing you're there. But we watched them out in the open too.'

'And then you killed the ones you watched?'

'Not all of them.'

'So how many?'

She sucked in a long breath; made them wait.

'How many, Audrey?'

'I don't know.'

'You don't know how many people you killed?'

She sniffed. 'Maybe half.'

'Half the people on those tapes?'

The whole room seemed to slant.

There were fifty-eight tapes.

That meant they'd killed twenty-nine people.

73

Twenty-nine people.

It took a second for the full horror of it to land.

'But, of course, there were others we *didn't* tape, like Amelia,' she continued in the same tone, the same rhythm. 'We learned from the things we did wrong on the dunes. We got very good at befriending people, luring them in, absorbing everything about them. And, pretty soon after that, we discovered that once you absorb everything you can about a person – their life, who they are, what makes them tick – it's actually quite simple to *become* them. I mean, Jasper Slade, Nolan Winter – you can guess why we chose them.'

'They were wealthy,' Parkes said.

'In Nolan's case *insanely* wealthy. And they had no family, few friends; Nolan was a germ nut – he barely went outside. I shagged him a few times, just to get him onside, to make him believe my story, and I've never seen someone shower as often, or scrub himself down so hard. But him being like that, it was a big help. He could go months and months without physically seeing anyone, and because Dean was so good at mimicking people, at *becoming* them, it was perfect.'

'Where did you put the bodies of the people you killed?'

'Beneath the places we ran.'

I felt a cold prickle in my skin.

'What do you mean "beneath" the hotels?' Parkes asked.

'In the basement, under floorboards, behind cellar walls.'

'How did you hide the bodies from staff?'

'We always put them in parts of the hotel the staff couldn't access.'

Parkes said, 'How many hotels did you run over the years?'

'The Coast Inn was our first. Dean inherited some money from an aunt, so we thought it would be fun to try our hand at hospitality.' She loaded *hospitality* with the weight of every heinous act the two of them had ever carried out. 'Then we moved to Bristol, because we read about this hotel owner there, and he had a pretty decent resemblance to Dean.'

'What was the name of the owner?'

'Gary Sealy.'

'And the hotel?'

'The Clifton View. It went well there for a while, but then the money started to run out. Sealy was rich, but not rich enough. So we burned it down and moved on.'

'Where did you go after that?'

'Epping Forest.'

'The youth hostel?'

She nodded. 'We thought we'd mix it up – plus, Jasper Slade was *rich*. His dad had left him a ton of money and Jasper's big plan had been to open a series of hostels across London. Those were fun years – but then an American kid got drunk and accidentally cracked the one-way mirror in his room, and the whole thing went south. We had to kill him, obviously, then had to get through a couple of weeks of the police turning up asking questions about a missing kid from Colorado who might have stayed with us. We had no records of him, so eventually they stopped asking questions but, after that, the whole thing was compromised. So we set fire to it all.'

'And then you ended up at the Fir Grove?'

'Correct.'

Parkes nodded. 'So who did the killing?'

'It depended.'

'On what?'

'On who we'd chosen to kill.' She played with the ends of her hair, her fingers twined with a cord of red. 'I generally planned it and all the things we needed to take care of before and after. Dean did the heavy lifting – he got rid of the evidence, set up the fires when we needed to get out. And then, when Christopher was old enough, he got involved. He was smart, like his mum' – she meant herself, not Amelia – 'but he had a temper like his dad. Difference was, he couldn't control it as well as Dean, which made Chris a difficult mix. So he had to be taught like a dog – but once you had him under control, he was *very* effective.' She waned a little as she talked about Harper.

'Why did you always stay in the background?'

'Because I liked it there. And because it made more sense to have just one of us out front. As the kids got older, and especially when Christopher started coming into the fold, it meant there was more potential exposure if we were all out there making ourselves known. It was better and safer if only Dean was visible.'

'And Michael never knew what was going on?'

'Not until recently. But as I said to David, it sadly turned out that he had a little too much of his mother in him.'

This time she did mean Amelia.

A knock at the door.

Naughton got up and opened it and it was the uniformed officer from earlier. He was holding two pill boxes and a bottle of water. Naughton took both from him.

'Finally,' Audrey said, and snatched the pill boxes from her. One was red and white and had *Ramipril* written across it. The other were statins. As she took out the pill trays, and swallowed a pill from each box, she said, 'I guess I won't be having a stroke tonight.'

'Let's move on to Cate and Aiden Gascoigne,' Naughton responded, and as she turned to another fresh page in her notes, I glimpsed the time on Parkes's watch: 3.31. If the idea was to keep Audrey talking through the night, to wear her out and force her into making mistakes, it wasn't working. She barely seemed to be flagging at all.

'Why did you target them?' Parkes asked.

'I think you know why.'

'Because Cate was looking into you and Dean.'

She took down another big mouthful of water. 'Like I said to David, she turned up at the Fir Grove one day asking the staff questions. The staff called me down, I talked to her, and I didn't like what I heard. She was smart. So we started keeping tabs on her. We got inside her house the day before we planned to take her on Gatton Hill and searched around – and in the wastebasket on her computer we found a picture she'd taken of Dean leaving the Fir Grove. There was nothing else; nothing saved to the Cloud, nothing that she'd emailed to herself. We couldn't find any notes, any recordings. It was a total blank. Of course, now I know *why* she covered her tracks so effectively: she'd told her husband what she'd found out, or at least what she suspected – that Dean was alive and well, maybe even still killing – and her husband's tiny brain couldn't handle it. I guess he thought it was too risky and would bring them too much trouble, so he told her to stop. But she didn't stop. She kept digging into Amelia's disappearance, into Dean, she got a list together of hotels she could target, and she ended up at ours. She hid it all from Aiden, basically from everyone. But, at some point, she must have forgotten to press 'delete' because, in the Trash on her computer, we found that photo.' Audrey paused. 'That was about the only mistake she made. Eventually, I suppose she must have got the sense that she might be in some kind of danger, because, as I understand it, she sent all her research off.'

'To Makayla Jennings.'

'Yes. I've often wondered why she didn't just post it online. I guess it wasn't in a coherent enough state. Or maybe she liked the idea of us chasing our tails trying to find it. I mean, that sneaky little bitch didn't even tell me she was writing a book until her final breath. I just thought she was playing amateur detective, in the middle of some sort of midlife career crisis.' Audrey was quiet, her silence almost respectful. 'Why would anyone think she'd send all her research to a woman who could barely even remember her own name? But it was smart. Eventually, when Makayla died, Cate knew it would be found. Maybe by that time she hoped we'd have already been caught.' Again, she played with her hair. The room descended into a hush, Parkes and Naughton waiting, Audrey caught for a moment somewhere else. 'I guess you want to know about Gatton Hill . . .'

The final piece of the jigsaw.

'It all got messed up,' she said, her voice smaller than it had been at any point until now. She cleared her throat. 'The plan was for me to pull into the layby on Gatton Hill, flip my bonnet, and make it look like I'd broken down. When Cate and Aiden came past, I'd flag them down, basically step out into the road and give them no choice but to stop. Dean and Christopher would be waiting. We'd pull them off into the trees, knock them out and then carry them the rest of the way down, through the ravine, into the pine forest on the other side, where we'd left a van parked on the access road. Both of them were big strong boys. It was a long way, and hard work, but it would have been fine for them if we'd had the time we needed.'

'So what went wrong?'

'We had access to their phones, so we knew exactly where they were headed and when they'd arrive. I'd worked all the timings out perfectly. The story I told you lot, about arriving *after* they'd already come off the road, was a lie. I was already in the layby by then – I'd made use of the fact that there was no CCTV at the bottom of the hill – and I saw the whole thing happen: their car came around the bend and, out of nowhere, this fucking rabbit darted across the road.' She shook her head, wiped at an eye, cleared her throat for a second time. 'Can you believe that? A *rabbit*?'

So it was an animal. Something so small, so random, had eventually toppled every secret the King family had buried over thirty years. I looked at Audrey. There was a definite subtle change in her, as if she'd realized that at the end of this was nothing. No more games. No more freedom.

Just a room in a block with no windows.

She continued, quieter than ever. 'Aiden swerved the car to avoid it and then they just vanished from the road. A second later, their car's in that ravine, on its roof.' She swallowed, voice hoarse, and sank another mouthful of water. 'And then that's when Zoe Simmons appears. I tell Dean and Chris to head down to the Land Rover and pull the Gascoignes out while I handle Simmons.' Audrey paused, her hands back on the table in front of her, fingers spread, thumbs touching. She watched them for a while, as if they were part of her she didn't recognize. 'By the time I actually get to Simmons, she's already dialled 999 and the clock's ticking, so I have to call them too, because it looks suspicious if I don't look desperate for the emergency services to come. I'd been with Stanley Gray for a few months by then, this whole thing had run like clockwork until that point, and then suddenly – within minutes of us arriving on Gatton Hill – I'm having to involve the police. Anyway, I'm literally hanging up when Dean and Chris appear at the bottom of the ravine. It takes about a second for Simmons to see that something isn't right – but by then I've got a knife to her throat.' She ground to a halt again. Another drink of water. It was all coming out now, the dam fracturing. 'Simmons was just a shit-scared kid. It wasn't hard to bring her in line. The hardest part was telling her what to say, coaching her on what she needed to tell the cops, and what would happen if she didn't in the ten minutes before the cavalry arrived. That was why I kept it simple for Simmons: the car was on its roof from the minute we got there and no one got out of it. That was all she needed to say.'

'Which is what she did,' Parkes said.

'We never had a problem with Zoe until David turned up.' She looked across at me. 'You want to know who killed Zoe? He's your answer.'

There was something in her face now.

But then she was talking again. 'Anyway, the whole time Simmons is standing there, my knife at her throat, I'm having to keep an eye out for cars. But we had maybe one pass us in the entire time we were there, and that was just a bunch of teenagers who barely even noticed us. So, really, it was just Simmons and me, and what was happening down in the ravine.'

'Which was what?' Naughton asked.

'Dean and Chris trying to get those bodies out of a car that was now on fire. Christopher burning his arm trying to pull that stupid cow out. Aiden, he was ruined. Broken bones. Blood everywhere. He never really woke up. Cate was broken too, but she could string a few sentences together. Dean and Chris, they got Aiden back to the van and he pretty much died on the spot. Cate, they managed to get back to the hotel, but she played us. After I'd finished giving my statement to the cops at Gatton Hill, I hurried there and she basically lasted about twenty more minutes. She knew she was dying. She could feel it. So all she did was string us along – and then she dropped the bomb about the book.' She glanced at me again. 'So we had two dead bodies, a witness – and no idea where the book was. It was a mess. I mean, why else would I stay with Stanley fucking Gray for five months after that?'

'And their bodies are beneath The Fir Grove?' Parkes asked.

Audrey didn't reply.

'Audrey.'

This time she said something. But her voice was small, head dropped, her fingers spread in the same position on the table.

'What?' Parkes said. 'What are you saying, Audrey?'

She repeated herself.

But still we couldn't hear her.

'Audrey? You're going to have to speak up.'

I could feel it settle across the room like a shroud, the certainty that there was a turn coming, something we hadn't seen. And then Audrey lifted her head from her chest, like a shipwreck raised from the seabed, and we saw it. Her eyes had watered, the whites stained red; saliva was bubbling at the corners of her mouth; her fingers, set in position for so long, had started to draw in, claw-like, as if she were in pain. And then – voice ragged, a hint of a smile on her face – she looked at me and said, 'I win.'

'*Shit*,' I said, getting to my feet.

'David,' Parkes started, 'sit dow–'

'Get a doctor.'

Parkes stared at me, Naughton too.

'Get a *doctor*!' I shouted. 'There was something in her pills.'

74

Audrey rolled in her seat and then slumped forward, her chin hitting her chest, her hands slipping from the table. Her solicitor, next to her, froze, uncertain what to do.

'Get out of the way,' I yelled at him, and – as he scrambled to his feet – I pushed him clear and moved in, lifting her head from her chest. She looked woozy, her eyes struggling to focus, but when she saw it was me, she smiled again and said something, her words wet, indistinct, saliva foaming at the corners of her lips.

I heard Naughton sprint out of the room.

Parkes moved in behind me.

'I win,' Audrey wheezed again.

'What have you taken?' Parkes said to her, her attention on the pill boxes, on the foil tray still poking out from under the flaps of the blood-pressure medicine. I watched as she pulled one of the trays out. They looked completely genuine.

But then that was the whole point.

If she ever got arrested, this was her emergency cord.

I dropped to my knees in front of her, my hand still trying to keep her upright. She blinked at me, her eyes fixed on mine. Everything else in the room faded away; for a moment it was just the two of us, two feet apart.

'What did you take, Audrey?'

A twitch of a smile.

I glanced at Parkes. 'Whatever she took, it needs to come up.'

There was nothing in the training manual to help Parkes deal with this. She didn't know what to do, what she was *allowed* to do. One wrong move and this entire case came crashing down. But in a couple of minutes there wasn't going to *be* a case – or, at least, it was going to be a case with no killer to charge. '*Martine*,' I said, 'the longer we wait, the worse it is. We need her to bring up whatever it is she's –'

'I get it, Raker.' She looked to the door, as if Naughton was going to magically appear there, a doctor at her side – and then back to Audrey. 'Okay,' she said. 'Do it.'

I brought Audrey's head forward, over the table, and moved my fingers towards her mouth. But then she started fighting me.

'No!' she screamed, pushing her shoulder into me, her strength surprising. I was struggling to keep hold of her. 'No, no, no!' she screamed again, then lurched sideways, off the chair, landing with a dull thump on the floor.

'*Shit*,' I heard Parkes say from behind me, but I was already moving again, to my knees, shuffling in closer to Audrey, trying to swat her arms out of the way.

'Get off me,' she slurred.

'Audrey, those pills are coming up whether you –'

'*It's too late!*' she screamed, her voice breaking apart.

I stopped, staring at her on the ground beneath me.

'It's too late,' she said again more calmly. 'They're already in my bloodstream. That's the whole point.'

I glanced at Parkes, and then back to Audrey. 'What did you take?'

The smile was still lingering there.

'What did you take, Audrey?'

'I would never let you win,' she said, her words soft, slurred. 'You've only known who I am for a few hours.' She coughed and swallowed. 'But I've known all about you for *weeks . . .*'

Her eyelids fluttered and a thin tear trail escaped from the corner of her eye, tracing the arc of her cheek. Her death was close now, her breathing slowing down.

On anyone else the tear would have looked delicate, even moving.

But not on Audrey Calvert.

'I know all about you, David,' she said again.

I looked at Parkes; she at me. And then Audrey started coughing, the noise drawing me back. When she settled, she found me again and – in little more than a breath – she said, 'Say hello to Marcus for me.'

My blood froze.

'What did she say?' Parkes asked from behind me.

'I don't know,' I lied. 'I can't hear.'

I leaned into Audrey, our faces almost touching.

'What are you talking about, Audrey?' I whispered.

But I knew.

I knew exactly what she was talking about.

Nausea scorched my throat.

And then that same smile clawed its way out to the corners of her lips, like a virus eating its host – and suddenly it was written there.

The last song of the Blackbird.

'When you see him,' she whispered, 'tell him I enjoyed our time together.'

Healy

Healy glanced between Paula's bedroom and the one on the other side of him and then to the bathroom up ahead. Suddenly, he could smell something: air freshener. And not just a hint of it – an almost overpowering aroma. In a socket were two plug-ins and both were on. And from the cord on the light fixture just inside the bathroom he could see a Magic Tree.

He edged closer, sensing something was up.

In the doorway he stopped.

Face down in the bathtub was a body.

His stomach clenched. Around him more Magic Trees dangled from the ceiling like an art show, twisting gently on their twine as flies knocked against them. But they couldn't quite disguise the stench of death.

The front of his thighs bumped against the tub.

He looked down at the body.

At this distance, there was no masking the stench of decay, the air fresheners lost in the ripe rot of decomposition. The body must have been here almost a week.

He covered his nose with his sleeve – the smell bringing back a flood of terrible memories, of walking into hundreds of crime scenes and seeing the absolute worst of what humans were capable of – and bent a little, leaning closer. He tried to see who she was, if it *was* Paula, because it was a woman – he knew that much. She was dressed in a pair of light grey running leggings spattered in blood, a running top and Nike trainers. One of the trainers had come off and lay next to her, and the right sleeve of the running top was torn. Her head was at the plug end of the bath, her hair splayed across her face, but he could see enough of her neck to know how she died.

She'd had her throat cut.

He fanned back some of her hair to reveal her face and then he immediately stepped back, his head full of static, and left the bathroom, hurrying through to the bedrooms. In Paula's room his eyes fell on the photo frames on the carpet. He thought about the lie that Paula had told him about not putting the house on the market, then the FOR SALE sign he'd found hidden in the woodshed, then the picture of this house in the estate agent's window. And suddenly something else landed with him – how he hadn't seen a single photograph in the house during the times he'd been here. Not of Paula. Not of her son.

He scooped up a picture frame.

He knew what was coming, but even as he saw it confirmed, and saw the face of the woman looking back at him, the feeling of betrayal shattered him. He reached out to the wall for support. The woman in the photo was the real owner of this house.

And she was the one lying in the bathtub.

A noise from downstairs.

Gently, he put the picture frame down on to the bed and padded across to the doorway, looking to the staircase. He could hear the sea, but otherwise it was hushed.

Inching across to the steps, he looked down, not able to see anything else but a square of flagstone floor in the space between the kitchen and living-room entrances.

He edged down the stairs.

They moaned softly under his weight, the crash of the waves on the beach not loud enough to cover his descent.

418

He stopped and peered around the frame into the kitchen. The front door, at the other end of a small enclosed porch, was shut. Through a window to the side of the room he could see the drive.

There was no car outside.

He stood there for a second, trying to work out *who* the woman he'd been talking to – having *dinner* with – was and what she wanted with him. And then there was a faint squeak behind him – it was so quiet, it took him a second to realize it was the door to the downstairs bathroom – and he turned.

He was already too late.

He staggered back into the kitchen, the woman who'd called herself Paula watching him from the bathroom door. The syringe was at her side now and she was looking at him from an angle, motionless as a statue. She'd dyed her hair red, and she'd altered herself in other ways – her make-up, her dress sense.

She was like another person.

Healy hit the table, the legs scraping the flagstones, and then touched a hand to his neck. A speck of blood came back. This time the woman came forward, into the kitchen, completely unconcerned by Healy, by any threat he might pose to her. He was physically bigger, and could probably put her down with one strike, but it seemed to make no difference to her, and Healy knew why. He could feel the answer already, spreading in his body, a frost forming.

He sat on the edge of the table, watching her approach, and then she pulled a chair out next to him and guided him down into it with a thump. He couldn't fight her, couldn't do anything. All he could do was follow her with his eyes as she walked to the opposite side and took a chair herself. As she sat, she placed the syringe on the table, staring at him, rolling the needle back and forth with a blue-painted fingernail.

419

'It's nothing personal,' she said. Previously she'd spoken in a strong Yorkshire accent, but now he could hardly hear an accent at all. It was only words with no clue to their origin. 'You're just a pawn in a game.'

'What game?' he said, his voice low, hazy.

'"What game?"' she mocked in a voice exactly like his, and started rolling the syringe again. 'I wouldn't try to speak too much. Save your energy for listening.' She paused, looking around the room. 'I've got to be honest, I enjoyed this life for a few days. I'd kind of forgotten what it was like to live in a house.' Her eyes lingered on the room, on the décor, on the life that had belonged to a woman whose throat she'd cut, and then they pinged back to Healy. 'That thing about seeing a man at your house. That was all a lie. But it worked perfectly. I knew as soon as I said it, you'd be on the phone to him.'

Him. Shit, she meant Raker.

She knows everything.

'Yes,' she said, as if she'd read his mind. 'I know who you are, *Colm*. I know all about you. We've been watching Raker for a couple of weeks, since Cate's parents began discussing the idea of calling him. We followed all the little arteries in his life and, before long, we started seeing a withheld number cropping up on repeat in his phone records. So we dug, and we dug, and we kept digging – but do you know what really got us there? All the research that Connor McCaskell had done. Before he ended up face down in the tarmac, we went through his life and we found his file on your pal Raker, and there it was: an anonymous call to police on Raker's last case from a man with an Irish accent. McCaskell never made the connection; probably didn't think about someone in Raker's life faking their death. But we did because, well, that's what we've been doing for years ourselves.'

She stopped rolling the syringe, studying him. 'But what I'm still struggling to understand is how exactly you pulled it off. That body they found that was supposed to be you – it said in the media it was matched to you through DNA. Now how did you two naughty boys organize that? I can't for the life of me figure it out . . . but however you and Raker did it, it wasn't legal.' She wagged a finger at him. 'You two have got a bit sloppy in the time since, though. You've been careful – but not quite as careful as you should have been. Over time that can happen. Standards slip. If you're not on your guard the whole time, it's the tiny little details that get you caught . . .'

Healy's legs were dead, everything from the waist down already in stasis. He moved a hand flat to the table, his nerves sparking, and tried to push himself out of the seat. But he barely moved an inch. The woman watched, amused. 'Anyway, I need to get back to London,' she said. 'My family are there, waiting for me. But I should tell you before I go about what I've just put in your body. We've been using it for years; we used to steal it from veterinary clinics but now you just go to the Internet and put in your order, like you're shopping for apples. Only thing is, it affects people in different ways. Your friend David, he was out for well over a day.' She stood and went to one of the drawers, fishing around for something. 'But I think it's unlikely you're going to fight this stuff as well as he did.' She turned, something in her hands now: a roll of duct tape. 'This drug . . . well, it's not good for people with heart conditions.' She flashed him a look, a response to his own flicker of horror – because, before he had faked his own death, Healy had spent weeks in a coma after a heart attack.

She put both his hands in his lap, Healy unable to stop her, unable to fight back, and started to wrap duct tape around his wrists. She did the same with his ankles, then tore off a separate strip and stuck it to his mouth. And then she looked from Healy to the back door, as if measuring up the distance from there to here.

'I'm sorry it had to end like this,' she said.

He tried to move, tried to force his muscles to work, but he was completely disabled. Swallowing, his head starting to swim, he glanced at the woman again.

But she was just staring at him now.

A hunter getting ready for the killshot.

And then she stepped closer to him, her hand clamping his neck – her nails digging in so hard his breath stopped in his throat – and she said, 'If you ever wake up from this, Colm, tell David Raker I won . . .'

PART SEVEN
The Silence

75

I sat by the phone for two days, waiting to hear from Healy.

All I got was silence.

With every hour that passed, the panic got worse. I paced my living room like a prisoner doing laps in a yard. I couldn't sleep, couldn't eat. I'd planned to jump in my car – which had been released back to me by forensics – and drive to north Wales the second I left the station in Walworth. But Parkes soon put paid to that. She told me she had no choice but to release me on police bail, and that meant – although I wasn't charged with anything – I had to return to the station at set times over the course of the next week, and if they asked me to come in for an interview outside of those times, I had to be available for that as well. If I didn't cooperate, they'd place me under arrest.

So the living room was where I encamped, watching my phone, pleading for it to ring. And in the background I watched the media feast on the suicide of Mariet King. I saw as they gorged on her and her family of killers, three people who'd got away with terrible crimes for thirty years, who'd been so effective in doing so, no one had even realized they existed. Their story gave headline writers everything they needed.

And after the headlines came the accusations: in the age of DNA and advanced forensic science, how *had* the Kings stayed so well hidden? At least *some* of what they did – the choices they made, the lives they ended, the names they used and IDs they conned government agencies into giving them – should have registered with authorities somewhere.

How could this family keep reinventing themselves, keep installing their alter egos in new hotels and hostels, watching and hunting, and the police never pick up their scent? By day two, the question that kept getting asked in print, on TV and online was had the cops fallen asleep at the wheel? Northumbria Police, in particular, were subjected to exactly the media storm they'd done their best to suppress ten years ago. But, in truth, the reality was more intricate. Mariet King and her family were highly intelligent and highly organized. Every decision they'd made had been meticulously planned and every single consequence, from every single angle, thought about in full.

That was what made them so frightening.

And I imagined it would only become more frightening the longer the search for bodies went on. Forty-eight hours after Mariet had killed herself, the cops confirmed they'd found six corpses beneath the Fir Grove, in a basement section of the hotel no one except the Kings had access to. All but three of the bodies – killed, forensics estimated, within the last twelve months – had been reduced to skeletons. That would make identification difficult and prolonged, and that went double for the bodies they were going to find under the other properties, long since abandoned, that the Kings had once owned and run in other parts of England.

The first time I returned to the station, Parkes – in the quiet of an interview room and never on tape – gave me unofficial updates. I got the sense that – fresh from what had happened in that interview room with Mariet King – she was struggling to deal with everything. For her, maybe I was some kind of reset button, a voice that wasn't someone else on her team, someone looking at the same heinous acts she was hour by hour, and increasingly – though desperate not to – becoming desensitized.

She shared some items with me too.

One was a diary that Amelia had kept, part of three boxes that her aunt had taken possession of after Amelia and her parents had apparently drowned in the North Sea. Inside were poems Amelia had written, ideas for stories, musings and sketches. Mariet had described her as simple, but there was nothing simple about the poems she'd written. They were beautiful, articulate and measured; the story ideas were unusual and genuinely inventive; and the musings were often a sweet, delicate and innocent insight into the mind of a teenager. But the part that got to me the most were the diary entries that Amelia had written. She talked about not having many friends, about not ever having met anyone she'd truly connected with – and she wrote about her parents: *They annoy me. They really, really annoy me sometimes. But then I think about a life without them and my world collapses.*

Her words reminded me so much of what I'd thought about my own parents at her age, how much they'd frustrated me, how distressingly uncool I'd found them both – but also, like Amelia, how much I'd loved them. It made me think of my own daughter too, of how she might view me, of how I just wanted to be there for her.

I didn't know whether, in the aftermath of what had happened with the Kings, I was just feeling vulnerable, a little alone, but the simple pristine elegance of Amelia's words brought tears to my eyes.

They were tears for her and her parents.

And tears for the time they would never have together.

At least, not in this life.

Parkes and I finally got on to the subject of Cate's shoebox.

She said it was being analysed extensively by forensics and it hadn't taken them long to gain access to the USB stick. On it, as I'd suspected, they *did* find a key for the bespoke short-hand Cate had used in her handwritten notes – and they also unlocked what Cate had researched and written of her novel.

In a 2,500-word opening chapter Cate had eloquently discussed the conflict she was experiencing by not being honest with her husband about her findings. She wrote, *I feel like I'm having an affair by not telling him and, when he reads these words, I hope he can forgive me. But no one has given these women a voice before – not the media, not the public and not the police officers, except, perhaps, for one.* And maybe, in the end, that was why she kept it all to herself: she didn't trust anyone else, apart from Makayla Jennings, to do what was right by the three victims that, for so long, Cate had wanted to give a voice to.

When I went to visit Martin, Sue and Georgia after finally leaving the station – I saw there would be no comfort for them in what I'd found out. Their daughter and son-in-law were gone and weren't coming back. And that was all that had ever really mattered to them. The small hope that Cate might still be alive.

In the notes of Cate's that Parkes allowed me to read I saw how committed, driven and brilliant she was. I also saw something in the atrocity of the Kings' crimes that no one else – even the cops – had noticed until then.

Every killing was carried out between January and July.

In gardens and parks and cities all around the country, January was when the earliest song of the blackbird tended to be heard.

And July was when it ended.

76

On the third day of not hearing from Healy, I finally gave in and called the number of the people we'd been renting the cottage from and asked if they could go and check on him. I sat by my phone, watching the screen, waiting for it to ping with a text or buzz with an incoming call. I couldn't think clearly about whether I'd set something terrible in motion, whether I was about to collapse every secret Healy and I had sustained by phoning the landlord, but it hardly seemed to matter any more. The longer I went without hearing from Healy, the more frightened I became. Then, two hours later, the landlord finally called me back. He was confused.

'There's no one at the cottage,' he said. 'It looks like he's moved out.'

I hung up, trying to think what that meant. Had Audrey – *Mariet* – just been trying to play with my head as she was dying? Had Healy made it out of north Wales as he'd planned? But if he had, why hadn't he called to let me know? The fact that he hadn't was what really scared me. Because I could only think of one reason he wouldn't call.

I just didn't know where she would have left his body.

All but imprisoned in my home, unable to go looking for him, enraged and resentful and afraid, I tried to distract myself, going back to the coverage of the Kings and then to a YouTube video that one of the newspapers had unearthed of Makayla Jennings. It had been recorded back in 2012, at the police and forensics conference in Newcastle, but had only now been uploaded. The NDA, clearly, was a dam that couldn't hold any more.

I watched as she talked about the Dune Murders, about her investigation, about Dean King being her prime suspect, and it struck me that another brilliant mind – just like Cate's, just like Amelia's – had been cut down before her time. The difference on this occasion was that the Kings had no say in Jennings's demise from a disease every bit as heinous as them. I'd watched footage of Jennings earlier on in the case, intermittently drawn to old television interviews with her, but this felt different. She was older, a little quieter, but less encumbered by the rules of her job.

Afterwards I thought about how there was a cruel kind of irony in the relationship that Makayla Jennings had formed with the three women in the dunes. Except for Leon Coetzer – who, I imagined, was in the crowd that day at the conference – there had been no one left in the police to carry the memories of Lilly, Felicity and Maggie.

No one except Makayla.

Until, in the last years of her life, she'd finally lost sight of them too.

In a newspaper article online there was an interview with Joshua Jennings about his mum, and he said it was tough on him and his brother in different ways, but that Isaiah had taken Makayla's death particularly hard. Even when she couldn't remember who her sons were, Isaiah had still craved the routine of going to see Makayla; the room she'd called home; even the long silences he and his mum had shared.

And then, as I scrolled down the page, I came across an audio file that Joshua had given the journalist, a file that Isaiah had recorded on his phone three days before Makayla's death. Joshua thought their mum would have liked it if people got to know the person Makayla Jennings had once been.

I clicked Play on the audio.

It picked up midway through a conversation, presumably because Isaiah hadn't thought to use his phone to record what was being said straight away.

'– *beautiful boys. I'm so proud of you both.*' She was speaking as if she were the woman on that stage back in 2012, at the front of that conference, not the woman who'd all but succumbed to an awful withering disease. '*I always said to your dad, "We've been so blessed with our boys." It seems like only yesterday that I was picking you up from school. "Be kind, rewind" – do you remember that? I always used to say that to you and your brother when you fell out.*'

In the interview Joshua said that, after he had listened to the recording for the first time, he'd immediately picked up the phone – emotional, confused – and spoken to his mum's doctor, asking him how Makayla could suddenly remember things so clearly. Her doctor had said it was likely to be a phenomenon called 'terminal or paradoxical lucidity', when for short periods of time – usually in the final days of their life – late-stage dementia patients could sometimes experience a sudden burst of clarity.

'*I know your brother will be all right, Zi,*' she said to Isaiah. '*But you make sure he looks after you, okay? If there's ever anything important, or you think you need help, you know Josh will always be there for you.*' She stopped. The silence lasted a long time, and I wondered if she was starting to lose herself again. '*My two beautiful boys,*' she said, and I could hear the change in her voice, the confusion setting in again.

'*Mum?*' Isaiah said, his voice tiny, distant.

'*Be kind,*' she said softly. '*In your life, just always be kind.*'

77

That night I finally got a call on my mobile.

But it wasn't from Parkes or someone at the Met. I lurched for the phone, almost dropping it, desperate to see if it was Healy. It wasn't.

It wasn't even a British number.

'David Raker,' I said, picking up.

'Oh, hi,' a woman said. 'Uh, David. Hi.'

A mid-Atlantic accent, nervous, small. Straight away, I vaguely recognized her voice and looked at the number on the display: it was American. New York area code.

'David, my name's Rebekah Murphy. We bumped into each other in New York earlier in the year. I don't know if you remember that.' As she paused, it flooded back to me: I'd been out there meeting a friend of mine who lived in LA, and Rebekah and I had got talking in Bryant Park. 'You mentioned your job – and you left me your card.'

'Rebekah,' I said. 'I remember.'

'Oh, good,' she responded, relieved. 'Great.'

'I have to be honest, it's, um . . .' *It's not a good time.*

'Shall I call back?' She sounded disappointed.

'No,' I said, not wanting to hurt her. 'No, it's fine.'

'Okay. Well, um, I don't know if you remember what we talked about.' I heard her pause, a child chatting in the background, a dog barking. 'I mentioned my mum.'

'You did, yeah.'

'I'm sure you remember all this too, but I was born in the

UK and lived there until I was eighteen. Mum, she walked out on me and my brothers when I was three.'

'You never saw her again, right?'

'No,' Rebekah said, 'just the occasional card. And that's fine, you know. I made my peace with that a long time ago.' But then she stopped. 'Or maybe I thought I did.'

'But not any more?'

'No, not any more.'

A beat. We both knew what was coming.

'I really need you to find out what happened to her.'

After the call from Rebekah, I headed straight to bed.

It was only 8 p.m. but I was absolutely exhausted – four days of barely being able to sleep was finally catching up with me.

Except I couldn't drop off.

I couldn't stop thinking about Healy.

At 2 a.m. my phone started buzzing again. Still wide awake, I reached over and grabbed it off the bedside table. Again, it wasn't Healy – it was the same London landline that Martine Parkes had been calling me from for the last three days. I took a breath, frustrated, annoyed.

'Martine?' I said. 'It's two o'clock.'

'I know. But you're going to want to hear this.'

I tried to still my thoughts. Was it something to do with Cate and Aiden? Why couldn't she just wait until morning?

'Okay,' I said, sitting up straight. 'What's the matter?'

'Do you remember a cop called Colm Healy?'

Instantly, the walls closed in on me.

'David?'

'Uh, Healy?' I said, shutting my eyes, putting a hand flat to the mattress, feeling like the whole house was moving.

Shit. What was the best thing to say? I did? I didn't?

'David, are you there?'

'Yeah,' I responded, trying to sound confident. 'I was just trying to think. Colm Healy.' I paused again for effect, but really I was spinning out to all the reasons why Parkes might be asking this. Was he dead? 'Yeah, I remember him.'

I waited. *Don't appear nervous.*

'What's Healy got to do with anything?'

'There's a police station in south London,' Parkes responded. 'Wandsworth. He used to work there, apparently. But the station isn't used much any more. Basically, it's just an admin team in there now.'

'Okay.' I shuffled to the edge of the bed. 'So?'

'So, with more homeworking going on now, no one's been into the office for four days.' Parkes stopped. 'He was left in a walkway at the side of the building.'

'Healy was?'

'Yeah,' she replied. 'Bound and gagged with duct tape. Which is surprising – because he's supposed to be dead.'

'So he's *not* dead?'

I sounded too desperate for an answer.

'No, he's not dead,' she said. 'Just dehydrated.'

I felt a second of relief. But only a second.

'You said he could have been there four days?'

'It looks like it.'

'Why are you telling me this?' I asked, having to strain every muscle to keep my voice even. But all I could think about was Audrey – *Mariet* – taunting me in her final moments, telling me she'd won. She'd worked out that Healy was my weak spot, and she'd made her move. She might not have known that I'd lied to the police about him, perjured myself in interviews, that Healy and I had covered up a DNA switch, an act of blackmail, but she'd worked out enough. Now she was burying the knife in me.

'So it seems he faked his own death,' Parkes said.

'That's crazy.'

A pause. 'Do you know anything about that?'

'No, of course not.'

I tried to sound outraged but I was lying so much now, piling one on top of the other, that I couldn't tell what was helping me and what was inflicting more damage.

'Why would you ask that?'

'Because when he was found there this afternoon,' she said, talking slowly now, deliberately, as if she didn't know if she could trust me, 'he had a message on him.'

'A message?'

'Hanging from a piece of string around his neck.'

I swallowed. 'What did the message say?'

'"My name is Colm Healy",' Parkes said, and then paused. All I could hear was my heart. '"Seven years ago, I faked my own death. And David Raker helped me do it."'

Author's Note

For the purposes of the story, I've carefully altered some of the working practices of UK police forces and have taken some minor liberties, especially in terms of the way interviews are conducted and evidence is presented. Any alterations I've made, or decisions I've taken, have been made solely to keep you turning those pages, and my hope is that all of it is subtle enough to have passed unnoticed – at least until now.

Acknowledgements

As with all my books, *The Blackbird* has been brought to life by the brilliant team at Michael Joseph. Chief among them is Maxine Hitchcock, my editor and publisher, who lets me go off for a year and write whatever I want (within reason, of course), and whose hard work, razor-sharp insight and endless patience helped improve immeasurably early drafts of this book when they landed on her desk. I also want to give a big shout-out to the amazing team elsewhere at Penguin HQ, including (but not limited to) Rebecca Hilsdon, Beatrix McIntyre, Helen Eka, Jon Kennedy, Lee Motley, Mubarak Elmubarak, Vicky Photiou, Elizabeth Smith, Colin Brush, Jennifer Harlow, Clare Parker, Deirdre O'Connell, Katie Corcoran, Natasha Lanigan, Kate Elliot, Hannah Padgham and Stella Newing. A big thank you as well to Jennie Roman for her copy-editing and to my annual life-saver, Caroline Pretty, who has become a black belt in unravelling my terrible timelines and always knows what happened to Raker when (and in what book).

A Weaver book wouldn't be a Weaver book without Camilla Bolton, who's not only an amazing agent but also a great friend and a calm, rational voice during the moments in a book's life when I start to doubt every single word I've written. I also want to say a big thank you to Sheila David in Film & TV who has worked so hard for me this year on a few different things, and to the lovely ladies in Foreign Rights: Mary Darby, Kristina Egan and Georgia Fuller. Thanks also to Jade Kavanagh and Rosanna Bellingham.

For helping maintain my sanity over lunches, coffees and

texts, a big shout-out to my great writing pals Chris Ewan, Claire Douglas and Gilly Macmillan.

For being endlessly supportive, thank you to my big, beautiful family: the amazing double act of Mum and Dad, who are (although I realize I might be biased) the best parents in the world; my sister, Lucy, and the Ryder crew of Rich, Hannah and Sam; the Linscotts – Boxie, Di, Delme, Kim, Declan, Nathan and Josh; and to Barry, and Jo and John.

And, of course, last but definitely not least, two people who have to put up with me every day and have the good grace never to complain about their lot: my wife, Sharlé, who is basically the rock on which I've built my entire writing career – thank you for everything you do; and my daughter, Erin, who makes me so proud every day (and makes me laugh) and who I love more than anything in the world.

Finally, to my wonderful readers, who buy my books, talk about them, tag me in on social media posts, send me emails and come to my events when I'm out on the road: thank you from the bottom of my heart. Without you, none of this is possible.